MIDNIGHT SKIES

A FANTASY NOVEL

Suspense & Romance You Can Fall For

L. J. Vant

All Around Publishing, Inc.

Midnight Skies
Copyright © 2025 by L. J. Vant

First Printing: December 2008 by Publisher BookStrand
Original printing under the author's name, Zequeatta Jaques, and title *Loving Anna*

Reprinted July 2025 under pen name L. J. Vant after extensive revision

Cover design by Zequeatta Jaques
Cover image: Breanna Peterson/Shutterstock.com
All cover art and logo copyright © 2025 by All Around Publishing, Inc.

This book is a work of fiction. References to real establishments, people, events, locales, or organizations were used by the author only to provide a sense of authenticity and used fictitiously. The characters, events, and dialogue are a product of the author's imagination and should not be taken as factual.

ISBN: 978-1-7344314-7-6

Printed in the U.S.A.

Publisher
All Around Publishing, Inc.
www.allaroundpublishinginc.com
God is good!

DEDICATION

To all who look up into those night skies and wonder at the vastness of it all, this book is for you. Let your imaginations soar.

MIDNIGHT SKIES

L. J. Vant

And It Begins

The year: Does it matter? The account has been told, and at the story's end, you may wonder if it holds all a tale or some truth.

Tom gazed upward at the stained ceiling above his head as he listened with half an ear to his wife of fifteen years, her voice loud and clear over the phone he held against his ear. The chair he sat in he'd tipped back with a precarious disregard on its two back legs. He yawned wide before he replied to her question.

"Yeah, sure, I'll stop and pick it up from the store on my way home. I promise. I said yes, didn't I?" He frowned as his wife expanded on her reasoning of the thing he was to buy, and of which he'd, with purpose, forgotten to stop and purchase two days in a row. Why she couldn't go to the store and get what she needed baffled him; he'd told her to. But nope. She'd refused with a frown directed his way and a shake of her head.

Nag...nag...that's all she knows to do, and she wonders why I want to play golf every weekend with the guys.

Tom glanced down to scan the monitor that was watched day and night. With a rapid eye blink of astonishment, he stared at what was coming across the screen. His chair legs hit the tiled floor with a thud.

"Got to go, hon," he said, his eyes glued to the monitor. He fumbled around and tried to find the base for the phone he held. He could still hear his wife's shrill complaining before he found what he searched for and hung up on her in mid-sentence. *No way,* he thought, his heart racing.

No friggin' way. He shook his head in disbelief. There it was again, clear as day. He'd sat before this monitor, night after night, with nothing but yawning silence all these years, and now, jackpot!

Bleep. Bleep.

There it was again!

With trembling fingers, Tom dialed the home phone number for his supervisor. He hoped the jerk was home. A lady's man in his small mind, his supervisor cruised the nightclubs every chance he could when able to sneak away from his wife. The revulsion the females at work displayed at his advances toward them failed to penetrate his thick skull that he wasn't quite the Casanova he believed he was. The man wasn't bad looking, but it was so obvious he wanted to screw someone, anyone, other than his wife, that they found him to be something of a joke. Tom drummed his fingertips on top of the desk before him as he listened to the phone on the other end ring for the fifth time.

"Come on, man," he said into the silent room around him. "Make tonight be the night you're with your wife."

"Hello," a faint male voice said over the line.

"Hey, boss. It's me, Tom. I have contact!"

***

"The hell you say?" Jack twisted upward in his bed. His wife rolled over against him, and with irritation, he pushed her to her side of the mattress.

"There it is again," Tom shrilled over the phone.

Jack, with haste, kicked back the bed covers over his legs. Standing, he looked at the clock on his nightstand, the phone he held he pressed tight against his cheekbone; it was one a.m.

"I'll be there in thirty minutes. Don't you call anyone else about this. And, Tom, when I say *anyone*, I mean no one. You comprehend me?"

***

"Sure, boss," Tom replied even as the phone connection ended. "Piece of shit," he mumbled as he watched the monitor before him.

***

Jack yanked his shirt over his head and, with his other clothing gathered, assured his wife as he dressed that it was a problem he had to take care of at work. He left the house at a dead run. His car started on the first try, and with which, he threw into reverse and swiveled to look backward. Facing forward again and the vehicle put into drive, he shoved the gas pedal under his foot down. *If Tom's pulling a prank out of boredom, I'll fire him on the spot.* Jack's fingers were clamped around the steering wheel before him as sweat dripped from his forehead. He arched a forearm upward to wipe it away, frowning as he maneuvered the car onto the highway.

A scant time later, he half-walked, half-ran down an empty hallway to where Tom's station was located in the United States Government-funded building and the ongoing program within it. Slamming through the office doorway, he scurried to where Tom sat, staring at the monitor before him. Jack slumped into the chair beside his desk and scanned the message, which scrolled across his computer screen. This was no prank pulled by a bored underling. The dispatch was clear as day.

...we wish to make connection with your leader...we wish to make connection with your leader...

Jack leaned over the metal desktop to drag the phone on it forward. His heart pressed against his ribcage, and its rat-a-tat beat made him shake. He dialed his superior's home number. At the male voice coming over the line from the other end, he rasped, "You need to notify the president. We have contact."

Chapter 1

Spring
College Campus

"I am telling you, Anna, it might be true. Quit laughing at me!"

Stylishly cut, short black hair bounced around the young woman's face in response to Anna's reaction to her stated theory, her agitation obvious.

"Charlee, you're my best friend, and I'm telling you, there is no such thing as aliens living among us. You've watched too many sci-fi movies over the years. Although I agree with you, it would be a huge psychological adjustment for us humans if there were such a thing, and it was proven."

Anna wiped with her hands at the tears that flowed down her cheeks as she sobered from her deep laughter. She gazed across the college dorm room at her best friend, a friend she'd had since she had gone to live with Molly and George. They had been best friends from that first day of grade school when Charlee walked up to her and took her hand in hers to pair them for a game of tag. Her friend Charlee was striking in looks and had always been so.

Anna had to admit she and Charlee both got second and even third glances when they were out on the town in the busy college club hangouts they frequented. Charlee was much more likely to jump into a relationship with the opposite sex, though, where she strayed toward caution's side when dealing with the male species. She was too guarded, her friend always said. *Loosen up, girl. Live a little*, Charlee frequently told her.

For the past two years, Charlee, with desperation it seemed, had searched for a lasting relationship. In and out of love at least three times in the past year alone. It worried Anna, her behavior. She felt protective of her longtime friend and wondered at her actions. Anna's hair swung forward over her shoulders as she bent to retrieve an armful of clothes from the dorm room closet. She turned to lay the items on the top of her bed. She packed to go home that morning.

Halting what she was doing as Charlee watched her in silence, Anna walked over to where her friend stood to hug her, smiling at her as she did so.

"You're still my best friend, Charlee White, even though you're a certified nut case. Aliens among us? Really? Where do you come up with these things?"

"Oh, shut up," Charlee said, coming out of her silence, and she laughed but then sobered. "Have you talked to Molly this morning? How's George?"

Anna swallowed back real tears, not her earlier tears of laughter. She shrugged. "Not this morning, no, but she informed me last night that the doctors said if the chemotherapy is ineffective in getting the cancer in remission, then he may have a year or less. Andy and I wanted to get home as soon as we could when we found out the news. Poor Andy can't get away from base for another two weeks, and he's worried out of his mind. George didn't want him to request leave from his Marine training or for me to leave in the middle of a semester, so they waited to tell us the news. I'm glad the semester is over, and I can go home now."

Anna folded the jeans she'd laid out and placed them in one of the tanned suitcases open before her. The past fourteen years were full of fond memories for her; Molly and George were the type of parents who showed loving affection toward her and her brother. They had made sure she and her brother grew into happy, well-adjusted adults. Nothing was ever said to them about their true parents, Frank and Sue, after that fateful summer day that had changed her and Andrew's lives for the better...*Much better lives. Funny, how I've never missed our natural parents as the years have slipped by,* Anna thought. The subject of how George and Molly had become her and Andrew's adopted parents had never been discussed. They had simply accepted it.

With a slight shake of her head, Anna looked up at Charlee and gave a sad upturn of her mouth. "You couldn't ask for better parents than George and Molly, Charlee. I hope George doesn't suffer with his cancer."

"I hope not either, Anna."

Anna lifted her pair of cases, packed with all of her clothes, from the bed with a handle in each hand.

She walked toward the door.

Charlee followed, pulling all the doors open for her. She then leaned on the last one as she strolled past it.

"When are you coming home?" Anna inquired, descending the dormitory steps to her car. Charlee had lost both of her parents in a car crash two years prior, and as an only child of parents who had no siblings themselves, she had no close living relatives. She'd always lived four blocks up the street from Anna and maintained her family home even with her parents' deaths.

"I plan to stay here another couple of days and talk to Lance before I head home," Charlee said.

Anna turned swiftly to look back up at her friend and grimaced.

Charlee gave a lopsided smile back down the steps at her.

Anna shook her head. "You know how I feel about Lance. You can do better. But, if he's what you want, I wish you luck. And if you're happy, then I should be."

Placing the suitcases into the trunk of her white compact car given as that year's birthday gift, she slammed its lid shut and turned to wave goodbye.

Charlee lifted a hand back.

Sliding into the front seat, Anna started the car and steered it home. She reminisced over the past years as she adjusted the radio to a favorite rock and roll station. Images and emotions rolled through her as she recalled the day she and Andrew came to live with the Summers. How scared she'd been, left with two strangers as a six-year-old. Yet, those feelings of uncertainty were soon replaced with sentiments of warmth and love. To this day, when she caught the aroma of new car leather, she felt that same emotional response experienced when Molly had helped her up and onto the front seat of the vehicle they drove that night. The feeling of homecoming that had washed over her had been overwhelming for her little six-year-old mind. She'd cried and cried as Molly hugged her close to her. She and Andrew had no words to say when they'd first glimpsed their new home. They had thought the sloped, green, manicured lawn leading up to the two-story white manor house before them was out of a fairy tale. Anna loved and still loved, the gleaming wide-planked pine wood floors throughout the house and the spaciousness of the two-story home. Still, even now, when away and walking through those front doors again, she felt the same awe as that first day she and her brother realized they were to live there. Their experience of a home up to that time had been two-room shacks with the stale smell of cigarettes and always the sound of loud fights and a parade of women, and sometimes men, in and out of the house. An open marriage, her parents mysteriously said to them. *Keep your damn mouths shut and get out of sight*; she and Andrew had heard often when they asked who the men and women were. With a flip of the lever on her car's steering wheel column and becoming aware of her surroundings, Anna signaled her wanted right turn. She eased the vehicle out onto the interstate and into its fast traffic flow as her memories flooded.

Molly spoke quietly to her and Andy that night, informing them their parents couldn't keep them. She and George were blessed, she'd said, as she had smiled down at them; they would get to have Andrew and Anna come live with them, and they were glad to have found them after such a long time of searching for them. George had looked huge to Anna from where she'd sat beside him and listened to Molly's lilting voice as she explained why they'd taken them from their parents. George, a broad-shouldered man well over six feet tall, had dwarfed the car's interior. Molly, a fine-boned woman with delicate hands and a soft-spoken voice, was beautiful then and still was, even after all these years. Molly and George both had aged well. They didn't look much older than they had shown fourteen years prior. George, always in shape, had been going strong until diagnosed with cancer.

Awareness of the scenery, she sped by registered, and with an appreciation of it, Anna took in the budded-out green-leafed trees that grew along the highway and the freshly mowed intermedium. The car indicated its low gas level, and she began to search for a place to refill. She also needed a cappuccino. Coming up to a large gas station with multiple services, Anna slowed the car to maneuver it into the station's far-east gas pump lane. Shutting off the vehicle's engine, she opened her door. When she emerged from the car, a man across the way issued a low wolf whistle at another pump. Anna directed a smile his way as she pushed her hair away from her face. As the gas flowed into the car tank, she leaned backward against the car to glance over toward the older man who'd whistled.

I bet he's married.

The number of wedded men who hit on her and Charlee was about the same as the single men who showed an interest in them. Shifting her feet and feeling somewhat contrite at her sour thoughts, Anna averted her gaze away from the man. He had caught her appraisal of him and now openly watched her.

What made me jump to the automatic assumption that he must be married? She thought, puzzled. *I don't trust people, just as Andrew says, so I've never found anyone who's made me want to settle down or become intimate with them. I've let my early childhood experiences affect my judgment. Although... now Charlee.* Anna smiled. *That girl. In and out of love at the drop of a hat.* Anna slid her gaze over to the man again, only to veer her glance from him. He was good-looking and seemed in great physical shape; she would admit that.

Molly and George disliked it when she talked about appreciating anyone of the opposite sex. Neither of them had ever verbalized anything, but she and Andrew picked up on their disapproval when they both had begun to take an interest in the opposite gender. She dated, but the tension radiating from them made her not date anyone for long.

Click.

The gas tank filled, Anna retrieved her purse from the front seat of her car and headed for the store entrance.

"See ya, honey. I love that tight ass. I bet it's a perfect fit for my hands."

Anna turned. The same man who'd whistled earlier, now with an arrogance displayed, smiled at her. He waved goodbye and blew a kiss as he drove off. His wedding band flashed. With a heavy frown, Anna rotated to continue walking across the parking lot. *Not so good-looking,* she mused. She strolled out from the Quik Stop a few minutes later, holding a large, steaming cup of French vanilla-flavored cappuccino and laughing at herself. Her Achilles' heel, always a hot cup of cappuccino, even on an unusually warm, early summer day.

Chapter 2

Planet Garr
Seven Months Prior

Striding up the massively wide stone steps and then past a row of large white pillar columns that led to the High Commander's private receiving chambers, Traun's polished, knee-high, black leather boots resounded with a clipped force upon the stone that made up the floor of the Government Palace. He was emotionally, as well as physically, exhausted that evening. Within just the past hour, he'd returned to the central city from a month-long, intense battle in Sector Nine, the High Commander having ordered him there a month ago to get an uprising under control. The Palace guards watched him in silence, and Traun knew they searched for any sign of weakness from their High Commander's Army Major. He hoped they saw a strong, confident man and none of his inner turmoil or physical exhaustion with those watchful gazes.

Nodding to the sober-faced men before the chamber doors, he strode past them, and when he cleared the doorway, the twelve-foot-high wooden doors were heaved shut behind him. The High Commander and his Lifemate watched as his stride brought him toward where they sat in regal pose; the backs of their royal chairs were bright red, trimmed in gold, and glowed behind them, highly polished. Traun felt a mother's love envelop him when he drew close enough to see the expression reflected on her face. Her posture became relaxed as he came near.

"Mother, I am glad to see your lovely face again after so long an absence." Leaning down, Traun kissed the raised cheek she offered him. She patted his face with a delicate hand.

"You're so tanned. I have been worried about you while you were in Sector Nine," she said.

"Son," the High Commander by her side greeted him.

"Sit, sit." He indicated the chair positioned before them. "Give your mother and me your report."

"Father, Mother, my report isn't all good. We lost well over five hundred lives in Sector Nine." Traun lowered his tired frame onto the high-backed chair as he felt the bile rise in his throat at the remembered battle he'd returned from. His usual stoical control slipped under his parents' watchful gazes.

Shifting to give himself time to control his emotions, Traun stretched his legs out before him. He swallowed. He kept his gaze lowered as he tamped down the unexpected reaction.

After a long and painful moment, he looked back up. "I am sickened lives were lost. The people attacked each other and my army. They ripped apart their towns and homes in their rage and fury. My troops and I worked our way through their destruction and gained control, but not without all those lives spent. Before we left, the leading council members there agreed to pass out the calming serum to everyone as needed."

Locking eyes with his father, Traun allowed the man before him to see some of the anguish he felt. "Father, there were over a thousand rioting citizens that my troops and I had to inject with the calming serum. Most are now remorseful of the destruction they caused in their countryside. For how long, though, Father? How long before the people rise again over the injustice done to them? An injustice done to all of us. I can't blame them for their despair and anger. What is life, after all, without an expectation of time ahead?"

His mother gave a deep and heartfelt sigh. "What errors we and our ancestors have made over our lifetimes. All in the search for the perfect living specimen, the perfect cure-all, the perfect world."

Her emotion was apparent on her delicate, aged face as she brushed away the moisture that had gathered at the corner of her eyes. She touched her chest. "My heart aches for the loss of all those lives and the demise of any future generations for the world of Garr. We destroyed ourselves with our arrogance of being superior to our Creator."

"Son," Traun's father said as he watched his Lifemate, his voice grave. "We received an urgent report from the Watchers of the Skies while you were in Sector Nine. It has been noted that the wormhole has begun its one thousand years of stirring."

Traun, with a foreboding feeling, stared at his father. "But we were to have another year before the wormhole path opened?"

"The wrong date must have been entered into the Book of Wisdom. We don't know what happened, but you must begin preparations to leave on the morrow. That is why I ordered you to report to me today. Your brother began the organization of the ships and supplies you'll need, as well as however many animals he can have loaded. By the time you go to planet Earth, pick up the Caretakers and their Transfers, and then travel back to the wormhole entrance to meet up with the other spaceships, you'll barely have enough time to unload your cargo and for the spaceships' crews and their ships to travel back through the wormhole before it closes again."

His father paused, but then he continued.

"Your aunt sent news from planet Earth that your uncle has contracted Earth's wasting disease. We received the report soon after you departed for Sector Nine. Your uncle needs the Learned Ones' healing medicine to get the disease under control. As soon as you reach Earth, go to him first."

Traun felt his anger swell. He was angry because he didn't have the next year as he'd believed he would to cut ties and say his goodbyes before leaving for his life in the new world. Anger also from the lost year with Avreen. If he were honest, he'd looked forward to having more time with her. He wasn't in love with her; he hadn't allowed any love to develop because he'd been aware of his expected life plan since his younger years. He did, however, enjoy her company. She'd been a faithful lover and companion during their relationship and, as such, deserved his consideration and respect in ending it. After a month of celibacy, he looked forward to seeing her again. With this news his father shared, he'd have to tell her that tonight would be their last night together. He hoped she didn't begin to cry when he broke the news. He was in no mood to deal with an emotional scene. Traun shifted in the chair as his tension made his neck cramp. A headache had started to rake its claws across his brow.

His father spoke. "Son, I know this is unexpected, and I'm sorry. Your mother and I can't tell you how devastated we are to not have another year with you as we thought we had. Your brother said to give you his love.

He doesn't think he'll be able to be back in time to see you off. He was disheartened when he, with his Lifemate, left here to organize the other spaceships."

Traun rose, and his height caused his mother to crane her neck to look up at him.

Rising, she continued to gaze upward at him. "I want to imprint your image into my mind. Once gone, I'll never be able to look upon your beloved face again," she said.

She pressed her lips to his cheekbone when he leaned down to enfold her in his embrace.

"My heart aches with my loss felt already," she said softly.

The High Commander rose to his great height from where he sat. "Son, I love you with everything I possess. I shall miss your presence here on Garr. Only through you and the others will our race survive. You are our last hope. From the written reports we received from Earth, your chosen Lifemate seems to be someone you can find happiness with."

His chest tight at the impending loss of his family, Traun replied, "Father, I shall be a High Commander you will be proud to call son. I solemnly vow that you and Mother will live on through my sons and daughters this night and be remembered."

With an abruptness, the High Commander rotated away. When he turned back around, his gaze glistened with moisture.

"You, my son, are a man worthy to command a new world. You will rule with compassion and intelligence. You have been bred to be a leader of men—"

He swiftly turned away again. When he turned around, he said gruffly, "Let us convene with the High Council members and brief them on your report."

Traun met with the leaders and then said goodnight to his parents. When he left the Great Hall and walked out into the cool night air, he realized he needed a bath and a deep massage before he proceeded to Avreen's. Moments later, he strolled into a nearby city bathhouse, and the women there clamored over each other to serve him.

Traun relaxed as his headache eased. The woman behind him worked magic on him, her fingers firm on his neck and shoulders. An hour later, when he stepped into his waiting, hot bath, he slid into the scented deep pool of water with a verbal sigh of appreciation. Steam rose and swirled up over his head as water sloshed around him.

***

More than one of the females in the bathhouse felt disappointment that the man they washed paid no special attention to any, his mind elsewhere. The dark-eyed female who held the large towel ready to dry the High Commander's son when he rose from his bath was envious of whatever or whoever had his thoughts so firmly captured.

Roughly, she began to towel him dry.

***

Unaware of the tumult of emotions caused among the women, Traun wondered what had angered the female who attended him. He noted the woman dried him rather briskly. She almost snapped the towel she held at his bare body; he realized in alarm as he stepped back from her. He reached to grasp the end of the towel to pull it from her fingers before she could cause damage to his exposed body parts.

"I believe I can handle it from here," he said. He smiled in question when she pouted up at him. Spinning on her heels, the woman exited through partitions, left swinging in her wake. Traun shook his head in bewilderment.

Making short work at drying off, he dressed in freshly laundered clothes and strolled into the brisk nighttime city air.

He was anxious to see Avreen.

When he reached the front entrance of her home, he took the steps two at a time.

With a raised fist, he pounded on her door.

***

Avreen had heard the news of Traun's arrival back into the central city several hours earlier. She had hurried to complete her errands in the busy downtown market and then rushed home. She bathed and perfumed her body and waited. Her excitement grew as the hours passed. She made sure his favorite drink was prepared and chilled. It was a beverage made as a specialty in the city: a drink few men could handle before its potency rendered them out for the night. Avreen knew Traun wouldn't stop to eat before he came to see her, so she made preparations for his favorite meal to be delivered when she called for it.

Humming to herself, she was happy with life in general. That day, she received the endorsement she'd worked hard to achieve. Three weeks prior, she'd learned the horrifying intelligence report of the wormhole opening predicted was sooner than believed.

As the news spread like fire across the city, she began to plead with the High Council members in charge of the sign-up to allow her to take the place of a Volunteer who had been scheduled to relocate to the new world and who'd taken her own life; the young woman's body found by her aging parents who still grieved over the senseless loss of their only child. They couldn't understand the note left by her bedside; she who'd approached them, they said, and who asked them for permission to sign up to be a Volunteer. Daily and unceasingly, Avreen worked to convince the High Council members why she, Avreen, would be an excellent candidate as the replacement Volunteer for the New World. That day, she'd received word of the Council members' consent.

And why shouldn't they have chosen me? Avreen thought.

She was the child of a Leading Council member of Sector Twelve. Moreover, she'd taken it upon herself to learn the language of the Earth people.

Although the Earth Transfers should have learned the language of Garr while they waited for relocation to the new world, she thought with a scoff. She sniffed with her disapproval of the hybrid-Earth people. She didn't know much about them, only that they'd been kept and raised apart from the world of Garr.

The High Council members had informed her that they were impressed with her intelligence and willingness to give of herself for the continued survival of their race. The one drawback of their decision, they had stated, was that as a new member of the army of Garr, she'd not trained under the appointed High Commander who was to rule over all who relocated to the new world. She was still in basic training. They'd frowned over that aspect. Nevertheless, they said, they felt she would be an asset on the new planet with her family's background and the abilities she'd shown so far in her training.

Avreen made certain none of the High Council members knew of her relationship with Traun. She was sure her bid as a Volunteer would have been denied if they'd known their connection.

Hesitant of how Traun would react, she planned to keep the news of her submission papers and her acceptance to herself. She felt confident that, with the rush of leaving, he wouldn't become aware of the change in the list of Volunteers to the new world until it was too late to adjust. The whole city was up in arms over the news of the wormhole opening early, and all in charge, it seemed, scrambled with haste to prepare.

In high spirits, Avreen wrapped her arms around her waist and twirled about in her private, small city home with wonder at what she'd accomplished.

I know once Traun sees me in the new world, he'll not take another Lifemate but me. He hasn't wanted anyone else in our two years together. He will be pleased to see me. So delighted, he'll forgive me my deceit. I love him, love him, love him….

She smiled wide when she heard a fist pound on her front door. Her silent singsong humming halted within her head. She knew she was a welcome sight when she opened her door to Traun's appreciative gaze. He grinned wide as he stepped forward past the threshold of the doorway and, in one swift move, grabbed her around the waist to pull her to him. He reached back with a booted foot to kick her door shut behind him, lifting her easily to stride toward her bedroom. He tossed her onto her bed. The evening gown she wore slid away as he tugged at it, her body exposed for his appraisal.

In haste, he stripped his clothes.

"Ah…," he groaned as he lowered his hard body next to hers. "I've missed this."

Avreen smiled upward at him when he grinned down at her. With eagerness, she met his lips with her own.

All will be right for us in the new world as Lifemates, she thought with satisfaction.

Later, lying beside him in sleepy contentment, she giggled when he reached out to draw her to him to wrap an arm around her.

"Again? So soon?" she drawled.

He turned toward her and shook his head at her. He raised her hand to his mouth to graze her knuckles with his lips.

She realized he planned to break the news to her of his leaving on the morrow.

"Avreen, this is our last night together. I'm sorry, honey. I learned tonight I'm to depart for the new world immediately and not in a year as we thought."

"I know, Traun. I heard the news in the city. I'm glad we have this night together since we won't see each other for a long time." Avreen held her breath at what she'd let slip.

Untangling his fingers from hers, Traun propped himself up on an elbow, and his gaze met hers. "This is the last time we will see each other. You understand that, don't you, honey? We discussed my obligations at the start of our relationship. I must take a Transfer from planet Earth for a Lifemate. And I won't be able to return from where I'm going."

Avreen raised her arms to wrap them around his neck. She let her eyes well with tears, and her voice kept subdued. "I know this, Traun. I can't help but to dream, can I?"

As he gazed down at her, his face softened in his regard. "I'm going to miss you and your gentleness," he said. He let her ease his head down to her raised mouth.

Chapter 3

Sioux Falls, South Dakota

Anna drove her car into the driveway of her home. She was bone tired. Stepping out of the parked vehicle, she leaned over to touch her toes and stretch her muscles. She decided that two full days on the road was enough for anyone when she straightened. Looking toward the house, a warmth of love washed over her as Molly walked out onto the front porch. Anna ran to her, and Molly opened her arms to embrace her.

"I'm so glad you're home, Anna. George will be happy to see you. He misses you when you're away," Molly said.

Wrapping her arms about her, Anna hugged her tight. She pulled back to look at her. "How is George?"

"He's holding in there. The chemotherapy is rough on him, though."

She and Molly turned to enter the house, their arms wrapped around each other's waists.

"Where's George now?" Anna questioned.

Molly patted her arm. "He went to lie down. We returned from the hospital only a few minutes ago. He received a round of chemo today, and when we got home, he said he felt tired and wanted to rest. But you go on up. I'll bring your bags in from the car and put them in your room for you."

Anna braced herself for any change in George's appearance as she climbed the stairs to the master bedroom. Molly had asked her not to show her shock at how much weight he'd lost. George, always in charge, didn't like anyone to feel sorry for him.

Knocking on the bedroom door and hearing, "Come in," Anna opened it to enter the light-muted room. She paused inside the doorway while her eyes adjusted to the darkness. When she could see George, who lay on the bed under a blanket, a ripple of shock coursed through her at how thin he looked. She schooled her face to mirror only pleasure at seeing him.

"Come in, come in," he exclaimed. He held out a hand to her.

With eagerness, Anna crossed the bedroom floor to grasp his hand. "How are you feeling?" she said with concern. "Molly told me you had a round of chemo today."

"I feel good, considering. Don't want to dwell on it, though. We must do whatever needs to be done to control the cancer. How was the drive down? Not too hard on you, I hope. Look at you. You're prettier every time I see you."

Leaning down to kiss his hollowed-out cheek, Anna replied as she sat down on the edge of the bed beside him, "I'm good, a little tired from the drive down. I wish you had let Molly call Andrew and me when you first found out you had cancer. We would have come home to be here for you."

"Now, girlie, don't you worry about me. I wanted you to finish your studies. Besides, Andrew will be here in two weeks, and you both will be here for the summer."

Anna shook her head at the man before her. "Still, we would have been here earlier for you and Molly."

George smiled. "You're here now."

Scanning his face, Anna could tell he was exhausted and not feeling well. "George, I'm going to go help Molly bring my suitcases in from my car. She says the chemo makes you tired, so I want to let you rest. In a couple of hours, I'll come back, okay?"

He squeezed her hand. "I do seem extra drained tonight."

She stood up from the bed and turned to leave when he said, "Anna?"

"Yes?" She looked back at him with concern.

"You know how much I love you and Andrew, don't you?"

"I've never doubted it since you brought us here to live. Why do you ask?"

"I wanted to make sure you knew."

"I know, George. I know…." She eased the bedroom door shut as she watched his eyes close.

Molly glanced up from where she stood before the pale gray granite kitchen countertops when Anna walked into the room where she was. She looked down at her hands as she tore leaves from a head of lettuce with slender fingers. She was preparing a salad with the evening meal. Anna had noted her suitcases left at the base of the staircase when she'd come down them.

"How did it go?" Molly asked.

Anna walked over to stand beside her.

"He was tired and, as usual, worried about Andrew and me. I'm glad you warned me about how much weight he'd lost. He has always been such a large force to me. I was shocked at how frail he appeared. Are the doctors predicting anything different from the last time we spoke on the phone?"

"They are still trying to get the cancer in remission, and if unable, it's the same prognosis. He might have six months to a year, they say—oh, I almost forgot to tell you. Andrew called while you were up with George. He says he should be here next weekend instead of another two weeks as originally thought. He finished his tests early, and his supervisors approved his leave because of George's condition."

"George will be glad to hear of the changed plans." Anna swallowed back her emotional response to the reminder of George's diagnosis.

Molly motioned to the table where she sat the salad bowl. "Come and eat. George won't be able to hold anything down, so we'll let him rest."

Anna pulled out a cushioned-seated chair.

She and Molly caught up on each other's news between their bites of grilled steak and salad. After the meal, they chattered away to each other while they cleaned up the kitchen. Anna retold Molly the tale Charlee had conveyed about aliens living among them and her wanting to do her college thesis on the theory. While she laughed over her friend's imagination, she noticed Molly didn't laugh in return with her. She looked down at the plate she dried and smiled rather sadly instead.

Peering closer at her, Anna took the dishtowel from her hands to turn her toward the kitchen doorway. "I'll finish up in here. You go upstairs and check on George, as I know you want to do. I'll stop by before I go to bed."

She glanced at the kitchen clock, which showed eleven p.m. "It's late and time for us to call it a night anyway."

As Molly walked out of the room, Anna turned back toward the kitchen sink, and as she did so, her eyes caught a movement of light out of the window, high up in the sky. She leaned closer over the kitchen countertop toward the clear glass window before her for a better view. Squinting and looking upward, she thought she saw another flash of light, but it disappeared. *Must've been a falling star*, she thought as she pulled back from the window. Drying her hands, she folded the dishtowel she held to lay it on the counter. Walking out of the kitchen, she flipped off the overhead lights.

With her light rap of knuckles on Molly and George's bedroom door, moments later, a low murmur of voices could be heard through it. Anna thought she caught the distinct, deep sound of a man's voice besides George's. Perplexed, she wondered when the visitor had arrived. Knocking on their door again, she waited.

Molly opened the bedroom door and, with a step forward, closed it again behind her.

"Molly, does George have a visitor this late at night? I didn't hear the doorbell ring."

Molly lowered her gaze from hers. "No, honey, it's the television. Why don't you visit with George in the morning? He's exhausted. Today's chemotherapy treatment was particularly hard on him."

Anna wondered why she seemed so edgy. *Probably just nerves with George's illness,* she decided. She'd let both of them get some rest. She reached out to hug her, and Molly patted her on the back. Anna smiled at her when they parted.

"Let George know I stopped by. A hot bath sounds delicious right about now. I'll see you both in the morning. Love you."

***

"Love you too, sweetheart." Molly watched Anna enter her bedroom before she turned to reenter hers. She saw Traun and George looking at her.

"Did she hear me speaking with Uncle?" Traun asked.

Molly sighed as she walked over to the bed to settle beside George. He reached out and took hold of her hand with his.

"She heard, but I told her it was the television set."

"Is she the chosen one?"

George squeezed Molly's hand as he glanced upward at her. He nodded his head at Traun. "Yes, she's the chosen one."

***

Traun wondered what the woman with the soft, pleasing voice looked like. Mentally, he shrugged and turned his attention back to George. It didn't matter what she looked like. What needed to be done, he'd do, just as he'd told Avreen during their last night together on Garr: he must do his duty for the sake of their people even if he didn't look forward to taking an unknown Lifemate. It was his choice not to know what this selected Lifemate looked like. He hadn't wanted to know. He would execute his obligation, no matter what.

Traun withdrew from his uniform pocket the bottle of small white pills he'd brought. He handed the container over to his uncle.

"The Learned One said you are to take two of these pills a day until gone. Don't miss any. There are enough for thirty days, which is the complete treatment cycle for the Earth disease you've contracted."

Molly took the bottle from George. "Don't worry, I'll ensure he takes all of them as needed. We were concerned you wouldn't make it in time. We sent the message eight months ago."

"Is that why you started the barbaric treatment for the illness instead of waiting for the Learned Ones' healing pills?"

"Yes," Molly replied. "The wasting disease spread fast, and we needed to do something to slow it down until you could get here."

"Move that chair over to the bed, Traun. It hurts my neck having to look up at you." George rubbed at the back of his neck with a large hand.

Traun fetched the chair indicated and lowered himself onto its polished wooden seat to stretch out his legs. He crossed his feet at the ankles as he returned his uncle's gaze.

"Uncle, I don't have good news to report. My delay for the eight months to get here instead of the usual six is because our world is in chaos. The people are unhappy. There was a rebellion in Sector Nine, which took time to quell. We restored peace and order for now, but only by giving the troubled ones a higher dose of injections to stabilize them."

Molly gasped. "How is the High Commander and my sister?"

Traun felt his throat tighten. "Mother is holding in there, Aunt. She and father both feel the pain of the people and their own for what has happened to our world."

He looked back over toward George. "Uncle, you all must be prepared to leave in three weeks."

George and Molly both drew back with their surprise at his announcement.

"But we have another year for our plan to be put into place," George said.

"No, Uncle, there was a miscalculation. The wormhole is open now. We have three months to go through the passageway before the door closes again. I have ships on their way as we speak with supplies and the Volunteers. We are scheduled to meet them at the wormhole passage by then." Traun stood to push the chair back. "Uncle, Aunt, be ready to leave when I return."

Rising from the edge of the bed where she sat, Molly hugged him. "Goodbye, Traun."

Nodding at her and his uncle, Traun reached across his midsection to press the device attached to his belt.

***

In seconds, where the man had stood was now air.

Molly met her Lifemate's gaze.

"I don't know how Anna and Andrew will respond to this, George, with it having to be sprung on them so fast and us leaving Earth right after. A year would have given them the time needed to come to terms, mentally and emotionally, with what we have to tell them."

George sighed.

He reached down to adjust the blankets which lay over his legs.

"Come to bed, Molly. We'll break the news to them next week and pray they'll come willingly with us."

Chapter 4

Anna leaped up from the lounge chair where she lay by the swimming pool when she heard the chimes of the front doorbell the following weekend. She grabbed her bathing suit coverup to pull it over her head, then paused to slip on flip-flops before sprinting through the house for the front door.

"Molly, George," she yelled as she ran. "Andy's here."

Sliding to a stop on the polished wood floors, she slung the door before her open.

"Andy, you're home," she squealed. She grabbed her brother by the neck to pull him through the open doorway toward her.

Laughing, he wrapped his arms around her.

"Come on, sis, it's only been a couple of months since we last saw each other. No need to be so dramatic."

Anna laughed and released her tight hold of his neck. "I still missed you."

They turned as one at the sound of George and Molly's approach from the living room.

"Andrew, glad you made it home," George said. He reached out to shake Andrew's hand at the same time Molly started to hug him.

Laughing over their antics, Andrew placed his arm across Molly's shoulders as she turned in his arms. "With this kind of welcome, I'm glad to be home. George, you look good. From Anna's phone call the morning after she arrived here last weekend, it didn't sound like you were doing too well?"

Anna, who stood beside George, patted him on his back. "He's gained three pounds this week."

George harrumphed, his embarrassment showing with all the attention.

"I'm a lot better than I was. Let's go to the living room and catch up on your training this past year."

"I'll go brew some tea for all of us," Anna said.

"Well, son," she heard George say as the others drifted from her toward the living room, "how's the Marines treating you?"

Molly jumped up from her chair to help her when she walked into the living room fifteen minutes later with a tray full of tall, iced glasses of tea. Anna set the tray on the end table beside George to hand a glass over to him. Molly had already taken one for herself and one for Andrew. Turning, she walked over to sink alongside her brother on the plush brown sofa across from Molly and George, who reclined in a matched set of rose-flowered patterned chairs. She took a sip of tea from the frosted glass she held.

Playfully, she punched her brother on the shoulder.

"Every time I see you, I swear, Andy, you're taller and broader in the shoulders."

With smiles directed at them, George and Molly looked on as Andrew punched her back on her shoulder with humor shown before he said, "What have you been doing with yourself this past week? Looks like you've gotten a lot of sun, as tanned as you are?"

Anna gazed with tenderness at George for a moment before she looked back toward Andrew. "George has been up and about and doing so well—looking better every day, I might add—that I've been taking it easy. You know, swimming in the pool and relaxing."

***

George and Molly made eye contact as the two continued to chat and tease. The time had come to begin their story. Molly kicked off her shoes to pull her legs up beside her hips on the chair she sat in, as if making herself smaller would protect her from the emotional onslaught about to occur. With a sudden awareness of the tension within the room, Andrew and Anna stopped their conversation to glance at them. George gazed back at the two. He swallowed hard. His dread rose within him.

Both young adults began to rise from their seats, their gazes fixed on him. He waved his hand at them.

"No, sit back down, the both of you." He took a deep breath and let it back out again. "Molly and I have something to reveal. We believed we had a year to explain the situation to you, however, due to circumstances beyond our control, it's to be done now and without delay."

Anna and Andrew looked at Molly, and when they noted her distress, their gazes swung back toward him. George saw their fear claw through them as they waited for him to continue.

Andrew burst out, "What are you trying to tell us? You're not dying, are you?"

"No, Andrew, I received the cure for my cancer this past week. I should be healed within a month."

The confusion experienced over his comment was apparent as the two young adults' stares leaped from him to Molly before they looked back at him again, their brows drawn together.

"Let me start from the beginning, and please, hear me out before either of you respond," he said.

George shifted his gaze from their bewildered expressions as he cleared his throat. He began the narrative after returning his attention to the young adults he and Molly had raised as if they were their own.

"Molly and I are from another world within Earth's galaxy, a far-away planet called Garr. The world we knew—our world of Garr, is in chaos because of choices our leaders made thousands of years ago and forced our people to abide by. Our people—as a result of government enactments—are now sterile between each other, but not outside of our race. Through searching and experimentation, it was found that we are identical to this planet's human race, except for an extra chromosome that we have. You both before me are a product of that experimentation, descendants of a people on the brink of extinction. There are ninety-eight others like you stationed in the United States. All of you are half of this world's origin and half of Garr origin. It is your destiny and that of the others to leave this planet and travel with us to another world, a new world where we as a people will have a chance to save ourselves from extinction."

An hour later, he trailed off into silence. Only once or twice had Andrew tried to interrupt him. He hadn't allowed it. Anna hadn't said a word. He and Molly, in silence, studied their faces as they waited for their reactions to what they'd been told and of the pictures displayed of the world of Garr and its inhabitants—people like them but not.

The two young adults stared back at them, unblinking.

Anna, who'd slipped from the couch to the floor as she'd looked over the stack of pictures brought out, gazed with a look of horror at them both. George knew she wondered who these strangers were before her, whom she'd believed she knew and had expressed a love for all these years.

With all the evidence shown to him, Andrew still peered hard at him in skepticism.

"So let me get this straight. My sister and I are of half-alien and half-Earth human genetics, and we're expected to leave here in two weeks… and not only leave here but marry and breed with one of your kind when we reach this unknown planet you speak of to help your people preserve your race." His voice and eyebrows were high with his disbelief.

"Yes."

"Shut up," Anna shouted. She lunged upward to her feet.

George, Andrew, and Molly jumped in reaction.

Molly burst into tears.

Anna gawked at them all, her eyes wide. She waved her hand over the pictures.

"You expect Andrew and me to believe this…this…whatever this is? Well, let me tell you something. This supposed half-alien isn't going anywhere. To be a breeder, of all things. Really? How sick."

She stomped out of the living room.

"Anna, stop. Stop right there. Please try to understand," Molly called out to get her to turn around as she rose from her seat.

Anna took off in a sprint for the front door of the home. It slammed shut behind her.

Molly turned back around.

"What have we done, George? What have we done?"

She whirled away to leave the room.

When she returned a few minutes later, he and Andrew still sat in awkward silence. She paused inside the living room doorway, streaks of tears displayed on her face.

George knew Andrew's stunned and bewildered gaze directed her way caused sorrow to shaft through her again at their deceit. He shook off his surprise at Anna's emotional outburst. With her continued silence throughout his disclosure, he believed she was shocked but was processing his narrative well.

"Where does the body monitor show she's headed?" George noticed Andrew spasm at his question. *Another mystery to explain to him and Anna,* he thought. He gave a silent sigh; so much deceit.

Lifting the heel of her hand to wipe at her eyes, Molly replied, "She's headed over to see her friend, Charlee."

Reassured of Anna's whereabouts, George leaned forward with a hand extended toward the young adult he'd raised from a child to manhood. "Son, please say you'll listen to Molly and me and try to understand our side of this story."

Andrew didn't move. George pulled the hand of friendship he offered back to his side.

"So, you've monitored our movements from the time you obtained us from Frank and Sue. I guess I can understand that. After we were conceived and you lost us, you couldn't afford to lose us again, could you? I never understood those words said that night you took us, but I never questioned it."

With his started and halting explanation of how their monitoring was done, Andrew held up a hand.

"I don't want to know the mechanics of our tracking devices, George. At this point, I don't think I can take much more. Right now, I want you to explain to me about Frank and Sue, who they were, and exactly who Anna and I are to them. And who you and Molly are."

Molly walked over to George's chair and sat on the arm. She burst out with anger, "Frank and Sue were horrible people."

"Molly, no." George patted her hand for her to be quiet. "Sue was your Earth mother, and Frank, her husband. You and Anna obtained our genetics from your male Donor parent on our home planet of Garr. He is getting up in old age. We don't expect he'll survive the winter. You and Anna are the descendants of a High Council member. He has served on the Council his entire adult life."

At Andrew's questioning look toward him, George explained, "A High Council member is an official who serves his or her world for the betterment of others.

"Molly and I would never consent to me being a Donor parent. We submitted our names to be Caretakers instead and were chosen by the Council for that role. Thus, we were assigned to your and Anna's cases when your original Caretaker failed to report in at his usual time. As I said earlier, we, as a race of people, are now sterile between each other. It happened swiftly and without warning. Around one thousand years ago, our Learned Ones were, with success, able to use germline manipulation for designer babies. This resulted in the people of Garr being mandated to use the technology for the betterment of our race. It resulted in less illness, less disease, and uniformity in the same color of hair and the same shade of eye color. The only differences allowed were our heights and our face and body structures. We now have a lifespan of around one hundred and fifty to two hundred years. Molly and I are approaching one hundred years of age. Molly's ninety-eight, and I am ninety-nine years old."

"Are you kidding me? You look and act like someone who's in their middle forties."

After Andrew's stunned outburst, George continued, "Our Learned Ones failed to realize until it was too late that a sterilization process was happening between our people. Now, we are dying off as each generation reaches its expected lifespan. I am the last of my family line. Molly has one sister and two nephews left in her family line. Our world is at war over the forced decisions made to make our people supreme beings."

George paused—his gaze he held steady on Andrew's.

"To save ourselves from a path to total annihilation and to preserve our kind as we know it to be, it was decided by our High Commander and the High Council members to select Volunteers and Caretakers to start over on another world with Transfers from Earth like you and Anna, who can breed with our people. It is to be a new beginning for the Garr race."

After a few seconds of silence, Andrew asked, "How did you come to be here on Earth? I mean your people, originally, here."

"Our High Commander and High Council members contacted the U.S. government and other leaders from this world many years ago. The people of Garr and the people of Earth genetically are a close match, but our government officials wanted to go slow with our experiments of interbreeding with Earth people. Our officials wanted nothing to go wrong. The U.S. government and others of authority around this world let us set up several bases scattered throughout the land to begin our work. They agreed to this in exchange for transferring our advanced technology to them. When everything was ready and seemed perfect, we incorporated artificial insemination on the female Earth subjects. We used the sperm from the Garr Donors to a participating Earth female in the program. The Earth subjects were paid for their contribution as birth mothers. We used volunteers only. The participants were told that a family who desperately desired children was sterile and would pay for their help. It was understood at the onset that the child would be handed over to the unseen family upon birth."

"And *this* is where Frank and Sue come into the story," Andrew said as he flopped back on the couch. The emotion George heard in his voice reflected the tension he felt.

George nodded. "The Caretaker assigned to your and Anna's case decided for whatever unknown reason, and without the High Council's knowledge or permission, to leave you with your Earth parent until Anna was birthed, which was eighteen months after you.

"From what we understand, in reading over the Caretaker's last written logged report, is that Frank began to demand more money right after Sue's conception with Anna, or he wasn't going to let us have either of you. It's not understood why the Caretaker didn't notify the High Council members of his demands or what Frank's hold was on the Caretaker. The night Anna was born, the Caretaker disappeared. He stopped reporting to the High Council members. And nothing else was logged in his written reports. We've searched for him, but he's not been located since."

Andrew frowned. "He's dead."

"How do you know this?" It puzzled George, his matter-of-fact statement.

"I overheard Frank telling Sue about the incident between them the same morning they brought Anna and me to you and Molly. They had gotten into a physical confrontation. From what Frank said, it was an accident. He worried that he had been found out. How much did we cost your authorities?"

"It had been agreed upon between Frank and Sue and the Caretaker. They were to be paid one hundred thousand dollars at your birth and another one hundred thousand at Anna's birth. In the end, two hundred and fifty thousand was paid for Anna, which was what I gave Frank the day we got you both back. He even tried to demand more money when he handed you over to Molly and me."

"Where are they now?" Andrew bit out.

George realized Andrew's anger at the two people in his life who'd mentally and physically mistreated him and his sister in their childhood rose within him again after so many years of dormancy, and he answered with a gentle tone, "They're both dead—robbed and killed while at a bar was our last report, two months after they were given their final payment. The police report stated they'd bragged to people in the bar about having lots of cash. Later that same night, they were seen sitting and talking with a man whom no one seemed to know, or at least who nobody was willing to say anything about to the authorities. The bar owner found them in their car, their necks broken, when he closed his establishment for the night. The money was never located."

Molly stood and walked over to where Andrew sat.

She reached out to touch him on the shoulder with her fingertips. "I'm so sorry for the pain we've caused you, Andrew."

He looked up at her and reached to close his fingers around hers. "Don't be upset on my account. I love you, Molly, no matter who you are."

He looked over at George. "I love you both. I'm confused, is all."

***

Anna ran until she reached Charlee's house. She was confident she was home since she had called earlier that morning and said she'd made it there. Pounding on her front door while ringing the doorbell simultaneously, Anna burst past the doorway when Charlee started to open the door.

Her friend staggered backward with her assault. Open-mouthed, Charlee stared at her. She watched as she gasped for air.

"What in the world is wrong with you?" she demanded.

Anna tried to catch her breath. She'd run full-out for four complete blocks with her flip-flops clasped tight in her left hand and still wearing her bathing suit and silky coverup. Her side hurt.

She finally wheezed out, "I'm an alien, Charlee."

Charlee erupted with laughter to pull her toward her and close the door behind her. "Have you been smoking wacky weed?"

"No, Charlee, I am telling you." Anna rose from her bent-over position to look her in the face. "Truth, I swear. Tonight, I found out Andrew and I are aliens."

"Ha, ha, okay, you got me. Damn girl, you had me scared that something was seriously wrong with you."

With the shock and emotional roller coaster ride experienced, Anna burst into tears.

"What in the world, Anna?" Charlee took her by the shoulders to turn her toward her living room. "Go sit on the couch, catch your breath, and calm down. I'll get you something to drink.

"Here you go."

Charlee handed her one of the cold sodas she held before she sank into the other end of the sofa from where Anna reclined. She drew her legs up so she could sit Indian-style and face her.

"Now, tell me what's going on here." She sipped at her cold drink and watched her take a drink from her own.

Anna retold the tale George had articulated to her and Andrew. When she finished, she watched Charlee. Her hands trembled as she took another sip of the soda.

"They even showed us pictures of their planet and people, Charlee. Can you believe we're expected to marry one of their people and breed with them? All because they screwed up their lives?"

When Charlee remained quiet, she exclaimed, "Well?"

"Well, what?" Charlee fired back. Her excitement was obvious. It seemed she was trying to stay calm, yet she couldn't contain her glee.

"Anna, this is so fantastic. What have I been telling you all this time? I knew *you* were among us. I told you, didn't I? And what did you do? You laughed at me for my belief. Molly and George, wow!"

Charlee grabbed her hand to hold it between hers. "I want to go with you to this new world."

In shock, Anna stared at her friend. "But I'm not going anywhere."

With clear surprise, Charlee retorted, "What will you do? Stay here without them? You're the type of person who has to have your family around you. And they are your family, Anna. I know you love Molly and

George. Why, you can't go for two days without talking to them. And what about Andrew? Is he going?"

"I don't know," Anna mumbled. "Why would you want to go, Charlee? What about you and Lance? I thought you two were serious?"

Charlee grimaced. "When I arrived at his apartment, he had another girl with him. I walked in on them, and they weren't talking when I walked in, if you get my drift."

"I'm sorry, Charlee."

She shrugged, concealing the hurt that Anna was positive she must feel. The phone beside Anna shrilled, and she jumped.

Charlee reached past her to pick it up and leaned back to her side of the couch. "Hello," she said.

Her gaze cut to Anna as she listened to the conversation on the other end of the line. "Yes, it would be best if she spent the night with me if you fought."

She attended again to the muffled voice on the other end of the line. "I'll let her know. Bye."

"Who was that?"

Charlee handed her the phone to hang up.

"Your brother, and he said to tell you everything will be all right and for you to come back home early in the morning. You two will talk then."

"How did he sound?"

"He sounded fine, as far as I could tell." She glanced toward the wristwatch she wore. "It's midnight. Let's go to bed. I'll wake you early in the morning. Everything will be clearer to you then, you'll see."

***

Gazing up at the white plaster ceiling above her head the next morning, Anna was wide awake when Charlee knocked, bright and early at seven a.m., on the door of the room she was in.

"Come in, Charlee," she called out. She raked her hair out from over her eyes as she sat up. Her remorse at George's stricken look when she yelled at him, and Molly had caused her to toss and turn throughout the long night. Molly's shocked expression haunted her. Anna didn't want to be the cause of pain for either of them, no matter their deceit over the years.

The door to the bedroom swung inward, and Charlee strolled into the room. "How you feelin' this morning?"

Swinging her legs to the side of the bed, Anna stood. She grimaced when the soles of her feet took her full weight. The pounding they'd received as she ran barefoot on the cement sidewalk to Charlee's the evening before had made them tender. Covering her mouth with her hand, she gave a wide yawn.

"Okay, I guess. I couldn't sleep a wink all night long. I did come to a decision, though."

Charlee held out the pair of faded jeans and shirt she'd brought. "And what have you decided?"

Anna took possession of the loaned clothes.

"I thought about everything said yesterday, and there is no way I'm going to leave Earth and travel to a strange planet to be a breeder, of all things. Yuck. Whoever heard of such a stupid thing to expect of someone? I doubt that Andrew will agree to go. I guess I'll be here alone if Molly and George have talked him into it." She shrugged her shoulders in a pretense of unconcern, although the thought of Andrew leaving bothered her. Suddenly, she sank onto the side of the bed behind her and looked up at Charlee with dismay.

"What if he does decide to go? And with Molly and George gone also in two weeks, I don't think I'll be able to survive. Andrew and I have always been there for each other, and I love Molly and George, even with everything they revealed last night."

Anna jumped to her feet.

"I have to hear what my brother has decided. I'm heading home as soon as I shower and get dressed."

Chapter 5

With her goodbyes said to Charlee and an extracted promise to call as soon as she talked with her brother, Anna was anxious to hear what he had to say. She hurried the four blocks home. All was quiet at the home front when she opened the front door and stepped through the entryway. Treading quietly toward the kitchen, she could hear a low murmur of voices as she approached the area. The three occupants who sat in the room stopped speaking to look her way when she stepped through the oval kitchen doorway, their breakfast remnants evident in front of them. Unable to meet Molly or George's gazes, Anna looked everywhere in the room but toward them.

"I want to talk to my brother alone."

Pushing back his chair, Andrew stood.

"Let's go into the living room. We'll talk there," he said.

At Molly's pinched expression, he laid a hand on her shoulder.

"She'll come around, Molly, you'll see."

"No, I won't," Anna snapped. Pivoting, she left the kitchen.

She waited, her legs curled under her on the couch where she sat. She closely examined her brother's expression when he strolled into the living room to sit in a cushioned chair across from where she reclined. She couldn't read him.

"I am going," he said, the silence within the room broken.

Anna drew her breath in. "But I can't stay here without you, Andrew!"

"Stay or go. You can't waffle with this, Sis. We must prepare to leave for our journey within two weeks."

At Andrew's sharp tone, Anna stared at him. Her brother had always been someone she could rely upon to support her. He was someone she ran to when hurt or when she needed a shoulder to cry on. He'd always been her number-one defender.

With her bruised feelings, she burst out, "I can't go, Andrew! I can't. It's barbaric, what's expected of us."

He sighed as he studied her. "Your decision is going to devastate Molly and George."

Anna wiped away her spurt of tears.

"I know it will. But I can't grasp that you and I are part of another world, another race of people. I don't know who I am anymore. Charlee accepts this tall tale of us being part alien. Anyone else would consider it, and all of us, crazy."

Andrew remained silent.

Anna fidgeted. She felt so guilty.

"Will you tell Molly and George I want to talk to them to explain my decision to stay? I love them, Andrew, even knowing they're not of our world. I don't want to hurt them, but the thought of leaving Earth and traveling to another unknown planet is too scary even to consider. And to think, we're expected to marry strangers when we get there. Strangers we're supposed to breed with?"

She shuddered with distaste.

***

Andrew studied his fingertips for a moment before he looked back up.

Rising from his chair, he gazed down at his sister. He wanted to enlighten her as to what he knew from talking with George long into the night. The choice of going wasn't his or hers to make. The decision to leave for the new world had been made years ago by the people of Garr and agreed upon by the powers that be on Earth. It was a signed and sealed contract between ruling factions and not to be spoken about or argued over. He hesitated with his indecision before deciding against trying to explain it to her.

"I'll inform Molly and George of your decision to stay and your wish to clarify it yourself."

Neither George nor Molly had moved from their positions at the kitchen table where he'd left them. The look of fear and upset on their faces caused Andrew to hurt. He sat across from them to splay his fingers on the tabletop before him.

"She says she can't go. The thought of being used as a breeder is repugnant to her."

"You didn't tell her there was no choice in the matter? She will have to go whether she wants to or not?"

"No, George, I thought it would be best if she believed the decision was hers to make. We'll have to find some way to convince her she wants to go."

George and Molly looked at him and then at each other. Molly dropped her gaze.

"We need to tell you something," George said.

***

Anna looked up when her family came into the room where she waited. *I'm going to miss them dearly once they're gone,* she thought as she watched them come toward her. Her heart felt heavy at her loss already, and her tears welled up.

Molly questioned if she'd eaten breakfast.

"I couldn't eat anything even if I wanted to," she replied.

"Then drink this coffee," Molly told her gently as she handed her the cup she held. Anna's tension began to ease from her shoulders as she sipped the steaming coffee. She glanced over at Andrew and George, and when her gaze met George's, he leaned toward her.

"Anna, Andrew tells Molly and me you've decided not to leave with us in two weeks."

"I can't go, George. I'm sorry if my decision hurts you and Molly." Anna looked at Molly.

Molly leaned over to pat lightly at the top of her leg. "We understand, honey. However, are you sure this is what you want to do? Why, last night, you said the thought of a cosmic journey was exciting."

Anna felt confused.

"I did? I don't remember that?" She looked at her brother. He nodded yes, she had before he quickly turned toward George. Anna followed his gaze to George, who nodded in agreement.

"You did, girlie, you said that very thing," he said.

How strange, my forgetting I said that? Anna thought with bewilderment. The tightness she'd felt in her neck and back since the evening before was gone. She raised the cup she held again and wondered why no one said anything. They all watched her. She sipped at the coffee. Molly finally spoke.

"I can see how you'd have second thoughts about going. You love your recordings of music collected over the years, and since you can't take the complete collection, well...." Molly shrugged. She leaned forward toward her, and her face reflected a certain sadness.

"We will miss you so terribly, though, now that you've changed your mind about going with us. And your change of heart will leave the one to have been paired with you alone in the new world. He'll have no spouse and no children. No one for him to love and no one to love him."

Molly shook her head with sadness.

Anna frowned. *What a stupid reason for not going to a new world, because I can't take all my music collection?* She felt extremely sorry for that poor, unknown man. All alone now. She looked around at her family as they watched her.

She looked back at Molly. "Yes, it's sad, really, isn't it, Molly."

Andrew choked.

"Are you okay, Andrew?" Anna worried about him.

"I'm fine, Anna. Finish your coffee." He coughed into his hand.

"Charlee's going with us, or I'm not going. She has no one here and would be alone if she didn't go."

The three before her looked at each other as if in alarm. Anna realized they hadn't expected her demand. George spoke up.

"Anna, we can't allow her to go. She's not like you and Andrew. You are part of our genetic makeup. She isn't."

"She goes," she replied stubbornly. She then begged, "Please, George. Please."

***

Molly grasped her spouse's forearm. "George, Traun will understand if we bring Anna's friend. And once she's on board the spaceship, he won't be able to send her back anyway."

She felt intense guilt over what had been done. Her only consolation was that if Anna were dead-set against going with them, they'd never have gotten her to change her mind, even with the laced coffee. What she, George, and Andrew did was better than the alternative, which would have been to drag her kicking and screaming with them. She would give the serum to her as needed and then cease the deception.

The drug would be out of her system within twenty-four hours after she stopped ingesting it. Unable to refuse her plea, George agreed that Anna's friend could leave Earth with them. Molly couldn't help but wonder if their deceptions would cause undue hardship later on for all involved.

***

"What about me?" Charlee asked as she combed her hair. She looked back at Anna in the mirror; her reflection was of hurt feelings. "You're all I have, too, you know," she continued.

"Oh, you're going," Anna said, surprised by her question. She had come over to inform Charlee she'd changed her mind; she would go with her family to the new world after all. She'd thought Charlee understood it was a given; she would go also.

Anna stood up from the side of the bed, where she reclined, as Charlee rotated to face her. Her expression was one of disbelief.

"I made it an ultimatum. You go, or I wouldn't." Anna made a motion with her hand to emphasize her determination of it. "Finish getting dressed, and we'll get the items Molly says she needs from Nyberg's Hardware."

Anna was still somewhat baffled with changing her mind about leaving. She'd believed she was dead set against it; only after talking to her family had she realized she desired to go and looked forward to facing the challenges of the upcoming journey. Even the thought of marrying a stranger and what was expected from that marriage had lost its touch of surrealness.

***

The two short weeks of preparation for the upcoming cosmic journey caused a whirlwind of activity in the two households. Anna and Charlee stayed busy going back and forth from their homes. George told them they could bring their clothes and ten or twelve personal items they felt they couldn't live without. Everything else would have to stay behind.

Anna and Charlee agreed they should each bring different books on how to make homemade soap, candles, and clothing. They discussed earnestly whether bringing books identifying plant life would do any good since the plants in the new world might not resemble Earth's. In the end, they reached an agreement: it couldn't hurt to bring one apiece, in case they might be helpful.

***

As Anna rested in her bedroom two nights before the scheduled departure, she mused over how fast the days had flown by since she'd sat down with George, Molly, and Andrew that emotional Sunday morning to discuss whether to leave with them. She remembered how anxious she'd been while waiting for George's approval for Charlee to go with them. After his agreement, she'd sat and talked with him and Molly and reached an understanding of their world and what they were experiencing on their home planet. Andrew relayed to her what George had explained to him about what had happened to Frank and Sue.

As she listened, Anna couldn't help but feel sadness for her Earth parents. They were two people so self-centered and evil-minded that they'd lost out on the goodness life could have offered them. Maybe George and Molly's influence as she grew from childhood into adulthood had softened her heart toward her Earth parents, two people she'd tried hard to forget.

Andrew and her life had been tough before Molly and George had taken them in. Andrew had experienced the brunt of their parents' brutality, protecting her the best he could, a child himself at the time.

Once she agreed to go to the new world, she decided to do so wholeheartedly. Her and Charlee's enthusiasm had seemed to take hold of the entire family. There was still one thing she was curious about, and she wanted to discuss it with Molly alone.

Rising from where she rested on her bed, Anna walked out of her bedroom to look for the woman who'd been her mother for the past fourteen years. She found her in the master bedroom, packing the last of her and George's wanted personal items.

Anna sat silently on the edge of the king-sized bed in the expansive room. The flower-patterned down comforter that draped it had dipped beneath her weight. She watched Molly's busyness as she sorted through clothes still hanging in the closet.

Memories flooded through Anna as she waited for the soft-spoken woman to take notice of her. She recalled the sound of George and Molly's laughter, which always floated from their bedroom, and her and Andrew's happy laughter throughout the home. Molly and George's marriage was the type she hoped to have with her unknown, soon-to-be husband. They were secure in their love for each other. They knew they could fight and disagree, but the other would always be there when needed.

Molly glanced to where she reclined on the bed.

"I should have started my clothes packing earlier. Now, two nights before we leave, I have to rush. What are you up to?"

"I've been curious about something and need some answers."

Molly stopped sorting through her clothes to turn fully toward her. "What's on your mind?"

"When George informed Andrew and me about settling on this new planet with the Volunteers from Garr, and the Transfers and their Caretakers from Earth, he said all Transfers were each expected to marry up with a Volunteer from planet Garr, whom, as I understand, the High Council members handpicked for us. What if we don't mesh with who's selected for each of us, Molly? What if we want to be paired with someone else? We should have a say in the matter. What if the person I'm paired with doesn't care for me or me him? Your people look like us, but what if I don't find the person I'm paired with attractive? What if I find his habits repugnant?"

Sighing at her worries, Anna watched Molly bend over to tape shut one of the boxes that held her and George's clothes. She wrote her name across the top of each one scattered about the room in an elegant handwriting before she rose to look at her again.

Anna continued, "When I decided to leave with you, I made up my mind to go willingly and with an open approach to it all. I'm excited about the challenges we may face when we reach this new planet. However, if I'm to marry a stranger, I'd at least like to know he's someone I can live with."

Molly laid her magic marker and boxing tape on the top of the container closest to her leg. She walked across the plush carpet-covered floor to sit on the bed beside Anna and reached out a hand to push a strand of Anna's hair behind an ear.

"Everyone who is transferring to the new world but you will have a Lifemate selected for them by the High Commander."

"Hmm…I don't understand?"

Molly frowned. "Let me explain this better. As you know, your Donor father is a high-ranking member of the High Council on Garr, and as such, his request upon being such was for a female child of his seed to be required to marry the current Leader's unwed son, who will be going to the new world with us.

"That chosen son is my nephew. And, sweetheart." Molly looked directly at Anna, her gaze unwavering. "I believe you will find happiness with him. I haven't seen him for the past twenty-three years, except for the night he delivered George's pills for his cancer, but I remember him as a child, being someone who cared for others. He was a sweet and thoughtful boy then, and I expect, knowing my sister, he has grown into a caring and morally proper adult."

Studying Molly, Anna chose the only option she had open: to put her faith in Molly's judgment. "What's his name?"

"Traun Gladumere."

"Traun Gladumere," Anna rolled the name off her tongue. It felt right somehow. She smiled at Molly, and her sense of humor took hold of her. Molly was easy to embarrass.

"Sounds like a name tagged to a strong and confident man." Anna raised her right hand with her palm outward toward Molly, and with a solemn expression, she chanted, "I hereby do swear to give my daily, utmost best to help populate the new world for the people of Garr and to enjoy it."

She wiggled her eyebrows.

"Anna," Molly exclaimed. Her laughter spilled out. She rose from the bed to point to the door.

"Go finish your packing, young lady."

***

Molly watched Anna stroll from the room, and she shook her head in amusement. She was secure in her belief that the young woman she'd raised and her nephew were a perfect match for each other. *If only my sister could see her grandchildren from their union. What beautiful offspring they will produce,* she thought, with a sigh.

A twinge of guilt was felt at what she'd done to convince Anna she wanted to go with them. *A few more doses will be required, and then I'll cease.*

Chapter 6

The Journey

"Are you girls ready to go aboard the spaceship?"

Andrew strolled into Anna's bedroom, having been directed there by Molly to collect the two. He observed the stripped-down bedroom with bemusement. It was a room Anna and her gangly friend, Charlee, had grown up in and where he remembered them mooning over boys in high school and playing Anna's music collection. Andrew recalled the giggling he'd always heard when walking by the bedroom. He had found it annoying, and it seemed never to cease when the two were together.

Anna and Charlee sat crossed-legged on the floor as if they were still teenagers while they thumbed through Anna's pile of music recordings.

"What are you two doing?" he asked when neither of them bothered to look up or answer his first question directed at them.

"If you must know…we're picking out our most favorite CDs to take with us. And yes, we're about ready," Anna drawled out. She held up a compact disc cover for Charlee to look at.

"What do you think about this one?"

Charlee leaned over to read the title. "Yes. We must take at least one recording of the *Rolling Stones*. They're classic."

"Hurry it up," Andrew ordered, his aggravation rising at their stalling. "George and Molly are waiting downstairs in the living room for us. George had the rest of our luggage transported on board the spaceship, and now it's our turn."

Anna and Charlee scrambled to their feet. His sister hoisted up her portable CD player. Charlee clutched a compact disc organizer in her hands.

"We're ready to go," they both sang out.

Andrew didn't move. He continued to gaze at Charlee. It felt as if he'd been knocked for a loop. He'd never noticed her beauty before.

"Let's get this show on the road, brother dear." Anna snapped her fingers in his face. He moved backward. His sister arched an eyebrow at him.

"Grab that box of batteries on your way out, will you?" she said.

He turned to leave the room and snatched up the batteries.

"There you all are," Molly exclaimed when they entered the living room where she and George waited. Three black belts dangled from her hands.

"All of you, come here and put one of these on," she said.

"What are they for?" Anna questioned before Andrew could. She turned the belt handed to her over in her hands to examine both sides.

"See those little black boxes on each one?" Molly said.

"Yes." Anna handled the box on her belt.

Andrew examined the one he held.

"Those are transport power boxes linked to the ship," Molly said.

His sister snatched her fingers from the area on the belt she'd been examining. Molly laughed.

"All three of you, come over here beside me and stand close to each other. Go ahead and put those belts on." She waited for them to do as instructed.

"Now, when George says to, push the front of the box down with your finger and hold it there. It will cause a message to be sent to the waiting spaceship to transport you up."

***

Anna and Charlee looked at each other.

"You scared?" Charlee asked.

"I am now."

Anna was careful not to touch the black box on the front of the belt with her fingers again. She didn't want to be transported up without the others. She knew her eyes were as wide as Charlee's as Charlee stared at her.

"Andrew, hold my boom box for me, will you?" she demanded.

Andrew turned toward her.

In an attempt to still her quivering insides, Anna gazed around the living room she and the others stood in. She had fond memories of growing up in the room. She felt a shaft of unease at the sight of the immaculately clipped and cared-for evergreen shrubs out of the room's large bay window. *What if this doesn't work out as planned? There's no turning back once we're gone. No more comfort of a safe place called home to run to.* She shivered at her thoughts. The soft murmur of conversation between the others in the room drew her attention back to George.

She, Charlee, and Andrew now stood shoulder-to-shoulder in a semi-circle before him.

"Are you all three ready?" he asked.

He chuckled as they looked at each other before they nodded their heads back at him. "Put your fingers on the front of the black box on your belts and push down after my count of three. One, two, three.

"You can all open your eyes now," he said moments later.

Anna gave a peep through her eyelashes at the area around her. Her eyes popped fully open in her surprised disbelief as she looked around.

Good grief. This is like the Starship Enterprise, except...wait a minute.... She looked down at the platform floor where she now stood; no, it was not the same. There were no lighted circles down there.

Quickly, Anna looked back up. *Where are Scotty and Captain Kirk?* she thought, with a bit of hysteria. *It's not right without them welcoming us aboard.*

When she turned toward Andrew and Charlee, Anna realized they were as stunned as she was. All of their mouths stretched into broad grins as their gazes connected. Anna raised her hands to wiggle her fingers back and forth and waggled her eyebrows at her brother and best friend. With an exaggerated drawl, she said, "Space travelers...we now are...."

George smiled. He pointed to the wall to his left. "Remove your transport belts and hang them up over there. Molly and I will show you to your assigned quarters."

It's so quiet, Anna thought as she looked around. Except for a soft hum, there was no other sound, and no other people were seen.

"Does anyone know we're on board the spaceship?" she whispered to Molly, who stood beside her.

"Yes, honey, they're aware we're on board. We should have broken from Earth's gravitational pull within the first few minutes of our boarding. We were the last to arrive. Let's all follow George and find our sleeping quarters." She turned to step in behind George, who strode out of the open doorway and into a dimly lit hallway.

Anna, Charlee, and Andrew fell in line behind her. They huddled so close together that they tripped over each other.

Five minutes later, George pointed to a door to the right of the hallway from where they all stood. "Anna, that is your assigned quarters. Charlee will stay with you. Andrew, you're straight across the hallway from them. Molly and I will be on Level Two of the ship, where the Caretakers are assigned. The ship's floor level we're standing in is Level Four. All the Transfers from Earth are stationed on Levels Four and Three, respectfully.

"Look for your floor Level and corridor number until you get oriented to the ship's layout. And as you can see here, your room numbers are above your doors."

Picking up where he left off, Molly said, "To unlock the door to your rooms, enter your name and birth date in the box beside the door. You can change the code anytime after you open the door."

She fell silent, and George took over again.

"Will you three be all right if Molly and I leave you and go to our assigned quarters?"

To Anna, it seemed relief surged through him when she and the others nodded. He turned toward Molly to cup her elbow in his hand. "Let's go, Molly. I need to check in with Traun as soon as I can. He's our High Commander now and will expect to hear from me."

Traun...? The spaceship's captain? My future husband? Anna wondered. She realized that she, Andrew, and Charlee stood still as statues to watch Molly and George stride away. The hallway's low lighting threw their shadows eerily out and up the wall, as they left them. Turning, Andrew handed her boom box over to her that he held.

"What do we do now?" she gave a nervous laugh.

"We go into our assigned quarters and wait. George or Molly will return and fetch us if we need to go anywhere." Andrew glanced toward Charlee, and he caught her gaze before he stepped across the small hallway to his room. Punching in his code, the door before him slid open with a soft swish. He stepped out of sight. The door closed with another whisper of air.

Anna punched her code into the box beside the door of her assigned room. She laughed nervously when she messed up and had to start over. The door before her whooshed open. Cautiously, she stepped forward into a darkened room, and Charlee followed. They both jumped when the door closed behind them, and the lights within the room flared bright. Anna assessed the two twin-sized beds across the room from where they stood. The flat headboards of the beds were fastened against the wall. There was barely enough room to walk between the two beds; they were so close.

As they stepped further into the room, she and Charlee agreed that the beds reminded them of hospital beds. The white covers were tucked in so tight that not a wrinkle dared to be present.

The room before them contained only the bare necessities.

As they glanced around at the sparseness, they thought the double doors against the wall to their left were most likely a closet; the single door to their right might lead to a bathroom. Neither was brave enough to walk forward to check out anything. Everything seemed made of chrome or some other type of shiny metal. All within the room reeked of function and nothing else. The only softness was from the covers on the twin beds. There was a small metal desk tucked up in the right-hand corner of the room with a metal stool shoved up underneath it. Anna and Charlee looked at each other, noting what appeared to be a compact, although complicated-looking, communication system positioned on the wall above and behind the desk.

"Yeah, like we'd know how to operate that," Anna said. Taking a deep breath, she stepped over to the closed door, which, as they previously discussed, must be the bathroom. With some nervousness, she reached out a hand toward a single black button on the wall and pushed it. A pocket door swished open. Giving a peek inside the small cubicle before her, she glanced around toward Charlee.

"It's the bathroom all right and for function only."

Pushing the button again to close the door, Anna walked over to the bed closest to her, and she looked at Charlee as she tossed her boom box down on top of the tightly tucked-in covers.

"All the creature comforts of home, you think?" She frowned at the austerity of the room.

Charlee ventured over to the double doors to the left of them that they'd noted earlier, and she touched the black button on the wall there. The doors glided back to expose the area behind them. She glanced inside.

"Yep, a closet."

She took a step closer. "None of my clothes are in here, though. Only yours."

"No?" Walking to the closet, Anna peered around her shoulder and into the small space before them.

"We'll have to ask Molly and George about that," she said.

Charlee closed the doors. "What do you think we should do now?"

Anna looked back at her.

"Heck, I don't know. Sit on those beds and wait for Molly or George to return, I guess?"

Moving the boom box to the floor from where she'd placed it on the bed closest to her, Anna kicked off her shoes to crawl into the small space.

Charlee followed suit on the other bed.

In silence, they sat across from each other, waiting for George or Molly to show up again and inform them what to do.

***

"Do you have to see Traun so soon?"

Turning, George met his Lifemate's gaze as they entered their assigned quarters. "I need to tell him what we've done as soon as possible. He's our High Commander now. And you know as well as I do, Molly, that it wasn't right I allowed Anna's friend to come with us without consulting him first."

"I know it wasn't proper protocol, but I couldn't continue to see Anna upset. I'm worried how he'll respond to our deceit."

Molly walked over to where he stood to wrap her arms around his waist as she frowned. George combed his fingers through the black, silky strands of her short-cut hair and kissed her upturned mouth. Reaching down, he pulled her arms from around his waist.

"The sooner I get this over with, the better for all of us. You agree, don't you?"

"Yes, I do," she said with a sigh.

She patted his chest with the palm of her hand and then waved that same hand toward the ship's intercom system on the wall above the small writing desk.

"Go ahead, call him. Put it on speaker, though, so I can hear what he says."

She turned away to kick off her shoes.

George pushed the sequence code for the Command Center, where he knew the High Commander would be, and then he said Traun's name into the system.

After a moment had passed, a deep voice came over the ship's communication system: "Uncle, how are you and your Transfers settling in?"

"We are all in our assigned quarters." George paused, and his gaze met Molly's.

"Traun, I'm checking in, but I called also because I need to speak with you about something as soon as you're free."

"Is there some problem, Uncle?"

"No, no pressing issue, but I need to discuss something with you at your earliest convenience."

"Meet me in my quarters in half an hour. I need to brief the oncoming crew right now."

The intercom system went silent.

Thirty minutes later, George walked with a brisk clip down Corridor One of Level One to the expanse containing the spaceship's Captain's living quarters. George also knew Level One held the captain's public dining room, the ship's sick bay, briefing rooms, and the ship's Command Center. Permission was gained to enter the private living quarters, and George stepped past the doorway's threshold before him. The High Commander's assigned room was much like the others on the ship: stark with only the bare necessities but larger, with a small dining table and a sitting area. Traun sat at his desk before his computer, and George recognized the ship's daily log report on the computer screen. Traun studied the monitor. He glanced over his shoulder at him as he stepped further into the room and motioned toward the small dining table.

"Uncle, take a seat," he said.

He turned back to the report to press a button.

George saw with his action that something was circled in red on the spreadsheet. Walking over to the table, he drew back one of its chairs. As he had on Earth, he couldn't help but notice that the man before him had grown from the small, mischievous boy he'd known on Garr into a self-restrained and formidable man who commanded respect with just his demeanor. Traun slid the razor-thin monitor back up against the wall and stood; apparently, the error he'd been looking for in the report was found and circled in red. George swallowed.

The High Commander walked over to sit down across the table from him.

"Uncle, we are finally on our way to the new world. You ready for this adventure of ours?"

George flashed a grin. It felt tight. "I'm ready. It has been over forty years in the making, although it seems as if it were yesterday that your father and I discussed the much-desired contact with planet Earth. Your aunt misses her sister. She wishes she could have seen her again before we traveled to the new world. I also wish we could've returned home one more time."

He continued to ramble…and knew he did.

***

Traun sensed his uncle stalling before he told him why he'd requested an audience with him.

"Uncle, what was it you needed to see me for?" he inserted within the streaming dialogue.

The rest of the report he'd been going over needed his attention.

His uncle abruptly fell silent and shifted sideways in his chair to cross his legs. He traced a large finger down over the pleat of his brown trouser pants.

"Traun, I approved a friend of Anna's to come with us to the new world. She is on board even as we speak and in Anna's assigned quarters."

Traun stiffened. His anger began to build.

His uncle raised his gaze to rush into a lengthy explanation, and he continued to expound despite his silence. He described how Anna, his future Lifemate, refused to leave Earth without her friend Charlee and how upset Molly had been throughout the episode. He described Anna's reaction toward them upon learning of her mixed blood: how she'd cried with her shock of it all.

"Enough," Traun interrupted, tired of listening to the justifications for his deceit.

"You've overstepped your authority here, Uncle. Not only did you go behind my back on this, but you waited to inform me of the situation when you knew there was nothing I could do about it."

Traun leaned back to rest an arm on top of the chair opposite from where he sat, and he studied his uncle. He suppressed the anger he felt toward him.

"I haven't had the time to review all my log reports to see if everyone approved to unite in the new world is still on the list. As you're completely aware, Uncle, one hundred Transfers from Earth and one hundred Volunteers from Garr will be paired. Suppose my total Volunteer number is the same, and I expect it to be. In that case, this woman you've brought along will be an extra female with no Lifemate for me to pair her with, which I'd hesitate to do anyway, her being of complete Earthly origin."

Agitated, Traun pushed the chair he sat in back from the table to adjust his legs. His uncle's disclosure cleared what he'd thought was a mistake in the ship's last boarded automated body count.

Errors were always made when things were rushed.

He had informed his uncle that when he and the others boarded, he'd immediately leave Earth's orbit. He had played right into his hands.

"Why was my future Lifemate allowed to think she could refuse to come to the new world? Was she not informed it was predetermined at her conception?"

His uncle responded, "Have you not read the reports sent to Garr concerning Anna and her brother Andrew?"

"No. Why should I have? If she hadn't suited, Father would've informed me. The choice of a Lifemate wasn't mine to make. Is there something wrong with this female? Am I to be burdened with a Lifemate who is faint of heart?"

Dread spread through Traun at the thought.

His uncle appeared shocked. "No, she's not timid. She's a strong-minded young woman. However, she and her brother had a rough start on Earth in the first years of their young life. By the time we obtained them, your aunt and I believed, with the approval of your father, it would be best to raise them in a single-family unit. And not, as you know from your visit to our home, at the compound where the other Transfers were raised and educated as to who and what they were. We felt it would be too traumatic to change everything in their lives from what they'd been used to. We wanted any ill effects of their Earth parents' early influences firmly squashed and believed it best to interact one-on-one with them.

"Molly and I are pleased with Anna and Andrew. We couldn't be prouder of them than if they were of our direct blood. After graduating from high school, Andrew joined the Marines at my instruction, and Anna studied botany in college at Molly's urging. They are both bright and intelligent and have tried hard to accept the truth of their birth and what is now expected from them."

His uncle seemed indignant that his Transfers should be considered weak. He continued with further details about their lives.

"Since the two were raised as other Earth children, keeping them from having close contact with the Earth people was impossible. Because of their interaction, Molly and I were afraid to explain who they were, what was expected of them, and who we were. We thought it best to wait and broach the subject when a year was upon us to leave our station on Earth for the new world.

"With the wormhole opening earlier than prepared, we had to inform them of us and their life direction and leave their world within two weeks of springing it on them. Our story shocked them both. It was especially hard for Anna to accept the truth."

George, his expression grave, took a breath. Traun had wondered when he would.

"I believe she is the right Lifemate for you, Traun. She is a loving and exceptional young woman. I'm asking not as one of the populaces you are to govern, but as your uncle, to have patience when she doesn't understand the ways of the people of Garr or what is expected of her. It's not her fault for her ignorance, but mine and Molly's. She's innocent, even at twenty years of age. We've protected her, and maybe we guarded too much."

"It's time for me to meet this chosen Lifemate of mine," Traun drawled when George fell silent and stayed that way. "And I'll decide about this young woman after I get to know her. You, Molly, and the others come to my public dining quarters tonight around seven. And Uncle…"

George stood up to exit the room, and Traun leaned forward to lock eyes with him. "I need to know if I can count on you in the new world to be behind me. I will not tolerate any additional overstepping into something that is my call to make."

George's gaze didn't waver from his. "Traun, you're the High Commander of the new world, and I recognize you as such. You have my loyal support and backing."

His shoulders were straight and rigid as he turned away.

Traun settled back into his chair to watch the man he knew as Uncle vacate the room. He was confident he'd meant what he said and that he did recognize him as his new High Commander. His uncle had always staunchly supported his father as the High Commander of Garr. Traun remembered him being known on their home planet as a good and balanced man, someone his father put a lot of trust in.

Rising, he closed the computer program he'd previously been studying. He would finish the review of the ship's daily operational log later. He wanted to read the reports sent to the High Council throughout the years concerning the two Transfers under his uncle and aunt's care. The information would help him gain some insight into his soon-to-be Lifemate. *It's time I went over the life reports on all the Transfers and Volunteers,* he thought, rubbing at the back of his neck. The muscles there were tight. Turning, he pushed the intercom button before him. He needed to inform the crew member responsible for preparing his meals that there would be five extras for dinner that evening and to set up in the main dining area.

***

"Anna, wake up."

Anna could hear Charlee's voice. She couldn't get her eyelids open, though.

"Anna, wake up."

Charlee shook her shoulder.

Anna and Charlee had both fallen asleep when no one showed back up to their room. Anna felt a tap on her shoulder.

"Anna, wake up."

"I'm awake, Charlee. What is it?"

"Someone is buzzing at the door."

"It's probably Andrew. Knowing him, he's tired of waiting for word of what we're to do." Anna sat up to swing her legs over the edge of the bed. Fully awake now, she stood to tread barefoot across the cool floor and pushed the button that opened the door to their assigned quarters. Molly's familiar and loved person stood in the hallway.

"Molly! Charlee and I thought you and George had abandoned us," she cried out.

"Now, you girls should know better than that," Molly said. Her smile encompassed Anna and Charlee both as she entered the room.

"What are we doing?"

Molly turned toward Anna at her question. "We will have our evening meal with the High Commander tonight."

"Is it him? Is the ship's captain my assigned Lifemate?" Anna's heart kicked weirdly as she waited for Molly's answer.

"Yes, dear."

"Did George inform him about Charlee?"

"Yes, dear."

"Well?"

"Well, what?"

"What did he say?" Charlee and Anna both waited for Molly's response.

"Everything is going to be fine." Molly smiled at Charlee before she looked back at Anna. "He wants to meet the both of you and Andrew. I spoke with your brother a moment ago. He agreed he'll wait for you two to get ready, and then the three of you will come to our room so we can all arrive together."

She motioned to the desk in the corner of the room. "Did you girls notice the communication system on the wall above your writing desk?"

"We did, but we couldn't figure out how it worked and were afraid to touch anything," Charlee responded.

Molly made a motion toward them. "Come over here. I'll explain it to you."

She patiently waited for their approach. Efficiently and with little fuss, she explained how it worked. She asked if they understood everything. When they nodded, she patted their arms.

"When you're ready, call Andrew's room. George and I are in room ten on Corridor Two, Level Two, if you remember. Now, I plan to go freshen up and get dressed for our dinner tonight. We're supposed to meet with the High Commander at seven. Don't be late. And dress up."

She turned to leave the room.

"Oh, Molly, wait. None of Charlee's clothes are here."

She turned around, and Anna continued, "She can wear mine, but she'd like her own, if possible."

Molly waved a hand toward Charlee.

"I'll see if we can't have some of your clothes brought to you. I'm sure they're in the ship's storage area. See you girls soon."

Anna, with Charlee, watched the door close at her departure.

"We've got to find you something extra nice to wear to meet your future husband," Charlee said.

Anna gave a nod. "I'm scared, Charlee. What if he's ugly, or even worse, a cruel man? None of us have a say in who we're to marry or even if we want to marry, and now that we're here, it's going to happen whether I like it or not."

"What has Molly told you about him?"

"She's never described his appearance to me, even though I've repeatedly asked what he looks like. She says he resembles her and George, and she believes the two of us will make good Lifemates. She has also said he's a good and decent person." Anna shrugged her shoulders as she tried to make light of her apprehension.

Taking turns in the small bathroom, both found (through trial and error) that the water in the tiny shower flowed a few minutes before the valve shut itself off. It caused them to soap and rinse swiftly between each water cycle. There was a large drying unit attached to the bathroom wall, high enough so they could stand under the warm air to dry; no towels were needed.

Anna and Charlee threw out possibilities about her future husband at each other from the bathroom as they took turns getting ready: what he could look like, what they liked in a man or didn't like.

Anna told Charlee, "I hope he resembles George. You know how I love tall, muscular men with black hair and dark-colored eyes."

Charlee grew quiet. Both she and Anna now stood in their underwear, individual showers done.

"What's the matter, Charlee?" Anna waited by the bathroom doorway for a turn in front of the mirror.

Charlee handed the hairbrush she held to her and walked past her to allow her access to the mirror secured on the wall of the small cubical room. She turned to lean against the doorframe as Anna had done.

"It occurred to me that I might be forced to marry. Wouldn't it be awful if we both were tied to men we couldn't stand?"

Anna stared at her for a moment and then gave a single shudder. She dismissed the horrifying thought.

"Let's not discuss it. If it does happen, we'll have each other."

Turning back to the mirror, she reached to fluff her hair one last time. "I'm glad you convinced me to cut my hair before we left Earth. It has more body shoulder length instead of down to my hips."

Charlee glanced at her hair and said, "Never in a million years would I have imagined when we were in high school that you and I would be standing in a spaceship and discussing marriage to aliens."

Anna laughed as she looked at her. "And yet, you're the one who was always telling me your stories about extraterrestrials among us?"

"Yeah, but I don't think I ever really believed in what I tried to convince you of all those years we were growing up." Charlee smiled back at her before she turned to walk away from the bathroom door. Going over to the clothes closet, she hit the button on the wall to open its doors and to peer inside the cavity beyond.

"Can you believe this? I wonder who hung up your clothes in here and why all of mine were put into storage?"

Anna walked up to look into the closet from behind Charlee. "Molly said to write our names on our boxes and to put an X on the two we would need while in transit to the new world."

"Yeah, well, I did that, and with an X, put on two of them."

With dawning comprehension, Anna threw a hand to her forehead and pretended to swoon.

"Since you weren't supposed to be here, they wouldn't have known where they were to go. That's why you don't have any clothes in here. The great mystery of the missing clothing has been solved. We can now rest from our worry."

"Oh, shut the hell up," Charlee said, laughing. "That smart-alecky sense of humor will get you in trouble one of these days. I wondered, is all. No big deal. I'll wear yours."

She reached inside the closet to pull out a short-sleeved tan and white dress with a scooped neckline and held the dress out to Anna.

"You should wear this. It'll show off the tan you have."

"You think so?" Anna frowned as she took the dress and turned it from front to back to look it over. She had packed the dress and one other to wear while they were on the ship because Molly had told her to.

"I don't believe I've worn this thing since I bought it last summer. Are the shoes I purchased with it in there?" She looked at Charlee, who stood in front of the open closet.

"I know I placed them in the same box because they matched the dress."

Charlee glanced at the closet floor and then bent down. She straightened. "Is this the pair in question?"

"Those are the ones." Anna took the shoes dangling from her fingers.

"And now, what for you to wear?" She stepped up to stand alongside Charlee and to hunt through the closet.

"Here it is."

Pulling the other dress, packed as instructed by Molly, out from the closet, Anna handed it to Charlee. "The bronze color will show off your dark hair and eyes. It'll go perfectly with those sandals you had on earlier."

"If you say so." Charlee began to get dressed.

Anna followed suit. She slipped her bare feet into the tan and gold high-heeled sandals that matched her outfit. Sitting on the edge of her bed, she bent to buckle razor-thin shoe straps around her ankles. She was pleased that her toenails were painted with a clear, glossy shine. They looked good with the sandals and the dress.

"We better call Andrew before he thinks we're going to be late," she said as she straightened, shoe buckles secured.

Charlee glanced at her. "Yeah, it probably wouldn't be proper to arrive late at the High Commander's invitation to dinner. Instead of calling his room, why don't we knock on his door?"

She shrugged a bare shoulder at Anna. "We're ready to go anyway."

"Lead the way." As Anna waved a hand toward the door, knuckles rapped.

"I bet that's my dear brother now. Too anxious to wait for us to come to his room," she said.

Walking over to the door, she pushed the button beside it to open it. When she saw Andrew, she looked back over her shoulder.

"What did I tell you?" she said, laughing.

***

"What did you tell her?" Andrew quizzed. He glanced past Anna to her best friend. His breath caught in his throat.

Unable to tear his gaze away from the woman before him, Andrew stared in disbelief. Her sleeveless dress sported a low neckline, letting him know she was sized to fit perfectly in his hands. His gaze followed the curve of her waist and hips before he stared down at her trim ankles and slender feet in her sandals. Charlee had always been his sister's gangly friend who'd hung around their home for years. He'd never paid her much mind. The first time she'd ever caught his eye was earlier that day when she and Anna had been sorting through Anna's music recordings. He had found her attractive then, but tonight, words he remembered from a storybook Molly used to read to Anna as a child echoed within his head.

The ugly duckling of gangly youth has turned into a beautiful swan.

Coughing into his hand, Andrew pulled his gaze away from her. He'd start to drool if he didn't.

He waved his hand.

"Come on, you two. Let's go before we're late."

He noticed Charlee glance down at the dress she wore. She ensured it was buttoned correctly before she followed Anna into the dimly lit corridor, and she whispered to him, "Why the strange expression? Do you think I'm not presentable?"

She frowned when he didn't respond.

***

George, Molly, Andrew, Charlee, and Anna walked down Corridor One to the High Commander's private dining quarters, each lost in their thoughts. Anna felt her apprehension building as she strolled forward beside Charlee. All halted when George did. He indicated for Charlee, from where she stood, to push the intercom button on the corridor wall. Everyone remained silent while waiting for admission into the High Commander's accommodations.

Anna shifted uneasily. *Why does everything the past two weeks seem to be a blur? What made me change my mind about coming on this journey anyway? If I didn't know better, I'd pinch myself to check and see if I'm sound asleep in my bed. What if I'm in my room back on Earth and having a strange dream or a nightmare?*

As she watched the door slide open, Anna twisted her arm with her fingers.

"Ouch," she gasped. She was in no dream.

"What's the matter with you, Anna?" Molly looked over at her.

"Nothing." Anna rubbed the tender spot on her arm.

***

Traun swirled his dark golden-colored drink around in the clear drinking glass he held, and he stared down at the spinning liquid as he waited for his aunt and uncle to enter the room with his future Lifemate.

He missed Avreen and his home planet.

The door to the corridor opened, and he glanced upward across the space of the room to watch as an attractive young woman stepped forward. She reminded him of the women on Garr, having the same beautiful color of black hair they were born with and kept throughout their lifetime.

She looked his way and then turned to whisper to someone who stood directly behind her and was blocked from his view. Traun watched as the dark-haired young woman stepped aside to admit whomever she spoke to access the room. The glass of liquid he'd absently raised to his mouth halted in midair; his gaze riveted on the fair-haired woman whose curves were outlined by a dress that skimmed her body.

Its hem stopped short several inches above her knees, and her bare legs seemed to go on forever.

Feeling a jolt hit him low in the abdomen, a plea raced across the inside of his mind. *Please let her be the chosen one.* His boredom with the evening had vanished.

***

Standing close enough to overhear what Charlee whispered to his sister, Andrew's anger sliced through him. His gaze found Charlee's, and her neck and face flushed crimson before she wrenched her eyes away from him. For a moment, it seemed regret flashed.

Good, Andrew thought. *She damn well should be ashamed. She'd take that man if he's not the one Anna's to marry?*

***

Anna glanced past Charlee to the man who stood across the room with a drink. Her chosen Lifemate, Molly had said. When their eyes made contact, she felt she couldn't breathe momentarily. *I know why I've never been interested in a relationship with anyone on Earth. I've been waiting for this man all my life.*

***

Traun pulled his gaze from the woman's. His uncle approached him to greet him in the age-old custom of the men of Garr, with his arm extended to grasp his forearm and fingers clasping firmly around his elbow.

With their grips on each other released, his uncle turned back to the others standing in the doorway, and he motioned for them to come forward.

"Traun, this is Anna, Andrew, and Charlee," he said.

Intense satisfaction coursed through Traun as the blonde gracefully walked forward with the introduction. She was his.

"Anna," he repeated, and her name seemed to roll from his tongue with an awareness of belonging there. He nodded his head at his future Lifemate. He glanced at Andrew and Charlee, who stood beside her. "I am glad to meet you all three."

"Aunt, as always, I am happy to see you again." Leaning down, Traun embraced Molly when she walked up to him. Her strong resemblance to his mother tugged at his heartstrings.

He turned back to include the whole group. "Why don't we all sit down at the table? The food is prepared and ready to be served."

Traun walked over to the large table and waited for the others to approach before sitting at the head. His uncle circled to the opposite end.

The woman named Charlee seemed to hesitate about where she wanted to sit. Her gaze connected with Andrew's, who now stood across the table from her. It appeared she pulled out the chair closest to Traun with reluctance.

***

Taking the empty seat on the other side of Charlee, Anna realized she seemed reserved…and had been since her teasing comment when they'd first entered the room. Her eyes were now downcast, and Charlee placed her cloth napkin onto her lap. Her gaze flicked Andrew's way. Anna glanced across the table to where her brother sat across from them. There seemed to be an underlying tension between her friend and her brother. He watched Charlee.

Could it be he's interested in her? Anna wondered with surprise. Twice now, she'd caught him staring at Charlee while he seemed unaware of the action.

"The food may not be what you are used to. However, it's the best we can expect while we're on the ship," her future husband commented from the head of the table where he now sat.

His gaze encircled the table to include them all. "It's edible and nourishing. I guess that's what counts."

He directed a glance toward her, and Anna's insides tightened with his slow, drop-dead, gorgeous smile. She inclined her head at his comment and then looked down at the plate before her.

"Let's give thanks," Molly said when their server departed.

With Molly's prayer completed, Anna picked up the eating utensil beside the plate and wondered what she was about to consume. Spearing a green-looking vegetable thing, she decided it was best not to know. She placed the fork tip with her impaled piece of food up to her mouth. She chewed the portion and then, mentally, shrugged. *Not too bad. A little bland tasting but edible.*

"Uncle, I'm glad you've recovered from the wasting disease," Traun said.

Anna listened as she ate.

George swallowed the bite of food he'd placed in his mouth. "Once I received the proper treatment, I was back in fine form in no time. Has the transfer of knowledge agreed upon begun from our planet to Earth?"

Traun gave a nod. "Father started the process when I picked up my passengers and left Earth's orbit. I hope the leaders of Earth didn't expect to receive the complete workings of our spaceships and how we travel through space. That was part of the agreement, but we want a new beginning without the worry of being invaded in the future and our own knowledge used against us."

George agreed.

Anna was caught up in the conversation.

"How long will it take to reach this planet we're supposed to inhabit?" Andrew asked.

"A month," Traun replied after taking a drink.

"We're scheduled to meet with three other spaceships at the wormhole passage. There are passengers and the Volunteers from Garr on board those ships, as well as supplies we'll need to survive on the new planet."

"Exactly what is a wormhole passage?" Andrew asked as he leaned forward.

"A wormhole is a tunnel in outer space that leads from one area in a galaxy to another. Some stay open continuously, while others open and close periodically. We've traveled for centuries through a wormhole tunnel from Garr to Earth at our leisure, as it stays open continuously. The one that leads to the planet we plan to inhabit opens briefly, and once in a millennium."

Andrew looked down the table toward George as he reached to pick up the glass before him beside his plate. "George told us about the wormhole opening only once every one thousand years. With the rush to prepare for when you came to pick us up, I never did get around to asking him to explain the whole wormhole thing."

As Anna listened to the conversation between the two, she noticed that what she, Charlee, and Molly had to drink was different from what the men had in their glasses, and she wondered why. She watched Andrew take a sip from his glass, grimace, and look questioningly at its contents before he placed the container back down on the tabletop.

Molly laughed at his behavior. "Traun, what are you men drinking?"

Traun looked over at her as she continued, "Are you drinking that awful beverage that's a specialty of the Palace City?"

"Yes, Aunt, why? It's my preferred drink. As I remember, Uncle occasionally enjoyed it while on Garr, so I ensured he had some. I figured Andrew would also like the drink."

"The girls might want to try it," Andrew said, smiling. Anna knew he'd noticed she and Charlee bristled at not being offered the drink as the men.

"I don't think so," Molly said, frowning. "It's pretty potent."

Reaching toward George's tumbler, Anna quickly grasped it to raise it to take a large gulp of its contents. At the golden-colored liquor's hit to the back of her throat, she gasped at its raw, slicing burn. Head spinning, she worried if she'd catch her breath again. Moisture collected in her eyes. She held the glass out toward Charlee, who shook her head at her. She didn't want to try it after observing her reaction. Anna turned to set the glass back down beside George's plate.

"I think that's all I want," she wheezed out with effort. Tears rolled down her cheeks.

George and Andrew roared with their laughter. Molly shook her head, and her lips twitched.

***

Traun watched the woman before him. She captivated him. A surprise, this half-Earthling he was expected to breed with.

Chapter 7

"Anna," Traun said when Anna answered the communication system's buzzing noise in her room. "Would you like to tour the spaceship with me, say, in about an hour?"

Anna hadn't seen or talked to her future Lifemate since she and her family had dined with him that first night on board the spaceship. She'd begun to think he must not care to see or to get to know her before they reached the new world. George and Molly told her he was a busy man when she questioned them about it. He has to prepare and plan what needs to be done once we land in the new world, they told her. His duties as High Commander were demanding, they'd said. Still, she'd hoped after meeting him that first night that they would have their month or more of traveling to the new world as a chance to get to know each other.

"I would like that, Traun," she replied.

"I'll see you in about an hour then," he clipped out before the speaker went dead.

Turning back toward the center of the room, Anna asked Charlee, "What will you do while I am gone?"

Charlee, who sat relaxed and stretched out on her bed, looked cute in her blue cropped pants and matching pin-striped top. "I think I'll stay here. Besides, some of the other Transfers we met yesterday said they might stop by later this evening. Getting to know them this past week has been fun and interesting."

Anna walked over to where Charlee lounged and pushed her bare feet over to sit beside her. "Isn't it weird how they were stationed isolated on Earth all those years?"

Charlee nodded in agreement. "Why were all of you kept on Earth and not taken to George and Molly's world, do you know?"

She crossed her feet at the ankles.

Anna frowned. "George told us it was because not everyone on their planet agreed with the decision to interbreed with humans on Earth. Even officials within their government fought over it. The officials who pushed the plan were afraid that if we were brought back to their planet, there might have been plots organized to exterminate us before the time came to journey to the new world."

"Why was there so much controversy?"

"From what I understand, the people in disagreement believed the government needed to focus within their kind for a solution to their sterilization issue."

Anna shrugged as she gazed at her friend. "You know, Charlee, all of us Transfers are all around the same age. I'm twenty. Andrew's twenty-one and a half years old, and in talking to the others, all their ages range from twenty to mid-twenties."

"At least they were taught English in addition to the Garr language," Charlee responded. "We would've been in trouble otherwise, unable to communicate."

Anna smiled. "I can understand some, although not a lot, of what they're saying when they begin to talk to each other in the native dialect of Garr. You should be able to understand a little of it, too."

Charlee sat up straighter and uncrossed her ankles. "How's that?"

Anna laughed at her confusion. "Don't you remember our secret language I taught you in grade school? Molly taught it to me and Andrew. Remember? I explained some of the words to you so we could communicate with each other in school without our other classmates knowing what we said."

Charlee gave a slow nod. "I remember...it's been a while...once we got out of grade school, we never used it. How did Molly teach you and Andrew without you knowing what she did?"

Anna laughed. "She's one smart lady. From that first day we came to live with her and George, she would play a game with us. She said she was going to make up a word for something to see if we could remember it. Then she would ask us what the meaning was when she'd repeat it back to us later. She was always pointing to something and asking, what is our pretend word for that? Or, what is our pretend word for this? Andrew and

I would always try to remember more than each other and string the words together to make sentences for her. A lot of it comes back to me when I hear the Transfers talking to one another. Now, I know it wasn't a game we played."

Charlee laughed. "I admire her underhandedness. Clever lady."

Anna smiled. "I haven't practiced in years, so I'm rusty. I don't understand many words I overhear, the Transfers using."

Rising from the bed to pat her hips with the palms of her hands, she asked, "How do I look?"

Charlee glanced at her tan slacks, white top, and shoes.

"Fine."

Anna's dark brown eyebrows and eyelashes enabled her not to have to depend on cosmetics to enhance them.

"There he is," Charlee said at the sound of their door signal.

"Open Ten," Anna said. The door to their room swished back. She and Charlee had learned that trick that very day.

Traun stood within the hallway.

Smiling, Anna moved toward him. She appreciated his form in his uniform, which was molded to his broad shoulders and lean hips. His black leather boots were polished to a high shine. Anna was six feet tall but noted that he was even taller.

His glance into the room encompassed her and Charlee, and he smiled at them both before he centered his focus on her. "Ready?"

"Yes," she said. His deep-voiced accent sent ripples down her spine. She turned toward Charlee.

"See you later," she said. She silently mouthed "Wow" to her friend before turning around.

Tongue-tied as they strolled down the long and narrow corridor, Anna didn't know what to say to start a conversation with the man by her side. He oozed confidence.

"Where would you like to go first?" he asked. He matched his stride to hers.

"How much time do you have?" Anna said cheerfully. "I don't know what to see first, but I'd like the complete tour."

He smiled down at her and cupped her elbow as he led her forward.

"Let's turn here. Tell me what you've seen so far, and then I'll know where to start."

He seemed to be staring at her hair, and Anna wondered at his sudden expression.

"I've been to the chow hall," she said.

He grinned. "That's the crew's slang you've heard. Where else have you been?"

"Molly and George's room, and of course, Andrew's room and your private dining area. Charlee and I have stayed close to our quarters. However, we've met many of the other Transfers from our corridor and visited back and forth this past week. All of us are wondering what the new world will be like."

Inclining his head, he responded, "Yes, I'd think everyone would be excited and want to discuss what the world we're going to inhabit will bring for us all."

He glanced down at her again.

"Why don't we stroll around the ship, and I'll explain anything you may have a question about. How does that sound? I have about two free hours to give you today."

Anna found herself admiring his head of thick black hair. "Sounds good. And I do have a question."

"What would that be?" he inquired.

They stepped into the nearby clear round enclosure to stand on its platform, a replica of the lift Anna and her family had used to arrive at his private quarters that first night aboard the spaceship. Their bubble rose from its current position to the next floor level.

"I haven't gotten to ask George or Molly, but Charlee and I wondered how large this spaceship is and what it's used for. We know there are several levels to it."

Traun lightly squeezed her elbow, which was still cupped within the palm of his hand. "This is a passenger ship. And yes, there are several levels to it. We have level one, where the spaceship's control center is located, and my quarters, briefing rooms, and sickbay. Then there are levels two, three, and four, which hold the passengers. Level five contains the staff and passenger dining hall, a lounge area, and the transport bay where you boarded the ship. Under that floor is the mechanics of the ship. Six levels in total. All of our spaceships are not designed the same way, though."

Anna listened as he continued.

"Two ships scheduled to meet with us at the wormhole opening are cargo ships. They have only four levels to them, although they are much bigger than this one we're currently traveling in."

"How many passengers can be transported on this spaceship?" Anna gave a vague wave of her hand.

"Around two hundred and fifty. It's much smaller than the other passenger ship we'll eventually meet with."

"How many spaceships does your world have? Are they common?"

"Not common, no. There are four total. The ones I just mentioned and this one. Our spaceships are expensive, and our government controls all of their operations. For common travel within our world sphere, we have almost the same as what you call airplanes. How would you like to see the Command Center?" He stopped walking to turn towards her and let his hand drop from her elbow as he gazed down at her.

"With all your questions, I believe you'd enjoy seeing the powerhouse of the spaceship," he said.

"Yes, I would like to see where all the decisions are made concerning this ship and its travel through space." Anna smiled.

***

Traun pulled his gaze away from the woman by his side.

"Then the Command Center it is," he said.

He was pleased with this Earthling of their mixed races, his soon-to-be Lifemate. A feeling of well-being settled over him.

They strolled into the ship's operating complex an hour later; having met George and Molly, they'd stopped and conversed with them for a while. George wanted to discuss the workings of the spaceship he commanded. Several dark-colored-haired heads turned as the crew at their workstations glanced up at their entry. Traun led Anna to the metal railing, which divided the Command Center into two parts: the Commander's area and crew members' areas. He halted at the top of the steps leading down to a large shallow pit—the exact location where his crewmembers now gazed up at him in silence.

"Crew, I'd like you to meet Anna, my Lifemate-to-be. Anna, some of my crew members on this trip." Traun smiled and indicated with a flick of his wrist the individuals who now stared at her. He thought she appeared ill at ease as his evening combined crew of twelve men and women turned towards her to bow.

Several men made eye contact with her, smiling a little too long. Traun scowled down at them. They became aware of his disapproval and quickly returned to their duties.

With apparent amazement, Anna gazed around the room. She grasped the top of his hand and squeezed his fingers. Turning his palm over, Traun replicated her action.

She turned toward him. "Wow," she said.

"Would you like to see what we are traveling through outside the ship and what it looks like?"

"Yes, I would," she responded. Her eyes shined with her enthusiasm. She turned as the crewmember, at his instruction, flipped a switch. The hidden and massive, flat-screened monitor rose from its razor-thin gap in the ship's floor. She watched, unmoving, while the monitor before them settled into its position. Traun motioned toward the crewmember again. The large screen lit up with an explosion of space's vast and inky blackness and the stars that flickered from a distance as the spaceship sped forward.

***

Anna clenched her fingers tight around the hand of the man who stood by her side. It felt as if she were being sucked forward toward the vast nothingness of that outer space now exposed. She wanted to say to turn the thing off but couldn't pull her horrified gaze from it to speak. She sensed that the man by her side looked down at her. Suddenly, she was propelled from the monitor toward the door they'd passed through earlier. Directed from the Command Center, her future Lifemate hit the button on the corridor wall beside him to close its doors, blocking the curious gazes of his crew members who watched them.

"Anna?" he said. With obvious concern, he looked down at her. "Are you okay? What's wrong?"

She swallowed.

"I think I'm going to be sick." Anna raised a desperate gaze as two crew members passed by, watching them. *How embarrassing to vomit on the floor with an audience.*

"Please get me out of this hallway," she begged.

Swinging her into his arms, he moved down the corridor with long strides. Opening the door to what Anna realized was his private quarters, he took her inside the room and away from prying eyes.

Laying her down on his bed, he turned to go into the lavatory. She watched as he found and then wet a splashcloth. Wringing it out, he returned to place it over her brow. He sank onto the bed beside her.

"What happened in there?" he asked.

Embarrassment made a slow crawl over Anna. Holding the wet cloth to her forehead, she avoided his gaze. He grasped her chin and urged her to turn her face toward him.

"Look at me," he instructed when she resisted.

She raised a reluctant gaze.

"Don't be embarrassed about getting ill in front of me. I'm sure over our lifetime together, we'll see each other sick plenty of times." He rubbed his thumb back and forth across her cheekbone.

"Now, what happened in there?" he asked again.

Anna shrugged. "I panicked. I suddenly realized we're hurtling through space and that there's nothing but a huge, never-ending blackness out there." Anna shuddered, and her nausea rose again with the image evoked.

Traun stared at her.

He moved to rub his hands up and down each of her chill-bumped-covered arms. "You were aware we are traveling through space, though?"

"Yes, of *course*, except you can't tell we're moving. I never envisioned what it looked like out there. This…this…uncontrollable sensation came over me when that screen lit up, where I felt like I was tumbling out into that inky blackness. It frightened me."

He stopped rubbing her arms to let his hands rest on her wrists. He studied her for a moment. He bent to capture her mouth with his. Anna's heart rate increased. A sigh escaped her. She reached up to encircle his neck with her arms. After a moment, he pulled them from around him and leaned back away from her. He smiled down at her.

She knew he probably wondered at the bemused expression she directed his way. It shocked her, the feelings he was able to encourage. He'd effectively lessened the sickness she'd felt.

"I have to return to the Command Center. Before I do, though, I need to get you back to your room," he said.

Anna watched his beautiful smile spread across his wickedly handsome face, and she wanted to experience more of those soft kisses.

"Come on, up with you," he said. She knew he'd been able to read her expression as he stood and then pulled her up into a standing position beside him.

"Better now?" he inquired as he pushed her hair from around her face.

She nodded. "Yes. But embarrassed."

"Don't be. It shocked you when you realized we were hurtling through outer space."

"Please." Anna held up a hand.

"Let's not talk about it. I don't want to have another vision of what I saw and become sick all over again."

Traun left her at the entrance to her room. He promised he'd try to make time to see her the next day. Anna smiled as she recalled his comment, how it was unfair that he and she had a chance to get to know one another before becoming Lifemates while the other Transfers and Volunteers didn't have the same opportunity.

"But," he'd said as he leaned down toward her, "I'm glad we've been given this chance before my duties on the new world will consume most of my time and energy."

Floating into her and Charlee's room, Anna felt happy and content. She wondered where her friend had gotten off to with the room empty. As her thought was completed, Charlee emerged from their shared compact bathroom. She halted in her stride into the area when she noticed she stood in the middle of the room.

"Charlee," Anna exclaimed with concern and hastened to her friend. "You've been crying?"

Charlee's eyes were red and swollen, her face blotchy.

"Anna," she wailed, "I am sick of that damn brother of yours."

Surprised, Anna dropped her hand from her.

"What has happened?" She didn't understand Charlee's heartfelt declaration. Andrew wasn't the type to make women cry? He always had them tripping over themselves to be around him. Anna walked over to sit on the stool in front of the desk and watched her friend begin to pace back and forth in front of her, clearly agitated.

Charlee stopped her striding to look at her. "He accused me of flirting with two of the male Transfers. Can you believe that? He said they'd begin to think I was easy if I didn't stop it."

She swung her arms out from her sides as she looked at Anna, her hurt feelings visible. "He even insinuated that maybe I am an easy lay. I'll admit I am not a virgin, thanks to that pig Lance. Who, I believed at the time, was the love of my life. But you know I'm not easy, Anna. And I promise, I wasn't flirting with anyone. I won't get into trouble by ignoring the order of no relationships allowed."

Anna stood. Her anger coursed through her at her brother for what he'd said. Embracing Charlee, she hugged her in reassurance.

"I know you're not that type. You don't have to convince me. What happened after I left to cause him to make such a wild accusation anyway?"

Charlee sniffed and walked over to her bed to sit down so she faced her. "After you left, he called our room and asked if I wanted to go to the ship's lounge with him. He said some of the other Transfers planned to go there to play card games. I told him I'd like to go since I was bored alone. Everything was going along fine. We were all playing this silly card game some of the male Transfers taught to Andrew and me. Anyway, I was on the team of the two male Transfers and Andrew was on the two female's team. We were all laughing and having a good time, I thought. When the two male Transfers and Andrew stood to get some refreshments for everyone, your brother overheard the two discussing me between themselves, saying they'd like to sample me before being stuck with an unknown Lifemate.

"It seems," she said, as she huffed, "that your brother remembers a lot from your secret word game Molly used to play with you two. The Transfers spoke the other world's native language when they said what they did."

She swiped at the corner of her eyes.

"After they all returned to the table with the refreshments, I noticed Andrew was quiet but didn't think about it. One of the men said something to me that I thought was funny as he handed me my glass, and I laughed."

Charlee sniffed. "That was when your brother abruptly told the group he and I had to go because we were supposed to see George and Molly. When we were out of sight and hearing of the others, he grabbed my arm, yanking me around to him, and told me what they said. He accused me of wanting their attention because maybe I was the type that delighted in it. Telling me that he'd better not catch me doing something I shouldn't. He kept on and on at me, dragging me down the hallway.

"I should've slapped his damn face then and there," she told Anna with her hurt obvious. "His accusations stunned me, though, that I couldn't think. I finally yanked my arm away from him and ran back to our room. I'm not easy. And I wasn't flirting with anyone," she repeated.

Anna watched the tears well up in her friend's eyes.

"No, you're not. And I don't know what's wrong with that stupid brother of mine acting that way toward you either," she said.

She was suspicious, though, that she did know. Andrew never behaved hateful toward anyone. He was unfailingly kind and thoughtful. *He must be falling hard for Charlee.* Anna had a hunch her friend felt something for Andrew, too. Otherwise, she wouldn't be so upset over what he thought of her. Moreover, she was the type who, in a heartbeat, would tell someone where he or she could get off if a person made her mad enough. *And she's angry enough,* Anna thought as she studied her.

Traun had informed her that, as the High Commander, he was responsible for pairing the couples once they reached the new world. No one had any choice in their Lifemate. It all had to do with genetics.

I'll talk to him about this situation and try to convince him to pair them. She hoped she could persuade him it would be the right thing to do, genetics be damned.

They were into the third week of their space odyssey before Anna had an opportunity to speak to Traun face-to-face and in private. Ever since she'd panicked on seeing what was outside the spaceship, they'd been surrounded by her family members or other passengers when they happened to be together, or his time was tied up with the duties required of the ship.

Although they'd not had an occasion to be alone together until that evening, he'd made a point to call her through the communication system device every evening. They seemed to be able to talk to each other about everything and, sometimes, talked long into the scheduled nighttime rest after everyone on board the ship but the working crew in the Command Center were fast asleep. Anna was positive he was her soul mate. Molly told her he should be since she'd been conceived for him when she confessed her belief to her one evening when they were together.

Laying her eating utensil beside her plate, Anna wondered what he was to say about her request. She wanted Charlee and her brother to be as happy as she thought Traun and she would be with each other during their marriage. He laid aside his fork to wipe at his mouth with the white linen napkin he picked up. He made eye contact with her across their eating table as he set the cloth aside.

"Why so lost in thought?"

He reached across the table to cover her hand with his and to give her fingers a light squeeze when she remained silent. "Let's sit on the resting lounge where it's more comfortable. And you can tell me what it is you're so hesitant to ask me."

Anna rose when he did. When she went to pass him by to take a seat on the opposite end of the couch from where he'd reclined, he reached out to grasp her wrist and gently, but with firmness, yanked her down next to him.

"No, you don't. You sit beside me," he said. He stretched an arm out behind her on the back of the couch as she settled beside him. He began to toy with her strands of hair that seemed to fascinate him.

"Now, what has got you chewing that bottom lip?" he said as he smiled down at her.

Anna stopped the nervous habit. "I have a favor to ask of you."

"Yes?" He smiled at her as if it pleased him there was something he could give her.

Turning toward him, she pulled her hair from his grasp. "You know how you told me you were responsible for everyone's safety going to the new world and that it's on your shoulders to pair the couples up once we reach the planet we're traveling to?"

Anna dropped her gaze from his when he began to frown.

"Where's this going, Anna? And yes, I said that."

That frown didn't bode well. She began to fidget.

"Could you pair my brother and Charlee as Lifemates?"

Anna looked up to meet his gaze with hers. She rushed to explain as he pulled his arm from behind her.

"I believe my brother is falling in love with Charlee, and she is with him. He's jealous of any attention given to her by the other Transfers, and she stays upset when she's around him. I've caught him staring at her several times, and he doesn't even seem to realize when he's doing it—"

Traun held up his hand.

"Anna, I can't. There are ninety-nine Transfers from planet Earth and ninety-nine Volunteers from Garr. An equal number of men and women I am to pair together once we reach the new world. There is no one, much less your brother, for your friend."

"You mean she's to be alone? Married to no one?" Anna's horror rose. She hadn't realized that possibility.

"I'm sorry. Your brother had better get those hormones under control. I hope, for his sake, he hasn't fallen in love with your friend. Unapproved relationships will not be tolerated."

Anna didn't respond. She felt sick at the thought of Charlee alone with no spouse in the new world. Her friend who wanted a family since she'd lost her parents. It was why she'd wanted to come with them. She, her brother, Molly, and George were all Charlee had.

Chapter 8

The ship buzzed with excitement and action. They were at the wormhole passage. The High Commander was to issue his order of the spaceship's descent through its eye and to the universe on its other side.

Traun had informed Anna the evening prior that the other three spaceships had arrived two days earlier than expected at the wormhole passage and now waited for their arrival on the planet they were to inhabit. At their request, he'd permitted them to travel through the wormhole ahead of them. And he'd released to them the exact coordinates as had been recorded in the Book of Wisdom many centuries past: ancient, written words passed down from ancestral space travelers of Garr.

"Are you ready for this, Anna?" he said when she walked up to stand by his side, where he gave directions in the Command Center. Anna listened to his instructions to the crew before her as she watched the men and women move in the shallow pit. They pressed buttons rapidly on the control panels before them as each watched the razor-thin monitors scattered about. She turned to smile at Traun and his question.

"I'm ready to have my feet on solid ground."

He slipped an arm around her waist to pull her up against him. "Don't look at the monitors," he said for her ears alone. The air around his murmur tickled her ear, making her shiver. He squeezed her hipbone where his hand rested, his touch gentle.

"Why don't you go back to where your family waits? If you're in the middle of the spaceship with them, you'll be unable to tell that anything is happening when we begin our descent through the wormhole or when the crew brings the ship down into the planet's gravitational pull.

"I confess," he told her in a whispered undertone. "I just wanted to see you once more before I began the descent, which is why I requested your presence." He squeezed her hip bone again. "Once transported to the planet's surface, things will be chaotic. I may not be able to see you for a day or two. Make sure you stay close to your family."

Anna nodded. She was reluctant to part from him.

"See you on the new planet," she said before she turned away.

****

Anna was once again in the spaceship's transport bay. This time, she waited to leave instead of arriving. Both instances filled her with wonder and apprehension of the unknown.

In silence, she stood alongside Charlee as they waited for their turn to walk onto the transport platform to be whisked away to the world below. She looked at the other passengers who'd made their way to the transport bay after the announcement that disembarking had begun according to the assigned deck level and room number. She wondered if the others felt the same apprehension as she did. Some talked to each other with excitement, while others stood quietly, no words spoken.

Anna and Charlee looked at each other when their names were called.

Charlee stepped forward but then halted. She turned to look back at Andrew. He'd pulled at her hair from where he stood behind her. Unsmiling, she snapped, "What?"

"Be careful and stay close to Anna," he said.

Taken aback by her brother's emotion-laden, soft-spoken command, Anna watched her friend's countenance warm toward him.

"I'll stay close to her," Charlee said.

Anna walked on toward the transport platform. When Charlee stepped onto the platform a moment later, she turned toward her. "What else did my brother say to you?"

"Nothing much. Only that he'd see me later." Charlee didn't meet her gaze.

Anna studied her.

She'd broached the subject with them both about what Traun had told her. Neither one had commented on it.

The transport crew indicated they were ready.

Her group waited, and as she'd done that first time when hurtled through space from one area to another, Anna slammed her eyelids shut.

"Anna! Charlee!"

Opening her eyes, Anna saw Molly and George. They hurried toward her through a swarm of black-haired people, locating others and personal property.

Molly waved toward her.

Anna waved back and then turned to look for Charlee.

She stood right behind her.

"Here we go again, amazing ourselves," she said. She laughed at her friend's bug-eyed expression.

Charlee giggled a nervous sound.

A pair of ladies with satin black colored hair hurried by. They suddenly stopped to turn around to face Anna and bent from the waist down.

Confused over their behavior, Anna bowed back.

The women smiled at her and said something to each other before they hastened away.

"I wonder what that was all about," Anna commented.

"I don't know, but they looked straight at you," Charlee said.

A few minutes later, the same two women scurried back toward them. This time, however, they had two other women in tow with them, and they chattered with excitement. The four ladies stopped several yards away to stare at Anna. All four curtsied to her. Anna looked at Charlee in surprise.

"Well, good grief?"

"Bow back," Charlee said.

Turning to the four women, Anna mimicked the extreme bend they'd given her. The women giggled amongst themselves before they turned to scamper away.

"Molly, did you see that? What in the world is going on?" Molly and George walked up toward her.

Molly laughed. "They are showing respect to the chosen Lifemate of their leader of the new world. You don't have to copy their actions. Nod your head as you've seen Traun do."

"But I'm not going to be married to their leader. I'm marrying Traun, the son of the leader of Garr."

"Anna, when you asked me about Traun, I thought you understood. He *is* our leader of the new world. Why did you think he was called the High Commander by everyone on board the ship?"

"Because he was the commander of the spaceship, I thought." Anna looked at Charlee. "Did you realize he was the leader of our new world?"

"Nope, I thought he was the commander of the ship. Same as you."

Anna turned back toward Molly, and she felt a disquiet within. Now she understood why he seemed to have so many duties. Duties she'd thought were excessive for a commander of a spaceship. He had never told her he was the leader of the new world. He must've believed she was aware of his status. She'd assumed whoever was in charge waited for their arrival.

She turned toward George, where he stood in silence beside Molly.

"I don't know how the wife of a leader should act or what I'm even responsible for. What if I insult someone by not knowing your customs?" She felt embarrassed she'd bowed to the women. Did the women secretly scoff at the response? They hadn't seemed to, but who knew?

"Be yourself, Anna. They'll love you as we do," George said.

Anna snorted. She wasn't so sure about that. It made her feel awkward and uncomfortable when several pairs of eyes cut her way when the individuals thought she was unaware of their scrutiny. It didn't excite, in the least, the sudden news of her status.

"George," Andrew called out.

He hastened up to their group to stand beside Charlee. "It took me a moment to locate you all. Pure chaos down here, isn't it?"

"Yes," George responded. "Although Traun is fast getting things under a semblance of order. He instructed me where he wanted us to mark off where to erect his and Anna's living hut and ours. And now that we're all here together, let's go to the area."

Anna wondered where Traun was.

Unable to pinpoint his whereabouts among the throng of people who swarmed around them, she followed the others. As she walked, Anna's breath caught at the unadulterated naked beauty of the natural scenery around her. It was raw and primitive. Her pace slowed until she came to a complete standstill.

Huge towering mountains, their tops capped in white, which must be snow, were to her far left. Trees were scattered in every direction from where she stood, and many were so mammoth that an eighteen-wheeler could fit sideways within them with room to spare. Knee-high bluish-green grass swayed and brushed against her legs with the soft breeze that caressed her cheek: its touch gentle. Yellow, purple, pink, and blue flowers bloomed in large, expansive swaths across the valley as far as her eye could see. Anna inhaled and shut her eyes; the scent of the flowers, trees, and grass blended to form a light melody of perfume. It was a pleasing effect.

"Anna, come on," Andrew called out. Smiling to herself, Anna opened her eyes; the area's beauty overwhelmed her. *There must be a Creator, as Andrew and I were taught in those Sunday morning church classes Molly insisted we attend as children*, she thought—*there's such an abundance of almost sanctity here?*

Andrew called out again. Anna hurried to catch up with her family.

George had stopped walking.

They all stood several feet back from an embankment that sloped downward to a clear, pebble-bottomed stream of water, its banks with narrow sand strips on both sides. Anna halted beside him. The water's movement below surged with sound as it flowed past them all. She silently mused as she studied its movement. *Those trees on the other side of that stream don't have much underbrush to hamper our way if we wish to cross that wide-flowing creek and investigate beyond.*

"I can hear a distant waterfall. Can any of you hear it?" she asked no one, in particular, who stood alongside her.

Turning, George pointed down the slope and across the rushing water to the grove of trees on its other side.

"Traun said it's about a mile or two further on. He said the valley drops downward from here on out. There is a sharp drop in some places, but in others, there is a gradual decline. The scouts found the waterfall while they explored the area before we landed.

"This large valley we're standing in, he says, is the best place to build our temporary homes."

George included everyone within his gaze.

"When I saw him earlier, right after Molly and I transported down, he showed me this site and said this is where he wants us to set up our family camp. He said to partition off a large enough section for our huts.

"Andrew, you can help me stake out the area." He turned toward him, rods clasped in hand for the task.

Anna, Molly, and Charlee watched as the two men worked. When they were done, the men returned to them.

"We need to locate our belongings that were transferred down," George said, and the five of them strolled back to the edge of the milling crowd.

He turned to Andrew.

"I'm going to find the servants that would've been sent to serve the High Commander. They can help us move our things to the area we've quartered off. You stay here with the women."

Andrew nodded.

***

Hours earlier, before anyone else, Traun had been transported down from the spaceship to the new world. The commanding officers of the other three spaceships briefed him on the supplies brought with them and the results of the area around them they'd had investigated.

He was also updated that he was short one Volunteer, a female. When the time had come for her to board the spaceship, she'd become hysterical, begging the authorities not to make her go to the new world. The female, inconsolable, was granted permission to stay on planet Garr. Her behavior was unexpected and shocking.

Traun's first thought at the news was that now he could give Anna her request. He could pair her brother as a Lifemate to her Earth friend. He didn't like the thought of her brother's offspring having more Earthly genetics than Garr, but it was better than the alternative, which was to leave Andrew or one of the other men without an assigned Lifemate.

Ninety-eight, instead of the original ninety-nine, men and women chosen as Volunteers by the High Council of Garr gathered around Traun at his beckoning. With careful consideration, each had been selected as Lifemates for the ninety-nine Transfers he'd brought from Earth. Before him stood men and women chosen from the army he'd commanded on their home planet: unwed men and women willing to come to this new world and serve him and help save their race. All were genetically guaranteed to produce a healthy, strong, and robust new race for the people of Garr.

Holding up his arm, Traun signaled for their quiet. All became silent and turned their gazes toward where he stood. He allowed a satisfied smile to stretch across his face.

"We are finally here on this planet we've heard so much about. It's an exciting time for everyone. I noticed all of you looking around at this crowd, trying to locate the Transfers from planet Earth, and I understand your curiosity and wish to get a glimpse of your potential Lifemates. But all that must wait for the time being. Our first obligation is to focus on the most immediate and required tasks for survival. You and I not only have our potential Lifemates to protect, but we also have the Caretaker couples that came with them. We also have two Keepers of the Book of Wisdom, the Learned Ones, and the other two hundred and twenty couples who wished to serve in this new world. There are six hundred and ninety-three individuals now on this planet, including ourselves, that we are responsible for...."

His followers listened in silence. At the end of his speech, each turned to begin their assigned duties.

Traun watched them all momentarily before he turned to stroll over to the group of servants sent by his father and mother for his household. The men and women had gathered as he'd instructed, away from hearing distance of where he spoke with his troops.

When he approached the childless couples, he instructed as he said to them, "Go out and locate and stand beside any storage boxes with my name, the name of Summers, or the name of White written across the top or the sides of them.

"A man, my uncle, will come and collect them and you. You are to move all items in an area he has sectioned off. He will direct you to it. Move your belongings to that area also."

The servants bowed before they turned and, with an excited chatter, began to read the names on each item or packed box they walked by. Traun knew they felt honored to be a part of something so monumental. Each couple saw it as a privilege to have been chosen to serve him and his Lifemate and the offspring of their union: children to guarantee the race of Garr would continue, even when the others on their home planet would be gone within an estimated three hundred years—a livable globe to be with no people. The servants brought from Garr had signed the official royal

Garr announcement ascertaining their loyalty to him and wish to serve him and his family.

Hearing a man behind him clear his throat, Traun wondered with irritation which one of his troop members needed a question answered. He thought he'd sent all away to get things organized. He turned, prepared to give instructions, and was surprised by who stood behind him.

"Bran," he exclaimed. He held an arm out to his one and only brother, and his smile stretched wide. Traun clasped his fingers tight around his brother's elbow, a brother still in his prime at the age of sixty-five years.

"What are you doing here?" he said with delight.

With an ear-to-ear smile that Traun knew he also displayed, Bran said, "Since I couldn't see you before you left for planet Earth, I asked Father for permission to travel here to tell you goodbye."

Looking around at the crowd, he said, "You're getting things organized in rapid order, I see." He and Traun watched as Traun's troop of men and women spread out, giving directions on who needed to go where and bringing order to the confused crowd.

Bran turned back toward Traun. "I wanted to surprise you, which is why nothing was said about my presence on board the spaceship I traveled on."

"I am glad you're here, Brother. I noticed the animals penned up across the valley as soon as I was transported. More than I expected. Do you know how they fared on the long trip here? Did we lose any?"

"All held up. Not a one lost. And I was able to squeeze on ten of Father's best riding animals, plus his prized male breeder for them. The live fish we brought were dumped into two lakes beyond your encampment. The water was capable of nourishing the fish, yet no indication of life was found before we transferred what we brought into them." Bran shook his head.

"In the two days here waiting for your arrival, there was no report of animal life or any other life. However, our arrival may have scared off what was in this area. With this hectic schedule, we hadn't time to scan a huge area only twenty circular miles from here. If we'd had the room to transport a few Lifters and their fuel, we could have sent air riders out to investigate further or left the equipment for you to use."

Traun scanned the green and lush land around him and Bran. It all appeared ripe for human life and growth.

"I can't believe there's no other presence on this planet. I hope we can live peacefully if anything is out there."

He turned back to his brother. "Did your Lifemate not travel with you?"

"No, she felt she should stay with her mother and father until my return."

Bran smiled. "How about this chosen Lifemate of yours? What are your feelings on her? Did I ever tell you that I saw her as a child of six? You were only fifteen when I traveled to Earth to help our uncle and aunt find her and her brother. We were worried we'd lost your future mate. She was a skinny little thing then."

Traun laughed. "No, you made no mention of her. At fifteen, I would have been away to study and train for my future here. I wouldn't have been happy to have to listen to anyone tell me about a lost six-year-old child. I was interested in the girls on our planet at the time. You can tell father and mother I'm pleased with the little Earthling."

Traun hesitated for a moment as he wondered over his state of mind. He'd never felt for another as he did for Anna. "Brother, I believe I love her. We've had time to get to know one another, and I can't seem to get her off my mind when I'm away from her. Even now, as I stand here with you, I wonder if she's all right."

Bran laughed in his deep, rippling way at his revealed sentiments.

"Sounds like you're experiencing either love or a powerful attraction, baby brother."

He smiled at Traun as his amusement subsided. "I'll tell you something I've not shared before, except to my Lifemate. I knew she was the one I wanted the moment I saw her."

Traun laughed and then sobered. The time had come for his brother to return to the waiting spaceship. He held his arm out to him even as his brother's communication device crackled again with the message to board the spacecraft.

"Bran, I...," he said, wanting to say goodbye yet unable to get the words past his lips. Bran ignored his outstretched arm to grab him by the shoulders and draw him in close to him. At that moment, Traun had no concern about the uncharacteristic public display of emotion between them before the observant eyes of the people.

"I shall miss you and our esteemed father and mother the rest of my days," he managed to say.

"I, too, shall miss you, little brother," Bran replied.

"And now," Bran said, his emotions under control as he stepped back from their embrace with a palm slap delivered to Traun's back.

"I must transport back to the spaceship. The anxious Commanding Officers and their crewmembers must start the journey back through the wormhole before its passage becomes too narrow to pass safely through."

Traun nodded as Bran reached for the transport button on his belt.

"I can't watch you leave." Turning, he walked away. His sorrow cut deep within him at the loss of his entire family, lost on behalf of duty and at science gone haywire. When Traun heard the slight yet distinct difference in the sound emitted from the spaceships that hovered above, he knew it indicated they geared up in preparation for a swift departure.

It's been a long and tiring day, he thought with a sigh given. He still had an enormous number of duties to be finalized before nighttime fell on this recently occupied planet.

***

With her eyes glued to the clear blue sky above her, Anna watched the spaceships begin their rotation as she waited for George to return with the servants he said would've been sent from Garr.

In the blink of an eye, all four spaceships were gone as if they'd never been. Her eyes squinted against the sun's light; Anna questioned the sudden loss she felt. Turning back to her family and best friend, she wondered how Traun fared with what the scene around her must demand of him. He, their High Commander, her future husband, and all this confusion to be regulated by him.

***

Loneliness gnawed within Traun's gut as he sought quiet solitude. He needed to gather an inner strength. Sentiment couldn't be displayed if he expected to command the people he was meant to lead. He looked around at the milling crowd before he stepped behind several huge wooden crates that held the material to erect temporary living huts. They were the shield he needed from his people's all-seeing gazes. As he took a deep, calming breath, Traun heard the slight snap of a branch breaking underfoot and looked up. A woman walked forward toward him.

He stared in shock as she drew closer, and then, when close enough, he reached out, yanking her to him. He wrapped his arms around her familiar frame.

"Avreen," he sighed. His pleasure at the sight of her was profound.

He kissed her upturned mouth with the same fervor toward her as she displayed to him. She wrapped her arms tight around his neck. She was his lover, companion, and friend: someone he knew cared about him and his wellbeing. Her vocal moan of desire caused Traun suddenly to realize what it was he was doing and with whom. It staggered him, his loss of control. He reached to pull Avreen's arms from around his neck and to hasten back away from her. An image of Anna rose within his mind's eye.

He hoped no one had come around to the backside of the crates and been a witness to his actions. Avreen surged toward him again. He held up a hand to halt her progress. Her presence on the planet shook him to his core.

"Avreen, what are you doing here?"

She tried to come toward him again.

"Stay back," he instructed, his voice firm.

"How are you here?" He couldn't comprehend her presence before him. He would never have allowed her to follow him. Traun noted her bewildered look and confusion as she gazed upward at him.

"What are you doing here?" he said again. She stood motionless, her face stationary, her eyes glued to his.

"How did you sneak onto and off one of our crafts and stay hidden without anyone catching you?"

Upon noticing her outfit, he said, "This uniform of a troop member must've helped you?"

Avreen beamed up at him, and her smile displayed perfect white teeth.

"Did you not see my name on the Volunteer's register? Is that why you pushed me away? Because it confused you about my being here?"

She didn't give him time to respond before she rushed on to explain about a Volunteer who'd taken her life in fear of coming to the new world.

She explained how she'd applied to the High Council as the woman's replacement and had been chosen.

Traun frowned. "Your name is not on the list of Volunteers, Avreen. I know. I've reviewed it many times in preparation for my selection to pair the Transfers with them. I've read all their likes, dislikes, all their genetic history, and not once did your name appear on any report."

Avreen smiled at him again, and her eyes sparkled. "In the rush of the wormhole opening sooner than expected, the High Council members must have failed to replace the other woman's name and life history with mine."

She moved forward, her expression one of intimate expectation between them.

"I have missed you, Traun—so terribly these past months. I know we'll be happy as Lifemates in our new world. You were afraid to ask me to sign up as a Volunteer, weren't you? Did you believe I wouldn't be happy here?"

Avreen laughed, and she reached out to grasp his wrists with her fingers.

"You must know now, after seeing me here, I'd go anywhere with you and for you, my love."

With a quick step backward and away from her hands, Traun frowned.

"Avreen, I can't have you for my Lifemate, you know this. My chosen Lifemate is someone I can create life with for the survival of our race."

"But you love me, Traun. I know you do. You wouldn't have grabbed me as you did and been so happy to see me if you cared nothing for me."

Traun took another step backward from the woman before him. Yes, he had affection for her, but he never told her he loved her.

"Avreen, I'll have to pair you with the Transfer I had selected for this young woman who took her life."

"But we can marry, Traun? You're the High Commander here. You can do as you want. None on Garr will ever know."

"Avreen, we can't. You will marry another."

"No," she shouted, her eyes locked with his in open defiance. Her hands became fists by her sides.

"You will." His tone was sharp as he stiffened in surprise at her reaction. It angered him, her refusal to understand the situation she'd gotten herself into.

"You lower your voice to me, Avreen. As your High Commander, I'm not telling you. I'm ordering you. You will marry whomever I select for you to marry. Our mission on this planet is to procreate life for our survival as a race of people. If I married you, there would be no children from our union. Is this the true you before me? You only care for your wants?"

Avreen stretched a slender hand toward him in the face of his anger, and tears gathered within her now soft and pleading gaze.

"Please don't be angry at me, Traun. I'll do the right thing. If you say I must marry another, then that is what I'll do. I want what is best for our people, like everyone who transferred here to this planet. I…I forgot myself."

She stepped back to stand up straight, a proud determination now displayed to give of herself for their people.

At her reversal of attitude, Traun felt his anger toward her dissolve. He didn't understand why she'd thought to follow him. She should have stayed home on Garr. He watched as she reined in her emotion, and when, with a soft voice, she asked if he wanted the Earthling chosen for him by others, he couldn't bring himself to hurt her further by admitting that yes, he wished his Anna for his Lifemate. It was a desire he'd never experienced with her. He now knew he loved Anna and was pleased to be married to her and her only.

"I must do what is best for our people," he replied. Avreen looked at him oddly before she turned abruptly to walk away.

***

I must do what is best for our people. Avreen mulled over Traun's short statement. Its vagueness and his use of the words our people puzzled her. Her spirits soared at her sudden comprehension of his hidden communication with her. Her heart grew lighter, and her steps developed a bounce as she walked further away.

She understood.

He wants me yet sacrifices himself for the people of Garr.

His concealed message was that she and he would be together. Duty first. He must create life with that Earthling; afterward, she and he would rule together.

Avreen shuddered in distaste at her thought of his to-be Lifemate.

She also would do what was best for their people until they could be together.

***

"Anna," Charlee called out.

Looking up, Anna, in irritation, blew a strand of hair out from in front of her eyes. The physical work, plus the heat of the day, made the sweat pop out on her forehead and run down the sides of her face. Anna frowned when she felt sweat move down the center of her back to the crack of her ass, as well. She'd been gathering up another armload of broken and dead tree limbs. Charlee's arms were heavy with the small branches she'd gathered. They had been tasked with amassing firewood for their small group: firewood needed for the cooking of the evening meal, and once nighttime fell on this strange planet of theirs, a campfire for their group to gather around. The others still moved personal items to their selected camping area.

"I have all I can carry," Charlee called out.

"Okay, Charlee, I'll be right there," she hollered back.

Anna bent to pick up one more small branch at her feet. She managed to fit it on top of the others she held, and with her arms piled high, she turned to follow Charlee's path.

Tromping up to stop beside her and to where they'd dumped what they'd gathered so far, Anna lowered her arms. The wood she held fell to the ground, bouncing this way and that. She snatched her foot back when one large piece almost landed on her bare toes. Sandals were not the most practical thing to wear. She and Charlee swiped at their forearms, removing the dirt and bark left behind from the wood. They both looked up and out across the meadow.

Anna frowned as she stared ahead.

A group of men surrounded a woman. They helped move her storage trunks into an area she'd picked out. The men scrambled to see who could bring the woman her things the fastest. Her joyful laughter was heard easily, as was Anna and Charlee's ability to see her beautiful features. She wore the same uniform they'd seen some other men and women who walked around and organized the camp setup wear. George had informed them they were the Volunteers from Garr, and all had been selected from the military units of their planet.

Anna glanced at Charlee and then down to their dirty clothing. They grimaced at each other. Anna noted Charlee's unguarded expression of watchfulness when Andrew halted in his stride in passing the woman to speak to her after she said something to him. He and George lugged a heavy container filled with articles from home between them, and they sat it down. After he and the woman spoke and she turned away, he and George began their slow approach again.

"What did that woman say to you, Andrew?" Anna questioned when they arrived at their campsite. Their breaths were labored from their work.

***

Andrew glanced toward Charlee and grinned at her as he set the trunk he had lugged with George's help into camp down. He found the smudge of dirt across her left cheek captivating. He rotated a sore shoulder. Charlee continued to gaze unsmiling at him.

He wondered if she might be jealous of his speaking to the woman. *That would be a nice change, her jealousy*, he thought, especially since he'd made a fool of himself the night he'd accused her of wanting to sleep with anyone and everyone on board the spaceship except him.

Turning back to his sister, he replied, "She asked if I was the brother to the blonde-haired lady who is to be our High Commander's Lifemate. She said she inquired because she noticed my hair color when I started to walk past. I told her, yep, I was, and she was welcome to come by our campsite tonight if she wished to make your acquaintance."

"What did she say?"

"Nothing. Her attention was taken by one of the men who helped to move her things. I might go back later to see if she needs more help." Andrew cut his gaze toward Charlee to gauge her reaction to his statement. It disappointed him when she turned away with no change of expression. Nothing else was said by his sister when the servants who'd been behind him and George walked into the campsite.

She and Charlee went back to their assigned duty.

Andrew watched them from where he sat and rested as they returned to stack dried pieces of wood, collected per Molly's instruction, by the shallow fire pit he'd dug out earlier. That pit, not the larger one, Molly informed, would be used to cook their meals over. She took control of the rations handed out for their group and now directed the female servants to begin preparations for the evening meal. With dusk creeping across the valley, all gathered around their areas selected to camp, and their voices grew quieter, more hushed. A sudden shiver of apprehension passed over Andrew as he gazed out over those scattered campsites, and he frowned.

Anna and Charlee went back for one more armload of requested wood.

***

Tired, hot, and sticky feeling, Anna expressed to Charlee a longing for a submerged bath in the creek, which flowed past close to where they still gathered the needed firewood. Its clear water looked inviting.

"After we take this last armload up, let's come back down here and wash up," she said.

"I'm ready to call it a night, and I think we have plenty of firewood, don't you?"

Charlee didn't reply but nodded her head in agreement.

Upon entering the family campsite to dump their armloads of wood, Anna turned toward her brother. "Andrew, Charlee, and I want to return to the creek to take a bath before it's time to eat. We're filthy. Will you come with us since it's beginning to get dark?"

Andrew stood, and Anna realized the large tree branch he, George, and the other men had struggled to pull to the campsite for seating had probably felt comfortable. He'd been sitting on it and listening to the conversation between the four older women who stood around the fire pit designated for cooking their meals. Molly and the female servants were engaged in an earnest discussion on how to cook the rations that were handed out, their pots in hand.

"A bath sounds good. I need one myself," Andrew said.

Molly stopped her conversation to look over at them. She laughed. "Dirty cheeks, lank hair, and sweaty faces. You've all three worked hard today."

She pointed with the base of the cooking utensil she held toward the left of the encampment.

"See that storage box to the very back of the others, Anna? It has towels and washcloths in it. Gather some for all of you. There's soap and shampoo in there, too. Don't waste any."

With the collected items in their arms, the three took off down the incline toward the creek.

Anna frowned as she shed her shoes. "How are we to do this? We can bathe with our backs to each other, but the others up there can see us."

Andrew glanced toward the campsites along the backside of the incline they'd scrambled down from. "It's dark enough now. No one should be able to see anything. But if it makes you both feel better, I'll stand here with my back to you both and hold my towel out in front of me. It should block anyone's view," he said.

Anna and Charlee darted behind him and the towel he held, his arms stretched out wide. Throwing their dirty clothes aside, they vaulted into the water. In unison, they hastened back onto the creek bank.

"Yeow," Anna squealed.

"What's the matter?" Andrew caught himself as he almost turned around.

"This water is so cold, it bites," Charlee exclaimed. "Mother!"

Andrew snorted. "Go for it, the both of you. I won't stand here and hold this towel while you two take your sweet time getting used to that water."

Anna looked at Charlee.

With reluctance, they both stepped back into the creek water.

Anna gasped. Charlee soaped down rapidly and handed the bar of soap she held over to her before ducking into the water. Anna mimicked her actions. With her hair and body clean, she stepped out from the creek behind Charlee.

Her teeth chattered.

Goosebumps covered her arms and legs.

Charlee was already dressed. After drying off, Anna donned clean underwear and lounging pants with a matching top. Rubbing the soles of her feet dry with the edges of her towel, she slipped bare feet into unlaced shoes.

"Your turn now," Charlee told Andrew, and she looked at Anna to flash a grin. Anna laughed before handing one end of her towel to her and turning her back to her brother.

***

In anticipation of Andrew's waiting shock, Charlee beamed at him. His blue-eyed gaze locked with hers after he removed his shirt.

"You want to watch me undress?" he asked. He flexed an arm muscle and grinned wide.

Charlee swiftly turned, embarrassed. She hadn't so much as blushed when he'd removed his shirt, but she hadn't been able to look away. *Any red-blooded American girl would stare at that broad chest and those well-defined arm muscles*, she thought in defense of not turning away but standing to stare at him instead. Her face burned even more when she noticed Anna gazing at her with what seemed like a look of censure.

***

With a curse at the sting of the cold water when he entered it, Andrew made short work of bathing and exiting the creek.

Drying off, he pulled his plaid-patterned sleep pants on and slipped bare feet into brown work boots. Rising, he reached to grasp a fistful of Charlee's shiny, wet hair to give the short, black strands a quick, firm yank.

"You can look at me now if you want to," he said, his voice deliberately husky. He laughed in amusement when she took off with a fast-walking clip up the incline toward the campsite. He followed, grinning widely as he pulled his fitted tee over his head.

"Leave her alone," his sister said from where she walked behind him.

He ignored her.

When they re-entered the campsite, Andrew caught the aroma of cooked food. It drifted from where Molly and the other women in their camp stood around a pot and its bubbling contents.

His stomach growled.

"Molly, that sure makes my mouth water," he said as he walked over to stand where she was. Molly spooned some of the contents from the pot onto the plate held. She handed it over to him.

"Don't tell *me*. Tell these women here." She pointed to the women who stood around her. "They're the ones who thought to bring all the spices with them we could use."

Andrew smiled at the group.

"Thanks," he said. He watched the women duck their heads before they lifted them to smile wide at him. He anticipated the taste of the food. With full plates handed over to Anna and Charlee, the two sniffed at their food.

"Thank you," they said in unison before they followed him toward the other campfire away from the makeshift kitchen. Andrew stalled on where to sit on the large tree limb positioned beside the fire as he waited for Charlee and his sister to decide where they were to land. He wanted Charlee on one side of him.

When the two started to sit close beside each other at one end of the log with no room for him beside Charlee, he quickly plopped between them. Anna almost lost her plate with his action and looked at him in exasperation. Charlee gazed at him in astonishment before quickly looking back to her plate at his wink toward her.

***

Anna fought to keep her eyes open as she finished her last bite of food on her plate. She didn't know what she'd eaten, but it had a flavor and a texture she'd savored.

"Give me your plates," she said as she stood. Her brother and Charlee had also finished eating. *Work and the open air made us all extra hungry,* she thought as she looked at the empty rectangular dishes she carried to the women who heated water to clean up the after-preparation mess.

"Let me help," she said when she reached them. She stepped up to the short-sided but large rubber tub, which had been set atop a tree stump and filled with hot water. Anna lowered the plates into the water and began to roll up her nightshirt sleeves. She paused in her movement. The women around her chattered in their native tongue. She was unable to understand the rapid-fire words they spewed. However, she did know that they all shook their heads at her, *that no*, they didn't want her help.

One stepped forward to bow low before her. The woman then repeated in slow and broken English, accompanied by animated hand movements, what the others tried to tell her.

"You no clean. We clean only."

Molly walked up. "Anna, don't try to help them. If you insist, they'll be insulted and hurt. They'll think you don't care for their work."

"But I know they're tired, the same as we are, Molly."

"It's not done, Anna. You are to be their High Commander's Lifemate. You're not expected to help them. They must serve you. In their eyes, being part of the High Commander's household is considered an honor and a privilege. They are doing what they can for the race of our people."

The women before Anna wrung their hands as they stared at her.

"Inform them, Molly, that I appreciate their hard work and only wanted to help with the chores. I didn't mean to insult. I don't understand how the world you come from can be so technically advanced, and yet you have such an ancient attitude toward your people and their statuses."

"Anna, it is the way it has always been. And we don't have a closed social class order. Anyone can move up the hierarchy when the opportunity comes to them. It is only that the ones on the lower end of the scale are servants. Go visit with Andrew and Charlee. I'll tell the women that you appreciate their hard work."

Anna walked back over to where Charlee and Andrew still sat beside each other. They'd observed the commotion between her and the servants.

"What was that all about?" Charlee inquired.

"I insulted our servants by wanting to help do the dishes." Anna looked at her friend and brother.

"I think I'm going to go to bed before I do something else wrong. Besides, I'm exhausted." She left them to walk to where the servants had spread out her bedroll earlier on the ground, its top folded back ever so neatly. With a sigh, Anna slipped her shoes from her feet to step onto her bedroll. Sitting down, she inched under its cover to pull it up under her chin. The night air felt cool against her cheeks.

She lay on her back, her arms folded behind her head, staring up at the stars. Her awe engulfed her. *To think? Another galaxy with a planet resembling Earth…and yet it's so different in so many ways.* Anna noticed what looked like two hazy, outlined spheres high in the darkened sky, beyond the planet's main moon and its smaller one behind it.

I miss Traun, she suddenly thought.

Anna yawned wide and realized it was the first night in several weeks that they hadn't seen or spoken to each other before they'd retired to their respective beds. Rolling over onto her side, she faced away from the lights of the other campfires. With her arm curved under her head, she closed her eyes.

***

Traun finished his rounds of checking on everyone and visiting with the patrol surrounding the new campsites. He now wanted to see 'his Anna' as he'd taken to thinking of her. On the morrow, all Volunteers and Transfers would be married by the Keeper of the Book of Wisdom, he'd decided that day. He feared letting too many days go by before he paired them. He didn't need relationships springing up between individuals who were not going to be Lifemates.

What a mess this is, joining individuals who may or may not fit, personality-wise. Even with all my knowledge of them, he thought, frowning. Nevertheless, the leaders of Garr and his father wanted the select pairings, and he alone, as the High Commander, knew the genetic makeup each individual carried within them: diluted Earthly genetics of the Transfers and the full Garr genetics of the Volunteers and their likes and dislikes. This would be the last time any tampering would be done. All that was left behind in the world of Garr. His people would begin again from the ground up—hand-to-mouth survival from here on out.

Traun strolled into the family campsite and, without making a sound, stepped past the sleeping and prostrate individuals in the camp until he spotted Anna's blonde hair across the flickering embers of a faded campfire. He made his way over to where she lay to squat down beside her, and he gazed at her sleeping form for a moment before he reached out with the backside of his fingers to stroke the side of her face.

Reassured of her welfare, he stood back up. As he searched the campsite, he wondered where the servants had placed his bedroll. He needed to catch a few hours of shuteye before it was time to circle the encampment again. He hadn't realized until he'd stood up that Andrew was awake and aware of his presence within the family camp area. Anna's brother rose from his pallet to gather an empty bedroll several feet away from his own.

He walked over to where he stood. "Here, why don't you spread this out on the ground beside her," he said in hushed tones. He held out the bedroll toward him.

Reaching over Anna's sleeping form, Traun accepted it.

Andrew studied him. "I noticed you have men patrolling the area. I have some training from while in the Marines. If you trust me, I can help."

"I am aware of your training, Andrew, which is why I wanted to leave you at the side of Anna and the rest of the group asleep here."

Andrew's broad shoulder was shrugged at him.

"I didn't know if you were aware of my background. I wasn't sure what was going on with you having the area patrolled."

Traun considered Andrew's unsmiling countenance. He liked Anna's brother and how he conducted himself as a man. He had a gut feeling he was someone he could count on should he need his assistance or backing. He spoke in a low tone. "The area we're camped in and miles beyond was scanned by the Commanding Officers from the spaceships before transferring the passengers down. The scanners picked up no life form even after all areas were examined several times. I don't believe there's any danger now, although I want us to stay alert in case something does show itself."

Knowing he was anxious to help, Traun took the time to explain his thoughts on figuring out their new home to him.

"In time, I'll send ground scouts to investigate the area beyond where we're camped. What they find will let me know if I should continue the patrol. I don't plan to send anyone out until after our huts are erected, though. First, I want to ensure we all have shelter from the elements and a safe place to sleep at night."

"Well, let me know if I can be of help. I'm willing to give my assistance toward anything." Andrew turned to walk back to his bedroll.

Traun spread the bedding he held beside Anna's. He stretched out on it, fully clothed and slipped into a light sleep with raising his arms to place them behind his head.

He stirred a few hours later. His bedroll he folded to place it back beside Andrew.

Chapter 9

Anna woke to the sounds of the female servants preparing the morning meal. As she became fully awake, she was eager to experience another day in this strange and new world. Rising from her bedroll, she paused to visually search across the valley and in the nearby campsites for a glimpse of Traun. *I wonder where he slept last night*, she thought, in her failure to locate him.

Andrew and Charlee argued again, which drew her attention to them. Charlee said something to her brother that, Anna could tell, infuriated him. She watched him turn abruptly to exit the campsite. She sighed and shook her head over their budding relationship. It frightened her, the hurt in store for them both.

I'm glad I know Traun and I are to be paired, she thought, anxious to see him again. Reaching down, Anna picked up her bedroll to shake it out. She began to roll it up when one of the servants walked over to stretch her hands toward her. With a smile directed at the determined woman, Anna gave it to her.

"Let's go search our boxes for something to wear and get ready for the day," she said when she walked over to where Charlee stood. She decided not to ask about the argument with Andrew.

"Good morning," Anna called out when George and Molly approached.

George smiled. "Anna, the High Commander has decided that all Volunteers and Transfers will be united today. We'll meet with the others in the valley in about two hours."

He looked at Charlee. "You're to come also. He said you should be prepared to be paired with a Lifemate. A Volunteer decided not to come to the new world at the last moment."

Peering over at her friend in surprise, Anna was elated at the unexpected news. She wondered if Traun would grant her request and pair her brother and her friend together. She hoped so, for both their sakes.

"Let's go get ready, Charlee," she said when George finished with his directives to them. She laughed, her spirits high. When Charlee stood unmoving, as if unsure of what to do, Anna grabbed her by the arm to force her into movement.

There were no bridal dresses or veils, and none were brought on their journey to the new world. She and Charlee dressed in their everyday clothes: knee-length shorts and thin-strapped sun tops.

After slipping on comfortable shoes, they were ready to go. They knew everyone was to report for work after the group wedding. George had informed them that the High Commander had said they had no time to spare for a celebration.

Shelters had to be built.

Anna didn't care about a missed gala. She was ready to begin life with Traun. She embraced their union on this beautiful planet. She tried to keep in step with the others who walked beside her, yet her eagerness made her want to run to where he waited. She noticed Molly and George smile at each other as they listened to her teasing of Charlee. She attempted to get her to smile over some silly bridegroom's joke. Her friend finally erupted into laughter when she messed up the punch line.

As their group approached the gathering crowd, Anna glimpsed Traun from where he stood on top of a large crate. By his side was a strange-looking old man; maybe not so old, she realized when the man turned, and his face wasn't entirely lined with wrinkles. His sported snow-white thick braid of hair, which hung long down to his waist, had given her the impression of an ancient age. His eyebrows were of the same white color and thick and bushy. He wore a long-sleeved, black, flowing robe that hid his hands and feet from view. *Good grief,* Anna thought as she studied the individual. *I wonder who he is?* She glanced over at Molly and George to gauge their reaction. They didn't appear to find anything odd about the man. She turned her attention back to Traun and watched as he spoke to the individual. When the man bowed low to back away and to stand behind him several feet, she was alerted that something was about to happen.

Turning toward the crowd, Traun raised his arms high for silence. The people grew quiet, their eyes glued to their High Commander. Anna watched as he lowered his arms to smile at everyone before him. His voice resonated out over the crowd with his words.

"It appears we were lucky, and we landed on this new world during its spring season. There is no recorded information in our history books as to the when, length, or severity of the planet's seasons, only that it has phases. Our first year here will be a lesson for us all. As such, we must be prepared for the worst kind of weather.

"With this in mind, following the wedding ceremony this morning, it is my order for all to help with the immediate start of the assembly of our shelters. Only after shelter is in place for our community will we have a day of celebration for what is to occur this morning."

He paused and looked over the crowd.

"Today," he said, and his impassioned voice carried out across the people, "is our much-anticipated day. It is the day our leaders of Garr planned for and worked diligently toward for decades. They had a vision for the survival of our people, and that vision has reached its pinnacle with all of you who stand before me this morning. Today, Garr's Volunteers will be united with the Transfers from planet Earth. Only by you, all Transfers, with your Earthly and Garr-combined genetics, did our leaders give our race the ability to survive into this next generation and beyond. All of our children from our unions will guarantee the survival of the Garr people."

The crowd around Anna cheered. Traun held up his hand, and his smile was wide. When all became quiet, he spoke again.

"Volunteers and Transfers, we are to forget we are from separate worlds. We are to forget that one world was more advanced than another. We are all of us now, of this world. A race of one. We are a world of new beginnings, a world for continued life, a world from henceforth to be known by Garrearth!"

The Garr population erupted with loud cheers and whistles. Anna looked around at the Transfers whom she'd traveled across the cosmos with, and she wondered if they, as she did, picked up on an underlying hint of superiority displayed against them. She frowned. Molly and George had never given her that feeling. She studied Traun as he stood so erect on the platform. It seemed he felt that way.

The High Commander, the man she was to marry, turned to the one who stood behind him. He spoke to him. Anna shifted her feet as she watched the two. Traun rotated back around to face the now-stilled crowd. His voice again resounded with passion as he spoke to everyone below him.

"I have commanded the Keeper of the Book of Wisdom to enter into its hallowed pages the name of Garrearth. He shall record the name from this day forth as meaning rebirth, life-giving. Today is the day of our beginning when two worlds become one. He shall record this important day in our history book."

The crowd shouted their approval.

He indicated for silence once more. When all grew quiet, he spoke again, and his voice boomed with authority, "Only after all other Volunteers and Transfers are wedded will my chosen Lifemate and I be united as one. The Keeper will call out your names and who will be paired from the list I've given him. When called, you are to come forward and stand side-by-side."

Anna watched in silence as each couple whose names were called out walked forward and toward each other. Some smiled with happiness, others had anxious expressions. She held her breath as Andrew's name was announced. Charlee White soon followed it. Charlee jerked beside her. Her expression showed disbelief as she turned. Anna raised her eyebrows at her and smiled. Andrew walked over to grab her hand and pull her after him.

Pleased for them both, Anna took her gaze from her brother and best friend and looked around at the crowd. She became aware of the exquisite woman who'd spoken to Andrew the night before, the one who'd asked him about her.

The woman stood only a few yards away, gazing over her shoulder at her; in fact, she stared unblinking at her. Anna smiled at the woman. A look of surprise shifted across the woman's delicate face. Her direct gaze changed to display what almost seemed like sympathy before she turned her back to her. She walked forward when the Keeper of the Book of Wisdom called out the name Avreen Bodane.

Puzzled by the woman's odd behavior, Anna watched her. Chill bumps rose on her arms, and she rubbed her hands over them.

"Anna."

Anna swiveled.

Molly hurried up to where she stood. "The High Commander has called for you to come forward before our holy man."

Turning, Anna walked toward the makeshift platform where Traun stood and toward who she now knew was a holy man dressed in the black flowing robe. They both watched and waited for her approach. Anna felt a sudden fear course through her even as she kept her gaze focused on Traun. She hadn't known him long, yet he was her future. She didn't glance at the woman she'd smiled at earlier when she passed her. The woman was paired with one of the male Transfers she had gotten to know en route to the planet.

He was a sweet man. She smiled at him, and he grinned back. When Anna reached the crate Traun stood upon, he reached down to help her up the makeshift steps toward him.

"My Lady Anna," a female voice yelled from the crowd.

Anna turned.

One of Traun's servants ran up to the crate to where she stood. The woman handed her a bouquet of long-stemmed blue florets. Smiling down at the woman, Anna bent at the knees to take the wildflowers. It was the same servant from the evening before, the one who'd explained to her that she wasn't to help clean up the dishes.

Anna straightened to look at Traun in surprise over the gift.

"You have a loyal follower already, Anna," he said.

He grasped her elbow.

"Come, let's go stand beside the Keeper. The crowd is anxious for their unions." He guided her to the holy man at the crate's edge. The sacred man looked out over the couples who faced him.

It seemed his expression was one of immense wisdom and love.

Anna listened as he began to chant in the foreign language of Garr to the ninety-nine couples below him. His singsong intoning fascinated her; it was almost hypnotic. She watched a younger version of the holy man below the large crate from where they stood work his way through the couples below them. He sported long black hair instead of white. Once the ritual with the ninety-nine couples was complete, the holy man on the platform with her and Traun stopped chanting.

Turning, he took Anna's left hand to place it over Traun's right and began chanting again the same singsong words he'd said over the other couples. When finished, he lifted her hand. Anna stiffened. She knew what was to happen next, having witnessed it. She gave a wince at the skin pierced between her thumb and forefinger with the slim needle the holy man held; a small, round black tattoo mark was left behind with his action. It was the same type of symbol that Molly and George sported on their hands. The holy man repeated the action on Traun's right hand.

With oil poured over their now clasped hands, he intoned foreign words before he backed away to bow deep before them.

The crowd cheered.

It seemed all were ready to embrace this new world with the leadership of their High Commander.

Once the people quieted and with his hold of her hand retained, Anna's now-Lifemate instructed his people, and groups formed; equipment and supplies needed from within the large crates around them were retrieved, even from the one she and Traun stood on top of.

The holy man exited the makeshift platform.

Traun gazed down at her.

"Hello, my Lifemate," he said in a quiet undertone.

"Hello," Anna responded, and sudden bafflement washed over her. *How is it that I wanted to be tied to someone from another world? My husband? This unknown person?*

"What now?" She drew in a breath of air.

"We go to work."

***

It surprised Anna how fast shelters were assembled. There were at least twelve created that day alone. The material the men stretched out over the frames of the huts reminded her of tent canvas material. To her amazement, when water was added to the tautly pulled fabric, a chemical chain reaction started, which caused it to thicken and harden and become impermeable to the elements once dry. The organically changed fabric could stand up to nature for at least ten years or so before it would begin to deteriorate, Traun had said.

It feels like cement, Anna thought, running her fingers down the outside wall of her and Traun's hut, one of the first to be built; each hut was around six hundred square feet, small yet livable for a time. It would take a month and a half, maybe two, Traun had informed, to erect all the living huts and other buildings needed, three hundred and fifty-one buildings to be exact. In the meantime, everyone would have to camp out as before. He hoped things would go as planned and nothing would hamper their efforts.

The women worked as hard as the men to build the huts. Several, including Anna, were tasked with toting water from the creek below the encampment; their drawn buckets of water were handed over to the men and women in their group who waited for them.

It was dusk now, and everyone was tired yet exhilarated over what had been accomplished in one short afternoon. Anna turned to walk beside Traun with Andrew and Charlee as they headed toward their campsite. When they entered the area, Traun and Andrew walked over to sit down to converse with George, who relaxed on a makeshift seat beside the blazing campfire that had been started earlier. Molly and the women servants had also returned to the campsite to wash up and start the evening meal. Anna strolled past the men.

She paused to talk to Molly.

Charlee walked on ahead toward her trunk of clothes.

When Anna approached Charlee a few minutes later, she said, "Charlee, let's go to the creek and wash off before eating. Molly says we have time. The meal isn't ready yet."

Charlee agreed.

"On second thought, let's wait until that crowd clears before we go down to the creek," Anna said in dismay. Individuals who attempted to bathe behind erected blinds were scattered along the creek bank.

"I agree. Let's wait," Charlee said, turning to where her trunks were.

Anna joined Andrew, Traun, and George as they talked among themselves. She smiled at George when he stood up and went to Molly. The hard day's work caused her leg muscles to protest as she settled beside Traun on the large tree limb. Andrew rose to walk toward Charlee during a lull in his and Traun's conversation.

When he reached her, he said something to her before fetching items from his chest of clothes. He returned to her. They spoke for a moment and then walked away together toward the creek.

"Well, I guess that leaves me to go by myself to bathe," Anna said as she watched them.

Traun glanced sideways at her.

He reached to pick up her tattooed hand to gaze at its mark. Turning her hand over, he studied the small blisters that had formed on her palm that day. He kissed the center of her hand. Anna couldn't stop her shivering in response to his caress.

"I wanted some private time with you tonight. I'll take you to the creek later once everyone's done," he said.

She tugged her hand from his and spoke quietly so the others in the camp couldn't overhear, "Traun, we can't. You know…not tonight. Everyone will know."

Leaning close to her with a low laugh, he replied, "We could, you know…but I want guaranteed privacy the first time I make love to you. You're safe for now. A bath is all we'll do tonight."

Anna felt her blush cover her face. She'd misunderstood what he'd meant.

***

Much later that night, after taking baths and everyone fast asleep around them, Traun reached an arm out.

With instinct, he knew Anna was wide awake as he grasped the edge of her bedroll to pull it and her against him. He rose on his elbows to look down into her wide, blinking gaze.

"What do you think you're doing?" she whispered.

"I want to kiss you goodnight, and now that everyone is asleep, I believe I will." He draped an arm across her waist.

"You're crazy," she whispered, though she wiggled closer. She smiled up at him. He met her lips with his and wanted more.

"I shouldn't have done that. Now I'll never get to sleep," he said against her ear.

"Me either," she said.

In the wee hours of the morning, Traun rose with a few hours of rest. He worried about his people's food, safety, and all the children to be born.

Moonlight enhanced the area around him.

The sun hadn't risen yet to announce another day. Everyone in the campsite was sound asleep, and several snored loudly. Glancing down at his Lifemate, Traun felt a surge of desire. Her nightshirt had become unbuttoned, leaving her breasts exposed. He bent to fasten the shirt back up and then repositioned her bedroll cover so it was up under her chin.

Rising, he took off for the creek bed. Its icy cold water could do double duty: curb his desire and wake him up simultaneously.

Chapter 10

"What do you think, Charlee?" Anna said after she and Charlee finished lugging the last of her and Traun's belongings into their hut built two weeks prior. Two weeks in which one hundred forty livable shelters had been assembled, Charlee and Andrew's home located six huts from her and Traun's.

No one occupied any.

Everyone was too busy getting shelter in place for each other and falling exhausted into their bedrolls at the end of the day, with no energy left to move belongings or set up personal houses, except that day. Charlee looked to where the male servants had assembled and placed the large bed Traun had brought with him from Garr and that Anna questioned her about.

"I think it should stay where it is, Anna. You can walk around both sides of it. And you can section that corner of the room off and hide the bed from the view of the rest of the room if you want. It's so heavy and huge that I don't want to try to move it. We've scooted it as far as we can."

Anna studied the bed and where it was positioned. It was large, but it needed to be to accommodate Traun's extra tall and wide-shouldered frame. She shrugged as she agreed with Charlee. She had eyeballed the distance from the fireplace to the corner of the bed and judged there to be plenty of distance between the two. Still, she'd wondered.

"Okay, we won't attempt to move it again. It stays where it is. It worries me, though, if it's far enough away from that fireplace. I don't want the covers to catch fire, even if the building can handle the heat."

Traun had assured her that a fire in the bumped-out fireplace wouldn't catch the rest of the hut ablaze. The chemically altered material of the hut could withstand any heat generated from within it, he'd said. Their hut and all the others that had followed were identical. They all had a single fireplace, one solar-powered light attached to the center of the ceiling, and one escape window at the back of each structure.

"Are your hands as blistered as mine?" Anna blew on a large and freshly busted bubble as she tried to stop the stinging sensation that spread across her palm.

Charlee glanced at her hands to whistle in sympathy. "Molly gave me some ointment for mine after that first workday. Have you not used it?"

"Well, it would've been nice if someone had told me we had ointment for our hands." Anna scowled at her friend.

"Well damn, Anna. Don't be mad at me."

"I'm not mad at you. I'm angry at myself for being so stupid. I haven't said anything since I've not heard anyone else complain. Help me rip this shirt into some strips. It's ruined already, anyway. I want to wrap my hands so we can get back to work. We still have the rest of your and Andrew's belongings to move. When we return to the campsite, I'll find that ointment."

Charlee helped her rip the soft cotton shirt and to wrap her palms with a couple of the small, clean strips. They had been able to move their things to their huts that day only because the men in the camp worked on raising a frame for a Communal hut in the center of the village. No help was needed from the women, they'd been told. Anna and Charlee had one more free day, and then they'd have to go back to hauling water and whatever else was assigned.

The large and expansive building the men worked on would be used to hold group get-togethers and conduct community meetings by a yet-to-be-elected High Council whose members would report to the High Commander and, under certain circumstances, he to them.

With her palms wrapped, Anna stepped to the open doorway of her home for some needed air. As she inhaled, Traun walked up the hill her way. She watched him hesitate in his long, confident stride to look to his right. He turned to walk in that direction.

Curious, Anna stepped out further from the doorway. Her Lifemate approached the home of the woman who'd called out to him.

***

As Traun stepped forward, Avreen emerged fully from the open doorway of her hut. She directed a smile his way. It was a beautiful and soft expression that made him recall their earlier days together while in their world of Garr: days of sunshine and picnics. It charmed, and yet, it angered him at the same time. That intimate smile of hers was inappropriate. He didn't know if he'd intentionally or unintentionally stayed from within her path after what she'd said to him four nights prior but this was the first they were face to face again since. It still bothered him her presumption that night when she'd strolled beside him to walk with him, her Lifemate, one of the night guards he'd posted on the other end of their encampment that evening. "I'm willing to meet tonight. I know how tedious your duty must be to create life with that Earthling," she'd said.

His shock had coursed through him, and he'd wanted to reach out and shake her that evening. He had understood exactly what she meant.

She was willing to meet with him for sex. Raw sex. Nothing more.

Aware of the others who could see them talking together that night, he'd restrained his urge to give her a sharp rebuke and a reminder of who he was to her. He was her High Commander. He could punish her for her impertinence. "Avreen, I explained the situation to you that first day we landed," he said instead.

He'd lowered his voice and continued, "We both have Lifemates now. You need to focus your attention on him."

She had seemed hurt by his response.

"I thought you posted Nevin on the opposite end of where we're camped so we could meet tonight?"

He had abruptly walked away and had wondered if he should explain to Anna about her but had decided against it. He loved his assigned Lifemate but was uncertain of her feelings toward him. She appeared content with him, although she'd not expressed any emotion for him one way or the other. They needed time to get to know one another better before they faced the complicated issue of Avreen. And now Avreen wanted to speak to him again.

"Do you need something, Avreen?" Traun warily observed his past lover.

"What is it that you require?" He knew his tone was terse at her silence.

Her welcoming smile slipped. "I want time with you, Traun. I understand you're busy, but it's only fair my request. I've done my duty to my Lifemate as instructed. Two weeks now. Don't become angry at me for asking you this favor."

Traun frowned. He didn't understand what it was she babbled about. This misunderstanding of hers that, somehow, they were still linked as lovers needed to be straightened out. It seemed she was determined not to accept that the relationship they had on Garr was over. He realized that they did need to talk privately and with frankness on his part.

"Tomorrow night, watch for when I pass your hut during my rounds, and then give me an hour. Wait for me behind your home. I'll put Nevin on night duty patrol again, away from the area."

Avreen laid a slender hand on his arm. Traun stiffened. She swiftly removed it.

"I'm sorry, no one saw me touch you." She smiled up at him as if they were co-conspirators.

Turning away from her, Traun gave a start of surprise. Anna's brother had walked past him and Avreen toward Charlee, who stood beside Anna outside their hut's doorway. Feeling distaste rise at the situation between him and Avreen, Traun wondered if Andrew had seen or heard anything. He had passed by close enough that he could have.

This misunderstanding Avreen has about the two of us will be cleared up tomorrow night.

On top of the other stresses, all he needed was an angry brother-in-law who demanded an explanation for something that wasn't.

* * *

Unclenching his jaw, Andrew continued up the incline toward Charlee as he forced himself to relax. He hoped his brother-in-law wasn't the kind to participate in any disloyal behavior toward Anna. He was unwilling to see his little sister hurt. Traun didn't strike him as an individual who would conduct himself unsavory. He seemed to be someone who valued family. Avreen's face tilted toward the High Commander, had held adoration for the person before her, and the hand laid on his arm had a possessive gesture to it. He hadn't seen Traun's face to gauge his expression as he passed by the unaware couple.

"Hey," Andrew said when he halted before Charlee. "How are you feeling this afternoon?" He was sure what he'd witnessed could be explained away.

"I didn't know you were feeling unwell?" Anna said, looking at Charlee.

Charlee shrugged. "I feel fine now. I didn't feel good this morning."

Placing an arm around his Lifemate's waist, Andrew flashed a smile. "Let's go see what you two girls have been able to move into our small home, hmm...."

He waggled his eyebrows, and Charlee laughed.

***

Anna watched the two as they left. *They get along fine now that they're married*, she thought at noticing Charlee's arm snaking around Andrew's back under his.

She was happy for them. She stayed where she was to wait for Traun.

He and her brother didn't say anything as they passed each other, only a slight nod of their heads. When Traun reached her, he pulled her into their hut to close the door behind him.

"At last, a moment to ourselves," he said as he backed her up to the inside of the door. Anna wrapped her arms around his waist to laugh happily at his devilish smirk. She anticipated his kiss. His breathing was affected, as was hers, when he raised his mouth from her. She smiled up at him.

"Anna, we're sleeping in here in two nights' time. I know I said I wanted privacy before we made love, but I'm beginning to believe we should've done like the other couples who sneak around at night thinking no one's aware of their doings."

He took an abrupt backward step away from her.

Unprepared for the sudden move, Anna's arms were wrenched from around his waist. A fingernail caught at the strip of cloth on her left hand to score across the raw and blistered palm. She hissed with felt pain.

"What's wrong?" Traun stilled his agitated movement.

"My fingernail cut through the blisters on my hand."

Only then did he seem to notice the white strips of cloth wrapped around each of her palms. He reached for the one she peeked at under the fabric to unwind the material. His breath sucked in when he saw her raw palm, bloody now from the deep scrape of her fingernail.

"What have you been doing these past two weeks?"

He reached for her other hand and removed the strips from it. With both of her hands grasped, he gazed down at her open palms. It seemed he was furious at her for her wounds.

Anna yanked her hands from his hold. His attitude irritated.

"I've been working the same as everyone else."

He continued to scold her as if she hadn't spoken, his tone accusatory.

"I don't have the time to pay attention to you at night, much less during the day. I'm too busy keeping everything on schedule as planned. I'm up before dawn and back after everyone's asleep. You should've made me aware of this, or Molly. We have salve to keep this very thing under control. What if those wounds get infected? We don't know what's in this atmosphere."

"Well, no one told me about any salve." Anna whirled to stalk across the room away from him. "Don't you have work to get back to?"

"Stay here," he ordered. He slammed the door on his way out.

He acted as if she purposely caused the blisters on her hands. *Really?*

Anna did feel foolish, though. She should have spoken up. It wouldn't do to become ill here, of all places. Rising to reopen the door, he'd banged shut, she saw the woman, Avreen, raise a hand toward him as he walked past her.

The woman continued to watch him even after he'd passed her by. Anna felt a sudden hypercritical anger. *I'm going to ask him about her. She seems too friendly.* She went back inside the hut to sit on one of the unpacked boxes that lined the walls to wait.

Traun opened the door.

He stalked to where she sat and instructed, "Give me your hand."

When she did so, he opened the tube he held to squeeze some of its contents onto her palm. The cream soothed the aching palm instantly as he rubbed the medication over it. Anna held up her other hand when told to do so.

"What is that?" she asked, still irritated by his attitude but thankful for the cream's blessed relief. It calmed the stinging sensation of the raw skin open to the surrounding air and dirt.

"Something from a Learned One. It will help to heal your hands and keep out any infection. You should have shown me these days ago," he said, his tone abrupt.

"How was I supposed to show them to you? This is the first time in two weeks that we've gotten to see each other except in passing, much less talk to each other. And I can take care of myself, thank you."

"Yeah. I can see that," he said as he put the cap back on the medication tube. He handed it to her.

Anna bristled at his condescending tone, and her earlier anger rose again.

"Who is this Avreen woman you talked to before you came to the hut? I noticed she happily waved to you when you walked by her to get this."

***

Gazing down at the medication tube, Anna was shaking at him under his nose; Traun wondered how their discussion of her hands had jumped to her asking him about Avreen. Did she suspect their past relationship with each other? He wasn't ready to explain that complication to her today, especially not in the fighting moods they both were in.

"You know what, little lady? You better get used to me talking to all the people under my command, male or female. I am the High Commander here, and if someone seeks me out day or night, I'll stop and listen to what they have to say. There is no room for jealousy from you as my Lifemate when duty calls, and I won't have it."

"Did I say I was jealous? I asked a simple question. I could not care less who you talk to, Mr. High Commander."

Her lips curled into nothing short of a sneer at him. Intense anger flared through Traun. It seemed his Lifemate didn't care for him as he knew he did her.

Well, so be it, he thought.

***

Anna jumped when the hut door banged shut again with Traun's departure. *So much for my misguided assumption of our compatibility with one another*, she thought. Her shoulders slumped. She wiped with the back of her hands at the sudden tears on her face.

Not feeling like seeing anyone, she stayed hidden and worked to organize the layout of the compact interior of the hut. Charlee didn't show up the rest of the afternoon, which she was thankful for. She didn't want to discuss the argument between her and Traun. It was dusk before Anna ventured from the hut to walk the short distance to the family campsite area. When she entered the camp area, she attempted to walk straight through it without acknowledging anyone. She didn't want to be there if Traun should, of all nights, come in early and want to escort her to the creek to bathe. She planned to wash—go straight to bed—avoid everyone. Under her arm, she carried a towel, pajama bottoms, and a t-shirt she'd brought from the hut. She didn't speak as she passed Andrew and then George. She was almost through the campsite, thankful Traun couldn't be seen, when Molly stopped her, demanded to see her hands, and told her Traun had informed her about them.

She tsked when Anna turned the palms up for her inspection.

"Honey, you should have said something. I would have known to get the medication for you."

"I didn't think there was anything you could do." Anna shrugged. Her tears threatened at Molly's concern.

"Keep the medication applied frequently throughout the next few days." Molly looked at her closer after the instruction.

"You feeling okay?" She pushed Anna's hair back away from her face.

Crap, Anna thought. She could see that Traun had strolled into the campsite from the corner of her eye. *Of all nights to come in early.*

"I'm fine, Molly. Really. I'm tired, is all. I'm going to go wash off now." She gave a forced, cheerful smile before she scurried away, relieved to have escaped Molly without acknowledging Traun's arrival. Upon reaching the water's edge, Anna plopped down on the creek's sandy shoreline and unlaced her tennis shoes. Her breathing calmed. She turned to her friend at his approach and tried to keep her unhappiness concealed from his watchful gaze when he halted to stand beside her.

"Hello, Anna, how are things going?"

"Fine, Nevin, and you?"

"Oh, okay. Avreen and I are all moved into our hut. How about you and the High Commander?"

"We're almost settled in. About another two nights, I guess."

Nevin hesitated for a moment, but then he said, "Being a Transfer and around the Garr people is getting some used to, isn't it? I mean…."

He looked away. "I shouldn't have said that. I'm sorry."

Anna studied the man before her. "It's okay, Nevin. I agree. It's taking some time to process."

"I'll see you around, Anna. Be careful."

Anna watched as he strolled away from her along the side of the sandy creek bank. He seemed disheartened in his attitude.

***

Traun realized at Anna's hurried exit from Molly that she wanted to avoid him. He still followed her as he wondered how she thought she was to accomplish her bath with no one to help block the view of her from the others. Several couples stopped to converse with him, which slowed his progress behind her.

Seeing Nevin pause in his walk to say something to her, Traun felt a slow burn begin when his Lifemate turned to flash a smile at the man as she unlaced her shoes. The Transfer was the one he'd paired with Avreen.

Could she be jealous of Avreen because of Nevin? Traun wondered. Anger clawed upward at his thoughts even as he nodded at the man's comment who stood by his side. He turned his attention to the couple before him, holding back from approaching Anna and Nevin. He watched them, though.

The couple who'd stopped him to chat moved on, as had Nevin.

Anna jumped when he sat down beside her. Traun wondered if she did so in guilt.

"I'll hold my towel out for you as you wash," he said. He wouldn't question her about the Transfer. However, he'd keep a close eye on them both. He kept his outward expression void of his inner thoughts and feelings. When Anna didn't move or respond to his offer, he glanced in question at her.

"Okay," she said. "And I'll do the same for you."

***

Anna woke earlier than usual the next morning but not early enough. Not before Traun was already out and about. She had thought to try and make amends with him before he left. Neither of them had much to say to each other after their baths were accomplished the evening before. They'd sat with family and the servants around the campfire and talked to everyone else while avoiding speaking to each other. She'd wondered what was going through his mind at his offer to hold her towel the evening before. He'd seemed reserved and still angry from their fight. She'd felt awkward with him for the first time in a long while. She had wanted to tell him she was sorry for their argument but was unwilling to make the first move.

The weeks are passing, and this planet's summer is upon us. Anna sighed at the realization and reached to pull her hair up into a ponytail. The back of her neck was damp already that morning. She looked down at her palms with the hair secured away from her face. They felt and looked better with one evening of treatments. She lifted her attention from them as she glanced around the campsite to search for her sister-in-law. When Charlee stepped out of her and Andrew's hut's entryway, she caught sight of her. She and her brother must have returned there the night before.

Traun didn't want to occupy their hut until everyone under his command had shelter. The men should complete the framework for the large meeting hall that day. She figured that was where he'd gotten off to so early. Andrew and George were also absent from the campsite. Traun had said the night before that he wanted the meeting hall completed before rain came in. Anna glanced at the sky. He had mentioned to George that he was afraid it was in the forecast, given the read-outs he'd been obtaining. She had seen the device he looked at and studied every morning and evening.

The weather had been lovely so far, although each day that passed was hotter and more humid.

***

Hoisting the large wooden beam over his head for Andrew to secure to its cross beam, Traun was thinking of the following evening for him and Anna. They would be in their home and away from the others tomorrow evening, their privacy secure. She would know him as her Lifemate before the night was over. He'd make sure of it.

I'll not allow any more time to slip away without that woman appreciating me as a man and her Lifemate. I'll keep her so busy every night she won't have time to think about that Transfer.

Traun's arm muscles tightened under the weight of the joist he held over his head. While lying awake the night before and thinking about Anna and the male Transfer from Earth, he'd decided that she hadn't had time to form a strong bond with the Transfer while they traveled en route together on the spaceship. He knew that when she hadn't been with him on the spaceship, she'd always been accompanied by a family member or her friend Charlee. He had decided, though, that she might still be attracted to the Transfer since they shared their half-Earthly genetics, and with that in mind, he planned to keep her in a constant state of awareness of her married status to him. In time, even if she were attracted to the Transfer, he was sure her feelings for Nevin would fade.

And to keep her aware of being mine, I'll clear the air between us this evening. Get things back on the proper footing, so to speak, before tomorrow night arrives.

Feeling better about the situation between them, Traun joked with her brother. "Hurry up there, boy. Get this thing bolted. I don't have time to stand here all day. We have more huts to build."

***

Andrew peered down at his brother-in-law as he laughed. "You go as fast as you want. I'll keep up, no sweat, old man."

Traun, only a little over seven years his senior, seemed older. His status as High Commander and the confidence exhibited gave him an aura of maturity beyond his twenty-nine years.

***

Working steadily throughout the day, Anna organized her and Traun's home. A couple of the male servants (she still had a hard time thinking of them as such) helped her to move and slide all of her and Traun's boxed-up clothing beneath his king-sized bed brought from Garr. Draped over the mattress and covers, an off-white cotton comforter was now placed. It was large enough that its edges hit the floor around the bedframe and hid the boxes. Two large fluffy pillows lay on the comforter and against the bed's headboard.

Two long braided rugs, which Traun had also brought with him, Anna spread out on the floor on each side of the bed. The thick rugs would protect their feet from the cold when winter set in. Traun had also brought two wooden storage chests and another extra-large rug. Anna centered the chests on the floor at the foot of the bed. She placed enough changes of outfits in them for her and Traun to wear for at least ten days before the servants would have to do laundry. The rest of their clothes, she decided, would stay stored away under the bed until the ones they used needed to be replaced. She didn't want to wear out too many clothes too fast.

The spare and extra-large rug was spread out in front of the fireplace.

She had brought the medium-sized wooden table against the wall beside the door. A favorite milk-white-colored flower vase had the honor of sitting on top of it. When a person entered the hut and looked left toward the large bed, they'd see, against the far corner wall behind it, an oval-shaped floor-length wood-framed mirror on wooden legs. She'd brought that with her, too, a gift from Molly.

Wiping the sweat from her brow, Anna gazed around at the interior of her small home. A curl of satisfaction rose that she'd been able to organize all of her and Traun's things.

The open room now seemed inviting and cozy.

There was even a high-backed wooden bench to sit on and a large wooden chair, both more than large enough for her Lifemate's frame. She'd arranged them on top of the beige rug before the fireplace.

The male servants had fashioned the two pieces of furniture out of tree limbs they'd gathered from around the valley.

Anna was delighted when they presented the gifts.

The pieces were rustic but looked good with the rest of the furniture. The legs, arms, and backs of the pieces were secured together by vines that had been found and then wound tight through predrilled holes; the trailing vines, when harvested, she was informed, shrank as they dried, binding tightly together anything they had been wrapped around.

Two buttery-yellow, flower-design silk throw pillows were brought to the laughter and question of Andrew. They graced each corner of the homemade bench. The pillows reminded Anna of home on Earth, precisely why she'd wanted to bring them. She swallowed back the sudden lump in her throat. A tree stump, perfect in its height and width, she placed beside the chair to use for an end table. The two male servants assigned to her for the day had helped to give its round top a highly polished shine. Her portable compact disc player currently held a place of honor on top of the tree stump, and the muted lyrics of a popular song from Earth sounded from it.

Anna clicked the CD player off and hummed the tune that had been playing as she walked out from the hut into the moonlit night. Turning, she shut the door to her new home behind her. She was ready to join the family gathering around the campfire, another day of hard physical labor behind them all. George had stopped by earlier to let her know to come eat. She was in better spirits that evening than the previous. Molly had commented to her that morning on how all couples fought from time to time; everyone was under pressure, she'd told her, *what with adjusting to our new life here on this planet, tension is bound to be high.*

She'd patted her arm before she walked away toward George.

Anna slowed her pace when reaching the family campsite. She glanced around it. Charlee and Andrew sat beside each other as they chatted with Traun. He sat across the fire from them, alone. *Another night in which he could come in early?* Anna decided to sit beside him. It was a move to make up on her part if he accepted it. In silence and with a display of indifference, she strolled over to settle on the ground beside his leg. She leaned back to rest her shoulders on the log behind her back, knees drawn up before her. In silence, she listened as Traun replied to her brother's query about the animals brought from Garr. He had posed a question of concern about the babies that the animals were scheduled to have.

"The animals must be bred again next spring as soon as possible. Hopefully, we'll not lose any of their babies during this birthing process. All the animals, except those brought here for riding purposes, are meant to help feed and clothe us if no other animals are found on this planet. The riding animals will be used to investigate the land for long journeys, but we'll have to go on foot until the herd is expanded. It would have been handy if we could have brought riding equipment. There wasn't enough room for them or their required fuel. There were many things left behind because of the time notice." Traun's features had a sudden drawn look.

As Anna listened to him and Andrew talk back and forth, their conversation turned toward what could be out in the unknown. She turned her palms over to inspect the dried and healing blisters on them.

They looked and felt so much better.

Almost healed overnight.

She shouldn't have any trouble carrying the water buckets for the Communal hut, which was scheduled for completion the next day. She tugged on a piece of loose and dried skin.

Traun reached down and took her hand, to hold it within his own as he continued to converse with her brother.

The action halted her activity. He stroked the soft skin on the inside of her wrist with his thumb as he listened to what Andrew was saying. Her fingers were squeezed lightly when she wrapped them around his and leaned her full weight against his leg.

It disappointed Anna when she and Traun couldn't find a private moment together before it was time for him to make his rounds to the other campsites. Yet, she felt they'd patched things up between them without having to discuss the fight. He walked over to squat beside her when she returned from her bath at the creek and was about to crawl beneath her bedroll cover.

"I should be back shortly. Pull your bedroll up against mine, and when I return, we'll talk if you're still awake and if you want?"

She gave a nod.

Reaching out, he ran his fingers through the wet strands of hair hanging beside her face.

"I'll see you when I return."

He lowered his hand to the top of his knee to push upward to stand.

Anna watched as he strode away.

Always, his rounds to be made, she thought. It seemed he was of the same mindset as she was about making up from their fight. He appeared pleased and in a good mood. Too restless to remain in the bedroll, Anna decided to wait for him at their hut. He'd have to pass by it on his way back to the campsite anyway, and it would be the perfect spot for them to talk. Rising, she crept past all the asleep individuals scattered about. Once clear of everyone, she wandered through the area with unhurried steps.

She knew that Traun wouldn't be too happy with her walking around at night without an escort, but the sky was clear, and she could see fine. Anna turned toward their hut.

Opening the door to the shelter, she stepped into its space and walked to the fireplace. She dragged the homemade chair before it to the open doorway; sitting in the chair and slightly out of breath, Anna stretched her legs to prop her feet on the doorframe—a perfect spot to see her Lifemate when he approached from his finished rounds.

Looking out at the surrounding huts, she felt a sense of pride and ownership in each one. She was proud of Traun and the people's willingness to follow him. His ability to lead was apparent to her as well as the others. It seemed they all worked hard to accomplish the tasks he laid out for them.

Lowering her feet from the doorframe to sit up straight, Anna watched from her home's darkened doorway as the woman, Avreen, exited her hut; the woman looked to her right and left before slinking around to the side of it as if afraid of being seen.

I wonder what she's about? Anna thought in bewilderment as she watched her.

She smiled when she noted Traun's form in the moonbeam night, returning from his rounds. He was almost past Avreen's home when he abruptly turned to walk down along its side and then out from sight behind it. Anna's smile dropped. She sat still for a moment.

Standing, she shoved the chair into the hut to shut the door.

Turning, she headed down the hill.

Even as she told herself she had nothing to worry about, unease rose with each step she took. She knew that Nevin patrolled that night on the other side of camp.

Traun wouldn't be a cheater, would he? No, he wouldn't.

With that last firm thought, Anna made it to the side of Avreen's home to step out from around the side of it to the back of the hut. She froze. Her breath stalled at the scene before her. She almost cried out.

Traun, his back to her, held Avreen within his arms, and her arms were wrapped tight around his waist; neither he nor she was aware of her presence as they murmured between them. With a step backward and then another and another, Anna turned and ran.

***

Traun held Avreen in his arms to comfort and shield her. His words were said to her only to try to understand her behavior.

When he'd rounded the corner of her home to its backside and strode toward her, she'd turned, and seeing him, she'd run to sling herself against him as she wrapped her arms around his waist, crying out his name.

"What is it, Avreen? Tell me."

"You're here, Traun. You're here." With a soft laugh, she leaned back to gaze up at him. He didn't move.

"You're not hurt? Frightened of something?"

"No."

In quick reflex, Traun took hold of her wrists to remove her arms from around his waist, wrapped so tight around him.

"Avreen," he said, and he made his voice harsh. He wanted her to understand that their relationship was over and done with.

"Stop this! You and I are no more."

"I...I...thought you, we...?" She gestured toward him and then to herself before she dropped her hand back to her side.

"But you said that you love me," she cried out.

"When have I ever said that I love you?" Her declaration took Traun by surprise.

"You said you were only doing your duty with that Transfer. You said it on Garr and again here. Your words let me know you loved and wanted me, not her. That we would be together."

"You misunderstood me, Avreen. I am doing my duty, but I want to be with Anna and only her."

***

Avreen stepped back and away from the man before her.

A man she worshipped with her entire being. She raised her hands to her hot cheeks as embarrassment ripped through her. She looked away, unable to meet his gaze. *Has he not ever said out loud that he loves me?* she thought in bewilderment.

Hunching her shoulders upward, she began to cry, and she couldn't stop the reaction.

"I...I...love...you. I thought you loved me, too. It's why I came to this planet, even though I knew you were assigned to marry another."

To comfort her, he pulled her back into his arms. "I am the one to apologize. I should have made my feelings clearer to you during our time together on Garr and that first day I realized you were here."

Avreen knew he didn't want to see her hurt, and it made her love him even more for it. He let her wrap her arms back around his waist and patted her back as she spilled her anguish against his chest. He didn't say anything as she cried. She gained control of the emotional response and pulled away from him through determined grit.

"Can we be friends?" She sniffed as she wiped her face with her hand.

"Yes. Always friends." Traun smiled at her.

"I guess I've made a fool of myself." Avreen looked everywhere but at the man before her.

"Let's agree to forget tonight ever happened," he said.

"Yes, let's," she mumbled.

***

Anna raced past her and Traun's home as anger boiled within her. Forgotten memories flooded her consciousness of how she'd had her fair share of married men on Earth who'd let her know they were willing to cheat on their wives if she were so inclined, believing they could get away with it. *It seems*, she thought with a deep sense of betrayal felt in the pit of her stomach, *that even alien species are of the same mindset.*

Slowing her running to a fast-walking clip, she stalked into the sleeping family campsite. She went to yank her bedroll away from Traun's and to move it to where it had been before, and then, for good measure, she moved it another couple of feet more away from his long-armed reach.

With her shoes jerked from her feet, she crawled under her bedroll cover to pull it up as high as possible.

Well. Slam, bam, thank you, ma'am, she sneered to herself when Traun strolled into the campsite without a sound. She realized he couldn't have been with that woman for more than thirty minutes after she'd left. *If he comes over here, I swear, I'll punch him right in the mouth.*

She closed her eyes in the pretense of sleep and curled her fingers tight to form two fists under the bedroll cover as she waited for his approach.

He went to the creek instead and then returned, having bathed and changed into night clothes.

Her first tear slipped to the blanket under her cheek when he made no step toward her.

***

Traun's disappointment coiled within him that Anna hadn't moved her bedroll up close against his. *She must have fallen asleep after I left*, he thought as he gazed over to where she lay almost concealed under her bedroll cover. He knew he'd pushed everyone as hard as possible to get shelters up; the next day was another planned work day. *Let her get her rest*, he thought, as he pulled his bedroll cover back and stretched out with a tired sigh.

Settling beneath his cover, Traun mentally replayed the emotional scene with Avreen. He had almost forgotten he'd promised to meet with her that night, anxious to return to Anna. As he was about to pass by her hut, it had dawned on him that he'd told her he'd meet with her that evening. He was sorry he'd hurt her. He'd not realized the depth of emotion she felt for him. *Hopefully, she'll turn to her Lifemate and find love in that direction,* he thought as he closed his eyes.

Chapter 11

The next morning, Anna, along with several other women, including Charlee, was assigned to carry water to the men and women who worked on the finishing work of the Communal Hall. They hauled buckets of water up the incline from the creek that flowed past the valley to the workers who waited for them; the others doused the fabric stretched out over the frame of the building with their hauled water.

The fabric was smoothed out with quick movements, and its curing and thickening process started, which was the last detail needed to complete the hall. Traun was one of the few men who still worked on the building. He had dispersed others to begin construction of additional huts further down in the valley; many more huts were still needed, and the finishing work on the hall that day didn't require numerous hands. The women who worked on the Communal Hall smoothed out the wetted material as far up as they could reach, with the men working downward from where they stood on their scaffolding.

Having managed so far that morning to avoid being the one who handed Traun a bucket of water, Anna felt her panic strike when she returned from the creek with a full pail to realize he was the only one who stood waiting. She tried not to look at him as she approached at a snail's pace. She still simmered with anger over what she'd witnessed between him and that woman.

"Let me step down, Anna, so you don't have to strain to reach me," he said when she halted below him.

Anna couldn't stop taking in his smooth movement from the scaffolding to where she stood. It nauseated her that she was still attracted to him after what she knew he'd done the night before. A slow, smug grin spread across his face when he saw she watched him.

Surely, he doesn't realize my attraction toward him? Oh, please, spare me that humiliation. Anna lifted the bucket of water and refused to meet his gaze with hers.

"Like what you see?" he said under his breath as he leaned close to her. His smile stretched wide when she snapped her gaze up to meet his. Shock coursed through Anna at his audacity.

Does he feel no guilt? No guilt at all? she wondered. The bucket of water she held slammed into his chest and bounced up to hit him under the chin. Cold water drenched him.

As the bucket fell back, seemingly in slow motion to roll to a stop at her feet, Anna stared down at it in stunned disbelief. It took a moment for her to grasp what she'd done in front of everyone around them. Her anger had wrapped with such an intense tightness that when she'd heard his comment, she'd struck out in blind rage and without thought. She looked back up. Fear slithered down her spine. Traun's smile of amusement at her moments earlier was gone. His expression was now hard and filled with chilling fury. Anna took a quick step backward, ready to take flight. He reached out with a swift move to clamp his fingers around her elbow and to pull her toward him even as he angled his body so the shocked spectators around them were unable to see his face.

He gritted out between clenched teeth, "Lady, don't you ever show me that kind of disrespect in front of my people again."

His fingers cut into the flesh around her elbow.

Ripping her gaze away from his, Anna hunted for her family and their support. Her fear paralyzed her. She found George and Molly's shocked looks directed her way. They shook their heads at her and lowered their gazes when she stared at them in a silent plea for their aid.

Andrew. He'll help me!

Anna swung her face toward her brother. He had stopped working mid-swing, apparently frozen at the public disrespect shown toward their High Commander. When his gaze met hers, he shook his head no at her also. He would not come to her rescue. He reached down a hand to stop Charlee from intervening when she stepped forward.

"Don't you look to your family to help you," Traun said, his lowered voice harsh against Anna's ear. "If they interfere, they'll bear the penalties, and rightly so. Do you understand me?"

Anna avoided eye contact with him.

"Look at me." He gave her arm a hard squeeze. She locked her gaze with his.

"You will continue to work the rest of the day as if nothing happened. And after we are done, you'll go straight to our hut and stay there. Do you understand me?"

His narrowed gaze pierced hers. In slow motion, Anna nodded that, *yes*, she understood. She wondered if she could stay upright when and if he should ever let go of her arm; her legs shook so.

"And, Anna," he continued in that unnerving soft yet hard voice since she'd thrown the bucket. "You will reap the consequences for your disrespect shown to me."

He loosened his grip from around her elbow. She stepped back away from him, every muscle in her body stiff. She tried to appear calm in front of the spectators who watched her and their High Commander. White-hot embarrassment coursed through Anna as she bent to retrieve the water bucket. She clenched her fingers around its handle and straightened to square her shoulders, and without meeting anyone's gaze, walked away from her Lifemate and the gawking group.

Once back at the creek's edge, she sank to her knees beside it. Her mind whirled from the public clash with Traun and his evident fury at her over it. Anna plunged her fingers into the cold water before her to bring their wet tips back up to her hot face to pat her cheeks. The other women, who'd been busy hauling their buckets of water up the incline, began to come back down to the creek for their refills. Quickly, Anna dunked her pail into the water to fill it back up. She rose from her kneeling position to turn and start up the incline.

The men and women who waited for water failed to meet her gaze at her return, as uncomfortable in making eye contact as she was.

Anna thought the work-day would never end, and when it did, she walked fatigued and alone toward her and Traun's hut. She was unwilling to try and test him by ignoring his command to go to their hut at the end of the day. Charlee made eye contact with her in passing and pointed to the creek as an indication for her to meet her there. Anna's eyes welled up at her sister-in-law's concern. She shook her head *no* at her.

"We will talk later," Charlee mouthed silently to her from beside Andrew.

Anna nodded.

Andrew stopped when she did. They stood before her small home. Charlee strolled on ahead, her expression sympathetic toward her.

"Sis, I don't know what happened out there today. I do know, though, that the public disrespect you showed our High Commander cannot and will not be allowed. This is a different world than where we came from. The rules have changed."

Anna gulped back the tears she wanted to shed. She gazed down at her shoes, refusing to look at her brother as he scolded her. He paused in his lecture.

"But you don't understand, Andrew—"

"You're an adult now, Anna! I can't come to your rescue in this. You need to work whatever this is out with your husband. And don't involve Charlee."

He walked away and followed the path his spouse had taken.

Anna turned toward the door behind her and, opening it, stepped inside of what was now her home. She shut the door behind her. She didn't want to see anyone. Her tears held at bay all that day burst forth when she noticed the two plates of food on the homemade bench and her nightclothes, folded with neatness, laid out on the bed. Alongside the clothes, a towel and a scented bar of soap had been placed: evidence of that sweet female servant, thinking about her when it seemed her family members were willing to allow her to suffer alone; no thought of her future well-being from them.

I must remember to thank Klinn when I see her again.

Anna wiped her face and wished she had the nerve to defy Traun and go to the creek to wash up. She felt sticky and dirty from the day's work. She left her plate of food untouched to curl up on the homemade chair to wait instead.

An hour passed.

Her eyelids began to droop.

She hadn't slept much the previous night, and with the tension felt all day, exhaustion took over, and she let it.

****

Traun paused in the doorway of his hut when he entered it well after darkness had fallen and noticed his Lifemate curled up, asleep. He closed the door with a quiet clink to walk into the room. The valley was secure with the guards at their posts, and everyone was accounted for. The overhead solar-powered light above him cast an intimate soft glow throughout the hut. *What happened between last night and today with her?* he wondered in confusion as he gazed down at her sleeping form. *Why the extreme anger with my teasing comment to her?*

Stepping to the bench across from the chair where she slept, he picked up the largest plate of food and turned to settle where it had been. He shoved the other untouched plate over as he stretched out his legs; he took a bite of the now-cold meal.

He didn't know what made his Lifemate wake up, but when she did, she sat up quickly in the chair to place her feet on the floor.

She refused to look over to where he sat.

Traun didn't comment as he watched her. She crossed one leg over the other and then uncrossed it, only to repeat the action. A lone finger tapped at the arm of the chair where she sat so straight and stiff.

He continued to eat until the last bite of food was gone. He set the plate beside him on the bench.

"Get up. We're going down to the creek." His tone sounded harsher than he intended. His Lifemate's eyes widened as if he'd relayed that he planned to drown her. Her fingers clutched at the arms of the chair.

"Gather your change of clothes and towel from the bed," Traun said firmly when she didn't move.

She shot from the chair to collect the items laid out on top of the bed. She was afraid to argue with him, he realized. Her objects were held tight against her breast as if a lifeline between her and him. She shifted from one foot to the other while he selected fresh clothes, a towel, and his toothbrush. She was still unwilling to meet his gaze when he glanced toward her.

Together, they walked down to the creek; unspoken words and angry emotions hovered between them. When they reached the water, Traun stripped naked without giving warning. He didn't care what his Lifemate thought of his behavior. After tonight, she'd know him through and through anyway.

She whirled to turn away.

He waded out waist-deep into the water.

"Undress and get in the water, Anna. There's no one down here, and it's too dark for anyone to see us clearly."

When she remained unmoving, he warned in a staunch tone, "Little lady, I'll undress you and wash you myself if I have to."

With quick movements, she undressed and ran into the cold water several feet from him. She soaped and washed, not wasting any movement.

With her back to him, she quickly exited the water and made a haphazard attempt to dry off. Traun watched as she grabbed her nightclothes abandoned on the sandy creek bank and hopped on one foot and then the other, shoveling each leg into her pajama bottoms as fast as possible. She hastily slipped on her top to button it up tight.

Beginning to towel dry her hair, she stilled.

She brushed her teeth.

He splashed the water behind her. She jumped in a flight reaction before she realized he was still bathing and not getting out of the water, as she believed.

With her breathing shallow and unsteady, she turned away again.

With amusement held at her actions, Traun, with deliberation, slapped at the water. His Lifemate jumped. She didn't turn around. He waded from the water. Drying off, he watched her as he pulled on his pajama bottoms. He slung his damp towel around his bare neck to slip his feet into his shoes.

"Put your shoes on, Anna," he instructed. He waited.

She complied with haste.

He turned to begin the walk back up the incline to the backside of their hut. When they reached the small shelter, he opened its door and motioned for her to go first.

She edged past him into the room. He followed her.

He shoved the lock home on the door with a deliberate loud and resounding click. Anna whirled over to stand on the other side of the chair made specially for her and him.

The chair, it seemed, gave her some measure of comfort as a barrier between them. Traun watched her in silence as he set aside his toothbrush and dirty clothes. He pulled the towel from around his neck to sling it to the basket to be used for it. He wondered where to begin with this Earthling. Should he ask about her behavior that morning and the cause of it? Or should he explain to her the standard of conduct that must be exhibited in front of the people that he and, yes, even she commanded?

At his continued silence, his Lifemate kept her eyes lowered onto the back of the chair that her fingers gripped.

His words were unhurried as he began, "Anna, I can understand your anger with me after our disagreement of the day before. But what I can't comprehend or grasp is that you came to me afterward in a gesture of forgiveness, and things were fine between us when I left you last night, I thought. Then today, you lash out at me in front of our people with behavior that was uncalled for and unbecoming of you."

He started to go on, but her gaze snapped upward toward him, and her eyes flashed.

"Don't you dare try to preach to me about what is unbecoming!"

Anger that had simmered under the surface all day in Traun flared. He took a quick step in her direction.

She immediately scurried to the wall behind her.

Traun knew by her frantic action what she believed he might do. Unbeknownst to her, she didn't need to fear he'd ever beat her. If a man in the world of Garr was caught abusing his Lifemate, the punishment was swift and harsh. The behavior was simply not tolerated. It was even taught against in the Book of Wisdom, which guided their behavior. He had been raised to find the action abhorrent. Yet, in that moment, he relished her fright of him. He wanted her to fear him.

He narrowed the distance between them.

She moved to dart around him, and he allowed it as he rotated to follow with slow, measured steps. With her gaze and attention fixed on him, she unknowingly backed toward the bed across the room. When he drew too close to her for her comfort, she attempted to dart around him again, and in quick reflex, he reached out to grab hold of a wrist.

"Don't you even think of hitting me. You alien beast," she yelled out.

***

Anna's breath caught in her throat as she strained backward on the arm, her Lifemate held tight within his grip. She dug her heels into the floor beneath her feet as slowly he drew her toward him, torturing her, as she'd seen her cat on Earth do to a mouse caught in the backyard. She hit with her fist at his hand, which imprisoned her arm. She kicked out and lost a shoe. He sidestepped her aim to his shins, even as he continued to tug her body to his. He kicked off his boots and grasped her swinging fist to hold it. Abruptly, he moved toward her, forcing her to step backward.

"Let me go." Anna's eyes met Traun's dark gaze as she took another step backward when he moved against her again. Her breath rasped. Fear clogged her throat.

"Make me," he mocked.

He kept pushing up against her.

With an abrupt move, he shoved her backward—the palms of his hands at her shoulders.

Unable to stop her sudden backward falling motion, Anna stared at her Lifemate in stunned disbelief at what he'd done. Her arms flailed about in the air. She expected to feel jarring pain at any moment. When she hit the bed instead of the hard floor of the hut as expected, she felt a quick surge of relief before she rolled over to claw her way up onto the bed's center, away from him, and to the bed's other side. He followed to pull her back toward him to flip her around so she faced him.

He slung one of his legs over both of hers when she kicked out at him again with her feet. Her other shoe now lost. Anna thrashed about in a bid for freedom. In silence, Traun watched her, holding her in place with ease. She didn't believe his breathing was any faster after their struggle while hers rasped. It hurt to breathe.

In increments, she calmed down as he didn't do anything but gaze down at her.

"Let me up," she demanded.

"Tell me why you're so angry at me, and I'll release you after that. Maybe," he taunted. Anna realized at that moment that she loved this man before her with every fiber of her being. Her heart hurt that he didn't feel the same way about her, given the evidence of what she'd witnessed the night before. Her eyes began to fill with tears even as she fought the reaction. She turned her face away from his, unwilling to admit to what she'd witnessed. He wouldn't ever know that she knew of his unfaithfulness to her.

"Anna, don't cry," he said.

He grasped her chin to urge her to turn her face back to his.

"Look at me, baby."

He kissed her forehead and then her wet cheeks. His touch was gentle.

"I bruised your arm today, didn't I?" he murmured. He kissed across the dark spots.

Anna's tears increased at his tenderness now shown.

He took possession of her mouth.

After a moment, she accepted his attention and lifted her freed arms to encircle them around his neck. She knew Traun felt her erratic heartbeat beneath his lips as he paused for a moment at the base of her neck before he moved them on across her collarbone.

He rose to meet her gaze with his and framed her face between two gentle hands.

"Yes?" he asked in a ragged breath. She knew what he wanted.

"I ache, Anna," he said, his tone low and soft.

"Yes," she responded, unable to deny him.

Her desire for his embrace drew her toward him.

Chapter 12

The next morning, Traun rose early, moving with stealth so as not to wake his Lifemate as he dressed. The stain of her lost virginity was evident on their sheets when he turned to straighten the top bed cover so that she was entirely under it. He studied her for a moment. The smudges under her eyes while she slept were a testament to the sleepless nights she'd experienced. Unanswered questions still lingered between them. She had refused to answer any inquiries directed toward her the night before, and he couldn't fathom the deep-seated anger she held against him.

There will be no work today, he thought, deciding to let her sleep in at hearing the soft plop—plop—sound of rain as it hit the roof of the hut. He was thankful that those without homes could stay in the communal hall, which had been finished the day before, or bunk with others in the village who had huts. Turning, he exited the secure enclosure.

***

Anna woke briefly. The pattering sound of rain outside the small home that cocooned her soothed and comforted her before sleep took her over again. Jolted back awake, she turned to see an open doorway groggily. With haste, she made sure her blanket covered her bare form. Whoever had opened the door to the hut had a clear view of where she lay.

Klinn stepped into the open doorway and looked toward her apologetically.

"Bring it in. My Lady Anna is awake now." She tsked at her Lifemate through the open doorway, and Anna heard him mumble something to the woman.

He had a metal tub grasped between large palms when he stepped forward.

"Put it beside the fireplace," Klinn instructed him. "Now go heat some water and bring it here." She shooed at him with her hands even as he backed away. He didn't glance over to where Anna lay on the bed in sleepy-eyed amazement, watching the two.

Klinn shut the door behind him. She shook her head before she hurried over to where Anna lay.

"My Lady Anna, I'm sorry we woke you. My Lifemate was supposed to place the tub down beside your door. It slipped from his fingers and hit the door, which caused it to open. I may as well get clothes out for you and make your bed now that you're awake." Her apology had turned to what she thought needed to be done in a heartbeat.

Anna rose to a sitting position in the center of the bed, and she clutched at the top blanket, making sure her nakedness stayed concealed as she tried to grasp what it was the woman rambled on about in her heavy accent. Something about clothes and a bath?

"Klinn," she said, interrupting the woman when she continued to babble on about rain and people who needed to mind their stuffy own business.

"Yes, my Lady Anna?"

"What time is it?"

"It is afternoon, my Lady Anna."

"What?" Swinging her legs over to the side of the bed, Anna worried why Traun hadn't bothered to wake her up. Everyone had required duties.

"Is everyone out working?"

She tried to bunch up the blanket around her as she stood. The fabric caught under her feet as she danced about. Klinn reached out a hand to halt her frenzied movements.

"No one works, my Lady Anna. Our High Commander gave everyone the day off because of the rain."

Anna started to laugh as relief flooded through her. "What are you doing here if everyone has the day off?"

Klinn smiled.

"I wanted to make sure you were taken care of, my Lady Anna. I heard what happened yesterday." With a sympathetic gesture, the woman patted her arm.

"Oh." Anna looked away from the servant, her embarrassment high. She had given fuel for all to gossip about her and Traun.

"Yes, well…I'm fine, Klinn. Thank you for being so concerned."

"They said they're curious about what happened between you and our High Commander. I told them never to mind that." Klinn nodded her head as if she'd settled something. But then she continued. "Your anger at our High Commander was obvious, they said. They said you earned their respect with the dignified manner when you went back to work after you clashed with each other."

She bent to pull the blanket out from beneath Anna's feet, then became a whirlwind of activity around her while she continued her endless hard-to-follow chatter.

"I told my Lifemate, our Lady Anna, and High Commander need alone time away from everyone. You would work out whatever's wrong between you if you had that."

She began to strip the bed. "I see I be right." She nodded at the blood stains on the sheet.

Anna wanted to die of embarrassment—nothing like an announcement about what happened privately between two people.

"With babies, everything be complete. You must keep doing what you're doing. Nightly, if possible." Klinn turned to smile at her as if she'd given a rare piece of wisdom.

Anna was mortified that the woman thought to instruct her sex life. The servant continued to ramble on and seemed unaware of her discomfort. Finished with her determined tasks, she turned to leave, her husband in tow behind her. He had returned to fill the tub with heated water. Klinn smiled at her before she closed the door with a firm click. Anna shook her head in amazement to lower the blanket she'd held around her. *Finally, alone again.* She'd consumed the plate of food Klinn had fetched and demanded she eat. The bed was made, her clothes laid out, and a tub of water waited for her, all accomplished in under an hour. She had tried to tell the woman she didn't need anything and to please take the earned day off, but she'd been ignored. Stepping over the metal bathing tub's smooth side, Anna eased downward into the hot water it held. She washed with the scented soap laid out, even her hair, and then rinsed. Stretching her legs out to hang them over the tub's edge, she leaned back onto the sloped end to close her eyes and issued a heartfelt sigh. Her feet touched the floor. The warm water surrounding her felt delicious, even if the tub was too short for her tall frame. It seemed she hadn't had a warm bath for ages and ages.

While she relaxed and half dozed, Anna thought about the previous night. Traun had been gentle with her; an extreme gentleness showed, in fact. When he'd reached for her that second time in the wee hours of the morning, she'd clung to him. Each time after their lovemaking, he'd wrapped his arms around her to hold her close as if he couldn't bear not to touch her. When he'd fallen asleep after that second time, she'd slipped her hand onto his chest over his heart and had wished the heartbeat she could feel under her palm beat for her and her alone. *How can this man make me feel loved and cared for after what I saw*? She'd wondered in confusion. She wouldn't confront him with what she'd witnessed. Her pride was too wounded by it.

Anna's eyes flew open.

Someone was at the door.

She hadn't locked it before getting into the tub, either. *Not again!* Anna glanced around the hut to find her towel.

She grimaced when she saw the large fluffy white cloth lying out of reach, slung over the arm of the chair.

"Wait," she called out when the door to the hut began to open. "I'm not decent!" She crossed her arms over her breasts and tried to scoot further down into the tub as the door continued to swing inward. Traun strode through the open entryway to shut the door straightaway behind him.

"Well, well, what have we here?" he said.

He laid the bundle he held onto the table beside the entryway.

Removing his raincoat to set it aside, he shook the rain from his hair. His eyes began to dance with his amusement found at her expense. He walked over to the edge of the tub to squat beside it. Dipping his fingers into the warm water, he brought them back up her side to brush them against the edge of a bare breast. He leaned forward to capture her lips with his.

"Good morning or good afternoon, I should say," he said when he pulled back from her. He smiled at her in response to what Anna knew was her pensive expression toward him. She was sure she looked ridiculous all spread out in the tub, and it embarrassed that he'd caught her in the unbecoming position.

"Good afternoon. Will you hand me that towel? So, I can get out of this thing." Anna nodded her head in the direction of the towel.

"But I like you in this thing. All lovely and cute with your long legs hanging over the edge." He reached out to run an open palm down the length of her leg closest to him.

"And so smooth and soft."

"Traun, please." Anna's face felt hot with her embarrassment. He quit his teasing to stand, and to walk over and pick up the white towel. He held it out to her after the few steps required back.

"Turn around." She kept one arm over her bare breasts as she took the towel and stayed where she was, slouched down in the tub of water.

His eyebrows rose. "I saw all of you last night, Anna."

"Please, Traun."

His lips twitched as he studied her. He turned.

Scrambling up and out of the tub, Anna dried off quickly and wrapped the large towel around her form, ensuring it stayed put.

"Does everyone have shelter from the rain?"

Turning at her question, Traun's eyes went to her bare feet and, from there, traveled up her bare legs to the bottom edge of the towel and upward to the top. Only then did his gaze meet hers. Anna had wanted to curl her toes into the floor beneath her feet with his slow appraisal.

"The Communal Hall is large enough to accommodate all without a home. Although some are bunking down with the others who have shelter," he said.

"What about the material still stored for the huts not built? Will it all be ruined with the rain?"

***

Traun reached out and pulled Anna to him, wrapping his arms around her waist. Her questions pleased him. They reflected that she was concerned for their people and thought of their welfare rather than hers. He hugged her to him.

"Everything is secure. Once the rain is over, we can resume the construction of the rest of the huts. Would you like to visit the Communal Hall with the people gathered there during this rain?"

Traun drew back to look down at her when she didn't respond. She seemed hesitant. It dawned on him that perhaps she wondered how the others would act toward her after her actions of yesterday.

"You may as well get the awkwardness over with as soon as possible," he said softly.

"Yes, I think I'd like to go and visit with everyone," she responded.

He bent down to kiss her, and she raised her arms to encircle them around his waist. When they parted, he said, "I brought a raincoat and a hood you can use. Go get dressed."

Traun gave a light slap to her bare bottom under the towel.

If he held her much longer, they wouldn't be going anywhere. He wanted to ask her again about her actions toward him yesterday. He still needed answers but was reluctant to start something that might end the harmonious mood between them.

Chapter 13

Anna hurried beside Traun toward the Communal Hall. As they entered through its doorway and paused to take off their rain gear, they still laughed between themselves over his comical hand flapping at his almost slip and fall. He took her coat, which dripped water onto the floor, and handed it, along with his jacket and their rain hoods, to a servant to hang up. He guided her around the puddle of water they'd made with a hand at her elbow.

"I'll be right back," he said as another male motioned to him from across the room.

Feeling somewhat abandoned, Anna looked around at the people who'd gathered. She smiled at the ones who would meet her gaze.

There seemed to be an air of festivity as the many there laughed and chatted.

She spotted George. She hesitated, wondering if he'd been embarrassed by her actions the day before. He strolled over to where she stood, and when he reached her, he pulled her into his embrace, which reassured her of his affection.

"Where's Molly?" she asked.

He glanced at Traun, who approached from behind them. He then grinned at her.

"Oh, she's around here somewhere," he said, over a burst of laughter from a group who'd gathered at the other end of the long building.

"Everyone has decided we need a party, and we're setting up tables so those who want to play card games can play. Some of the others who have musical instruments went to fetch them. Even the Keeper of the Book of Wisdom has gone for his wind instrument to play for us."

"Sounds like we came at the right time then, Anna," Traun said. He stepped up close to rest a hand on her waist and held a glass filled with an amber-colored liquid in the other.

Anna glanced downward. She remembered that liquid's alcoholic burn to her throat when she'd tried it.

"The men broke out the drinks for the occasion," Traun said. He chuckled at her grimace of distaste toward the glass.

George laughed. "How much of that drink did the men manage to bring from Garr?"

"Not enough, but they've assured me they managed to bring plenty of seeds to grow the plant for the main ingredient it's made from."

"I have married a drunk," Anna said to George. She smiled at Traun and hoped he knew she only teased. Molly had told her on the spaceship that he never allowed himself to get intoxicated. She said her sister informed her that he enjoyed the strong drink and put away more than most men but knew when to put it down.

Traun squeezed at her waist with his hand as he smiled down at her.

George watched their behavior with each other.

"I am going to go find Molly in this crowd," he said before he strolled away.

Others within the building began to walk up to them, eager to speak to their High Commander. Before long, Anna and Traun had drifted apart as Traun visited with all who beckoned toward him.

Standing alone, Anna watched the musicians from across the room where they'd set up and began to perform. The musical instruments they'd brought from Garr looked strange. None attempted to sing; the group teased and plucked out the sounds that rose within the building. The rising and falling notes held a haunting, poignant quality to them.

"A beautiful composition, don't you think?"

The low-voiced comment surprised Anna. She'd been absorbed in the song played.

"Oh, hello. Yes, it is," she said when she turned.

Nevin took his gaze from the musicians to meet hers from where he stood beside her.

Anna hoped his Lifemate wasn't nearby. With a quick glance behind him, she felt her relief and knew she rambled in her conversation, as she wondered where Avreen was when she couldn't locate her. "The rain slowed our work, but we all needed a break, don't you think? I mean, we're all exhausted. Although everything we've done was needed...."

"I agree," Nevin said when she trailed off, embarrassed and nervous. He continued.

"Avreen wanted some time alone, and this rain gave her an excuse. She's having a hard time adjusting to this planet and the change of lifestyle she enjoyed on Garr."

"Oh?" Anna didn't know what to say to the unexpected and personal disclosure. She glanced over to where Traun stood, his back to them. Nevin suddenly seemed uncomfortable at his admission to her.

"I'm sorry, Lady Anna. I shouldn't have said anything. Only I feel so comfortable with you, and I'm at a loss on how to bond with my Lifemate. I know you haven't had an easy time of it either, from what I heard happened yesterday."

Anna's blush rose, and she couldn't stop it. *Had all the people discussed amongst themselves over what had happened?* She looked down at the floor.

"Don't be embarrassed, please. I brought the incident up because I hoped you could help Avreen somehow. She's so withdrawn into herself. Maybe you could talk to her and explain your difficulty adjusting here?"

Anna shook her head in denial and looked back up to meet his gaze. "No, Nevin. I'm sorry. I can't be of any help with this."

His expression seemed to hold a hopelessness to it. "I've overstepped my bounds by asking it of you, but I had to try. I won't bother you with it again. Would you like to join me in a card game, Lady Anna?"

With his obvious concern for his Lifemate and feeling sorry for him, Anna felt an emotional tie with the Transfer, knowing what she did of Avreen and her husband. It tugged at her heart.

"Let's go play that game of cards," she said, smiling at him.

***

Traun watched the two from across the room and wondered what they discussed with such earnestness between them. He didn't like the engaging smile Anna bestowed upon the man before they walked away together to sit at one of the card tables.

Sometime later, he excused himself from the men he conversed with. It was time for his walk around the settlement to check on the four individuals posted as night watchmen for the evening. He needed to see what they had to report. He began to move toward where Anna still sat and played her card game. He halted from time to time when approached and conversed with the individuals or couples. When he arrived at the card table and the players who sat around it, Traun heard the Transfer, Nevin, say that Lady Anna must cheat to win every hand.

Anna, with merriment, laughed and told the Transfer that he was being a big baby loser; that's what his problem was. The others around the table burst out laughing with glee at her words. No one noticed him or his approach, all too absorbed in the teasing back and forth between the two.

Nevin reached out to grab hold of the hand she'd laid over the winning cards on the table before him. He lifted it to him with a pretense of searching up her shirt sleeve for the cards he swore to the others she'd switched on him to win. The others at the table laughed with him.

Traun frowned at the man's familiarity.

He stepped up to lay a hand on Anna's shoulder from behind her.

In a quick reaction, Nevin drew away from her. It was apparent he didn't want to invite disfavor from his High Commander. The others at the table grew quiet. Their eyes darted between the three of them.

"Anna, now that the rain has ceased, I will walk around camp. I want you to come with me."

Anna rose and smiled at him before turning to the others, who sat silently around the table. They watched her and him.

"Thank you for an enjoyable game," she told the group. "And next time, maybe I'll let you win," she said teasingly to Nevin.

He half-smiled back at her. He didn't look toward his High Commander.

Traun nodded to the group before turning her for them to stroll away.

***

"Man, I wouldn't wish to be in your shoes. You know better than to touch her," the man who sat at Nevin's right shoulder said. The others at the table shot sympathetic looks in his direction.

One of the other male card players leaned forward so none but those around the table could hear him. "I guess our High Commander took care of the problem between them. Did you see how fast she jumped up to leave with him?"

His assigned Lifemate, who lounged beside him, laughed low at his comment.

"Well darling, if he wanted me to go with him, I'd leap up too. Look at him." She licked her lips with suggestive vulgarity.

The others around the table laughed, most in embarrassment, although some in amused enjoyment of gossip.

Nevin didn't laugh. He gazed in dislike at the female Transfer from Earth and her Lifemate from Garr, who sat across the table from him. The two smiled at each other at their comments.

For all the gene manipulation the people of Garr know about, they failed to isolate the gene for crudeness, he thought as he pushed back his chair, ready to call it a night.

***

Anna walked beside Traun as they crossed the hall's floor toward its front exit door. Many within the room approached to say their goodbyes. *All in all, the evening wasn't so bad,* she thought, as they stepped out from the Communal Hall into the night air. She inhaled to take in the fresh scent left behind after the recent shower. Rain, dirt, flowers, trees, and some other hint of something, she wasn't sure what perfumed the air. She wondered at Traun's quietness as she tried to keep up with his long stride as he walked away from the building and her briskly.

Confused, she wondered if he wanted her to walk with him or to leave her behind. With a half trot forward, Anna reached out to grasp his hand.

"Stop."

He looked down at her in question as he halted.

"Is this a marathon?"

"What?"

"I can't keep up with you."

Anna took in his frown. "Have I done something wrong? If I have, I'd appreciate it if you'd let me know what it is."

He gave a light squeeze of his fingers around hers.

"Let's talk about this after we return to our hut, okay?"

Puzzled, Anna studied him. She didn't want another fight between them. She couldn't take more drama. Her muscles tensed as she thought over the evening; nothing unusual had happened that she knew of. She'd not caused a scene; her one and very public display would provide enough gossip for the people to talk about for a long time to come.

"I am not angry at you, sweetheart," Traun said. He slipped an arm around her waist to pull her to his side to start their walk again. This time, he shortened his stride to fit her own.

Anna realized the posted guards were friendly, although they kept a reserved distance from her. With his rounds done, she and Traun arrived at their small home to be met by Klinn and her spouse. An evening meal had been brought to them. Klinn's spouse had nothing to say while, as usual, Klinn talked non-stop.

"I hope this meal is to your liking, High Commander and Lady Anna. We thought to set it inside for you until we saw your approach. Did you have a nice time at the Communal Hall? Everyone needed rest, and the rain provided it for us, don't you think?"

Anna smiled at Traun's confused expression as Klinn rattled on with no apparent pause for air or a wanted response from either of them. She spoke about the rain and clothes to get out for them…. Anna knew not to try to interrupt her flow of words; Klinn did what she wanted and talked the whole time while doing it. She ordered her spouse to hand over the plates of food that he held. Anna accepted them. Klinn then made short work of turning down the bed covers and laying out their nightclothes; after all, was done, she looked around the room, shook her head as if in agreement with herself at something, and then motioned to her spouse that she was ready to leave.

"Goodnight," she said to Anna and Traun, a smile directed their way before she turned toward the door; babies were mentioned as she exited the hut. Her Lifemate nodded his head as he followed behind her.

"Goodnight," Anna called out. She wanted to laugh at how the woman ignored everyone around her as she did what she wanted and spoke her thoughts out loud while she scurried about.

"Is she always like that?" Traun hurried over to lock their door as if he feared the woman might return. Anna laughed at his actions and handed him one of the two plates shoved into her hands.

"Yes, and telling her you don't want her to do something doesn't do any good. She won't pay any attention to you."

She sat on the bench as Traun lowered himself into the chair. Crossing her legs, she took a bite of the hot food to settle back onto the bench.

"Did she mention making booties for our baby that would be here in nine months?" Traun took another bite of his food, his gaze on her.

"She thinks I'm pregnant already after last night."

At his surprised expression directed her way, she hurried to explain, "She saw the blood stain on the sheets this morning when she stripped the bed. You don't believe I'd discuss that with her, do you?"

"Well, I didn't think so. So, she's convinced after one night with me, you're pregnant, huh?" He pulled back his shoulders.

"Oh, please. Don't get puffed up."

Anna rolled her eyes at her Lifemate and his broad smile directed her way. *It was as they were when on the spaceship. An easy banter between them again*, she thought.

"Come here," he said. He set his plate on the floor beside his chair.

Rising from the bench, Anna turned to lay her plate aside. She stepped over to where he sat, and he reached out to settle her down sideways onto his lap. He worked a hand beneath her shirt to spread his fingers out over her stomach, his gaze on hers.

"I hope she's right. I hope for all our sakes babies are birthed right and left in nine months."

Anna's smile slipped at his reminder that their marriage was for the precise purpose of her breeding. There had been no romantic meeting and falling in love for them with a marriage to follow; all between them had been arranged for the continued existence of the people of Garr. *What if, for some reason, I'm unable to bear children*? She studied Traun's face in silence.

"What are you thinking, Anna?"

"I remembered there was something you wanted to discuss with me." Only at that moment was their earlier conversation recalled. She wasn't about to tell him what she'd been wondering. She would probably not like his answer. He lifted her hair from her nape to kiss the now-exposed spot.

Anna shivered at the tingle which raced down her spine.

"There are certain standards of conduct as the Lifemate of a High

Commander that you need to be aware of, Anna. I understand from George that you weren't taught these things, and I've been too busy to school you in them."

He continued to kiss at her neck between his words. The hand he had under her shirt he worked up to a breast. Anna arched toward that hand.

"Oh really? What type of standards?" She wasn't paying attention.

"First of all, other men are not allowed to touch you. If you reach out to them, that is fine."

"Wait a minute?" A spurt of anger rose in her. Drawing back, she met his gaze to push his hand from underneath her shirt. He let it lay where she dropped it to her lap.

"What brought this type of topic up?"

Traun's gaze held hers.

"When I walked up to the table tonight where you played cards, the Transfer from Earth had your bare arm within his hand as he peeked up your shirt sleeve. He knows such intimacy is against the rules of social conduct toward the Lifemate of a High Commander. He will be punished for it as is fitting."

Anna frowned. She detected a glint of anger within Traun's dark gaze. Her concern rose for her friend.

"Traun, he only teased me about having the winning card hand again after three times in a row. It was nothing. He doesn't deserve punishment. If Nevin stepped over some weird boundary line, the fault lies in my direction, not his."

Traun shifted beneath her. "Why are you so concerned about this Transfer, Anna? George and Molly may have been remiss in teaching you our social class rules, but he was schooled in all aspects of it. And he knowingly broke those directives. A relative or a holy man can touch you. That is all."

At his biting tone, Anna's heart sank. She didn't want discord between them again, and it seemed their evening would escalate to that level if she didn't do something fast. In a quick decision, she picked up his hand, which still lay in her lap, and laced her fingers through his. Kicking off her shoes, she turned to straddle his lap, with her feet positioned under her rump so she could face him.

Traun seemed surprised at her abrupt move, even as he adjusted her position so she fit better against him. Anna returned his hand up beneath her shirt.

He brought his other one to her hip as he silently watched her. She cupped his face within her palms to replicate his action toward her of the night before when he'd attempted to calm her down after their struggle.

"Nevin is my friend. I'm sorry I broke a social class rule. He is a nice man, whom I'm sure didn't mean a thing by his actions." She leaned forward to press her mouth against his. Anna's frustration rose when he didn't move or make a sound.

She bit down on his bottom lip with her teeth and surprised herself with her action.

***

Traun hardened with desire between Anna's legs positioned on each side of him, and he pulled her closer to him to take over the kiss. A knock sounded on their door behind them. He groaned out loud, unable to stop the reaction.

"Go away," he whispered against her mouth.

He lay his forehead against hers as he waited to catch his breath. Anna's breath rasped. She moved to press her face against the side of his neck. The rap of knuckles on the door was repeated. Traun lifted her from his lap to rise from the chair.

"We will finish what you started as soon as I get rid of whoever this is," he said. He watched as she straightened her clothes on her form from where she stood beside the chair where he'd set her. He went to yank open the door, intending to tell whoever was on the other side that whatever they needed could wait until the morrow. Traun paused when he saw his aunt and uncle outside the door.

"Uncle, is there some problem?" he said, concerned.

"No, no problem. Your aunt wanted to speak with you. She has a worry that she believes couldn't wait until the morrow to bring up to you."

Anna strode over to the open doorway.

"Molly, George, come in. Sit. Sit," she said. She motioned toward the bench.

"I hope you two weren't getting ready for bed," Molly said when she and George entered the small hut.

They walked across the room.

Traun met Anna's gaze behind their backs. He gave a lecherous grin at her, which caused her smile to spread at the innocent comment she made.

She quickly pulled her gaze away from his.

"We were just sitting here talking," she fibbed, not looking in his direction again. She walked over to pick up her half-eaten plate from the bench. She retrieved his plate from the floor and placed both on the small table beside the door.

Traun settled back down into the chair they'd vacated. Anna came back to sit on the floor in front of his legs. He spread them so she could move back between them; with an acceptance of his silent invite, she scooted backward to drape her arms across the tops of his thighs.

"Aunt, what concern do you have that couldn't wait?" Traun reached down to toy with the thick strands of blonde hair before him, which fascinated him.

Molly watched his actions for a moment before she spoke. "Traun, I was talking with the Keeper of the Book of Wisdom today, and he's worried you've forgotten about a House of Reflection for the people. I promised him I'd approach you with his concern, mine too, I might add. We must not forget our spiritual needs in this new world."

Traun knew his aunt and his mother were deeply religious. His own beliefs in a higher power weren't strong. Yet, he understood the need for people to be convinced that there was an entity that created life and who watched over their daily struggles. He hoped it was true.

"I haven't forgotten the need for a House of Reflection, Aunt. Tell the Keeper to pick where he'd like it built, and I'll assign a team of men to begin its structure. It will need to be small for now until we settle into a permanent area."

"I knew you would understand, Traun. It will be a great relief to him to know that a spiritual house, even a small one, will be built. We better go, George. It's late."

Anna lifted herself from her position on the floor. Traun told George and Molly goodbye as she walked with the older couple to the door to shut it behind them, saying her goodbyes to them.

"Lock the door, Anna," he instructed as he approached her from behind. He lifted her hair to twist the loose strands between his fingers before he bent to kiss the back of her neck. It startled him how much he desired her.

She reached out to slide their door's lock in place.

He smiled down at her when she turned in his arms to face him. "Now, where were we?" he said.

He let her hair drop from his fingers.

Chapter 14

All the living huts and a House of Reflection for the Keeper were completed. Six weeks had passed since that first night Anna knew her husband intimately. She was content with their life together even though he had yet to tell her he loved her. He was passionate behind closed doors with her and let her see a softness and tenderness inside of him that he kept hidden from the discerning eyes of the people he ruled over. She didn't know what Nevin's punishment was for breaking the social class rule of not touching the spouse of a High Commander. She knew, though, that he'd received some type of punishment. He still smiled and spoke to her when he saw her, although now he maintained a reserved distance from her. Her heart had contracted with his formality toward her with that first meeting again after the card game. She knew he'd approached Traun the day after the game; before her Lifemate had a chance to demand an audience with him, Traun had told her that much. The Transfer, he said, seemed to be sincere in the apology he gave him and had assured him that the behavior was all his doing and that Lady Anna should not be held to blame for any of his actions. When she inquired what type of punishment he received, Traun was mute, unwilling to discuss it further.

"So, is there anything I should be doing?" Anna looked to the female Learned One who stood beside her. The woman had examined her and confirmed her pregnancy.

The Learned One and her spouse were two of several Learned Ones sent from Garr to ensure the best of care for the new mothers-to-be. The woman was friendly but matter-of-fact in her words and actions.

She was pregnant, as Klinn had predicted from her and Traun's first night of lovemaking. *Six weeks pregnant*, Anna kept thinking. The rush of tenderness she experienced toward this unknown human being inside her astonished her.

Assured by the Learned One that all she needed to do was take one of the pills given to her daily, eat well, and rest if needed, Anna left the examination room, a small room built into the side of the couples' private living quarters. She walked across the valley bottom toward her sister-in-law's home with a spring to her step. She wanted to find Charlee and share the news with her. Charlee had been keeping to herself for the past few weeks, and Anna was beginning to worry about her. The confirmed pregnancy was a good excuse to see her friend and to check up on her. When Anna approached Avreen's hut with the need to pass by it to reach Charlee's, the woman happened to be exiting her door simultaneously. Avreen noticed her and halted in her leave-taking to stare at her; the door of her home was left open as if she'd forgotten about it; a scowl scrolled across her features.

Anna tensed, faltering in her step forward.

The loathing for her Avreen had taken to letting her see when no one else was around to witness always stunned. Traun may have had a relationship with her at one time, but Anna was sure that whatever had been between them was over. He may not have expressed that he loved her, but he made her feel loved. His detailed instructions on how to act before their people weighed heavy on Anna, as she strived to keep her expression deadpan before Avreen's obvious show of dislike directed her way. She hadn't mentioned the woman's behavior to Traun, afraid he might not believe her. She had no witness on her behalf if she brought the issue before him. The woman was careful to exhibit the utmost respect towards her whenever anyone else was around.

***

Avreen watched the Lifemate of her beloved, and her hatred for the woman swirled through her as the half-Earthling strolled up the incline toward her brother's hut as if she hadn't a care in the world. *How can Traun love that ugly hybrid Earthling?* she wondered in bewilderment. She whirled to stalk back into her home to slam the door shut.

All the men of Garr preferred dark-haired women; it was a known fact; their government had deemed it so. The Earthling's hair was the most hideous, palest color ever seen: blonde with streaks of an even lighter color threading through it, almost white from being out in the sun.

The errand she'd planned to do was forgotten.

Her hatred for Traun's Lifemate twisted her insides and made her want to vomit. She paced around the small interior of her detested home. A picture within Avreen's mind materialized out of thin air as if divine-given. Astonished, she halted her movement. Two things were required of her to correct all the wrongs in her life.

It was so clear—her vision.

Traun would turn to her when she did what was shown. The certainty of it was whispered to her. Avreen plopped down to sit on the rocker constructed by a male servant from Garr. Her smile spread as her happiness bubbled forth. She laughed with glee.

You love me. You always have. Why did I not see this? I was blinded.

Her smile faded. Her shock and embarrassment the night her beloved told her he didn't love her rose within her again. Her hatred after that night had switched from only being felt toward the hybrid Earthling to including him also.

"But not now. No, not now," Avreen exclaimed within the surrounding space around her. *The Earthling is a breeder and has always been so. I am so sorry for my thoughts against you, my love.* She tilted her head backward to let it rest against the back support of the chair, and she closed her eyes as she mulled over the passing weeks since her arrival on a planet she hated with her entire being. Avreen knew all that had happened to her was the fault of that Lifemate assigned to her beloved. Seeing him and the hybrid Earthling going about together within the village, she had to fight back her urge to pull at her own hair.

With everything she'd planned and organized, for that ugly, white-haired Transfer to lie with her beloved, night after night, while she had to endure her assigned Lifemate's lovemaking wasn't fair. *Not that Nevin's not shown me care,* Avreen thought with a reluctant fairness. *But he's not my beloved. And I didn't come here to be a stupid breeder. I will be called Lady Avreen. I will rule these people alongside Traun.*

Avreen opened her eyes to stare with an unseeing gaze across the compact space of the hut. She wiped away the tears that sprang forth and that she couldn't hold back. She missed her life on Garr and the privileges enjoyed there as an elite. She had always gotten whatever she wanted before her arrival on this planet. Her mommy and daddy had guaranteed it. The name Bodane meant something to the people on Garr. She yearned for her parents, whom she'd had to leave behind to follow her beloved. She reached up to rub her forehead, which hurt. She could feel her heartbeat against her fingertips.

Avreen lowered her hand to frown as she recalled Nevin's punishment received from Traun. She had expressed concern for his well-being when she saw the wounds on his back, left by the four lashes he'd received for touching *her,* a High Commander's Lifemate.

She had been livid on his behalf. What did he do! He'd scolded her for her words. Her hatred for the ugly, white-haired Earthling had spilled forth unchecked that day as she'd doctored his back.

"Shut up," he'd said to her. Everything was his fault, no one else's. He could have received more than the few wounds she doctored had the High Commander decreed it.

Well, of course, it wasn't his fault. It was the fault of her! Always her!
Nevin seemed under the hybrid Earthling's spell, the same as Traun.
Avreen rose with a quick reflex from where she reclined.
Her Lifemate was home early.

***

Nevin's smile slipped as the angry woman tied to him swept past him in sullen silence to leave their home. He swallowed back the hard knot that rose within his throat as he entered the now-empty room to close the door behind him. As he looked about the hut, a hollow, vacant sentiment swelled within his breast. His life on this planet wasn't what he'd dreamed it would be or even what he'd been taught to expect in the compound he and the others were raised in from birth. He sat down in the vacated chair.

Avreen was a beautiful woman, stunning, and he'd believed he was lucky to have her chosen for him. Now, he didn't know what to think. Her constant anger displayed towards life in general was a source of confusion. She disliked the High Commander's Lifemate, and he couldn't figure out the why of it. He had asked her one evening if she'd been forced to be a Volunteer, thinking that might be the cause of her anger. All he'd received was a clipped *no* in response. With a sigh, Nevin stood. He didn't want to stay in an empty hut.

***

Anna knocked a third time on the door before her, and when Charlee finally opened it, she was surprised at how wan her friend looked.

"May I come in?" she asked as Charlee stared at her in silence.

"Can we go down to the creek instead, Anna?"

"Yes, I don't know why not?" Anna stepped back, confused by her tone. It had been abrupt. Her friend took off to the backside of the house, and, in silence, she followed her. When they reached the creek, Charlee squatted beside it to splash water onto her face; she paused, and her hand lowered to her side when she sat down alongside her at the water's bank.

"I'm pregnant."

"Oh, Charlee, that's wonderful. So am I."

Charlee gazed back at her. Her facial expression was solemn.

Anna gave a little laugh. "Is the pregnancy hard on you? You look very peaked. You've even lost weight."

She reached a hand with concern to her sister-in-law's pale face, puzzled by her subdued behavior and sad-looking expression when she should be happy.

Charlee's tears rose. "I'm four months pregnant," she whispered.

Anna knew her eyes widened. They'd left Earth three months ago.

"Are you sure? You're not showing."

"I'm positive. After being sick several mornings in a row, I realized I hadn't had a period since the last time Lance and I were together."

"Does my brother know?" Anna already suspected the answer.

"No."

Charlee raised her hands to cover her face with them, and her words were muffled when she spoke. "I love Andrew. I don't want to hurt him with this. And he will be. You and I both know it."

Anna was at a loss for words as she sat in uncertainty beside her. Yes, her brother would be hurt and hurt badly. Nevertheless, he needed to know the truth; the sooner, the better.

"Dry your tears," she said sternly, taking command of the situation.

"Tell my brother tonight. Don't let any more time go by. He'll be angry, but when he has time to cool off, he'll realize this isn't something you planned and not a betrayal. You had no idea what the future held when you believed Lance was your one true love."

Anna softened her tone.

"Lean over here, and let me dry your tears. I'm still your friend, no matter what. We will get through this together. Do you want to walk back up to your hut now?" She rubbed Charlee's face dry with her shirt sleeve.

"No, let's sit here for a while," Charlee said. It seemed some of the pressure she'd been under had lifted from her shoulders.

"How far along are you?" she inquired after several minutes of silence between them passed.

"Six weeks, the Learned One said." Anna smiled in wicked humor at her. Charlee knew what the servant Klinn had said to her.

Charlee laughed and then hiccupped as she caught back a half sob.

"The first time, huh? That fight must've revved you two up."

Anna laughed outright at the comment. "I passed her coming up to your hut."

"Did she do or say anything this time?"

"Glared at me. Of course, no one was around to witness it."

"You still don't want me to tell Andrew what you saw that night or how she's acting toward you?"

Anna picked up a round pebble that lay close beside her and rolled the small rock across the palm of her hand. "No, I don't want him to know. He'd go straight to Traun with it."

"If the woman is glaring at you, I'd say she's not getting any action from Traun now."

"I should hope not." Anna looked at her friend, shocked.

"She would be smiling instead, from what you've told me," Charlee teased, and then, on seeing Anna's fallen expression, she added with haste, "I know he's not messing around with her. Good grief, Anna, he's crazy about you. It's so obvious when we're together as a family. Besides, I've watched him when she's nearby, and he doesn't even notice her."

"He hasn't said he loves me."

"Have you told him you love him?"

Anna shook her head.

"One of you needs to make the first move, Anna."

"Maybe." Anna threw the pebble she held out into the creek. *I won't be the one to make that first move.*

"I am so tired today."

"You're pregnant, all right," Charlee said, and she stood. "Come on, let's get you back home so you can take a nap. I need one myself."

***

Anna barely managed to kick her shoes off her feet, crawl atop the bed, and lie down. She was asleep as soon as her head hit the pillow. A tickling sensation at the tip of her nose woke her. Reaching upward, she rubbed the end of it with her palm, eyes closed. She drifted back to unawareness.

There it was again. She frowned to reach upward again.

Traun's laughter sounded.

Raising heavy eyelids, Anna realized the sensation she felt was him blowing down onto her face. She swatted at him with her hand.

"Stop it."

"Wake up, sleepy head. Why asleep so early in the evening? The sun's scarcely down."

Anna woke fully at his question. Sitting up, she slid backward with her back to the bed's headboard and gazed upward at him. "Guess what."

"What?"

"I'm pregnant."

Her Lifemate's expression changed from one that contained his humor to one of reflected satisfaction. His gaze lowered to her stomach area. He reached out to lay a hand against her shirt and still flat stomach beneath it.

"How far along are you?"

"The Learned One said six weeks."

Leaning down, he captured her mouth with his.

***

Traun's love swelled for the woman before him. The one who would give birth to his children and save his family line. He wished his parents and brother could know the good news of this first hybrid descendant in their family line. He climbed up onto the bed to stretch out beside his Lifemate.

"I haven't seen you sick in the mornings. I know that's one of the symptoms of pregnancy. I was watching for it."

Anna snuggled up against him.

"I haven't had an ounce of sickness, thank goodness, but I've been so tired lately, and when I mentioned it to the Learned One during my regular exam today, she ran the pregnancy test. Pregnant, plus low on iron, she told me."

Traun turned to reposition her hair so the thick strands lay behind her shoulders instead of at his face.

"Are you happy, Anna?" He wanted her to be happy with him and her life here, a life she hadn't known was preplanned for her.

She gazed up at him. He frowned at her continued silence. She sighed before she half-smiled at him.

"I'm happy, Traun. I—"

"What?" he urged.

"I'm content to have children for you and the people of Garr."

Her words seemed sincere. He was disappointed that she failed to express a fondness of feeling toward him. He'd leaned toward her in anticipation of it. Traun gathered her into his arms as he scooted downward so he and she could stretch out to lie flat on the bed. She placed an arm across his waist, and he tightened his around her.

She drifted back to sleep, and soon, he followed her. They were both unaware of Klinn bringing in and leaving their evening meals for them.

* * *

Charlee paced around the compact enclosure of her home as she waited for Andrew to be relieved from his night watch post duty. Having taken his evening meal to him, she'd walked back to their home and stayed there for him to stroll jauntily through the door like he always did when he returned at the end of his work day.

She was sick with dread at what she had to tell him. If only she'd known the future when she'd met Lance. Compared to the depth of emotion she felt for Andrew, her feelings for him were nothing. They had been shallow and fleeting. Yes, she'd been upset and hurt over his betrayal but bounced back quickly with no lasting residue of emotion. Unable to restrain herself, Charlee walked to the door again for what seemed like the hundredth time and opened it to peer out into the approaching darkness of the night. She was anxious for Andrew's return, and yet, at the same time, she feared it. She clutched the edge of the open entryway with her fingertips.

He walked toward her.

He had noticed her, too. She stayed where she was, even though she wanted to duck back inside the hut and hide. Trying to calm her nerves, she whispered to herself, "He loves me. He'll understand. He loves me. He'll understand."

He smiled broadly at her as he drew near.

"Hey, baby. Waiting for me?" He halted before her to reach out to pull her toward him. "I—love—you," he said, between his kisses against her mouth. He placed an arm around her waist to lead her through the open doorway and back into their home. "You are sweet to be so anxious to see me," he said.

Charlee couldn't help it. Her tears burst forth.

"Hey, what's this?" He shut the door behind them as he gazed at her. He frowned.

"I'm pregnant, Andrew."

He gave a half-laugh.

"Sweetheart, that's good news. It's what we want."

Charlee lowered her gaze from his to stare at the floor. He raised her face with a finger he placed beneath her chin. Her heart contracted when he smiled with tenderness. She could tell he was confused by her upset.

"Hush," he said, brushing away the tears on her cheeks that she couldn't stop.

"Are you scared? Is that what is wrong here?"

"I am four months along." Charlee watched Andrew's smile drop from his face at her abrupt disclosure. He shoved her back from within the embrace of his arms to look down at her shirt-covered stomach, and then he looked back up to meet her returning gaze. Spinning on his heels, he exited their home, its door not slammed behind him but shut with a firm click.

Charlee stumbled to their bed and crawled on top of it. Her legs were folded tight against her chest as she stared dry-eyed at the far wall across from where she lay.

***

You unfaithful bitch. Andrew knew even as his rage coursed through him that his judgment of Charlee was untrue. How could she have been disloyal when she became pregnant before they noticed each other? He brushed aside the realization as he stomped through the settlement past the huts scattered about the valley, and his jealousy of the other man whose child grew within her seethed through him. Andrew didn't know how or when he settled where he was: hidden and secluded, at the base of one of the giant trees behind his home as he rested his head against the massive tree trunk behind him. He stared out into the darkness of the surrounding night, his arms draped over the top of drawn-up knees.

His insides were twisted in a hard knot at Charlee's revelation.

A child to be born within their marriage that he didn't know if he could love or accept as his own? The intensity of his anger toward Charlee frightened him. Andrew recalled all the times his Earth parent had told him how worthless he was, a man who'd made sure he knew he wasn't his offspring.

Chapter 15

Four days had passed since Anna had spoken to Charlee and realized their dual pregnancy. She wondered how her brother took her friend's news. She had been occupied daily since that day: up and out by daylight and not home until dusk. That day, she and Molly supervised the storage of the produce that had been harvested that week from the community garden planted soon after they'd landed on Garrearth. She had to ensure seeds were saved from the garden's yield for next year's plantings. The ground was fertile, and the crops were abundant. They grew fast, so fast that it was startling.

Anna gazed across the large area before her, which had been sectioned off for the community garden, and worked up with equipment from Garr.

Her smile settled at everything her little group of workers had accomplished.

It still amazed her that she was accountable for the maintenance and harvest of the garden, plus the thirty individuals assigned to help her. Traun inquired about her plans for storing the harvest and saving seeds for next year's crop and gave her some advice. He had also given her direction a couple of times when he came by to check on the garden's progress, but other than that, he left everything to her discretion.

Charlee helped with the garden; however, that week, she'd been reassigned to tend to a servant woman who'd somehow tripped and broken a leg and an arm. She had taken over the woman's chore of collecting eggs laid by the poultry brought from Garr and the required feeding and watering of the noisy things. She also had to ensure all newly hatched chicks didn't escape their confined pen area; they couldn't afford to lose any, Traun had said.

Anna didn't care for the birds. They weren't like most chickens found on Earth. These things were twice as large, and all sported large yellow beaks and black-colored satiny feathers that covered their bodies, even their legs, and they squawked all the time. It was an earsplitting sound that got on Anna's nerves. The males of the species had a different shriek than their female counterparts. They drew out their calls in several loud bursts, even more annoying.

Closing the door to the storage building, Anna locked it. She felt foolish padlocking the building as if no one could be trusted, but Traun had instructed to keep their food supply secure. He'd informed her that throughout the coming winter, a set allotment of food would be handed out to everyone to safeguard that they'd all have plenty to eat until next year's harvest could be brought in. When they settled into a permanent place, the people would grow their own gardens, he'd said.

Molly walked up to where she stood.

"We put in a good day's work today, Anna."

Anna turned to smile. "You should be exhausted, Molly. I don't think you slowed down all day today."

Molly laughed. "Oh, I'm feeling my age today, sweetie."

The comment made Anna remember how old she was—ninety-eight years old. It was easy for her to forget because neither she nor George looked or acted their age—their age in Earth years, that was. Anna guessed they were middle-aged in the world of Garr. Either way, the thought of losing them scared her.

"Since we're done today, why don't you go home and rest, Molly? I will go home after visiting with Chloe and then Charlee."

"Yes, I believe I'll do exactly that, dear. Tell Chloe I'll come by later, will you? Poor thing. To think both an arm and a leg broken."

Anna watched her turn away.

"Molly," she said. She suddenly needed her to know how much she cared for her.

"Yes, dear?" Molly turned back around to meet her gaze with hers.

"I love you. I count my blessings daily for when you and George found Andrew and me." Anna smiled with tenderness at her, feeling sentimental for some reason.

"Why, I love you too, dear." Molly smiled back at her before she turned away once again.

Anna walked through the village and to where the injured servant lady lived. She felt tired that evening, but not excessively so, unlike some days she'd experienced; besides those few days of extreme tiredness, she was as healthy as a horse. Seeing Traun across the way, Anna raised her hand to wave at him. He lifted his back to her before he returned his attention to the group of men he stood with. It seemed they were reporting something important.

Knocking on Chloe's door, Anna opened it at the woman's loud voice, calling out, "Come in, whoever's pounding on that door!"

"Lady Anna," Chloe exclaimed when she stepped forward into the open space of the hut.

The woman raised her one good arm to fuss with her hair. "I'm sorry. I didn't realize it be you at my door."

Anna walked over to where the woman lounged; her bound leg was propped up on a homemade stool before her.

"I wanted to stop by to see how you are doing. I won't stay long."

"Please, Lady Anna, sit down." Chloe pointed to another rocker, a replica of the one she reclined in. "I be sorry about my leg and arm. Now, one of you must help care for me and take over my assigned duties."

"Good grief, you didn't break them on purpose." Anna sat down where indicated, uncomfortable with the woman's subservient demeanor. "We are all to pitch in when it's needed. You worry about your body's healing, nothing else. Charlee doesn't mind helping out with your chores."

The woman directed a smile her way, and Anna smiled back. She thought she and the woman were probably close to the same age. The woman looked maybe in her twenties, *but then again, as with Molly and George, she could be much older than she appears,* Anna thought.

"What did the Learned One say about your leg and arm?" She felt her sympathy stir for the woman.

"He said both be clean breaks and will heal fine."

"That's good news."

After they chatted for a while, Anna stood.

"I am going to go now and let you rest. Please have your Lifemate let me or the High Commander know if there's anything you should need." Anna meant the words she said; she wasn't just giving lip service to the woman before her.

"Lady Anna, I don't need anything, but I have concern, and I think I should mention it to you."

Anna waited.

"It be about your friend, Charlee."

"Yes?" Anna's face tightened.

The woman rushed to say, "Please don't think I be complaining about her. But she's different now. She so sad and not happy as before. She hasn't had much to say these past four days. She and I got to know one another before my mishap. She laugh then, but not now." Chloe shrugged a plump shoulder and frowned as she looked up at Anna.

"She say she not be hungry when I ask if she sit and eat with me. She goes all day without eating. Poor thing has no life in her, no spark. As you and her are friends, I thought I let you know so you check on her. I asked if you and she get to visit often, and she said not in several days. I be afraid something seriously wrong. She be of total Earthly origin, you know."

Anna thanked Chloe for her concern and told her she planned to visit Charlee that very evening. As she turned to leave, she remembered to inform the woman that Molly would come by and see her later that same day. She promised Chloe that she would also drop back by and visit with her in the following days.

Leaving the woman's home, Anna thought about what was said, with Charlee looking sad and not eating. She knew four nights ago was when she had informed Andrew about the pregnancy. Anna had seen her brother only in passing since then; his duties kept him busy on the opposite end of the village from where she worked in the garden.

She couldn't help but smile at Chloe's whispered comment about Charlee being of total Earthly origin, as if that must be the root of her problem. Maybe it was good that she'd decided to visit with her that evening.

Anna knocked several times on the front of Charlee and Andrew's door, and she started to turn away, thinking Charlee must be out and about when the door was cracked open, but barely enough for her to make out Charlee's face beyond it. It was pitch dark behind her within the interior of the hut.

"Anna," Charlee mumbled upon seeing her, "Can you return later? I am not in the mood for company right now."

She started to push the door back closed.

Anna stuck her foot in the doorway to prevent it from closing. She was alarmed at how drawn Charlee's face looked, the little bit she could see. She shoved her hand on the door.

***

"Damn it, Anna. I want to be left alone." The spark of anger Charlee felt evaporated as fast as it had come upon her. She sensed Anna step up inside the darkened room behind her as she turned to go back to bed. She crawled under the bed covers she'd had to emerge from to answer the door, pulled them over her head, and turned her back to her friend.

"Turn off that light when you leave." The room was too bright now because Anna had flipped on the overhead light to the hut and even opened the window curtains.

Charlee closed her eyes. She would be alone for the rest of the night when Anna left. Andrew came home to change his clothes in the mornings once she was gone from their hut. Where he stayed during the night, she didn't know. He hadn't spoken to her for four nights and days now. It was as if she'd ceased to exist as far as he was concerned. He had even turned his back to her when she attempted to approach him the morning after he'd walked out on her.

All she wanted to do now was sleep, blissful sleep, without awareness or pain. Charlee winced when Anna stomped across the hut's floor to the bed. The bedcovers were yanked down from over her head.

"You get up from there right now, Charlee, and you tell me what happened when you told my brother about the baby," she demanded.

Rolling over onto her back, Charlee gazed upward at her. *I wish everyone would leave me alone.* Chloe had kept asking if she felt ill that day, and now Anna was to pester her also?

"Anna, I am fine. I'm tired and want to rest. Come back later. Okay?"

***

Anna studied her friend's hollowed-out cheeks.

She had lost more weight in the past four days since their last time together. It wasn't good for the baby if she wasn't eating, as Chloe said.

A baby who was blameless of any wrongdoing on its part. Anna knew Charlee wouldn't, with deliberate intent, do anything to harm the child, whether she wanted it or not.

"Charlee, when did you last eat?" She pulled the covers away from her friend's fingers. Charlee had always been a fighter who went for what she wanted with gusto. Anna didn't recognize the person who lay on the bed before her. There was no life, no spark, in her friend. This wasn't the Charlee she knew, and it scared her.

"I don't know. I haven't been hungry." Charlee closed her eyes and ceased trying to pull the covers up over her head when, each time, Anna pulled them back down again.

"Go away and leave me in peace, Anna. Can't you take a hint," she mumbled.

Anna stared down at her for a long moment before she turned. Charlee was fast asleep before she walked away.

Molly seemed surprised when she opened her door at her knock to see her standing before her.

"Anna, I thought you were going to go visit with Charlee this afternoon?"

"I did."

"Why the long face, dear? Did you two have words over something?"

"Molly, may I come in and talk to you?"

"Yes, dear." Molly stepped back so she could enter the home.

Anna noticed George and hesitated.

Molly saw her indecision. "You may as well say, in front of George, what you've come to talk to me about. I'll tell him later, anyway."

Anna went to sit down beside him. "I wasn't trying to keep anything from you. It's just that I haven't even told Traun yet, although it won't matter that much to him anyway."

Molly walked over to sit down, and then she faced her.

"What is going on, dear?"

"Charlee is pregnant." Anna held up a hand when they both started to tell her that was good news.

"She is pregnant by someone she was dating on Earth. She's four months along. She told Andrew four nights ago, and I don't know what happened between them, but whatever it was, it must not have been very pleasant." Anna couldn't stop her eyes from watering at how Charlee had seemed so defeated.

Molly and George glanced sharply at each other.

"I don't think she's eating and is so lifeless. She didn't want to see or talk to me. All it seemed that she wanted to do was sleep. She's not the same person, and I don't know what to do for her."

Anna hunched her shoulders at Molly and George's continued silence.

"It can't be good for the baby or her not to be eating."

Molly stood. Her face had become set with a decision made. She looked at George and then at Anna.

"Come on, the both of you. We are all three going to go and talk to her and Andrew, too, if need be."

Anna rapped her knuckles on the door before her. When her repeated action remained unanswered, she reached out to the doorknob to see if Charlee had locked the door behind her at her earlier departure. It was unlocked. Anna glanced at George and Molly, and they followed her when she opened the door to step inside the hut.

Their gazes swiveled to where Charlee lay sound asleep. She hadn't woken to turn off the light she'd left on. Anna went to the bed to place her hand on her shoulder and to give it a shake.

"Andrew?" Charlee rolled over.

"Oh," she said when she realized it wasn't him. Her dejection was evident.

"No, honey, not Andrew," Molly said, stepping up close to the side of the bed, as did George. Charlee's gaze moved across them. She tried to sit up. "Is something wrong?"

With a sympathetic hand to help her up, Anna grasped her arm, and Molly took hold of her other arm.

"Let's get you up from here," Molly said with a firm tone.

"Anna, pour her a glass of water," she instructed.

Anna hurried to do as told. Molly directed Charlee over to a chair.

Charlee looked up at Anna with obvious bewilderment as she took the container held out toward her.

"Drink," Anna instructed and watched as she obeyed without question.

With frankness, Molly said, "Honey, Anna informed George and me about your pregnancy. I wish it weren't so, for your and Andrew's sake, but it is what it is, and life continues. I understand you informed Andrew about the pregnancy four nights ago?"

Charlee gave a nod.

"Am I right to assume he didn't take the news well?"

Charlee glanced up at Anna, and then she looked toward Molly. It seemed she couldn't meet George's gaze.

"He hates me," she said, her tone flat. "He hasn't spoken to me or stayed in our hut since the evening I told him."

"Well, dear, I can't speak for Andrew or even reassure you of his eventual understanding. However, I am going to tell you that you must pull yourself together and out of this depression you appear to be under. It is obvious you're not taking care of yourself and it could hurt the baby your neglect of self-care.

"Do you want to cause harm to the child?" Molly's tone now held a chill to it.

***

No, I don't want to harm my child, Charlee thought with sudden clarity as she shook her head at Molly.

A protective emotion for the baby rose within her, as did anger—anger at herself for the self-pity she'd wallowed in and intense anger at Andrew. The way he acted wasn't reasonable. His fury or jealousy or whatever he felt over her pregnancy was his to deal with, not hers.

Charlee sat up straighter within the chair she'd been directed to, and energy flowed through her. It was a strength she hadn't felt for what seemed an eternity.

***

Andrew opened the door of his home. After his rage-filled blowup that morning toward one of the men he worked with, he realized it was time to come home to Charlee and hash out their problems. He knew that, as he decided to talk to her that day, she was most likely taking the situation between them hard. Yet, he hadn't been able to face her or the baby issue until today. He still didn't know if he could accept her child from another man or find love in himself for it, and the thought scared him.

Four sets of eyes belonging to the most important people in his life swiveled toward him when he stepped up to enter the hut. To Andrew, it seemed they all stared at him in accusation, and he stiffened in defense of it. It surprised him to see Charlee's resentment reflected toward him in her gaze. He had believed she would be glad to see him, maybe even cry at his return. With that look, he didn't know what to expect, and fear shot through him.

"What's this?" he sneered. He slapped the door toward the wall to strut into the open space. Legs spread wide, hands on his hips, he glared at them all.

Anna shouted at him, her fury clear, "Someone has to be here for Charlee since you abandoned her."

Her accusation chafed Andrew. There was a truth to it. He swung his gaze toward Charlee. She stared at him in silence.

He turned back toward his sister.

"Your husband was looking for you earlier. So why don't you go home and mind your own damn business and stay the hell out of mine for a change."

Molly gasped.

George pulled back his shoulders. "Son, that attitude and language is uncalled for—"

"And why don't you grow up?" Anna yelled as she went to stand close beside Charlee. Her stance was combative toward him.

Andrew couldn't stop his eyes from widening. *What does she think? I plan* to *do physical injury to Charlee?* He looked at Molly and George. They also moved toward Charlee as if protective of her. It hurt him that his family believed he'd do bodily harm to his own wife.

"All of you," he ground out between clenched teeth and jabbed a finger without turning toward the open doorway behind him, "go home. Sonofabitch. Let Charlee and I work out our problems on our terms."

"Traun," Anna cried out, "tell Andrew he needs to calm down."

Andrew whirled around as Traun stepped into the open doorway, and his gaze swept over the room and all who were within it. *Hell*, Andrew thought, *now even the High Commander will get involved in this mess.*

***

Traun studied everyone huddled around Anna's friend. He had heard Andrew wanting them to leave him and Charlee alone. He didn't know what was happening here, but he for sure knew that they all needed to let Andrew talk to his spouse in private. A man didn't need his entire family involved in a personal squabble with his Lifemate. Traun motioned toward Anna and his aunt and uncle.

"Let's leave these two alone to work out their problems between them," he said sternly.

Anna looked down at her friend.

"Please, Anna, go. I want to talk to Andrew and alone," she said.

Anna started across the room, her narrow gaze directed and held at her brother. Andrew, in turn, glared back at her, and her gaze contracted even more. Traun placed a hand on her shoulder to guide her toward the doorway George and Molly had already passed through.

"Let's go," he said. He shut the door behind her when he pushed her past the hut doorway. He was ready to laugh at her fighting stance toward her brother.

"Come on, you can release all that pent-up energy on me when we get home," he teased as he chuckled down at her.

"Oh, shut up," she responded, although she laughed.

***

Avreen, returning to her own home, couldn't catch the words between Traun and the hybrid Earthling, but she could hear her merriment drifting her way, and she ground her teeth together at the sound of it.

She had not had an opportunity to implement her vision; however, she was positive that the time would come when everything would fall into place. *I need to bide my time and be patient.*

She watched the couple walk together toward their hut.

Soon, that will be me and Traun. I always get what I want.

Chapter 16

With everyone gone and his anger over the situation with his family draining away from him, Andrew was at a loss for what to say to Charlee as he stood awkwardly before her. *She has lost weight*, he thought, with concern.

He sensed she wouldn't let his apology to her be easy for him. Her anger-filled gaze as she watched him let him understand that much, but it needed to be said. Stepping over to their fireplace and standing before it, Andrew turned to settle on the large round rug beneath his feet after a moment in the quiet between them.

Charlee had brought it from Earth: a sentimental thing with attached memories of her mother.

"Come over here and sit with me, Charlee." He patted at the rug. He didn't think she was to come when, at first, she didn't move. She finally stood to come forward and to sit Indian-style before him. He reached out to clasp her hands, and she let him. Andrew moved his thumbs to caress the tops of hers. He had missed her and their nights together, their loving, their laughter, and her tenderness. He took a breath.

"First, let me say I'm sorry for walking out on you and for my actions toward you when you came to try and talk to me. I never should have turned my back on you that morning. I'm not trying to excuse my behavior, but I will say my childhood memories reared their ugly head between us." Andrew directed a self-conscious half-smile her way. She knew his history. He'd spoken to her of those first parents and their harsh treatment of him and Anna, not only verbal mistreatment but physical as well. He wondered at her thoughts as she studied him in silence. It scared him, her stillness. Maybe she was unable to forgive him. He had acted cruelly toward her.

"I love you, honey. With all that I am, I say that to you. I'm sorry for what I did to you that night, how I shoved you away from me. Over the past four days, I've done some serious thinking about that, the baby, and us. My untrust of others is my issue, and mine alone to work through. I was unfair to you, Charlee. My jealousy over this other man has nothing to do with you or the baby."

Andrew reached out to place his hand against the slight swell of her stomach, and he felt her tense. He knew his voice held a pleading note as he spoke, and his emotion choked him, "I can't live without you by my side, Charlee. Please, say you can forgive me."

When she remained quiet, he started to rise. She couldn't forgive him for his behavior, and he suffered. She reached out to stop his upward, stumbling movement away from her.

"I thought I was dying these past few days, Andrew. I felt so lost and alone."

She shook her head 'no' at him and even leaned backward away from him when he moved to try to embrace her. Confused, Andrew let his arms fall back to his sides to sit back down. Charlee drew a breath and straightened her back as she leaned toward him again. "I love you, Andrew, but if you can't find room in your heart for this child, I want you to leave me for good tonight. I will not subject this innocent babe to a lifetime of trying to earn a love you may never give. I refuse to be a victim, and I'll not let this child be one either."

She watched him. Andrew could tell she was terrified he'd get up and walk out on her, yet she held her ground. He reached to pull her to him and onto his lap. With her yielding stillness and watchful gaze, he wrapped his arms tight about her.

"I love you, honey. I promise you. I'll raise this child as my own."

She teared up with his declaration, her arms snaked around his neck, and she held tight to him. Lowering her onto the rug, Andrew stretched out alongside her. He moved to seek her mouth with his, and when their lips met, he knew he was home where he belonged. He made a silent vow as he drew Charlee tighter and closer to him. *If I can't love this child of hers, she and the child will never realize the truth of it. It will be my cross to bear and mine alone.*

Chapter 17

"What was all the commotion about last night?" Traun asked as he and Anna prepared for their day the following morning.

"Your brother must have had a bad day all around," he continued, shrugging his shirt over his shoulders to button it up. He looked over to where Anna sat on the edge of their bed.

"He tore into one of the men assigned to his group yesterday. It was relayed to me that when he asked Andrew how his Lifemate was doing, Andrew jumped up in his face and told him his wife was his concern, not his. The other men informed me they thought they'd have to pull Andrew off the man before he could explain to your brother that it was an innocent question he asked. He hadn't seen her around much the past few days, so he inquired after her."

Anna slipped her shoes onto her feet and listened to him with half an ear. She began to tie her shoelace. She hadn't been able to discuss what had happened the prior evening since a problem had called him away right after they'd returned home. She didn't think the news would make much of an impact on him anyway.

"Charlee is pregnant by her old boyfriend from Earth, and she told Andrew the news five nights ago. He hadn't spoken to her or been home since she informed him. She wasn't eating or taking care of herself, so my family and I got involved in the fight between them. I hope they worked things out last night after we left."

Anna re-tied her shoelaces, not satisfied with the knots she'd made. She glanced up. Traun had grown still at her words. She was surprised at the anger displayed on his face.

"Exactly when did you plan to tell me this news? Or were you planning to let a Learned One inform me?" His tone held an edge to it.

"I didn't think you would care one way or another. It's nothing to you." Confused by his behavior, Anna let her foot fall from where she'd propped it on her knee.

"Nothing to me? A full-blood Earth baby being born to another full-blood Earthling is nothing to me?"

"What has that got to do with anything? Charlee and Andrew can still have children with Garr blood in them." Anna was baffled by his attitude.

"Anna," he bit out, "all here were selected because of genetics. And even with that, I looked over everyone's files to pair them with the best partners to guarantee strong, healthy babies. Babies of strong Garr blood. Your Earth friend was snuck on board the spaceship without any hereditary risk check done or approval obtained.

"And now this? She wouldn't be here if I'd known she was on the spaceship in time. This baby of hers could have possible inheritable diseases. Even her genetic material could contain defects. Who knows, since she was unchecked. I had to pair your brother with her. I had no choice in the matter. No other would have wanted her as a Lifemate. Now I know why she missed her scheduled appointments with the Learned One. She knew her secret would be found out. I had planned to speak with Andrew about the missed checkups this morning."

Staring at Traun with her new-found knowledge of his disapproval of Charlee, Anna was upset. She'd not realized his strong outlook held against her best friend and now the baby she carried.

It seemed Traun recognized her distress. His tone was softer when he spoke, "Anna, the people of Garr are genetically healthier and stronger than Earth people. Through our gene manipulation ability, we live longer, and for most of us, without any trace of disease."

"Well, you sure needed Earthly human help when you made yourselves sterile with that precious gene manipulation," she fired back.

Traun stiffened. "I will tell you now, little lady, no child of mine will be paired as a Lifemate with that full-blooded Earth child she's carrying. I don't know of any others here who would want their offspring to be coupled with it, either. All will want strong Garr blood within their family line."

Anna sat in stunned silence. She couldn't move or even respond to what he said. *He is prejudiced against Earth people,* was all she could think. Her suspicion of it on their wedding day was now known for sure. If he held such a bias, how could he love her? She was, after all, of half-Earth genetics.

"I didn't mean to hurt your feelings over your friend and her child. It worries me, Anna, the trouble that might follow with her being here. There's no way to know her or the child's genetic liability to future generations born. Our leaders on Garr wanted no written knowledge or equipment for genetic checking brought with us."

His tone held an apologetic note to it.

Anna felt defeated. She had convinced herself that he loved her, even without his expression. *Do Molly and George hold the same viewpoint?* She wondered. If they'd been able to keep their birth origin secret from her and Andrew for all the years they'd lived on Earth, who was to say they didn't have the same prejudices but never voiced them? Anna felt sick at the thought.

"I will see you this afternoon," Traun said.

She nodded. She didn't meet his gaze or move from her position on the side of the bed. The door clicked shut behind him as he left the hut. It caused her to stir.

She went to the closed door. When Anna opened it to begin the work day, Molly strolled toward her. She halted in her leave-taking to watch her approach, and as she did so, she felt as if the woman coming toward her was a stranger. When Molly reached her, she couldn't stop asking, "Do you think I'm less of a person because of my Earthly human lineage?"

"Honey," Molly exclaimed as her eyebrows rose, and then in the next breath, she said, "Traun knows about Charlee's pregnancy now, doesn't he."

Anna nodded.

"Let's go inside and talk." With a gentle hand, Molly pushed her back into the hut to shut its door behind them. Guiding her over to the bench, she sat beside her to face her.

"First of all, no, I don't think you are less of a person because of your Earth origins."

"Traun does," Anna mumbled. She studied her hands.

"Honey, I don't believe he thinks you're less of anything. He was raised with the belief that we of Garr are genetically superior to the Earthly race, is all. We have been able to eradicate all defective inheritances within our makeup. Something Earth humans have yet to do."

Glancing toward Molly, Anna challenged her, "Well, shouldn't you all be afraid that some Earthly genetic hangover could still contaminate that perfect Garr blood when all of us lowly Transfers begin to have children, even with our clear medical diagnoses made by your people?"

"Anna, I refuse to sit here and listen to this. I love you, no matter what flows in your veins or what might show up."

"Oh, do you really? Or maybe all of us half-breeds brought here was just a necessary evil to accomplish your people's want to survive as a race? Maybe later, when all our children are birthed as you need, you plan to get rid of us?"

Molly's eyes widened as she gasped with obvious shock. Her shoulders slumped, and tears rose within her gaze.

"Oh, Molly, I'm sorry," Anna cried out. With a quick movement, she hugged the woman who'd been a mother to her since the tender age of six years. She was sorry for the spiteful words said to her. Molly had given her and Andrew nothing but care and love over the years.

"All is forgiven." Molly patted at her back. It took her a moment to meet Anna's gaze when she pulled away from her embrace.

"Now," she said with a catch in her voice, "why I came by to see you this morning was to tell you to take the day off from your assigned chores. George says he wants to work in the garden today and will oversee your weeding and watering. You and Charlee, he said, are to see if you can find any plants similar to those on Earth. But don't go too far."

Anna's spirits soared at the thought of a day off from work to explore, but then they plummeted. "We can't. Charlee still has to take care of Chloe and her chores."

Molly shook her head at her.

"I plan to check in with the woman and to take her meals to her. And George said he will take care of Charlee's animal chores."

"I love you, Molly."

Molly smiled at her. "I know you do, sweetheart. And I love you. Now go collect your friend. You two have some fun today. A gift from George and me."

She urged Anna toward the door when she hesitated.

***

"You don't want to go?" Anna felt her disappointment rise.

After Charlee reassured her that she and Andrew had worked out their problems the night before, she excitedly informed her that they had the day free from their usual workload. She explained that Molly had graciously decided to take care of the injured woman for her, and George would see to both of their chores.

"Anna, I'm sorry, but if we have a free day, I'd as soon stay home and rest."

"Well, I'm going." Anna jumped up from the padded chair she reclined in. Charlee looked at her from where she sat, and her apprehension at her decision showed in her expression.

"Do you think you should walk away from camp by yourself? I thought we were supposed to go in pairs?"

Anna frowned. "We haven't seen any other people, or for that matter any animals, in all the time we've been here. I'm going. I'll stay close to the areas already explored."

"Where do you plan to go?"

"Oh, I think I will walk to the waterfall and look around at the vegetation there, and then I'll investigate the woods to the left of it. After that, I'll return to the waterfall and have lunch there before returning."

At Charlee's doubtful expression, Anna gave a carefree laugh. "I'll be fine. Don't worry. I overheard some of the others say they'd walked past the waterfall. I'll head straight back home after my lunch break. Will that make you feel better, mommy?"

Charlee laughed at her drawled-out mommy title directed toward her.

"Be careful, dingdong."

Anna smiled back at her. She wished Charlee would go with her, but since she didn't want to, she wouldn't let it keep her from enjoying a beautiful summer day free from work.

"I promise. I'll be back right after my lunch. Besides, Traun will probably come and ask for me if he doesn't see me during the men's noon break. So, I better be back here by then."

As she strolled the trodden path toward the wide creek that was the lifeblood of their settled encampment, Anna hummed the tune of the song she'd listened to that morning. With careful precision, she placed one black tennis shoe-covered foot before the other when she stepped up to begin the walk across the length of the expansive tree trunk that lay over the swift-moving body of water arrived at. Anna kept her eyes on the tree trunk and her feet; if a person watched the fast-moving current below the log, it made you dizzy. All who wished to visit the waterfall had to use the naturally placed bridge to get from one side of the torrent of water to its other side; the wide creek that flowed beneath the sprawling log was used for bathing and washing their clothing, and it provided their drinking water: its constant movement forward always ensuring clear and clean water.

Stepping down from the log onto the rocks beside the log on the opposite side of the natural bridge, Anna continued toward the sound of the waterfall not yet within her eyesight. She paused often as she strolled to bend, examine, and note the vegetation that grew away from the footpath. She wiped at her brow as she straightened once again. The heat of the day had climbed. No breeze wafted through the thick trees or plants that grew around her. Anna could hear the roar of the plunging water ahead, and it was a mesmerizing call.

After several minutes and several turns of the pathway, she reached the powerful water tumble. She stood along the side edge of the natural rock basin beneath the waterfall and admired the area as she always did when there. The stone basin before her overflowed with water, and its spill followed the drop of the mountain range beyond where she stood. She always figured even more waterfalls would be found if someone followed that water's meandering path. A mist of water sprayed up and out into the air as the water from above cascaded down to hit the water held in the rock basin. It cooled her hot brow.

As she settled on the mossy bank alongside the basin, Anna discarded her tennis shoes and socks to stick her feet into the cold, clear blue pool of water.

Sighing with pleasure, she lay backward onto the thick carpet of green moss she'd settled on. Anna folded her arms behind her head to gaze up at the blue sky above her. *I think I'll lie here for a while before I continue.*

The roar of the waterfall was hypnotic. It made her want to catch a nap. She drowsily thought of how everything she'd ever known was gone, never to be again. For a moment, it saddened the loss of Earth and what she'd known there. She remembered how she and Charlee had frequented the nightclubs while in college. *Not too many months ago and yet a lifetime ago, it seems,* she thought sleepily.

She and Charlee had always had so much fun in those days, with no realization that the carefree times they enjoyed were soon to end. No one on Earth would believe her story if, somehow, she could go back and tell what she now knew.

Anna giggled, recalling the man at the service station who'd whistled at her the day she headed home to George and Molly. She'd journeyed that day toward a lifestyle change she could never in a million years have dreamed up.

Wouldn't that idiot have been shocked if he learned he whistled that day at a female who was of half-alien and half-Earthly origin? Anna yawned as she pictured the look on the man's face. *Shock, disgust, interest?* she shrugged. Who knew how he would have reacted to the knowledge?

I better get up, or I'll fall asleep right here. My clothes are wet from that mist.

Rising to sit upward, Anna pulled her feet from the water to dry them with the socks she'd removed. Her socks and shoes on, she reached for the backpack brought with her to open it and pull out the slice of wrapped-up sweet bread Klinn had given her to snack on; taking a bite from the soft bread, she rose to slip her backpack straps up and over her shoulders. She flipped through the pages of the plant book brought with her for a moment and studied its pictures between her bread bites. With the book placed under her arm, she took off with a hunt for plants in mind.

Anna frowned as she straightened again from scrutinizing the greenery at her feet. She hadn't seen anything vaguely familiar to any of the pictures in the book she'd brought. She'd wanted to find something she could tell Traun might be edible.

She wasn't sure how much further she'd gone than intended, but suddenly, it dawned on her: the wooded area she now stood in was much denser and darker. As she surveyed the area, Anna felt a shiver of unease rise. She had the odd sensation that eyes looked back at her.

A surge of adrenalin shot through her.

Something had grunted to the right of her.

She took off at a run.

The hair on the back of Anna's neck rose, and the space between her shoulder blades twitched as she zig-zagged around trees and bushes. She didn't have the nerve to glance backward.

The impression was strong that whatever was behind her was close and ready to pounce. The low limbs of a tree branch reached down to slap her across the face. *Dammit, that stings,* Anna thought, even as she continued with an all-out sprint. Out of breath and with a stitch developed in her side, she fought to drag in each breath.

I have to face whatever's behind me. I can't run anymore. I can't breathe. With a loud yell, Anna twisted about midstride to raise the book held in her hand, planning to use it to hit out at whatever was behind her. Her right foot sank into a ground cavity, and the ankle of that same foot popped. Her scream of pain resounded as she lost her balance. As she tumbled backward, Anna threw her arms over her head before she landed on the forest floor to curl up into a fetal position when she hit the smallest target she could make of herself.

With her face pressed toward the ground and her eyes squeezed together tightly, she waited in expectation of an attack. Her heart slammed against her ribcage. With each indrawn labored breath, Anna drew the musty scent of the forest floor into her nostrils. After several long moments with nothing but her rasping gasps heard, she cautiously opened her eyes to lower her arms from around her head. She glanced around.

Her heart's thundering slams slowed.

Something was right behind me? I felt it.

Realizing no creature stood ready to pounce, Anna stood to test the injured foot. Pain shot through her ankle. She plopped back down to the forest floor. Her tears spurted as she examined the injured extremity.

Is the thing broken? She wondered. Her ankle and foot had expanded rapidly.

Her shoe was now tight and pinched.

Anna glanced over her shoulder to take in the massive tree she'd darted around earlier. If there was a creature out there, she didn't want the thing to be able to grab her from behind. She began to pull herself over to the tree's base. She desired its wide security up against her back. Reaching the tree, Anna laid her head back in exhaustion against its bark-covered trunk. Sitting with her eyes closed, she prayed to the heavens for her and her baby's safety. She held the injured foot perfectly still. Any movement on her part sent waves of pain throughout it and up her leg.

Opening her eyes at the end of her prayer, she looked around. She recognized nothing.

Traun is going to be livid. I'll have to listen to another one of his lectures on how I am to act and behave as the Lifemate of a High Commander. Anna grimaced.

She knew he would search for her when she wasn't home during the men's noon break. After what seemed an eternity of watching and waiting for rescue, Anna began to nod off to sleep even though she fought to remain awake; the aftereffects of her adrenalin rush, she realized. Every so often, she'd wake, thinking she could hear something, and each time, in quick reflex, she raised the book held in her lap, ready to use it to defend herself if need be.

The day passed, and dusk crept over the forest's top. She began to believe she'd spend the night alone in the woods. Her fear at the thought of it threatened to overwhelm her. She shivered.

Was that a sound in those bushes?

Anna whipped her head around. She watched the area to her left. She waited.

Nothing emerged.

What if no one finds me, and I die out here? She thought as she took a deep breath. *My family will forever wonder what happened to me. I never told Traun I love him. If I'm to die, I wish he would have known that I did. Why didn't I tell him?*

Anna placed a hand on her stomach. *I deserve one of his awful lectures.*

"Traun, here I am," she screamed.

***

Traun went home early on purpose, having missed his check-in on

Anna during the middle of the day. His duties to the people never ended: someone was always calling out for his attention. He had wanted to talk to her at noon after he'd hurt her feelings that morning over his comments concerning her friend, Charlee. He had realized how she must have taken his words when he thought about the conversation later that morning. She would view herself as of Earthly origin, not of Garr blood, since she was raised on Earth. He opened the door to their hut.

They had taken to a ritual of eating their evening meal together at home with only each other. Traun frowned when he saw the two steaming plates of food on the bench, but no Anna. Maybe she was still hurt at him and had gone to Molly's or Charlee's to avoid him. He would check with Molly first.

"No, Traun, I haven't seen Anna since this morning. She planned to walk down to the waterfall today with Charlee. They were going to examine the plant life around the area."

"There's Charlee now." Molly pointed, and Traun turned. Charlee had stepped out past the door of her home to greet Andrew as he walked up to her.

"Anna must be around here somewhere if Charlee's here. I'll go with you," Molly said. She shut the door to her hut to follow behind him.

Charlee put her hand on Andrew's arm to draw his attention to him and Molly as they walked toward them. Andrew directed a smile their way. Traun knew he had talked to George and Molly earlier that evening. Andrew had apologized to him for his behavior from the night before and said he'd also apologized to them. He still needed to talk to his sister.

Traun smiled at his brother-in-law as he walked up to him.

"I'm looking for my Lifemate. I always seem to find her here, so I thought I'd come and get her out of your hair for you."

Andrew looked over at Charlee as he laughed at his statement. "Charlee, where's Anna? Is she inside?"

"She's not here. Have none of you seen her all day?"

Molly's eyes widened at Charlee's excitement. Her words had almost been shouted at them.

In an instant, Traun knew Anna had left the village alone, against his orders for no one in the community to do so.

"You didn't go walking with her this morning, did you?" he said, afraid that he knew the answer.

"No. I didn't feel like going anywhere this morning. Anna said she wanted to explore and go to the waterfall anyway. She promised she'd be back a little after lunch and said you would come here to look for her if she weren't. I assumed she'd arrived back since you never showed up." Charlee looked accusingly at him.

"Where did she plan to explore?" Guilt tore at Traun that he'd been unable to come home during the middle of the day as he'd made a habit of doing lately.

"A little way further into the woods than normal. Left of the waterfall. But she promised me not much further than others have walked before." Charlee wrung her hands together in her anxiety.

"Andrew, go find her," she demanded.

"No," Traun said when Andrew started to take off, his face losing its color.

"You stay here. It's going to be dark soon. I'll go and try to locate her by myself. I don't need more people lost. If I'm not back by morning, pull together a search party and come look for us both."

"I will," Andrew replied, and his voice caught on his words.

Traun started to turn away but then stopped to turn back to Molly.

"I am going to gather a weapon and some camping gear. Molly, will you fetch me food and water, and a medical kit from a Learned One in case she's not only lost but hurt, too? Bring everything to my hut." He turned away again, anxious to be gone.

Molly took off. Traun saw her grab George on her way to gather his listed items.

George wanted to go with him when he came to his hut with Molly, but Traun refused. Within an hour, he was ready to leave the small group who walked to the creek with him.

Andrew, his expression bleak, listened as George reassured Molly and Charlee that Anna would be fine, "Traun will bring her safely home," Traun heard George tell the two as he left them behind.

Able to make out where his Lifemate had lain in the moss that grew along the outer edge of the waterfall basin, Traun turned to search left from there. He hoped she'd gone in the direction she had told Charlee she planned to. Traun came across a piece of paper in the grass, and he recognized Anna's handwritten notes from a prior date during her college days. He folded it in half to put it in his pocket and continued. He began to call out for her.

He paused now and then to listen.

Dusk crept forward, and the sky overhead began to darken. Traun never felt as fearful as he did at that moment or as thankful when he noted her backpack lying on the ground. He bent to pick it up. He was going in the right direction. He wondered what could've happened to keep her from returning home.

He called out her name as before and listened for a response.

Nothing but quiet and stillness came back to him. He began to move once more. He estimated he'd covered around a five-mile distance from the waterfall.

Why would she have gone so far by herself? he wondered. She'd gotten herself lost and turned around was all he could figure. It was what he hoped for anyway.

He halted his stride. There it was again. His name was called out. He turned to follow its direction rapidly. He finally cleared through enough brush to spot where she sat, leaning up against the base of a giant tree. She appeared to be sound asleep, which he knew she couldn't be because her calling out his name had drawn him to her.

Relief flooded through Traun. He didn't know whether to kiss his Lifemate or bend her over his knee and give her a good, sound thrashing.

With a sudden move, she grabbed the book that lay in her lap and raised it over her head as she looked in his direction. Dirt was smeared down two scratched-up cheeks. Her hair stood on end, and leaves poked out on both sides of her head. Her eyes were round with fear, and they engulfed her face. Traun guessed she thought to defend herself with the book held high over her head. He started to laugh at the picture she made.

The book lowered.

"Don't you dare laugh at me, you alien beast."

Her tears flowed down her cheeks when he walked up to squat before her.

"I was so afraid you wouldn't come," she said.

"Alien beast, am I?"

"Yes, you are.

"I thought I was to die out here. I am so glad to see you." Her voice sounded hoarse.

Traun reached to cup her chin within the palm of his hand, and he examined the scratches on her face.

"I don't know whether to kiss you at finding you or to give you a good beating. I thought I gave everyone strict orders never to leave our camp alone?" His voice was stern.

Anna grasped hold of the hand he had against her face.

"Kiss me, please," she said. Her smile spread wide across her dirt-covered face.

He leaned in to kiss her parted lips. She wrapped her arms around his neck.

"I love you," she said when they drew apart.

With his hand on the tree trunk behind her head to brace himself as she clung to his neck, Traun looked down at her in surprise, and his heart soared at her declaration, even though he'd begun to suspect her feelings for him. He had realized she wasn't the type to respond to his lovemaking with as much eagerness as she did if she didn't have a care for him. He hadn't realized that for her to say those words aloud would cause him to feel overwhelmed with joy.

My Anna, he thought. *My beautiful Anna loves me.* She spoke on in a rush, even as she kept her arms locked about his neck, "I don't expect you to voice it back to me, Traun. I know you don't feel the same way for me. But after what I went through today, I wanted you to know my feelings. And I plan every single day, from now on, to tell you that I love you."

She smiled tremulously up at him. A moment later, she frowned at him when he didn't respond. He couldn't. His throat was closed tight with his emotion.

"So, now you know," she said firmly, lowering her arms. It seemed her feelings were hurt even though she'd said he needn't voice his care for her back to her.

It astonished him that she believed he didn't return her affection. He may not have told her with words, but he'd shown her repeatedly, through his behavior, how important she was to him.

Shifting his feet under him with his intent to tell her how much he did care for her, his foot bumped against her leg, and she cried out.

"What is it, sweetheart?" He looked down toward the leg beside his boot.

"It's my ankle. I think it may be broken."

It surprised Traun that he'd not noticed how still and stiff she held the leg. Now that he took the time to look, he could tell that the ankle she pointed to was hugely swollen even in the growing darkness. His relief at finding her and at her being alive had made everything else fade into the background.

"Here, let me remove that shoe. It's cutting off the circulation to your foot." He untied the shoelaces to the shoe to ease the footwear from her. The damaged ankle was why she hadn't returned to the settlement. She issued a sigh with the tight restriction removed.

"Better?"

She nodded.

"By the way, I love you too, little lady."

She smiled with a wobbliness to it up at him.

"That's nice to hear, even if I had to tell you first.

"What are you doing?" she asked when he rose to take items from the bag he'd brought with him.

"I plan to set up a tent for us to sleep in. And then, I'll look closer at that ankle and doctor your scratched-up face.

"How does your face and that ankle feel now?" Traun had maneuvered her into the raised tent with a blanket spread across the tent's floor. Her face he'd cleaned and doctored by flashlight. Her injured ankle was now propped up on his rolled-up shirt.

Sighing, she lay backward beside him. She'd eaten a snack while he'd worked on her. Traun took a bite of the food he'd shared with her.

"Yes, better," she said as she watched him.

***

Although she was tired and sore, and her ankle throbbed painfully, Anna was restored now that her husband was with her. She felt safe.

He gazed down at her as he swallowed his bite of food, and his expression turned somber; the slender flashlight he'd laid between them gave off enough light for her to see his face.

"Now, tell me again, sweetheart. Did you see anything before you started to run?"

"No, but I swear, Traun. I felt eyes watching me." Anna gazed upward at her Lifemate. She shivered and felt again that awful sensation that had taken hold of her earlier that day.

Something had followed her. She was positive about it.

Traun seemed to believe her; after his meal, he placed the weapon he had brought on the tent floor above her head.

"I want it within easy reaching distance, in case it's needed," he said as she watched him. He turned to pack away the food he'd brought with him.

"I'm going to take this bag from our tent and place it in a tree. We don't need food in here with us." Careful not to bump into her leg, he scooted from the tent. Upon reentering it, he stretched beside her to click off the flashlight.

"I love you, Anna," he said, kissing her clean cheek. She sighed. She was so tired.

Drawing back from her, he gave a slight shake to her shoulder. "I am still of the mind to give you a good, sound thrashing for coming into the woods by yourself and scaring me half to death."

In the tent's darkness, he began to work his fingers through her tangled mess of hair. He threw aside the leaves removed that were caught up in it.

"Traun?" Anna said in a whisper, wanting to talk. The cover of darkness and his professed love for her gave her the courage to ask him questions to which she needed some answers. He paused in his grooming of her.

"What is it?"

He shifted beside her.

"Rock under me," he mumbled.

"What you said this morning to me, do you not like Charlee?"

Traun began to stroke her arm with his hand. "I like your friend fine, Anna. I'm sorry I hurt your feelings this morning. However, I do have strong concerns over the child issue with her. If we don't survive on this planet, the Garr people will cease to exist, and what was planned for all those years and executed will have been for nothing. My duty as the High Commander here is to ensure our survival and for our race to continue."

Anna stayed silent as she considered what he said. She realized it was useless to argue with him over the issue. She hoped Charlee never realized Traun's inner thoughts about the child and her friend's full Earthly genetics.

As he continued to rub his palm up and down her arm in a soothing gesture, he suddenly inquired, "Anna, why were you so mad at me when you hit me that day with the water bucket in front of our people?"

Anna stiffened, even though she'd planned to ask him about that night between him and Avreen since he'd said he loved her.

Traun said from beside her, "We've come far enough along in our relationship that you can tell me what I did to you, can't you? I've been baffled by your actions ever since that day."

Terrified of what she might learn and yet answers needed, Anna responded, "I saw you with Avreen the night before that awful day. I had gone to our hut to wait for you when I saw you slip behind her and Nevin's hut moments after I'd watched her go behind it. When I went to investigate, I saw you two together."

"I don't understand what you could have seen that would have made you so angry?"

Anna frowned in the darkness of the tent.

"Wait, sweetheart, did you see her in my arms that night?"

"Yes," she whispered.

"I wish you would have told me what you'd seen," he scolded. "You should have stood your ground that very night."

"I was too scared to confront you with it. I was afraid of what you'd tell me about you and her. I still am."

"It's time I explain something I should have told you as soon as I found out Avreen had come to this planet."

Traun began to describe his relationship with the other woman. Anna stiffened and tried to pull out from his embrace, but he pulled her back against him.

"I let Avreen know that night that I love you and you alone. And I made sure she understood that what had been between her and me before was over. Anna, I love you. I've known my feelings for you since we landed on this planet. When you saw her in my arms, she'd run to me as if something were wrong. Once it was clear there was no problem, I let her know she and I were no more. She has her Lifemate, and I, mine."

Anna relaxed in increments. She rose on an elbow to kiss the base of his throat. His tone and words seemed to indicate that he was honest with her.

"I love you, Traun, and I knew my feelings for you that first night of our being together, which, incidentally, as you well know, was the night you made me so very pregnant. I'm glad our baby was conceived in mutual love, after all. I was afraid it was my love alone felt that night when he or she was created for us."

Traun hugged her to him, careful of her ankle.

They talked on. Anna was content as she lay beside him.

***

Lying awake in the tent's darkness, Traun felt Anna's body relax beside him as she fell asleep after having grown quiet. He listened to the sounds of the night outside of the tent; the wind had picked up, and the creaking of tree branches sounded as they swayed in response to it. A soft spatter of light rain began to fall onto the tent's roof. He dozed off with her held tight against him.

***

Anna woke to a hand up underneath the front of her shirt. She smiled when she felt Traun's fingers begin to stroke over the skin of her stomach. His hand moved upward. It stopped when it found her bra-covered breast. She felt the light pinch of fingers on a nipple. Opening her eyes, she looked directly into her Lifemate's laughter-filled eyes.

"Did I wake you?" He flashed a grin. Spreading his fingers, he palmed her breast to give it a light squeeze. With an abruptness, he removed the hand.

"We need to get moving. A search party will be out and about this morning and led by your brother."

"You're a tease," Anna responded. Her injury jarred her when she moved. She grimaced with the pain.

"Your ankle?" Traun questioned as he rolled away from her.

She nodded.

"Let me look at it again."

When he seemed confident he wouldn't bump her foot, he scooted down to her ankle to scan it and gave a whistle.

"It should hurt. It is even larger this morning and a pretty multicolor, too. You did a good job," he drawled as he looked up to meet her gaze with his.

He moved to reach past her head.

"What are you doing?" She watched him check the small weapon he'd retrieved. He glanced upward.

"I'm going to look around the surrounding area."

"Don't leave me!" Anna clutched at his pant-covered leg and rose to sit alongside him. She began to shiver and couldn't stop her reaction.

Traun captured her chin with his free hand and forced her to look at him. "Anna, calm down. I only want to see if I can find anything. I am not going to go far. I'll keep the tent in sight, okay?"

With a reluctant nod, Anna released her hold on him. Her shaking began to subside.

He leaned forward to favor her with a kiss and smiled when he pulled back.

"I promise I won't be long."

She watched as he sidled out from the tent to stand upright.

He walked away.

Anna inched over to the tent flap left open and stuck her head past it. Traun strolled around the area as he studied the ground before him. He disappeared into the thickets. The minutes seemed to crawl as Anna waited for his return.

Finally, she thought, and her relief flooded. His long stride was bringing him back toward the direction of the tent and her. He stopped beneath a tree to look upward into its branches. Anna glanced at her wristwatch; no more than twenty minutes had passed, and it had seemed longer.

"Did you see anything?" she questioned when he approached.

"I did," he said as he bent to lift her from the tent. He eased her back to the ground to settle her beside it. Anna scanned the wooded area around them. Traun began to dismantle their shelter. He folded the tent material up tight to stuff it back into its case and then placed the case against the base of the tree where she'd waited for rescue the evening before.

"To be collected later, along with your backpack," he informed her when he returned. He fell silent again.

"What was out there?"

He paused in his movement, and he glanced over toward her.

"I have no idea, but it seemed to be a human with a dog, and both left sometime this morning after the rain ceased. The prints each left behind were easily distinguishable. Our food is gone from the tree I stashed it in, too."

***

Traun didn't let Anna realize how shaken up he was. It scared him to think that whatever had been out there had sat and watched them long into the night. *What if I hadn't found her last night?* He watched her glance over her shoulder again as she searched the area around them.

She gave a shiver.

"The human and dog seemed to be together, and both tracks were heading away from our village." Traun didn't want to terrify her, but he didn't want to give her a false sense of safety. He couldn't help but wonder if that one set of human tracks was headed to get reinforcements.

"We must stay cautious and be on the lookout if the pair circles back around us."

Anna gave another worried glance around them.

He squatted down before her. They needed to head back to the settlement, and the sooner, the better.

"I'm going to carry you on my back. Do you think you can handle it?"

"I guess I'll have to. Help me up."

Traun stood to pull her upward and then held her steady with a hand to her elbow while she balanced herself on her one good foot. She rested her weight on that one leg while she watched him put his weapon's safety lock in place and the firearm in its holder attached to his belt. The small rectangular blaster didn't look lethal, but his Lifemate knew it was, having seen him show Andrew how to operate it.

Turning with his back to her, Traun squatted so she could lean forward to lay up against him. When she did so, he brought his arms up and under her rump to stand.

"You're heavier than you look," he said with an exaggerated groan. He let his knees give way under him before he straightened them.

She laughed at his antics.

"Walk," she ordered. He felt her wince at his step forward.

"You okay back there?"

"I'm fine. Let's go home, my handsome alien beast."

Traun grinned at her words. His fast pace soon ate away at the distance between them and their small community. After a while, Anna began to nuzzle at the back of his neck.

The touch of her lips sent goosebumps down the length of his arms.

"Stop it," he said, and he tightened his hold of her, "or hurt ankle or not, I'm going to finish what you are starting."

Anna's laugh sounded behind his back. "I love you," she said.

"You're not making it easy for me to walk, Anna."

"I know of a technique Earth humans do to each other that you might enjoy, and you can still walk as I do it," she whispered.

She blew a delicate swish of air at his ear.

"How do you know of this so-called technique, little lady?" he demanded.

"Oh," his Lifemate exclaimed, innocent-sounding behind him. "I haven't ever done it before. Although I've heard it discussed, Earth women say men love it."

She had piqued his interest.

"I'll give you a small sample of it," she said as she kissed his neck again. "It's called a Wet Willie."

Traun was suspicious of her but didn't say anything. *A Wet Willie*? he thought, as he wondered about it.

"Anna," he roared.

Halting his stride, he quickly removed her from his back while he attempted to get the wad of spit out from his ear. She'd stuck a generously wetted finger down into it.

***

Andrew and the three other men with him stopped advancing when they heard their High Commander bellow out Anna's name. Her laughter pealed a few seconds later. The men looked at Andrew. Andrew shrugged his shoulders back at them before he took off toward the racket the two had made. Relief flooded through him at his sister's happy laughter and knowing she was safe. His smile spread when he realized she must've pulled some prank on her unsuspecting Lifemate.

***

"Ow. Ow," Anna gasped between her gales of laughter. Her injured ankle throbbed with hot spikes of pain at her placement of the foot down onto the ground.

Traun held onto her to steady her while he wiped at his ear.

"You will pay for that, sweetheart," he threatened.

"You should have seen your face," she exclaimed. They watched her brother and the men with him come toward them from the surrounding thicket. Anna wiped at the tears that streamed down her cheeks. Her laughter subsided. She returned her brother's smile and that of her friend Nevin, who watched her and his High Commander.

Andrew shook his head at her. "Sis, I'm glad you're safe and sound."

He realized her lopsided stance and Traun's support of her.

"Well, maybe not so sound after all. What happened?"

The other men crowded around him to look down at the foot she held so still and up from the ground.

Traun answered for her. "She fell as she ran from a human and its animal."

The men snapped their gazes up to their High Commander, and all reached for the weapons strapped to each of their belts.

"No need to panic," Traun said as he eased her downward so she sat on the ground. He squatted beside her. Andrew and the others copied him. Their gazes flicked from him to her.

"Your Lady Anna went further into the woods yesterday than we have before. She felt something watching her and took off at a run back toward home. When she heard movement, she veered away from the trail and got lost."

Anna nodded at Andrew and the other men. "When I couldn't run any further and whirled to face what it was that chased me, that was when I twisted my ankle."

"What did you see, Lady Anna?" Nevin's gaze met hers.

"I didn't get a look at whatever it was."

The men before her frowned.

Traun leaned forward. "I didn't see anything either. But this morning during daybreak, when I checked the area close to our tent, I found a distinct set of human footprints and that of a single animal who walked beside the human. A pet, I presume. They looked to be doglike tracks as we know them. The human footprints were fairly large. The human and the animal stayed and watched us until early this morning, only leaving after the rain had ceased. Their footprint impressions left behind were clear and easy to detect."

"Where did the tracks lead off to?"

Anna knew Andrew realized they must not have led back to their village; otherwise, Traun wouldn't have been so calm as he replied to his question.

"Opposite direction from our settlement. You men, go check the tracks out for yourselves. I want a report as to what you think about them when you return to our settlement. Collect the camping gear I left behind and bring it back with you. You'll find everything propped up against the massive tree alongside where we spent the night. I plan to take Lady Anna to the settlement so a Learned One can examine her injury."

He turned to point a lean finger.

"Head west, and you'll walk right into where we spent the night. When you return to the village, come straight to the Communal Hall. I plan to call everyone together for a meeting there."

Traun stood and then helped Anna to stand. He turned back toward Andrew and the other men.

"I expect you four back within the settlement as soon as possible with your reports."

Andrew glanced toward her. "Take care, Sis," he said before he turned with the others to walk away.

Anna knew he was sorry for the harsh words he had said to her the night before.

"Be careful, Andrew," she called out. Her brother turned to bow toward her, and Anna watched him once he straightened until he and the other men disappeared into the woods before she turned toward Traun. She didn't look forward to the ride on his back again.

***

Finally topping the incline at the back of his and Anna's small home, Traun was bone-tired and his legs shaky. His Lifemate might be of slender build, but after two and a half hours of her hoisted up on his back, she felt like she weighed a ton, and to make matters worse, she'd dozed the last half hour or so, becoming a dead weight on his back. As he stepped around the corner of their hut, it seemed the whole village ran toward him to surround him. George, Molly, and Klinn led the pack.

"Oh, my," Klinn gasped, noting her Lady Anna being carried by him. She ran to the door of their home and stood back so George and Molly could hurry through the opened doorway, following him through it. Traun slid Anna feet first to the floor beside their bed. She was awake now. He turned to face her and, with a hand under each of her armpits, lifted her to set her up on the edge of the bed. He knew she was in pain; her ankle and foot were bigger and fatter than even that morning, and her face held a pinched look.

"I'll get my Lady Anna a glass of water," Klinn said to no one in particular. She frowned at Anna's swollen and purple-colored injury.

"What happened?" George looked to Traun.

Molly walked around him to hug Anna. She looked down at her ankle. "Oh, you poor, poor baby," she exclaimed.

***

Biting down on the inside of her left cheek, Anna was afraid she was about to pass out or, worse, embarrass herself by giving in to tears in front of everyone who surrounded her. With all their sympathy displayed, she wanted to howl like a baby. She could feel each beat of her heart within the injury. Several times, her foot had bumped against Traun's leg as he walked, and it was jolted again when he'd lifted her onto the bed. Anna knew he wouldn't want her to break down before the crowd around them. Giving in to her emotions in front of others was something he'd made plain was unacceptable. And now, even more, individuals had crowded into the small hut. It overflowed with bodies.

Anna looked up to meet her Lifemate's gaze. *Please make them leave.*

He turned to the crowd: her unspoken plea understood.

George spoke. "Where are Andrew and the other men? Did you not make contact with them?"

Traun looked toward him. Anna realized George was worried, but she wished he'd wait until later to ask his questions.

"Yes, we met them. I sent them to look at some human tracks found," Traun responded.

"Wait," he ordered when the occupants in the room gasped and, with excitement, began to rapid-fire questions at him. "I will explain everything later. Right now, I need a Learned One and everyone to clear out of here so Lady Anna can be examined."

"I'll fetch a Learned One," George said. He herded all from the home who had swarmed into it. Klinn handed Anna the glass of water she held in her hand.

"Thank you," Anna said, surprised the woman was quiet.

Molly instructed Klinn as Traun handed the servant Anna's now emptied glass, "Let's start heating water and get a bath ready for Lady Anna. And we must prepare something for both of these two to eat."

She turned back around.

"We were so worried about you," she said, kissing her cheek before leaving behind Klinn.

With the room emptied, Anna looked at Traun, unable to keep her tears at bay. He, in silence, positioned his bed pillow so she could lie backward on it and then leaned forward to grab the other one to ease her distended and bruised ankle onto the top of it.

"The Learned One will have some painkillers she can give you," he said.

Anna nodded.

He looked down at her ankle and reached to pull her one remaining shoe from her uninjured foot. The other one he'd stuffed into the bag left at the tree where they'd camped the night before. He looked back up from where he stood at her feet.

"I'm going to have to cut your pants from you. Otherwise, if I don't, I'll hurt your foot with their removal."

"I don't care." And Anna didn't. All she wanted was those pain pills.

She pointed to the small brown box across the room left on the table by the door the morning prior. "There's a pair of scissors in that box."

Traun moved to fetch the needed tool. With her jeans cut and removed, he dropped the now rags to the floor beside his feet. He turned to drape her housecoat down over her bare hips and then leaned to meet her mouth with his.

"Better?" he asked when he straightened.

Anna knew his duties as High Commander needed his attention. Reaching for his hand, she looked up at him. "You need to go, don't you?"

He squeezed her fingers beneath his.

"I'll wait for the Learned One."

He broke their contact to move to stand at her shoulder and to place his hand there when they heard George speaking to a Learned One outside the door of their hut. The woman entered behind George. She hurried over to the bed.

"Do you hurt anywhere else besides this ankle?" she asked.

Anna was surprised by the woman's curt manner. It was the same Learned One who'd informed her of her pregnancy and who she'd been assigned to. She had always been friendly before. "No. Just my ankle."

The woman looked at Traun. "I will do a complete physical first thing in the morning, but right now, I'll examine Lady Anna's ankle and give her the treatment for it."

Traun didn't say anything, although he inclined his head. A moment later, the Learned One ran a hand around Anna's injured foot and held a small, shiny medical device between her fingers as she did so. She had removed it from the large bag brought with her, which now sat at her feet.

She looked up at her audience to give what she must've thought was a smile. With puzzlement, Anna met the woman's gaze. She seemed tense.

The woman glanced down at the instrument held and studied its digital readout for a moment before she looked back up at her.

"You have a severe sprain and a hairline fracture across the middle of your ankle. I have ointment that will help to get the swelling down. I'll allow a couple of painkillers for you to take, but no more than that."

With the medicated cream retrieved from her bag and which she spread over Anna's ankle, the Learned One handed the tube held over to

Traun. She shook out two white pills from a container to give those to him. Anna wondered if the woman was nervous before her High Commander. It seemed she was. She watched as the Learned One bent again to the medical bag on the floor.

This time, a slender, silver-colored wand was retrieved. Its tip was made of metal, and the cord attached to its bottom connected to something in the satchel at the woman's feet. The Learned One flipped a hidden switch within the bag, and a low hum sounded; a narrow, purple plume of light shot out from the wand's tip.

Anna tensed and glanced up at Traun. He shook his head, indicating for her not to worry; it wouldn't hurt. After a few minutes of the spiral of light being moved in slow motion back and forth across her ankle, the Learned One indicated to Traun that she wanted to move up to Anna's face. He stepped out of the way but watched the Learned One as she continued to work.

Finished, the woman shut off the machine to fold up her equipment. She stuffed all back into the bag at her feet.

"What was that tool you were using?"

The Learned One rose back up, her medical bag clasped in her hand.

"It's a plasma pencil."

At seeing what Anna knew was her blank look directed back at the woman, the Learned One patted her shoulder.

"It helps to speed up the healing process of wounds. Now, make sure to take one of those painkillers tonight. It will help you to sleep. And have that ointment rubbed into your ankle three times daily."

"The painkillers and salve won't hurt my baby, will it?"

The Learned One lurched backward, and her reply was sharp, "Of course not! I wouldn't use anything that would harm the baby."

It seemed it offended her that she'd been asked such a question, especially with the High Commander beside her. Anna could almost hear the woman's thoughts: *Did the High Commander frown? Is he displeased?*

"I'm sorry. I meant no insult toward you, but I needed to ask," she said.

The Learned One's stance relaxed. She braved a glance at her High Commander.

"You two will produce a beautiful race of children for the people of Garr," she said.

She turned back to Anna. "You will have to use crutches for several days. I'll have a pair brought to you."

She gave a tight-lipped smile before departing abruptly.

"Well, so much for the friendly doctor routine of before," Anna said with a short burst of laughter.

Traun smiled down at her.

"I think I make her nervous. My father wasn't a fan of the Learned Ones of old and was vocal in blaming them for our current predicament. Her family was part of the original Learned Ones' who guaranteed the safety of our Germline Manipulation requirements.

"She and her Lifemate are two of the best ordered here from Garr, so I'm willing to overlook her bedside manner as long as she does what she's supposed to do."

George, who'd remained silent and in the background during Anna's examination, walked up to the foot of the bed to look down at her ankle.

"You sure did a number on that ankle, girlie."

He grimaced before he looked back up. "Charlee said to tell you when she saw how everyone was crowded in here earlier that she decided she'd come back by later to see you."

"I wondered where she was," Anna murmured.

Traun turned toward him.

"Uncle, I need you to gather a couple of others and have them help you spread the word that I want a meeting of the entire village at the Communal Hall tonight."

George nodded. "I sure will. I'm anxious to hear what happened out there with Anna. Many have questioned me about it. When should I tell everyone to gather together?"

Traun looked at the face of the wristwatch on Anna's arm.

"Two hours. Andrew and the men with him should be here by then."

With George's departure, Traun gathered a glass of water to give her. He watched as she swallowed one of the pain pills.

With the empty glass set aside, he said, "I need to go. I'll send Charlee to keep you company. Aunt should be back soon, too. I love you. Don't you forget it."

"I love you, too. And when you return, I want to hear about everything that happens in the meeting."

"If you're still awake," he said, turning away.

Chapter 18

Traun motioned toward Andrew upon noticing him and his three companions entering the packed Communal Hall; the verbal chatter within the building deafened a person to all but the closest individual. People were lined up, shoulder to shoulder, against all four inside walls of the building. Others sat squeezed together on the honed benches made for the hall, and some gathered outside the building's opened doors and windows. Everyone discussed what they had heard had happened or believed had occurred.

"If it weren't for the rain falling again, I'd move this meeting back outside," Traun told Andrew and the other three men when they strolled up to encircle him. They had to lean in close to hear him with the volume of the voices around them.

"Did you get a good look at the tracks?"

Andrew, with the other men who stood close beside him, nodded. Traun studied them. Andrew seemed to be considered the group's spokesperson, so he zeroed his gaze in on him.

"Thoughts?"

The crowd noise lowered.

"As you instructed, we inspected a large swath of the wooded area around where you and Anna camped. The human footprints were significant, just as you said, and it looked to all of us as if whatever it was out there circled your camp several times. We concluded that it was curious of you but afraid to come out into the open. The animal tracks, we believe, as you belong to a domesticated dog. Its tracks didn't look feline, as we know them.

"We followed the humanoid trail for quite a while, and whoever or whatever it was appeared on its own. Maybe a lone hunter, we thought. It seemed to know where it was going back to. Its tracks headed in a definite westward direction."

Andrew met the other men's gazes. They all nodded toward him. He looked back at Traun.

"We discussed it and think a search party should be organized to try to follow the humanoid. We believe we should investigate how many more there might be and if there is a possible threat."

Traun nodded his head in agreement.

"My thoughts exactly. Do you four wish to be included in the search party?"

"Yes," they all responded. Each seemed excited at the possibility of encountering other beings. It worried Traun, though, what might be learned. The planet hadn't been visited since its first discovery, and a thousand years had passed since then. When the first Garr explorers found it, they'd been unable to stay long but had reported that it could sustain human life, although none were noted during their stop and exploration. Turning back toward the crowd, who'd begun to chatter again, Traun held up an arm for their quiet. When conversation ceased, he explained to them what had happened to their Lady Anna and that there was proof of life forms on the planet. With a pause to allow what he'd said to be absorbed, he looked out over his people.

"What I request now are volunteers for a search and encounter mission. Counting myself and the four men beside me, I have five already to go. I want seven more for a total of twelve."

One of the women in the crowd called out, "Can a woman volunteer for this?"

Her Lifemate from Earth gaped at her in disbelief. Traun wasn't surprised by her inquiry. She had been under his command when getting Sector Nine under control, and he knew she had excellent marksmanship with any weapon that could be placed in her hands. She would be an asset on the journey. He wanted to smile in approval at her. He tamped the reaction down.

"Any female from Garr and from the army on Garr who hasn't been identified as pregnant can volunteer to be in the search party."

Traun knew four females from Garr had not conceived yet, having spoken to the Learned Ones on the issue a few days prior. He watched for a moment as the woman spoke with her Lifemate before he turned to the rest of the crowd. Two other female hands went up, one which included Avreen's. Traun looked toward Nevin, and he gave a slight nod back toward him. It looked like there would be three females on this trip.

Traun pointed to some of the other raised hands as he selected four male Volunteers he knew could track or had some beneficial skill.

***

It surprised Nevin when Avreen's hand shot into the air. His nod of agreement for her inclusion was done without thought. When he moved to where she sat, she looked up at him with a smile.

"Thank you for that. I want to go with you on this expedition."

Nevin studied her rapt expression. Her excitement was clear, and her attitude puzzled him. He never knew what to expect from this woman of Garr. The night prior, when he'd attempted sexual relations with her, she'd rebuffed him with a harsh word.

And now she's excited to be included in this journey with me? He had quit his attempts to find ways to please her or to get to know her as an individual. He had decided to do his duty to produce offspring as required, and that was all. When she'd accused him of having feelings for their High Commander's Lifemate the day of his punishment, he'd turned from her with a wish that he had been paired with someone like Lady Anna and not the beautiful but cold creature he'd been matched with.

Maybe I am half in love with the High Commander's Lifemate, as she accuses. At least Lady Anna smiles for me when our paths cross and speaks to me as though I'm someone of worth.

Avreen reached out with a slender hand to place it on his arm, and she smiled with a prior unshown sweetness toward him: that smile promised much. Nevin's heart lurched.

"A new beginning for us," she whispered. Nevin heard in that soft tone what he'd longed for since he and the woman before him had been joined as Lifemates—for her to wish to know him as a person and to acknowledge him as a man: her man.

He grinned.

He couldn't help it.

Avreen curled her fingers around his, and her eyes displayed a soft warmth within their depths.

***

It was late into the night when Traun left the Communal Hall to return home. He scowled at the plate of food left behind on the bench when he entered the shelter. It seemed he always ate food that had gone cold. He had had the volunteers stay behind after the rest of the crowd departed, and he and his small group discussed what might be encountered on their journey and the supplies he instructed each to bring.

He'd informed all to be ready to leave within forty-eight hours and stood up on that last directive to dismiss them and call it a night. He wanted to check on Anna.

She was sound asleep, as he'd expected her to be. The tub of water she'd washed off in had been left in front of the fireplace. The water in it looked more appealing than that cold plate of food.

In silence, Traun quickly stripped off his clothes to enter the water. The tub was too small for his frame, so he stood upright to bathe. Using the washcloth left hanging on its side, he soaped down. Water splashed on the floor as he scrubbed and then rinsed. When he stepped from the bathing tub to the bare floor, he made short work of drying off. He eased down beside Anna onto their bed.

Is she snoring?

Leaning over her, Traun listened, and then he chuckled. He had heard a definite snore that time.

She isn't going to like it when I tease her about her snoring, he thought on a smug note. He lay back beside her with the bedsheet drawn up to his shoulders. Turning, he draped an arm across her waist.

Chapter 19

The screech of a single rooster from the gamut from planet Garr woke Anna; the sound grated, and she cringed. She couldn't understand how Charlee found the early morning screeching comforting, usually from several male birds, not just one. She said hearing the noise each morning reminded her not to take life for granted, and she looked at the cries as a call to get up, embrace the day, and enjoy life.

Anna flinched when the lone thing let out another harsh cry. *Has it gotten out of its cage?* she wondered. It sounded as if it were right outside her door. She slapped her pillow over her head. It was not even daylight yet, and the bird was already at it. Soon, the others of his kind would join in. *I'd like to have the thing cooking in a pot*, Anna thought under her pillow.

Wide awake now, she felt across the bed for Traun. She grinned when her fingertips encountered a naked hip beneath the sheets. Lifting her pillow, Anna looked at her husband, visible to her in the pre-dawn light. She rolled sideways toward him to lift a hand and to trace her fingertips across his chest. The men of Garr couldn't grow hair on their chest or face, and both areas remained smooth and hairless throughout their lifetime, she'd learned. Anna trailed her fingertips down over Traun's ribcage. The muscles across his chest rippled with the light touch. Flattening her hand out, she slid her palm back up his ribcage and then downward over his stomach.

"Hunting for something?" His voice held a gravelly sound to it.

Anna laughed and withdrew her hand from him. "Wake up, sleepy head, and tell me what happened last night."

Yawning, Traun rolled sideways to face her. Anna could tell he wasn't ready to embrace the day yet.

"You are cheerful this morning. How's your ankle?"

"Better. Now tell me what happened at the meeting." She reached out to smooth the frown from between his brows with her fingertips. He caught her wrist to pull it upward to his mouth and kiss the inside of it. Tingles raced up Anna's arm from where his lips touched her skin.

"There are twelve of us leaving within forty-eight hours to track whatever watched you and me the other night." He sat upright on the bed, and Anna followed suit.

He continued. "I'd like to make contact with whoever lives on this planet with us. Hopefully, they're friendly, and since we're the interlopers here, we're the ones who need to reach out for their friendship."

Anna agreed, yet she was fearful that he and the others would enter the unknown. "How long do you think you all will be gone?"

"I don't know for sure. Hopefully, not more than four weeks, but it could be longer."

"You could be gone a month or more?" Anna reached out. All of a sudden, she felt terrified. Traun patted her hand on his arm.

"It may not be that long. But whatever is out there already has a two-day head start on us before we can even begin to track and follow it. I don't know how long it will take us to catch up with it or if we will. It depends on how fast it's traveling."

"You don't think it might live nearby and has stayed hidden from us?"

He shook his head at her.

"No. I don't believe what watched us the other night has lived alongside us all this time, and we're only now encountering it. Whoever or whatever it is, I think, happened to be crossing this part of the country at the same time you were traipsing through the woods."

Anna sighed at his reminder of her thoughtless venture. "Who are the men going with you?"

"Not only men. Three women are going as well."

"Really? And you agreed?"

Traun laughed when she eyed him in surprise. "Why the shock? Two of the three were under my direct command in the regiment services on Garr, and both were as capable in everything as the men except what might have required brute strength."

She shifted so she faced him. "But the planet you come from is so backward in so many personal areas that I never dreamed you'd allow any woman to be involved in this type of adventure."

He frowned at her.

"Garr is not 'backward,' as you call us. We are an advanced race of people, and you very well know it. I agree. Yes, there are certain customs we as a people continued to cling to as our technology evolved rapidly, but that doesn't make us socially backward."

"Whatever." She frowned at him as she rolled her eyes.

"Anna…."

"Okay, I'm sorry." He was sensitive to criticism of his people's ways or customs. Honestly, she guessed she was as unreceptive as he was when he disagreed with what she'd known on Earth.

"So, who are they? These individuals. And I know the women must not be pregnant, or they wouldn't be included."

Traun reached out to undo the top button on her nightshirt and began recounting names as he reached for her pajama top's second and third buttons. Anna knew some of the ones he named very well. She'd talked to the others but didn't know them personally. Of course, she wasn't surprised her brother was going. Her eyes narrowed at the last female's name that passed her Lifemate's lips.

"You have got to be joking with me!?" Angry, Anna rolled away from him to scramble off the side of the bed and then winced in pain when her forgotten hurt foot hit the floor. Traun dragged her by her arm back onto the top of the bed to pin her down beneath him. He lay halfway over her with her arms held above her head as he gazed down at her. He looked over the length of her form and then moved his feet away from her injured ankle.

"You had better release me this instant," she spit out. She glared upward. He always seemed to manhandle her when she wanted to get away from him.

"Anna, did you not hear me say Nevin's name after hers?"

Looking sideways past Traun's shoulder, Anna avoided his gaze.

"No." Her anger lessened within her. She still didn't want Avreen anywhere near him.

Before she knew what had happened, her Lifemate rolled away from her and had her turned sideways so that she faced him, and on her side, one of his legs he'd positioned on top of her thigh to keep her pinned in place. He raised a large hand, and her bare bottom received a sharp and painful slap.

"Ow," Anna yelled out.

"Stop it. What do you think you are doing?" Her rear end burned.

"That was for not believing in me," he said, and his face had a forbidding look. He held her in place as she struggled against his restraint. He raised his hand upward again.

"Don't you dare!" Anna tensed when his hand lowered.

It made contact and stung.

"That is for going into the woods alone when I left specific orders for everyone to go in pairs," he said.

"I will get you for this. I am not a child to be disciplined by you or anyone else." Furious, she tried to jerk out from his tight hold of her again.

"Be still before you hurt your ankle," he ordered. He rolled her over onto her back so that he could once again lay half on and half off the top of her, and he gazed down at her.

"I love you," he said, his voice husky.

"With what happened to you, Anna, you must listen when I give an order as the High Commander. And what is this jealousy displayed? Place a little faith in me, would you please? Our relationship together is much more important to me than to risk it on what Avreen and I may or may not have had on Garr."

Leaning down, he nuzzled the side of her neck; his lips made contact with her skin.

"Hmm, you smell delicious," he said.

In increments, Anna's muscles began to relax. Traun loosened his hold of her wrists.

Flexing his hips, he said, "Do you feel what you do to me, Anna? I promise I do not have a desire for anyone but you."

Raising her arms, Anna encircled them around his neck, and her words were whispered, "I still don't like the thought of you and her being that close together."

Traun reached up to caress her face with his fingertips.

"I love you," he said.

Anna felt the last of her anger at him drain away. "I love you too."

"What?" she asked in alarm when he turned her to raise his hand once again.

"Traun, stop, please." She tried to grasp at his hand as it began to lower. This time, his slap to her derriere was light with no sting.

"That was for your Wet Willie," he told her, smiling handsomely down at her.

Anna's laughter pealed as she remembered the shocked look on his face at the time.

"Make love to me," she said. "Please."

Chapter 20

"Don't let our people see your fear of my leaving," Traun told Anna as they began to walk toward the group waiting for their arrival. He knew that if the people picked up on her fear, they would become fearful. The crowd parted for them as she hobbled beside him. Tilting her head slightly downwards at his words to her, Traun knew she realized he would not show any emotion toward her at his leaving, as he expected her to keep her feelings in check. She understood he wouldn't kiss her goodbye before the people, either. They had said their farewells behind closed doors.

Feeling an overwhelming need to touch her one last time, Traun, under the guise of steadying her as she hopped along on her crutches beside him, slid his hand down the inside of her tanned, bare arm. *If she were not hurt and pregnant, I'd be tempted to take her along with me.* With a glance of curious review toward him, his Lifemate slanted him a small smile.

The crowd that had gathered and circled the group that planned to venture out into the unknown quieted when their High Commander and Lady Anna arrived together and turned toward them, becoming one solidified unit.

From beside Anna, Traun spoke to the gathered people, "While I am gone, you are to bring any problems you may have to the attention of your Lady Anna. She will act on my behalf for all concerns while I am away. I expect everyone to continue their daily duties to prepare for the upcoming winter."

The crowd nodded. They had presumed no less on all he said.

He had prepped Anna earlier to anticipate his announcement that she would act in his stead and also had instructed her to seek his uncle's advice on anything she felt unsure of handling. He had confidence in her, with George's help, to make sound judgment calls.

Traun wanted to give her one last hug and kiss before leaving as she remained quiet and still, her emotions under control. Her expression didn't reflect her earlier voiced fear for all their safety.

Her brother and the others selected for the journey began to hoist their gear onto their backs. They laughed and joked with each other and the crowd around them. Andrew, with no care what anyone thought of his exuberant display, grabbed Charlee from where she stood beside him to kiss her soundly. The crowd hooted at his show of vigorous passion.

Traun gazed down at Anna before lifting the heavy gear at his feet onto his back. He adjusted the backpack's straps over his shoulders.

"Make sure you keep the guards posted around the village," he instructed quietly. "And as I told you, Uncle will help you. You be sure to keep him informed of everything."

"I will," she said as she watched him.

Traun tightened the backpack's straps about his waist.

"I love you," she whispered.

"I love you, too," he mouthed in silence back.

***

Anna watched the group as they left the remainder of them behind. Her fears for their safe return almost overwhelmed her. She remained after everyone else drifted away, her eyes on Traun until she couldn't catch even the tiniest glimpse of him. He'd not looked back once. Sighing, Anna turned to face her now extra responsibilities.

Her gaze met Charlee's. She had been unaware that her friend had remained to watch Andrew leave.

"They both will be fine," she said to reassure her and herself.

That first day of being in charge was a long one.

Not an hour after seeing Traun off, the male poultry outside her door bright and early the past two mornings escaped from his cage again, and this time with four female accomplices who trailed behind him. Standing outside her front door, Anna realized the rooster and his entourage strutted toward her.

Molly and Charlee ran beside the animals and tried to return the pack to their caging areas.

Hobbling out to meet the runaway gang, Anna raised one of her crutches to help turn the flock around. In alarm, she watched the rooster make a beeline straight toward her. When close, he jumped into the air with a loud squawk, his clawed feet outstretched toward her.

Anna swore to Molly and Charlee that she saw a definite gleam rise in the rooster's eyes before he attacked. "I'm convinced," she exclaimed as they doctored the leg he'd pierced with a claw foot, "that bird has it out for me, and me specifically!

"Why else would he pick my hut to scream his loud call these past two mornings? And now, the hateful thing with intent attacked me, and to add insult to it, he brought others with him to show them what he was going to do!"

Molly and Charlee held their sides, doubling over with their laughter at her outraged expression and words.

"I'm going to see that his neck is wrung and have the thing plucked and cooked for our evening meal!" she declared. Anna started to grin in embarrassment when Molly and Charlee laughed even harder.

She knew her belief that that particular rooster held a personal vendetta against her was ridiculous; it wasn't capable of holding a grudge. Anna also knew that she couldn't kill the darn thing. Traun would be livid at her if she did.

Molly wiped at her eyes as her laughter subsided.

"Well, at least we have the villain and his followers locked back up," she said as she stood from where she'd been beside Anna's pierced leg, doctoring it. Anna worried aloud about how long it would take before the thing made a break for it again and came searching.

Molly doubled over with her laughter once more.

"I...I...have to go see why...why...George wanted me earlier," she said between her caught breaths.

"Charlee, you stand guard over Anna in case that rooster returns with his evil intent," she teased as she turned away.

The gouged hole stopped its bleeding. Standing back outside her home, Anna inspected it. Charlee stood beside her and said she wanted to go and finish her daily chores.

Anna started to nod when, in alarm, she straightened.

Two women yelled at each other below the hill from where she and Charlee stood, their verbal fight loud. Others turned to look. The argument, overheard with ease, was whether the scarf being tugged between them belonged to one or the other. Both screamed for the former to let loose.

The women noticing her ran up as each clutched an end of the scarf. Anna glanced from one shouting female servant to the other, bewildered as to what to do as they yelled for her to order the other to let go.

"Quiet! Give me the scarf," she finally said with a firm tone.

She had an idea. She held her hand out for the scarf that they still tugged between them. She had to give it a yank for it to be released. Anna placed the scarf behind her back and looked at the woman who'd shouted the loudest.

"Describe the scarf to me."

With arrogance and self-assurance, the woman responded, "It be blue silk, trimmed in gold."

Anna turned to the other woman. "Describe the scarf to me."

"It lightest of blue silk, trimmed tightly in gold thread. It be four feet long, and a slight discoloration be in one corner. My father gives it before leaving Garr, and it holds his love."

Anna handed the scarf over to her.

"Thank you, my Lady Anna," the woman said. She held the scarf to her cheek, and tears brimmed.

"You may go," Anna said in a gentle tone. Turning, she looked at the other woman, and her expression grew hard with the disgust she felt over the incident.

"I do not expect to see you before me again with this same type of issue."

The woman lowered her gaze.

"I be ashamed, my Lady Anna. My temptation be too great. The scarf extremely lovely, and when I see it on clothesline, I cannot keep from snatching it. My sin not happen again. I make promise."

The woman turned, and, with quick steps, she escaped the censure in Anna's gaze.

"Wow, how did you know to do that?" Charlee had stood in silence beside her during the entire episode. It seemed she looked at her with new respect.

Anna shrugged a shoulder. "I don't know. It came to me all of a sudden."

In truth, she had astonished herself that she'd known what to do. It shocked her that within their small and select village, some exhibited behavior she would've said, if asked, would not ever happen. For some reason, she'd believed that with all being hand-picked from Garr, they'd be above the baser instincts known to humankind. People were people, no matter where they were from, who they were, or why they were where they were, she realized.

Later that night, alone and behind a locked door, Anna lay curled up in a ball in the center of her and Traun's bed. Wide awake, she drew his pillow to her to inhale his scent. She wondered how his group was doing and how far they'd walked that first day. *Please keep them all safe,* she prayed.

***

Traun raised his arm to the ones behind him as he halted in his stride. The night was fast on the approach.

"Let's stop here for the night," he informed his weary group. He knew they were all exhausted. He was fatigued himself with the miles they'd covered that day. It had been a whole week since he and the others had left their families and friends behind. They'd scaled down the backside of the mountain their village was nestled into that first week as they found and followed the path of the unknown thing ahead of them. There were a few days they'd lost its trail, but each time, with excitement, they'd picked it back up again: whoever or whatever the two-footed thing was ahead of them, it traveled light and fast.

Easing his backpack from his shoulders to the ground beside his feet, Traun watched as the others around him did the same with theirs. Looking up at the clear sky, he decided to sleep under the night stars; no tent would be set up that night.

"It should be safe to have a fire tonight. We are far enough behind whatever we're following that it'll be unable to see the light of it. In this rocky enclosure, something would have to be right upon us before it, knowing we're even here."

Traun's group became active.

Before long, a warm fire crackled, the men set up tents, and the women were preparing hot food for their evening meal. As he'd instructed, the women kept set portions for everyone from the provisions brought. If their rations ran low, whether they found the thing they hunted for or not, they'd have to turn back home. They had enough for two months of dried and processed sustenance from Garr, light enough to carry as almost nonexistent in weight. Although not the most palatable thing to eat, it was fortified with everything a body needed to survive.

***

With a sideways glance across the camp from where she stood, Avreen scrutinized the men as they settled around the campfire. They waited to be told the food was served. She had been careful not to allow anyone, especially Nevin, to see her love for their High Commander, and she wanted to be the one to serve Traun his meal that night. One of the other women had beaten her to the task ever since they'd been on the trail.

Traun will notice me this night, Avreen thought with a firmness of determination.

That evening, she'd taken extra care in combing her hair and freshening up for the night. Nevin said with a smile that she had a very becoming glow when he passed her. Avreen felt excited as she fiddled with and stretched out the time to pack the cooking supplies. The other two women, now occupied with handing the steaming bowls of food to the men as they lined up, ready to eat when called over, paid her no mind. Nevin stepped into the line as Traun remained where he sat on the log beside the campfire.

She made a fast move toward the women. "Our High Commander has no bowl of food. I'll take one to him."

The women looked past the line of men to where their High Commander sat; a bowl was filled with quick reflex and handed over.

***

Checking the laser beam strength on his firearm, Traun waited for his men to be served. With his weapon set to safety, he raised his gaze from it to take in the encampment and his small group. Avreen walked toward him with a bowl of food held between her hands.

She halted before him. He returned her smile.

"Thank you, but you had no need to bring me my meal."

He reached to take the bowl from her, curling his fingers around the bottom of it. She moved her fingers so they lay over his. He pulled the bowl and his fingers out from under hers. She didn't comment as she turned to walk back toward where her Lifemate stood. She stopped beside him and spoke with him briefly before she continued on to where the other two women were still doling out the evening rations.

How strange life is, Traun thought as he watched her. *A year ago, she would've had me ablaze with such a come-hither look and touch and that sway of hips.* He didn't think she even realized what she did. Anna's reaction wouldn't have been calm if she'd witnessed that touch and look of hers. *My Anna,* Traun thought with an inward smile as he dipped the spoon he held into the warm bowl. He missed her.

***

Avreen smiled to herself as she lay beside Nevin in their tent. Traun *had* noticed her, and she knew he had by the way his eyes skimmed across her face and hands when he'd taken the bowl of food from her. Nevin turned to place an arm across her waist. She stiffened and then made herself relax. *No suspicion.*

She turned to accept his embrace, and with her eyes squeezed shut, she lost herself in her world. She imagined it was Traun who kissed her, and it was he who caressed her under the cover of darkness.

"My love…"

With a low, broken moan of despair given at Nevin's whispered endearment jolting her back into an unwanted reality, Avreen's urge to puke rose in her throat. He believed she was excited by his entry into her person.

Avreen curled her lip into a sneer at him and his belief. *I hate this wretched place and you. You stupid, stupid man. I am the daughter of a Leading Council member, mating with a half-Earthling.*

"My darling. My darling," he whispered low against her ear, his breath heavy.

Avreen's rage rose. Her beloved Traun should have held her and said those words, *not him.*

***

"It sure has started to turn cold these past few days," George said to no one in particular from where he sat before the fireplace and its warmth that radiated into Anna and Traun's home.

When darkness had fallen that evening, everyone's worry over their loved one's failure to walk into camp, as had been expected, reached a high point—as of that day, a month had passed since the eager adventurers had left their small settlement. Anna replied to his statement, which had broken the silence that had fallen upon their group who sat with him that evening.

"I think fall weather has set in. Winter will be close behind. The dark blueness of the sky almost looked like it could've snowed today. Didn't you think so, George?"

"I noted its color and thought snow possible. I suspect this planet may have hard winters, and with us being sandwiched between four mountains, we'll probably see early snow."

Listening to their conversation from beside Molly, Charlee dreaded returning to her empty hut. She shivered at the sound of the wind outside the shelter as it swirled, dipped through the trees, and sang forlornly on its way past. She'd dreamed such strange imaginings the previous night and even got up twice to double-check that she'd locked her door and window opening. In her last dream, Traun kneeled with his back to her when she suddenly stood before him. She'd watched his face twist in shock, fury, and anguish as he cried out for mercy from the heavens. At his displayed grief and sorrow, she'd tried to stretch out a hand to comfort him, and each time, Andrew had pulled her back with the order for her to "Turn away.... Turn away." In another imagining, Lance approached her and Andrew, repeating over and over, "The child is mine," while he laughed and laughed.

Chills raced up Charlee's arms at her memories of those nightmares. The echo of Traun's cry for mercy from the Creator had been so heartfelt and pierced with such sorrow that she'd woken from her dream with tears.

George stood to turn toward Molly. She was lost in her thoughts, worried about Andrew and Traun and the others, as they all were.

"Molly," George repeated before she looked over at him. "We better head back to our hut. It's getting late."

When she rose, he turned. "We will walk you home if you want."

"See you in the morning, Anna," Charlee said and stood.

***

Anna locked her door behind her family's retreating backs. They had agreed amongst themselves that all the explorers were fine. Traun, Andrew, and the others would stroll back into the settlement before long. She returned to the pillow she'd risen from to sink onto it before the fireplace and pulled her knees close to her chest to wrap her arms around her legs. She rested her chin on her kneecaps to watch the flicker of the fire. No matter everyone's assurances that all were fine, she worried about Traun and the others and how they fared, especially with the change in the weather pattern the past week. The nights and days grew colder with each day passed, and a frost had covered the ground the last few mornings when she'd ventured out.

Anna issued a heartfelt sigh. She was exhausted from the worries and demands that seemed to crop up daily. She didn't know how Traun, with little effort, appeared to handle the pressure. The duties of a High Commander were constant and never-ending. Even with George's help, some days, she wanted to hide from the stresses of it all.

The wind outside the hut picked up its howl.

As it whistled through the tree branches and past the hut, Anna thought it almost sounded human. She jumped an inch off her pillow when a loud thump sounded. She turned toward her door, her mouth dry.

"Who is it?" Her voice had squeaked.

"Me. Let me in!"

With a laugh, Anna breathed in. She rose and felt silly at her fear; she yanked open the door with a swift stride across the bare floor.

"Charlee, you scared me half to death. What are you doing out there?"

"Lock the door, Anna."

Anna shut and locked the door with her quick entry into the hut past her.

"What's the matter?"

"That wind, it gives me the damn creeps. Is what's the matter."

"It does sound like it's calling out to you. It sounds like it's saying, 'Follow me. Follow me. Do you dare?'" Anna cocked her head to one side as they both listened; Charlee grabbed her hand with hers.

"Can I stay here tonight? I'm too scared to be by myself."

"Of course, you can. I sat here scared myself after you left me," she responded.

Charlee turned to pull her after her. "Turn on your CD player. Maybe we'll be able to block out that eerie wind by talking and listening to music."

She released her hand to sit on the bench, kicked off her shoes, and pulled her feet onto it to lean against its silk throw pillows. Anna went to pick out a recording of easy-listening music and turned the volume down on the CD player so the music, in quiet softness, surrounded the room. She sank back into her pillow before the fireplace.

"I am glad you're here, Charlee."

The shadows caused by the flicker of flames from within the fireplace bounced on the wall beside her as she adjusted the pillow underneath her bottom for a more comfortable position. She and Charlee said nothing else to each other as they watched the flames within the fire move in time to the music. Anna began to feel melancholy with the soft notes that floated about the room. Charlee looked down at her from where she sat.

"Do you miss Earth or what we left behind there?"

Anna sighed and didn't reply for a moment.

"There are days that I do. The other morning, I was trying to decide what to wear when I started thinking about us shopping in our hometown and wished we could go again. I would love a cup of French vanilla cappuccino, too." She grinned up at her friend.

Charlee smiled back down at her. "Those were carefree days. Weren't they?"

"What about you? What do you miss from Earth?" Anna asked.

Charlee looked at her for a moment. "I miss being able to visit my parents' gravesides."

"Oh, Charlee, I'm sorry." Anna reached to pat her knee.

Charlee continued, "I do miss Earth and what we left behind, but if I had a choice to go back or be here with Andrew, I'd pick Andrew without hesitation."

Anna felt foolish about the things she'd told Charlee she missed. She knew she'd also take Traun over what they'd left behind. Yes, she wished for the modern conveniences she'd known on Earth, but not so much that she resented being on this strange planet.

Chapter 21

Traun inched cautiously toward the rise of smoke from below, which rose to where he lay in tall grass on an incline above it. Andrew and the others were behind him on their stomachs, also. He motioned toward them to halt. All stopped to wait for another signal. He gestured for them to ready their weapons. He wasn't close enough to see what was in the valley below, but he could now see the campfire glow from which that smoke spiraled into the clear night air, alerting him and his group to the presence of others. The sound of voices, coarse and low, carried upward to where he lay hidden. It was a garbled, unknown language, and he could hear an animal yelp every so often as if it were being kicked. He motioned left with five fingers and then pointed right to indicate the remainder to move there. His group behind him split and spread out. With everyone in position, he signaled again and heads down all crept forward as he'd done; the tall native grass covered their actions as they approached; they halted, stretched out on each side of him. Together, they crawled as one unit forward to the edge of the ledge to see down into the camp below.

A gasp sounded from one of the women.

With a quick slash of his hand, Traun signaled for quiet. He was afraid they'd been discovered when one of the creatures below them stood to look upward toward their position. He breathed again when the thing squatted back down by the fire. He glanced toward Andrew, who looked back at him, eyes wide. The scene below caused mutual alarm to race through them both.

Traun turned to gaze back down the outcrop. Giving a quick scan over the area, he counted twenty primitive male species within the campsite; several of the things were squatted around the blaze of the fire from which its smoke had drawn him and his troops, and a medium-sized animal skinned and gutted cooked over the open fire; others of their same kind were bent over more animals away from the fire working on slaughtered creatures who they'd bound with feet tied up within tree branches, heads down toward the ground. With efficient skill, the savages skinned and gutted the animals—short work made of the job.

Traun caught the odor of blood, guts, and body stench. The source was indistinguishable from that of the animals and the savages. The smell assaulted his nostrils with each lift of the wind current. He watched as some of the beings, too impatient for the animal carcass to finish its cooking, approached the fire to cut off hunks of bloody raw meat from it to eat; every so often, one of them would kick away a huge furry white dog which circled the fire as it tried to get at the meat the men consumed.

All the men in the camp were unclothed and barefooted, most with long, bushy, ratted, thick black hair that surrounded their faces; some had that hair pulled back behind their necks and tied with rawhide string, faces exposed; bushy black eyebrows slashed across their broad foreheads. All were short and stocky, no one more than five feet tall. It seemed they didn't feel the evening's cold air as they talked. One motioned excitedly as he spoke in their guttural, choppy language to the others around him. Traun suspected the excited one was who they'd hunted and trailed. Another savage responded from across the fire pit from where he'd squatted; his gesture and facial expression indicated he disagreed with or didn't believe what the other being said; a sharp reply given back to him caused laughter to erupt from the rest of the savages.

The disbeliever jumped to his feet and kicked the white dog with obvious intent in its ribcage as it passed him; it yelped to roll across the ground. The storyteller leaped across the fire toward the other savage. They rotated over and under each other on the ground, throwing hard and swift punches at each other. With an abrupt and strategic move, the storyteller straddled his opponent, his short, thickset legs planted on each side of the other being's waist. He bent down to grasp the other being's hair with two huge fists and then proceeded to lift and slam the other savage's head down to the ground. The disbeliever was knocked out by the action, unmoving afterward; his head was lifted and slammed to the ground one more time, for good measure, it seemed. The other savages in the camp, unfazed by the commotion, never ceased eating or working as the two fought or when the winner rose from the unconscious man. The conqueror pulled a long-bladed knife from its holder strapped to his bare thigh and marched back to the fire.

Bending at the waist, he cut a large chunk from the cooking meat and threw the piece toward the white-haired dog. It lunged upward, catching it between massive jaws, and turned afterward to slink off to lie outside the circle of the men with its prize.

Traun made a motion to his group to stay put. He wanted to see the direction the Neanderthal men headed. It didn't look as if they planned to spend the night where they'd gathered: several began to lower the gutted and skinned animals that hung from the trees, and the bloody carcasses slung over their broad backs as they grunted out their language to each other. The dog owner walked over to the one still sprawled on the ground; he looked at the being for a moment before he kicked him in the ribs with a large foot.

The audience, still hidden up on the grassy ridge, wondered if perhaps the savage was dead when no movement was made.

With a second kick delivered, the being rose to a sitting position. Shaking his head as a dog would when clearing water from its fur, he staggered upward to follow the others as they exited the camp.

Waiting until the entire group was out of sight, Traun stood. Andrew and the others rose also.

They gathered around him, all silent.

"We will not attempt to make contact with what we witnessed here. If they got the jump on us, we'd be done for before a fight started, even with our high-tech hand weapons."

"What do you make of what we saw?"

Traun turned toward Avreen.

"It looks to be a hunting party headed back home. This is a young planet, and unless there are other, more advanced people elsewhere, those may be all we have for neighbors. Not a pretty picture, is it?" Traun took in the expressions of his group. He felt the same way as they did: alarmed.

"At least we know from the animals they killed and dressed out that there's edible meat on this planet. We are not wholly dependent on what we brought," he said with their continued silence.

He glanced down to the trail the savages had taken with their departure. It worried him, the wild man who'd crossed paths with Anna. He didn't believe they'd seen the last of him. Traun turned back to the others who waited for his next directive.

"Let's gather our stashed gear and start our journey home."

***

Avreen, with the rest of the group, turned behind the High Commander to follow him. Nevin stepped up to walk alongside her. She glanced sideways at her Lifemate; they'd be back in their settlement within three weeks. An unexpected sadness rose at what needed to be done. Surprised by her emotion, Avreen smiled at her Lifemate when he glanced her way.

With irritation, she slapped his hand away when he reached out with the intent to help her step over a fallen tree branch.

***

Nevin issued a silent sigh. He never knew what to expect from the woman by his side. One moment, she appeared to want his attention; the next, she acted like she couldn't abide him. It seemed he was in the middle of a game and didn't understand the rules he was to go by. Stepping over the fallen tree limb behind Avreen, Nevin followed her as they brought up the rear of their group. His mouth twisted with his puzzlement and emotional hurt as he studied her backside.

He had hoped he and she had found some common middle ground within their arranged marriage. It didn't look to be so. Upon the return to the settlement, he planned to petition the High Commander to no longer be Lifemates with her. A life of solitude would be better than to endure this constant perplexity and emotional ups and downs.

Even with his resolve, Nevin knew his request to the High Commander would be denied.

***

Disappointment lay heavy within Traun as he walked ahead of the others. He had hoped, as he'd told his father, that they'd find civilized people on the planet if any other humans were discovered. He realized how naïve his expectations had been.

No mention of human life form had been made within the records of that long-ago visitation by his ancestors. Deep within his gut, he knew the savages would return to investigate what the one had seen and told the others about. He wasn't arrogant enough to believe he and his people were safe because of their superior weaponry. The Neanderthals might seem simple people and have crude tools, but with the number of animals they'd pulled down with those same armaments, their hunting and stalking skills must be superior to anything he'd ever witnessed. Traun gazed down at the compact weapon he'd removed from its pouch at his hip and of which he'd palmed within his hand; it was lethal, able to cut a man in half when powered to only medium capacity. *But what will happen to us when our high-powered, advanced weapons begin to wear down?* His jaw clenched at his thought.

He didn't have the essentials that made up the weapons' structures; those items were found on Garr. Their lasers were a plus, but he and his men needed homemade weapons to practice with and to carry at all times. If caught without their high-powered firearms and it came down to hand-to-hand combat, he was afraid he and his men would be on the losing end of the battle. Yes, he could give the order to his men to sneak up on the barbarians and to fire on all without thought or feeling, and the savages could be wiped out, problem solved. It was a directive he couldn't give. The Book of Wisdom taught that all races of life were precious. If the savages attacked his people, then there would be no hesitation on his part to give the order to kill all who struck. He hoped to live in peace alongside the Neanderthals, but his instinct warned him that it was wishful thinking on his part.

Andrew strode up to walk beside him.

"I don't know about you, but what I saw back there scared the living hell out of me."

Traun glanced toward his brother-in-law at his low-voiced comment. "I was thinking our high-tech weapons are a plus for us, and as long as they remain in good operating condition, we should be fine. I don't believe we've seen the last of those savages. They will want to investigate what the one told them about."

"My thoughts, exactly," Andrew said.

They arrived at the spot where their gear was stored. Andrew bent down to grasp his belongings and heaved his backpack onto his shoulders.

He seemed anxious to get back to Charlee and to let her know what he'd witnessed.

That evening, as Traun's troupe made camp for the night, the mountain they would climb the next day loomed. Traun dreaded its ascent, and he could tell the others were also worried as each glanced toward the mountain. He wished it were behind them already.

Accepting the mountain's power, Traun stretched out on his bedroll to prop his arms behind his head and gazed upward at the night sky. He'd not wanted his tent set up. That day, the sky had been a heavy, dark blue.

It would have been nice to know what type of weather they could face on the morrow. He'd left his weather sensor behind for George to use. Traun took the sky's color as a sign of snow falling before they could reach their settlement. He hoped not. The passage through the mountain range was hard enough without his group having to contend with snow.

The camp grew quiet as the others settled in for the night. He was anxious to see Anna. He wondered how she'd held up to the demands of a High Commander's duties. Shifting to find a more comfortable position, Traun began to speculate about the children they would have together. He hoped their firstborn would be a boy child and the next, a girl. A girl child who would look like her mother. He'd have to raise their male children to be rough, tough fighters who could ensure their kind's survival.

The girls we have, I can spoil, Traun thought with a smile he couldn't stop spreading. *Father, Mother, I have your first grandchild on the way.* An empty feeling in his gut settled. He missed his parents and brother. He would never see them again, and in turn, they'd never know what had happened to him or the rest of the travelers.

My Anna is my world now. My Anna and the children we are blessed with were his last thoughts before sleep claimed him.

The next morning, the air had a sharp bite that had been absent a week ago. A thick frost falling overnight had blanketed everything on the ground. The crunching noise everyone's shoes made on the rocky bottom of the canyon floor sounded loud in the quiet of the early morning. Traun turned to begin to step up the slanted slope of the mountainside trail. The exact route they'd descended from when tracking the savage.

With caution and the day now most passed, Traun maneuvered around the rocks before him on the mountain trail's footpath. They'd all stopped for a quick drink of water and a snack before rising to hike again. The trees had been sparser lower down the side of the mountain from which he and his group had hiked, but they'd gained in density the further up the steep trail they'd climbed that day. Traun glanced over his shoulder to take note of everyone staying up with him. Avreen and her Lifemate brought up the group's rear, with Andrew a step or two in front of her and Nevin right behind her. Keeping close to the backside of the trail and the now-approaching bend in it, Traun was careful not to look toward the exposed sharp drop on its other side. With several hours of steady climbing behind him and his group, the height was dizzying from the high vantage point. There was enough room for a grown man to walk on the trail, yet even with that, an individual needed to be vigilant: one wrong move could mean tumbling down the mountain's sharp drop. They had been gone a month from their settlement and still had several weeks of foot miles ahead. He knew his entire group was as fatigued and eager as he was to arrive at the place they considered home.

A shriek ripped through the air.

Jerked from his thoughts, Traun quickly halted his step forward.

"Stay here," he ordered as he squeezed past the ones who'd got past the curve in the trail. When he rounded the bend where he and the others had successfully walked only a few minutes prior, he noted that Andrew had two fistfuls of Avreen's shirt within his grasp as he gazed down the side of the mountain. Avreen looked down over it also.

With a hurried glance past the two, Traun failed to locate Nevin. Andrew turned as he approached, and his face reflected his horror.

"Son-of-a-bitch, Traun! He fell down the side of the ridge! Son-of-a-bitch," he repeated in a slow and hoarse drawl, his shock palpable.

Drawing close to where the two stood, Traun maneuvered past Andrew to stand beside Avreen. He spotted the broken and sprawled body of Nevin below them. The Transfer lay face up, eyes wide open, with a blank stare directed upward. Traun's nausea rose.

Avreen seemed to become aware that he stood beside her, and she reached to clasp him around his waist and to hold tightly to him as she sobbed into his shirt, her face pushed into his side. Traun pulled her tighter to him to step backward, removing her and himself from the danger of the ledge's edge. His compassion rose at her obvious distress over what had occurred. He couldn't imagine her pain.

"Shh, Avreen, shh," he murmured, tender emotion rising. He ran his hand down over her hair to calm her.

"Traun, hold me. Please, hold me," she said, even as her weeping increased.

He enfolded her in his arms, feeling the waves of shuddering that passed through her body. The shock of what had happened to her Lifemate held her in its grip. Their history together tugged at Traun's heart. He ignored Andrew, who stood in silence beside them, even as he registered Andrew's astonished glance between him and Avreen at her use of his name and the intimacy it implied. Traun urged Avreen toward the others up the trail who waited for his return.

"I'm right behind you," he reassured her, convincing her to release her hold of him and walk ahead.

"All of you go on to where the trail widens out. We will gather together there," he ordered the others at their approach to them. He briefed everyone on what had happened when reaching the large area he knew had been ahead. All gazed in horror at Avreen.

The two women in the group hugged her and spoke softly to her.

She continued to weep.

***

Andrew watched Avreen and couldn't shake the impression that her emotional breakdown was an act for the benefit of her audience. From what he'd seen and heard in those few seconds before he grabbed her, he couldn't banish the unholy consideration that Nevin's fall wasn't an accident, as everyone assumed it to be, and even he'd taken it to be. *Something doesn't feel right here.* Andrew glanced toward Traun.

How does he fit into the scheme of things with her and this accident? Shit. What am I thinking?

Andrew jerked his gaze from his brother-in-law.

***

Traun noticed Andrew's slanted look toward him and wondered what was going through his mind. Not only Avreen but Andrew also experienced shock. He hoped his brother-in-law could hold up to the strain of what he'd witnessed…and would have to witness even closer.

"I want everyone to continue up the trail to where we camped when we came down the mountainside. It's not much further," Traun told his stunned group. "Andrew, you and I are going to go down and bury the body. We should be back with the rest of you by tomorrow evening."

Avreen cried out, "What? No. I don't want you to go down there."

***

Andrew's gaze narrowed, and his thought flashed as Avreen looked up at their High Commander pleadingly with her eyes wide and luminous: *For someone overcome by grief, the lady sure seems to pay attention to everything said around her.* Traun moved to where she sat between the women who comforted her and squatted before her to take her hands within his. "Avreen, we can't leave Nevin as he is. We must bury his body. I refuse to walk away and leave him as if he meant nothing to us."

Andrew studied the two. Traun's voice was low and soft toward her. The others' gazes darted between the two; they obviously had a past between them, and the others saw it too. Avreen reached to grasp his forearms with slender fingers, beautiful even in her sorrow.

"I don't wish to leave him as he is, but I don't want you or…or… Andrew, to risk your lives by climbing down the side of the mountain to where he fell. He is dead already, you…you…two are not," she ended with a sob. She fell forward into his arms.

Andrew watched as Traun returned her to the two women who sat and flanked her. Their compassion toward her was evident as they nodded to their High Commander, promising to take care of her. He stood.

"It is something that must be done," he said firmly when Avreen looked up at him, a plea still in her gaze for his reconsideration. With a sharp motion, he turned away toward where Andrew stood.

With the supplies they needed gathered, Andrew followed behind him as the High Commander strode away from the subdued group. At the site of Nevin's fall and with ropes twisted around their waists, Traun went first over the edge of the mountainside. Andrew followed and, with each step, calculated.

The sun had begun to set by the time he reached the last tread to step down and to stand beside Traun and the twisted and mangled body of the man he'd liked and respected. Andrew fought his rising nausea at the closeup view of Nevin's body.

***

"You alright?" Traun questioned, seeing his brother-in-law turn away from the body, his face a pale shade of gray. He wondered if he could handle the required gruesome task.

"I'm fine," Andrew said.

"We're not going to be able to bury the body as I wanted." Traun felt his regret as he looked around at the surrounding rocks. The small shovel he'd brought was useless. He had wanted to give the man a proper burial. Nevin had been a good man, eager to work and willing to put his weight in whatever he needed to do. He knew a man loyal to him was lost that day, and he felt his anger rise at the senseless death, the first loss of life on this new planet of theirs. As Traun studied the surrounding rocks, large and small, he reached a decision.

"Andrew, since it's impossible to bury Nevin in the ground, we'll cover his body with rocks. That way, he won't be left exposed to the elements. Help me move him over to the area left of you, where the ground dips into that shallow hole." Traun nodded in the direction he wanted to lay the body.

In silence, Andrew bent to grasp the dead Transfer's feet. Traun leaned over to grip the body under its armpits.

"Ready?"

Andrew gave a quick nod.

Traun's arm muscles contracted as he and Andrew heaved the limp body up and over into the natural, shallow pit; blood soaked the ground where the Transfer's head had been, and a trail of it followed them. The back of his skull had been crushed from the impact of the rock it hit. His brain had even begun to seep out over the rock.

Traun tore his gaze away from the sight. He heard Andrew take several deep breaths. He knew he fought his urge to vomit. In the end, his brother-in-law couldn't stop his stomach's rebellion. Traun began gathering the smaller rocks around them and placed them over the body. Andrew seemed embarrassed that he'd witnessed his reaction. He felt ill over the gruesome sight, so he understood his response.

Andrew turned, swiping at his mouth with his hand before bending, gathering up rocks, and placing them over the body.

They worked together in a quiet reserve.

"Do you want to try to climb back out of here in the dark or wait till daylight? Traun questioned, studying the placement of the rocks. The corpse was now covered. "The moon is bright enough to make out the path back up."

"Let's get the hell out of here," Andrew responded. It was apparent he didn't relish a night spent with the buried body or the blood-soaked ground around them as he glanced across the area.

"I don't know how to bring this up, Traun, but I need to ask it anyway, and it concerns you and Avreen. Do you two have a history?"

Traun frowned. Andrew watched him as if he wondered how he would react to what he'd said.

"That is none of your business. Your sister knows about her, which is all that needs to concern you."

"You are my High Commander, Traun, and I respect your authority. However, Anna is my sister, and I refuse to see her hurt."

It angered Traun, Andrew's distrust. His reply was sharp, "I love your sister, Andrew. What was between me and Avreen is over. I consider her a friend now, nothing more."

Andrew studied him.

"I'm glad to hear it. I don't think you're going to like what I have to say next, but I am going to express my thoughts on what happened today and that dead man in that makeshift grave over there."

He jabbed a thumb toward the pile of rocks they'd stacked over the body.

"What are you talking about now?"

Andrew turned to look him square in the eye. "I don't think this was an accident. I think it was planned."

"You are accusing me of having something to do with this death?" Traun took a step toward his brother-in-law. He wanted to strike out at him with his fists. Knock some sense into him. He pulled himself up. Anna would never forgive him if her brother returned home beaten black and blue from her Lifemate's own hands.

"No. I didn't say that," Andrew said. He seemed to brace himself for the possible blow of fists.

"What are you saying then?" Traun gritted between clenched teeth.

"What I am trying to say is that something isn't right about this whole incident. Avreen may be your friend or a past lover, but her emotional breakdown seemed false to me. Shit, Traun! She didn't start to cry until you arrived on the scene."

Traun flexed his fingers, and his anger coiled tight. He'd reacted as he did before because of his feelings of guilt over the man's death. He'd not protected one of his people, but for Andrew to accuse Avreen of his death? That didn't make sense either.

Andrew took a step back. "Look, man," he continued even in the face of his obvious desire to strike him, "I was only a step or two in front of her when she screamed. There was nothing in our path that he could have tripped on as he climbed. You and I, all of us, were able to walk that trail without incident. I whirled as soon as I heard her cry out, and Traun, I am telling you, Nevin was holding on to her arm as if she'd pushed him. I saw his face in the split second before he let loose of her, and he had such a confused, surprised look directed at her. Her scream was not because she'd realized he was tripping and had tried to catch him. It was because of her belief he was to pull her over the rock face with him. When I spun around and grabbed her, she was not only scared, she was angry. I know enough of the Garr language to understand cursing when I hear it, and the lady swore a blue streak at him."

Traun's shock rocked through him at Andrew's charge against the woman who'd been his lover.

"Andrew," he rasped out, his jaw clenched so tight it hurt, "I don't care what you think you saw or heard. Avreen is the gentlest-natured person I know. She doesn't have it in her to hurt anyone. It was an accident, plain and simple, nothing sinister."

He and Andrew returned stares. Andrew was the first to break eye contact.

"Maybe I am wrong," he said. He seemed uncertain.

"Hell, you know the woman better than I do. Maybe I saw something that wasn't there. I guess my adrenalin rush caused my judgment to take a twisted and irrational turn."

There was no way Traun could imagine Avreen involved in something so evil. He thought back over their two-year relationship, and he couldn't recall her as anything but charming and gracious toward others. Yes, she'd been upset and confused when they all landed on this planet, but even with that upset after he'd made it plain that their relationship was ended, she'd not shown Anna or him anything but respect. Avreen was a gentle, sweet woman. *She should've never been selected to come to this planet in the first place,* Traun thought, with sadness experienced for her and Nevin.

"You are wrong, Andrew," he said, his conviction strong.

Chapter 22

Clang…Clang…Clang!

Anna, in a quick reaction, rose from inspecting the last of the fall harvest she and the others had gathered. Her eyes met those of Charlee, whose gaze shined with her excitement.

"They're back," Anna shouted to George as he, too, turned toward the sound emitted from the bottom of one of the metal tubs hanging in the trees. Someone pounded on it in the agreed-upon rhythm if an alarm was not sounding but an announcement was being made. The tubs were spaced out around the edges of the village, as Anna ordered them to be; several of them now reverberated with sound announcing the long-awaited arrival of the twelve who had left the settlement over a month and a half ago.

Anna took off and ran toward the backside of the village, where the sounds came from. Charlee and the others were not far behind, as all who worked the garden with her left their harvest baskets where they fell to the ground. Breathless, Anna laughed with Charlee as they both tried to catch air in their lungs when they skidded to a halt. They watched with the rest of the village as the long-awaited group straggled across the same log they'd crossed at their departure. Anna counted the number of heads coming toward them.

"Charlee, I count only nine people crossing that log, and none of them are Traun or my brother."

"Me too," Charlee whispered. "Wait." She grabbed her arm to stab the air with her finger.

"There. There they are."

Andrew, along with Traun, had emerged from the density of the tree line a little further down the creek bank from the others. With a sigh of relief, Anna's breathing eased, but then she realized there were still only eleven individuals. No one else had emerged from the tree line to cross the log over the creek's rushing water. The people around Anna surged down the incline toward the approaching group. She couldn't continue to scan for the missing individual.

****

Traun lifted his gaze toward the top of the incline to take in everyone gathered there. He searched for Anna as the crowd began to rush down toward his returning group. He was the last to step onto the log, starting the walk across it, and he was glad to be back within the settlement. He knew the others with him felt the same way.

All he wanted was Anna, home, and a locked door behind them. Traun smiled when he spotted her in the rushing crowd. Their gazes locked as she found him, too. He stepped down from the log behind Andrew to start toward her. A hand grasped his arm, halting his movement forward.

Avreen stood by his side.

He hadn't realized she was close.

Her eyes shimmered with unshed tears as she gazed upward at him.

"It is so hard to come home without Nevin," she said, her words a mere whisper. She wiped with slender fingers across the top of her cheeks at tears that threatened to overflow but that remained contained. Traun didn't know what to say that he hadn't already said. Patting her hand on his arm, his relief rose at his aunt rushing forward after tackling Andrew with a bear hug.

****

Anna's haste forward slowed as she watched the interaction between the two. She halted completely and didn't advance further when Avreen, with an abrupt move, was within Traun's embrace, and her arms wrapped around his waist as he patted at her back. Anna looked around for Nevin and realized that he was the missing twelfth. His absence was felt in the depths of her spirit as she swallowed back an instant rush of tears.

Something awful had happened, or he'd be with the others. She'd miss him and that smile he always flashed. He had been a champion for her as she'd been for him: he'd been a sweet, charming man.

****

Traun watched his Lifemate. He hoped she understood what was going on. He noticed her facial expression change as she glanced around at the crowd, and he knew the moment she grasped the situation. *My Anna*, he thought. He wanted to rush to her side to comfort her. Molly checked her haste toward him at the sight of Avreen clinging to him. She looked at him with an inquiring expression. When Anna approached, Molly realized that her eyes shimmered with tears, and she frowned.

"What happened?" Anna questioned, her gaze on Avreen still within the circle of his arms.

"There was an accident on the mountain that resulted in Nevin's fall to his death," Traun informed both of them.

"I am truly sorry, Avreen," Anna said.

Molly voiced her dismay.

Avreen didn't reply as she continued to cling with no plan to release her hold of him for all appearances, it seemed.

Anna glanced at him in question, and Traun realized the extent of her insecurity as she watched them. He began to feel irritated at the arms Avreen had clasped so tightly around him. She had been fine while on the trail back home and had seemingly adjusted to Nevin's death. Now, she appeared to be falling apart and unable to stand unless she held onto him. He was uncomfortable with her public and emotional display and realized the others around them had grown silent. They looked on, listening to the conversation between their High Commander and Lady Anna.

"Aunt, please escort Avreen to her hut and make sure she settles in with no problems. Go with my aunt," Traun ordered when it seemed Avreen was about to voice a refusal to leave his side.

Molly reached for her, and her expression reflected her concern. His aunt would know what to do and be able to comfort her. Taking her by the shoulders, Molly pulled her from him. She motioned to two other nearby women, indicating their assistance was needed. She turned as the pair began to walk away, with Avreen being herded forward between them.

"Traun, we are so glad you and the rest of your group have returned home."

Traun gave a tight smile. It was all he could manage. "Aunt, we are glad to be home."

***

Molly overtook the two women who walked on each side of Avreen.

They spoke soothingly to her, letting her know they were there for her in anything she needed. Molly was surprised when Avreen regained control of her emotions once they cleared the surrounding crowd. Her tears abruptly dried up.

"Thank you," Avreen said to her and the other two women. It was obvious she didn't want their company. She lifted her mouth into a heartrending slant, and her gaze reflected her sadness.

"Please, go back to your families. I need time to myself. Please," she said again when Molly and the other two women exclaimed that they would be glad to stay with her.

"Are you sure, honey?" Molly inquired.

Avreen drew further back from them. Her eyes kept downcast.

"Yes, thank you," she said, her tone soft. She returned Molly's hug.

Molly, along with the other two women, voiced their sympathy to each other for her as she walked away.

***

Traun turned toward Anna. His heart pounded in his chest. Everyone around him ceased to exist as he met her gaze.

He couldn't wait to distance himself and his Lifemate from all the others—to leave behind their laughter and joyful chatter. It was a relief to have Avreen's clinging hands from him. Traun felt a shame rise within him, even as he took a determined step forward. Avreen would have a tough time until her hurt and sense of loss lessened. She would now be alone on the planet. This wasn't something he'd wanted any of his people to endure.

"Come on, sweetheart, let's go home."

Anna wrapped her fingers tightly around his.

She seemed to fight for her breath, and Traun wondered if his desire for her smoldered in his gaze when he looked at her. When they reached the doorway of their hut, he ushered her in before him. Turning, he shut the door and locked it. They were secure, away from the all-seeing eyes of the others. He yanked his Lifemate to him.

Their gazes met, separated, and met again.

A jolt of heat sliced through Traun at Anna's final look directed toward him, and he lowered his head to capture her mouth with his; his hands and breath were unsteady when he broke away from the kiss.

He began to loosen her clothing, dropping each removed piece to the floor at their feet. She helped him to shuck his shirt from his shoulders. He turned her toward their bed. The moments and seconds were lost, and the evening moved forward as everything faded to the background except for his and Anna's reunion.

"It is apparent you missed me."

Anna, who now lay sprawled half on top and half off of him as they rested atop their bed, raised her head from where it had been on his chest. She slapped his bare chest with an open palm.

"I missed you? You missed me, mister."

Traun, his contentment deep, couldn't stop his laughter as he reached to pull her upward so that her face was even with his. His amusement ceased when their gazes met.

"I missed you," he said.

Anna smiled down at him, and he placed a hand behind her head to draw her to him for a caress of lips.

"More, please more," she whispered against his mouth.

***

"What happened out there? Did Nevin's accident have something to do with what you were tracking?" Anna studied her Lifemate's profile.

Traun glanced toward her from where they sat beside each other on the floor before their fireplace. The fire within it emitted a warm and inviting heat outward toward them. The hut had taken on a chill after darkness fell, and the temperature sharply dropped outside. Stretching forward, he placed another piece of wood within the fireplace on the fire. Straightening, he leaned back to prop his elbows onto the pillow behind him as he contemplated his bare toes before him.

"No, his accident wasn't connected to what we finally caught up with. We were crossing a treacherous trail on our way home, on the backside of the mountain behind our hut, when somehow, he slipped over the side of the steep ridge we walked on. Andrew and I climbed back down to where he fell and buried him before we continued on home."

Anna couldn't stop the tears that rose in her eyes. Her Lifemate reached to rub his hand up and down her bare arm within her housecoat.

"It happened so fast. I don't think he felt anything, sweetheart."

Anna lay back on the pillow positioned behind her, shifting sideways toward him. She was glad he and her brother had returned safe and sound.

"What was the individual like when you finally caught up to him? I'm assuming it was male?"

In detail, Traun described what they'd witnessed.

Anna couldn't stop her eyes growing wide when he went over the appearance of the beings and the fight between the one they'd tracked and his companion. She'd been lucky not to have been found dead or dragged off with the apparent wild man the day she'd gone out alone.

"What were the loud, clanging noises I heard announcing our arrival earlier?" Traun said when he finished the story.

"That is our alarm system."

"What's wrong with the system we had?"

"It quit working one day." Anna shrugged as if it hadn't worried her, but it had. "None of the men could figure out what happened to it. And the hand-held communication devices went dead after our first real cold night. When George and the men checked their charging units, they found none worked. The men couldn't find anything wrong with them either."

Traun frowned.

"I'll look at everything in the morning. So, what is rigged up that the guards were pounding on?"

Anna knew he thought there should have been enough stored energy in the control base units to last for years. The hand-held communication system was used only by the guards when on duty to communicate with each other, and he'd informed her that the alarm system set up around the settlement only pulled energy when it was activated.

"You know those extra metal bathtubs we had stored?" Anna smiled.

Traun nodded.

"We pulled them from storage to hang them in the trees around the village to use. We tested how their sound carried when pounded on, and you could hear each one from any position in the settlement. Not as loud in some areas, but still heard."

"Since the system works, we'll leave them up. I can't figure out what could have happened to those power-base units. What worries me is that the men on guard now can't radio each other if they see something. It leaves us open to a surprise attack if someone can't get to a tub."

With an abrupt move, he stood. "Come on. Let's go to bed."

He reached to pull her up, so she stood beside him.

"Are you worried about those wild creatures coming here? Do you think they'll try to attack us?" Anna shivered as her fear rippled.

Traun draped an arm across her shoulders as they walked to their bed.

"I think there's a good probability they'll come to investigate what the one saw. As for a formal attack, I'm not sure. I hope not. If they decide to visit us, I don't believe they'll come until spring. I can't imagine they'd travel over that treacherous mountain range with this winter weather moving in."

* * *

Traun pulled Anna tighter against him. She'd snuggled up to him when they'd climbed onto the bed. What he'd been unwilling to voice aloud to her echoed silently within him.

I hope we have until spring before the Neanderthals come to investigate what the one told the others about. It will give me time to plan a defense strategy and allow us men to practice with weapons besides our handheld lasers. I'm worried they will also stop working, just as the security and communication equipment did. I'm afraid that the savages will come with an intent to wage war when they visit us. I'm terrified over it all, Anna.

Shaking off his unvoiced, internal dialogue, Traun turned his attention to the naked leg thrown across his waist, and unable to resist, he slid a palm up that smooth limb.

Chapter 23

"You will go and apologize to Avreen this instant!"

Anna looked up from the table where she worked to gape in astonishment at Traun: his words snapped out at her from where he stood in the open doorway of the storage building that housed their garden's produce. She had been busy within the building all morning, packaging and labeling seeds saved from the summer and fall garden harvest. Angry and upset when she arrived that morning, she had since worked through it. The work before her had had a calming effect on her emotions. She had decided as she'd worked that it was time to inform Traun how Avreen had behaved toward her before he'd left on their journey and then that morning. What she'd spouted to her was unthinkable.

As she'd calmed down, Anna had wondered how her Lifemate could have been attracted to such a bitch. She hated to think like that, but that was what the woman was. She was a hateful, malicious person.

Dressing early that morning, soon after he had left, she'd made the spur-of-the-moment decision to see how Avreen was holding up and if she needed anything. Traun had informed that she'd confessed to him that she cared deeply for Nevin. Avreen's obvious suffering she'd witnessed had tugged at her heart and had made her realize how lucky she was to have Traun safe and home. She had felt wretched for Avreen, who'd fallen in love with Nevin after all, only to lose him to a cruel twist of fate.

She had wanted to express her condolences to her again in private. She'd decided it was time to leave her jealousy over Avreen's and Traun's history behind her. The woman needed a friend, someone to help her through this hard time—or so she'd thought.

She'd knocked on her door that morning and then worried she'd dropped by too early. She had turned away, deciding to come back later. She didn't want to wake her.

The door behind her had swung open, and she'd rotated back around. Avreen stood before her.

She looks beautiful, even with uncombed hair; her thought flashed as she directed a smile at her.

"I am sorry. I didn't realize how early it was until I knocked on your door." Anna's hesitation was experienced when Avreen stared, only giving a deep frown with no reply.

Suddenly, she seemed to emerge from a blankness and gave a glance behind her. She stepped backward to wave her hand toward the interior of her home.

"Please, please, come in," she had said, and her tone was polite.

Anna had stepped through that opened doorway, and with a glance around the inside of the home, she'd thought it had a homey feel. She had suspected the impression of the hut had a lot to do with Nevin's influence. There were several beautiful cut-glass crystal vases on two shelves. Costly by the looks of them. Those, she had guessed, had to be Avreen's.

"Your vases are beautiful," she'd said to try and break the awkward silence between them. Avreen slammed the door shut, and Anna jumped in response.

"Why are you here?" Avreen's words were sharp and abrupt, and all her earlier politeness was absent.

Anna had swallowed back her unease that rose, and she'd wanted to give Avreen the benefit of the doubt that grief over Nevin's death had caused her tone of voice and action.

"I…I wanted to come by and see if you needed anything and tell you how sorry I am about Nevin. He was a good man whom everyone will miss."

Avreen stared at her in silence for a second.

"Be missed by everyone or missed by you?"

"Maybe I had better go," Anna had said. It had been a bad idea for her to try to offer her condolences. The woman didn't like her and wasn't going to hide that fact in the privacy of her home. Avreen stepped in front of her to block her exit.

"Answer the question, Lady Anna," she'd said as she pushed her face close to hers. "What do you know of my Nevin?"

Anna had bit back her wanted angry response of knowing that he'd been an unhappy man.

Instead, she'd replied, "He was my friend and someone I will miss terribly. Now, get out of my way."

She was ready to shove the woman aside if needed.

Avreen had stepped sideways, which had surprised her, and she'd felt relief. Her heartbeat had thundered in her chest.

"Oh, before you go, Lady Anna, let me inform you of something. Traun is mine and always has been. We were lovers on Garr and will be here also. You are a breeder to him, nothing more, and don't you forget it."

Anna hadn't acknowledged the voiced declaration. The woman was vile and didn't need her or anyone else's sympathy.

***

"And what am I supposed to apologize to her for?" Anna shook off her recall of that early morning visit with Avreen. Traun shut the food storage door behind him as he entered the building.

"Don't you act the innocent with me, Anna? I'm ashamed of you and your behavior. Avreen told me of your order to her this morning when you woke her up with your visit to her."

Anna stiffened as hurt and confusion spread. Her Lifemate continued.

"I know you're jealous of her, but what possessed you to go to her home and accuse her of trying to lure me into her bed? And inform her that you never wanted to see her talking to me or crying on my shoulder again. What were you thinking about saying such a thing to her?"

"So, she walked up to you and told you that I did that, and you believe her, no questions asked?" Anna's lips felt so stiff that she had to focus on shaping them for her words. She was shocked that he'd taken what Avreen had told him at face value without asking for her side of the story.

"No, Anna, she didn't come to me. She didn't want to tell me anything. I checked on her as she hadn't been seen today. When she answered her door and saw me standing there, she burst into tears. She told me how sorry she was for what had occurred between you and her. When she realized my confusion, she didn't want to confess to me what you'd done, but eventually, I got her to tell me what had happened. She begged me not to be angry with you. It was all her fault, she said. She knew she'd clung to me yesterday in her sorrow, and obviously, it made you jealous of her. She expressed her torment that you feel threatened by her. You will go with me now and apologize to her for your actions. I demand it."

Anna slammed the empty pan she held in her hand down onto the wooden counter before her. Her anger surged at Avreen for her lies and Traun for believing them. Her entire body shuddered with her rage.

"I will not apologize to that woman! She is the one who said hateful things. She told me you were hers and always had been."

Traun walked swiftly to where she sat.

"Don't try to turn this around and blame it on Avreen. Did you or did you not go to her home this morning?"

"I did, but—"

"Stop it," he said, and his teeth were gritted together with his anger.

"You will apologize to her. Don't make this worse by denying what you did. Now let's go." He grabbed her elbow as if he planned to force her into movement.

Anna jerked it from his hand to grasp the edge of the table.

"Avreen is a liar, and even if you drag me to her doorstep, I will not apologize for something I didn't do!"

Her Lifemate studied her, his gaze intense and dark. Their breathing within the storage hut sounded harsh. It seemed he realized she meant what she said, and Anna knew he wouldn't want a public squabble between them to be witnessed by the others in the village.

"All right, Anna, have it your way. However, I'm telling you now that you will bear the repercussions if you disobey me. I better not catch you anywhere near her again. She has enough hurt to deal with without a jealous shrew who accuses her of wanting a relationship that she put behind her when I told her I loved you, not her."

Anna turned her back to him.

He didn't move. "I'm mystified over your actions, Lifemate. I know you're jealous of her. You've made it plain to me several times. But for you to be cruel to her during this time? I don't understand it. I wouldn't tolerate the behavior from any of the others, and I definitely won't from you, as you command the people through me."

Anna refused to look his way, her back rigid as she remained silent.

"It is time for you to grow up, Anna. I know you're a generous and loving individual."

At her continued silence, he left the storage building. Anna laid her arms on the table before her and dropped her head onto them. Unable to stop her tears, she wept at his accusation. *Why would he believe her over me? Unless deep down he loves her,* her thought flashed. She rose from the table to wipe her face. A determination had risen. She locked the door to the storage building and left it to set off at a fast clip for the House of Reflection. She avoided going past Avreen's hut, taking the long route around the settlement to her end goal.

***

Traun watched Anna from a distance and wondered at her actions. He continued watching her as she turned to take the rocky sloped steps up to the House of Reflection he had ordered to be built.

She's decided to go up there and think about what she's done, he thought, and he smiled with relief. *She plans to ask for forgiveness. She let her jealousy gain control of her instead of her controlling it, and she's realized it.* It had shocked him to realize her actions toward Avreen.

***

"Father—do I call you Father?" Anna looked inquiringly at the holy man she sat before. She recalled Molly always referred to him as Keeper. She hadn't been up to the House of Reflection for some weeks now, although Molly came faithfully, if not every day, at least every other day.

The holy man smiled, and his expression carried kindness to it.

"I am called Keeper."

He reached out a gnarled hand to lay it on her knee. "What troubles you, child?"

Anna's eyes welled up at the soft question. She was sure he'd noted their redness and puffiness from her earlier bout of weeping.

"Keeper, I want a divorce. I didn't know whom else to go to besides you, and since you're the one who married my Lifemate and me, I thought you were the one to help me get one declared."

The Keeper looked at her, his confusion evident. "What is this divorce you speak of, child? I have not heard this word before."

"A divorce is when a married man and woman legally separate and go their own way."

"No, child," he exclaimed. He drew back from her with obvious alarm.

"But I can't stay with my husband. My Lifemate," Anna corrected, knowing husband was also a foreign word to the man before her.

The Keeper waved his gnarled hands before him, his eyes wide. "No. No. Don't speak so, child."

Anna's tears flowed. She couldn't stop them. The holy man was going to be of no help to her. He dropped his hands down onto his lap, and, in silence, he watched her. He reached forth with one of those contorted hands again to pat at her knee with it.

"Does our High Commander beat you, child?" His tone of voice held his disbelief.

Anna, shocked by his question, spurted, "No! He doesn't beat me." If she declared physical violence, her accusation would have to go before the newly elected eight High Council members, two of which included her brother and George. If deemed guilty, he would face public flogging, lose his position, and be forbidden from seeking another Lifemate. The charge would be a disgrace to him and her whole family. He would lose all respect within the community. She didn't want revenge or to lie against him; she just wished not to be his Lifemate. The Keeper leaned forward toward her again.

"Why do you request this separation from our High Commander? He seems a kind man. An honorable man. He understood the need for a House of Reflection for our people to gather within."

Anna, remaining silent, tried to gain control of her emotions. She couldn't confess what he believed of her or expose his past relationship with Avreen. What if the Keeper didn't believe her version of the events of the day? He was from Garr, just like her Lifemate, just like Avreen.

"I'm very miserable with my life now, Keeper. I can't accept what he accused me of doing."

"Child, this trial you face will pass. Go home. Weigh up this request you've placed before me and what it will do to your family, our community, and our High Commander if we proceed."

Anna realized how foolish it had been to think she could obtain a divorce decree. She wasn't on Earth. She was tied to the ruler of this world, and he commanded the man before her.

"Please don't mention my appeal to anyone." She feared how Traun would react should he find out about her request. It seemed the Keeper took no offense by her plea as he inclined his head toward her.

"I will beseech the Creator during my meditations to him to look down with compassion on you and your troubles," he said as he stood.

***

Anna avoided everyone within the settlement, even her family, and went home to huddle in the large chair before the fireplace. The day had been crisp and cold. *Fitting*, she thought.

The sun had dipped, and night was approaching, she realized, glancing toward the window. The door to the hut opened. Anna turned with a glance given over her shoulder. She didn't speak as Traun entered the hut to close its door behind him with a soft click of its latch. She dropped her gaze from his to turn back to face the fireplace and the fire built within it. She sensed his attention was still focused on her as she swiped at her wet cheeks. She hoped he didn't try to talk to her. She would not, *no, she could not* forgive him for the accusations he had made toward her that day.

A knock on the door sounded. Anna didn't move from her position, with her knees pulled under her chin, arms locked around her legs, and bare feet up on the chair.

She heard Traun sigh. He reopened the entryway.

Klinn's cheerful voice filled the room. "I have your meals for you and my Lady Anna."

He must have motioned for the servant to put the plates on the bench where she always placed them because she walked forward to set the food-laden dishes down. With a single glance given toward her, she left.

Unfolding her legs, Anna stepped forward to pick up the smallest plate and then returned to the chair she'd claimed. She wasn't hungry but hadn't eaten much the entire day. At her scheduled medical checkup the day before, the Learned One had advised her to take care of herself. The baby was growing fine, she'd reassured her, though she thought she needed to eat more. Anna took a bite of food from the plate she held. It was like eating sawdust. She narrowed her gaze to jab her fork into another piece of the food. *I'll make sure to take care of this baby, even if its daddy is a jerk*, she thought with fresh anger rising.

Traun settled on the bench across from her. He began to eat. He glanced her way a couple of times as she remained silent.

"I saw you go to the House of Reflection today."

Anna jerked her gaze up. "So?"

He paused in his eating. His eyebrows rose. Anna could tell she'd angered him. "I thought you might want to talk about your visit," he said.

"Why?" she snapped. Her heartbeat picked up speed. Had the Keeper gone to him after all? Had he spilled the beans on her request to him?

Traun shrugged. "It was just a thought, Anna."

An oppressive silence fell between them. It continued to stretch as they each prepared for bed after their meals. Anna crawled under the bed covers to hug against the edge of the bed, her back given to him. Traun lay beside her momentarily before he rotated to his side, his back to her.

***

Fourteen days and nothing has changed between us. Silence. She goes about her daily chores, unwilling to speak or look at me. Even her friend studiously avoids me. Across the way from where he worked, Traun watched his Lifemate. She drifted back up to their hut after visiting with Charlee that evening. He laid the equipment part he held down on the bench before him as he watched Anna enter their home.

He was still dismayed by her actions toward Avreen. As his Lifemate, she had to realize the power she had over the people he commanded. Avreen had been shaken by the thought of her disapproval and, as such, his own. Traun slapped his hand down onto the work table before him with the decision made.

Enough of this silence. We will talk this thing through and move on with our lives.

***

Anna turned when the door opened to her home, which she'd just entered. She stiffened as Traun stepped into the hut; a determination was stamped on his face.

"It is time for us to talk this thing out between us," he said. He closed the door behind him.

"There is nothing to talk about. You believe Avreen. End of

conversation."

He stepped toward her. "Then you tell me what happened that morning between you two."

Anna gave no care if anyone outside of their home heard her. Her anger soared. "Tell you now?"

"Lower your voice," he ordered.

"I wish I had never agreed to come to this planet. And I wish I never laid eyes on you. I hate you with all that I am." Anna's body shook all over. She hurt at Traun's desire only now, after all this time, to want to hear her side of the story of what Avreen had told him. She could tell her hateful words shocked him.

"So you wish you weren't here with me. Well, you had no choice in the matter, little lady."

"I did, too. I agreed to be here only if my friend Charlee was allowed to come with me."

Traun's lips curled to display his scorn.

"No. You're wrong, Anna. A serum would have been given to you if needed. You would be here. Gagged, bound, and dragged if it came to it. You had no choice in the matter. You were mine even before your conception."

Anna shook her head in denial.

"Go ask my aunt and uncle if you don't believe me." His tone was sarcastic.

"I hate you. I really do." Anna knew she lied, yet she continued, "You're nothing but an alien beast to me. You have what you want. I'm pregnant. Your job is done. Go back to your lover. You deserve each other. You and she are both contemptible."

Traun spun on his heel, leaving. Anna knew Molly joked about her being born for him, but to not have had a choice in coming here? She didn't believe it.

When Molly opened her door at the knock on its entryway, Anna knew in an instant that she realized she and George were going to be questioned about something that they wouldn't want to answer.

"Come in out of the cold, Anna," Molly said as she tucked a strand of her short black hair behind an ear.

"George, give Anna something warm to drink," she said.

George tipped the container he held to pour some of the milk he'd been heating into a cup; he handed it to Anna as she sat in one of the chairs at their compact table. Holding the warm mug between her chilled fingers, she looked down into its white liquid. No word was said to either of the people who had raised her. Anna sensed George glance at Molly with his unvoiced question about what was wrong. In turn, Molly shrugged her shoulder back at him before pulling out a chair to sit beside her.

Anna raised her gaze.

"Did I have a say in being here?"

Molly and George's eyes met.

When they both failed to respond, she said, "I can see that I didn't. Was I drugged?"

Unwilling to believe that the intense emotion felt for her Lifemate could be drug-induced and not a natural love for him as she thought, Anna leaned forward to beg the two before her, "Please, tell me that whatever drug you gave me to get me here is not still being given to me?"

Molly reached to lay a hand on top of hers.

"Darling, I admit we did slip you a mind-altering serum after you returned from Charlee's home, the night after you learned who you and your brother were. But I stopped giving it to you the evening before we boarded the spaceship. I've not given you anything else. I promise darling, every emotion and every thought you've had since our leaving Earth has not been influenced by any drug."

Anna felt numb.

She didn't feel anger at Molly or even at George. She understood they had had no other recourse. Her destiny was predetermined; there had been no turning back for any one of them. She and her family sat silently at the table, drinking warm milk. None of them had anything to say to each other as they wondered at the hurt their actions had caused others. Anna knew her earlier hateful words had stung Traun. She also knew without a shadow of a doubt that he loved her and had even been attempting to bridge the ever-widening gap in their relationship. However, she couldn't seem to forgive him for believing Avreen's lies.

She stood abruptly. Looking down at the astonished expressions of the two beside her, she bent down to hug her foster parents.

"I love you both," she said. "And I've decided to repair my relationship with my Lifemate."

Anna watched Molly and George's surprised expressions change to wide grins.

Chapter 24

Anna waited long into the night for Traun's return to their home; finally giving up, she dressed for bed. She was tired, and she was scared he'd taken her words to heart and was, even now, as she waited, enjoying the embraces of Avreen. *No*, she told herself as she lay awake and watched the door. Traun wouldn't do that to her or Nevin. *Or would he?* Anna slung back the bedcovers that covered her, too agitated to sleep.

I could get dressed and go hunt for him, she thought.

She poked at the coals in the fireplace with the tool she'd picked up.

***

Traun sat across a tabletop space from Anna's brother in the Communal Hall. Upon returning from his round of duty, Andrew found him alone there, drinking in the dark. Traun wasn't drunk, but he wasn't sober either, and he soon found himself confiding in Anna's brother all that had transpired between him and Anna the past few days. Her brother listened to him as he sipped at the strong-tasting liquor offered to him. Traun knew the drink took the chill of the night off him.

"I don't know how to repair the damage I've done. I made a grave error in judgment by not asking her side of Avreen's story before I jumped on her." Traun fell silent. He felt he'd told Anna's brother things that should have been kept to himself.

"What you've said Avreen accused my sister of doing doesn't sound like the Anna I grew up with," Andrew said in the sudden quiet. "And you know my feelings on Avreen. I think she is very capable of lying."

Traun looked down at the tumbler he held in his hand. *Am I blind to her?* he wondered, feeling baffled. Avreen had always been charming, seeking to please. *Maybe it's just me she strives to please.* Traun frowned. He now questioned what he thought he knew of the woman. Glancing across the table toward Andrew, he realized Anna's brother had sat with him all night after his security shift and had let him ramble on.

"You better go home and get some rest, Andrew. I plan to work on our alarm control units again now that the sun's coming up. There seems to be nothing wrong with them, although I can't get either to power up."

Andrew yawned as he rose. "Let me catch a few hours of sleep, and then I'll come and help you with them."

***

Anna caught glimpses of Traun throughout the long day the next morning as she completed her daytime duties. She wanted to go to him but was hesitant to interrupt his work on the security units he worried over. Having torn apart the two units, he and her brother were now beginning to reassemble them. Traun looked up to catch her gaze on him. Anna locked her eyes with his for a moment before turning to head for their hut. Klinn would be there in a few minutes to gather their laundry. She needed to get it ready for her. She also needed to ask Klinn if her Lifemate had finished the large bathtub he was constructing for the High Commander. He had a soldering tool to fuse the two tubs he'd cut in half back together into one long one. Picking up the basket beside the bed containing her and Traun's dirty laundry, Anna dumped its contents to the floor. There wasn't much that needed to be washed.

"So, you do have to do something after all. Can't get the servants to sort your laundry for you?"

Anna whirled at the sneered question.

"What are you doing in my home?" she asked in stunned surprise.

Avreen strutted further on into the space as she looked around at it.

"Thought I'd drop by and see how you took it that Traun believed the story I told him. You realize now, don't you, that he trusts whatever I say."

It seemed Avreen was confident in herself and her approach to intimidating her. The woman's bold behavior left Anna dumbfounded.

"Get out of here," she ordered, and her anger made her tremble.

***

"High Commander!"

Traun looked up at the call and frowned as he watched the house servant assigned to his Lifemate run at breakneck speed toward him. He glanced toward Andrew, who'd also stopped his work to watch the woman.

"Lady Anna. Your hut," the red-faced servant gasped when she stopped before him. "She needs your help."

Traun felt his heart skip a beat. Anna was losing the baby. He dropped what he held in his hands to take off at a run. Andrew and the servant followed him.

Reaching the front door of his hut, Traun slid to a confused stop. He could see Anna through the gaped doorway to where she stood in the middle of their home, and she was speaking to someone he couldn't see. He frowned when he heard the distinct sound of Avreen's voice replying to her. He pushed the door wider open; Anna and Avreen were so engrossed in each other that they failed to notice they now had an audience. Avreen leaned in close to his Lifemate, her face inches from hers.

"Traun and I were lovers for two years before coming here. We still are. You are a breeder for our race. Something he has to force himself to mate with. I don't have to tell you where he was last night."

Traun watched Anna with alarm, afraid she was about to pass out as she swayed on her feet. Rushing through the open doorway to grab hold of her, he urged her to sit in the chair before their fireplace. He looked up.

"Get out," he ordered. The sight of his longtime lover and her spewed lies sickened him. He couldn't believe he'd lain with the viper that stood before him. When Avreen didn't move, Traun motioned toward Andrew and ordered, "Take this woman from here. Move her and all her belongings, this very day, to the hut furthest away from mine on the opposite end of the village."

He turned back to where Avreen stood. She stared at him, unmoving. It was as if she'd frozen up with fright. He didn't care. She should be scared. "You are forbidden access to this half of our village. If you ever again set foot on this side, you will be punished, and it'll be swift and severe. Do you understand?" Traun watched until she nodded her head in slow motion. Andrew grabbed her elbow to guide her from the hut and out of sight as he shut the door behind them. Traun knelt in front of the chair before Anna. She didn't look up at him.

"Anna."

He reached to her clasped hands on her lap.

"What she said was a lie. I stayed in the Communal Hall last night, and

I was there because I dreaded coming home to another night of tension-filled silence between us. Your brother found me there alone, nursing a bruised heart after he'd finished his duties and was heading for home. He stayed with me till early this morning. Please ask him. Please."

Anna turned her hands to grasp his fingers tightly with hers.

Traun breathed a sigh of relief.

"I am sorry, Anna, for believing what she told me without first hearing your side of what happened that morning."

She raised her arms to encircle his neck. No tears flowed. Clasping her around the waist, Traun stood to hold her tight in his arms, and turning, he sat down in the chair he'd removed her from to settle her onto his lap.

"I love you, Anna," he said as she studied him.

"Why would she lie to you and then come here to taunt me?" His Lifemate's bewilderment was apparent.

"I don't know," he whispered.

She continued. "I'm unable to grasp such malice. I knew she didn't like me from how she acted toward me when no one was around, but I didn't realize the extent."

Gazing at Anna, Traun was confused by what she said. "How has she acted toward you when no one else has been around?"

Anna shrugged. "Hateful. I smiled at her the day of our wedding as she stared at me. She turned her back on me. When I've ever crossed paths with her and alone, she always sneered at me, no respect shown. One time, she complimented the color of my hair and then smirked and said how the men of Garr found the color distasteful."

Traun reached up to stroke her hair. "I love the color of your hair."

"After I saw you two that night behind her hut, I thought she acted that way because of your relationship with her. Charlee told me that if she were getting any action from you, she wouldn't behave as she did. She would be smiling at me instead of being jealous."

Jerking slightly upon hearing what Charlee had said, Traun looked at Anna in surprise. "What made your friend think that?"

Anna smiled as if embarrassed. "I guess I've told her how wonderful you are in bed."

Traun felt the heat rise up his neck. "Anna. What are you doing talking about something as personal as that?"

Anna shrugged. "We tell each other everything. Charlee won't repeat anything I tell her. Same as I don't repeat what she tells me."

Traun shook his head. He didn't like the thought of her friend having such intimate knowledge of their relationship. "If Avreen's always acted hateful toward you, why did you go to her home that morning?"

"I thought with the grief she'd shown over Nevin's death that she would need consoling. I felt sorry for her. You said she had fallen in love with Nevin, and I thought if I extended my hand in friendship, she would too. She was rude that morning and told me you were hers and would always be hers. For a moment, her manner toward me actually scared me."

Traun hugged Anna. "I have never been Avreen's. You are the person I belong to. Before she and I began our relationship, she knew I was coming here to marry another. I have never seen the side of her you described until today."

A knock sounded on their door, and Anna sighed. She started to rise from his lap.

"Where do you think you're going?" Traun pulled her back to his lap.

"You know it's the servants, Traun. Do you want them to see us sitting like this?" Anna looked at him, her expression one of confusion.

"I haven't held you in over fourteen days. So, in this instance, I'll keep you right here. And if anyone dares to spread rumors of what they see, I am sure your loyal servant Klinn will set them on the straight and narrow."

"Come in," he barked out. Traun grinned at her. She was the love of his life and where she belonged.

The door opened, and Klinn stepped inside the hut. Her eyes twinkled when she saw her Lady Anna on his lap. She turned to frown at her Lifemate and the other male servant behind him.

"Bring in that tub and hurry about it. Now go fetch that hot water." Both men jumped to do as commanded. Their smiles were broad when they walked back out the door and glanced at each other after quick peeps toward Traun and Anna in his lap. Klinn, in quick succession, had food brought in, the bath filled, and the room cleared of all afterward. Anna seemed embarrassed as the servants worked. Traun could tell Klinn felt proud of herself. Through her help, Lady Anna was back where she belonged.

He chuckled as the door behind the servant Klinn shut with its final click. "Your face is red, sweetheart."

Anna looked at him with a frown.

"It's your fault," she said, slapping him playfully on the shoulder.

"You're the one who's made me so sensitive in how we act before the people under you. I hope they don't tell the others in the village about me being in your lap."

Traun grabbed her hand to draw it toward his mouth.

"Are you hungry?" he asked once he kissed the palm of it. "Our dinner and our bath are both getting cold."

Anna slid from his lap.

"I'm starving," she said. She moved to hand him his plate and then turned to sit on the rug before the fireplace. Bending her knees, she crossed her legs at her ankles and dug into her meal. Traun smiled as he watched her. It was good again between them. With her meal finished, she stood to lay her plate aside. He took his last bite of food still on his plate and then turned to set it aside. Anna walked to the basin of water they used at night and glanced his way before pulling her hair upward and off her neck to secure it with a hairclip at the back of her head. She brushed her teeth. With another glance and smile directed his way, she began to strip her clothes as she walked to the tub. It was the large tub that Klinn's Lifemate had constructed for him at his order.

With his mouth going dry as each article of clothing was thrown aside, Traun watched her. She was now nude. She stepped into the steaming bathwater. He stood to brush his teeth in several quick moves.

"I love you," Anna told him much later. "I am sorry for the hateful things I said to you."

Almost asleep, Traun rotated to his side from his back on their bed so he faced her. He reached out toward her with tender emotion rising as he pulled her once again into his arms. This was the generous, loving Anna he knew and treasured. He slid his palm across her bare back. He loved the feel of her skin. It excited him.

"I want you all over again," he said—his voice husky.

Chapter 25

Anna laughed at Charlee's antics, content with life. She shut the door to her home behind her friend as they both entered the small enclosure. At her five-month checkup early that morning, the Learned One had informed her and Traun that they were to have a baby girl. Anna had been convinced her Lifemate wanted a boy, but he seemed to not mind the news. He spoke with excitement as they'd left the Learned One's office of all he planned to do for this child of theirs.

She had told him that if he was bent on indulging the child so much, the girl would grow up to be a rotten brat, and no one would be able to stand to be around her. He had smiled that slow, drop-dead gorgeous smile at her, causing her pulse to quicken before he'd walked away to resume his duties.

"Charlee, stop," Anna begged, holding up her hand. "You're making my side hurt. I can't quit laughing at you."

Charlee halted her impression of the hateful rooster stalking her once again that afternoon. It had become a family joke of the seemingly mutual hostility between her and the bird. The animal did appear to make a beeline for her when he escaped his pen, which he seemed to be able to do regularly, according to Anna. She had begged Traun for permission to have the thing for a meal after one particularly trying day of the rooster getting loose and giving her chase, not once, but three times that day, before his escape route was finally figured out.

Charlee plopped down on the bed, and her laughter subsided. "Andrew says the rooster makes you a target because you're scared of it and try to run from it."

"Well, if I didn't run, the thing would flog me to death," Anna huffed. She sat beside her friend.

"Have you talked to Molly this afternoon?" Charlee asked with a sudden change of subject.

"No. I haven't seen her. Why?"

"She wants us all, as a family, to get together one last time around the campfire before it gets too cold to eat outside."

"Tonight?"

"Yes, tonight. She said to make sure I told you if she didn't see you first. It looks like another snow-front is coming in, and she's afraid once winter fully sets in, she and George won't be able to get out as much."

"Oh…." Anna couldn't stop her disappointment from showing.

Charlee frowned at her. "Don't be so enthusiastic about it. I'm not supposed to say anything, but she wanted to celebrate your twenty-first birthday."

"That's just it, Charlee. Traun said he had something planned tonight for the two of us."

"You can't disappoint Molly."

Anna nodded. "I know."

***

"Happy birthday, girlie," George said as he settled beside Anna on the tree trunk before the campfire, which radiated outward heat. The family meal was over, and her presents had been received and opened.

Anna smiled at him. She had been thinking of her pregnancy as the others around the fire talked and laughed.

"Thank you, George. Did you see what Klinn gave me? Aren't they adorable?" Anna lifted the white knitted booties she held.

George took one, and his hand dwarfed it. "I can't envision such a tiny foot fitting into this."

Anna watched Traun over the campfire flames as he conversed with her brother. Andrew glanced her way to flash her a wink. He nodded before Traun rose from where he'd been sitting beside him. Traun spoke to him again before he turned away. Anna wondered what the low conversation was about. *Traun must be going to check on the guards*, she decided as he strolled away. No glance was given in her direction. He had probably instructed her brother on something he'd need to know before his turn of duty. Her Lifemate worried over every small detail. Anna turned back toward George.

Andrew stood, yawning after several minutes of conversation had passed. "Come on, Charlee, it's getting late. I'm ready to go home."

His action prompted the others to prepare to leave as well. As everyone said their goodnights, Anna thanked them for their thoughtful gifts. She turned to head for home. Humming a favorite piece of music under her breath, she opened the door to her hut.

"Close the door and lock it," Traun demanded from where he stood before the blazing fireplace. As her surprise coursed, Anna hurriedly stepped inside the hut to shut and lock its door.

She began to giggle.

"Don't you dare laugh at me? I am trying to be romantic here," her Lifemate said, his tone rough. He seemed embarrassed. Anna couldn't help it. Her laughter pealed out from her. He was barefoot, wearing only his snug-fitting uniform pants, and scattered across the rug where he stood were pink petals from the flowers she'd carefully collected, dried, and filled a bowl with for decoration. He must have used the entire bowl, as more of the petals had been thrown over the top of their bedcovers. Music played softly in the background from her stereo. Anna lowered the birthday gifts she held to the table beside the door.

If he weren't so masculine, maybe he wouldn't look so ridiculous, she thought. She noted a pink flower petal across one of his big toes, and her laughter sputtered again. She couldn't help it.

"Come here," he ordered. Anna walked over to where he stood and smothered her wish to tease him.

"Here," he said. He held a fist out to her, and when she stretched her palm toward him, he dropped what he held onto it. She stared down at the ring she now had. Its inset stone sparkled even within the dim light cast by the fireplace. She looked back up.

"Where did this come from? It is gorgeous."

Traun took the ring from her and slid it onto her finger.

"It was my mother's. She gave it to me before I left Garr with instructions to give it to my Lifemate at the birth of our first child. I couldn't wait, though. And I don't think I can match this gift for the births of the rest of the children we will have. I believe she would understand my giving it to you early."

Anna's eyes teared.

"I wish I could have met your family, Traun. They must be wonderful people from listening to you talk about them."

He continued. "It was given to my mother by my father at my birth. She felt it was right for you to have it."

He pulled her into his embrace. "Happy birthday, sweetheart."

Anna smiled up at him, wrapping her arms around his bare waist. "I desire you for my birthday."

"That's what I hoped for when I planned this whole flower thing." He motioned to the petals around the room and then began to sway with her to the softly playing background music rhythm.

Anna realized it was an old Rolling Stones song, 'Beast of Burden.' They quietly moved together as Mick Jagger belted out the words, *I'll never be your beast of burden, my back is broad, but it's a hurting. All I want is for you to make love to me.*

Looking up at her Lifemate, Anna hoped he didn't think he was her beast of burden. She remembered the words she had said to him during their fight over what Avreen had led him to believe.

***

Traun squeezed his Lifemate's waist span with his fingers as he listened to the lyrics of the song playing. *Music on the radio, come on, baby, make sweet love to me.* He hadn't realized what was on the compact disc he'd placed in her stereo. Not long ago, he had felt she had every right to call him an alien beast. Someone she wished she'd never met. She had eventually confessed to him that she had asked the Keeper to be separated from him. He guessed she'd thought, at the time, it had been her only option.

Come on, baby, please...please...please.

Taking her hand, Traun led her to their bed. The song playing on the stereo changed to another as she gazed up at him.

"I love you, Traun. You may be my alien beast, but never a beast of burden to me."

Gazing down at her, Traun didn't reply. He couldn't imagine ever tiring of this half-Earthling that he seemed to crave.

Chapter 26

Avreen brooded in her hut. She was a nobody in this village. She was invisible. She felt a hatred deep inside her bowels for Traun's Lifemate, and it was a living, breathing thing that gnawed at her gut. She twisted her fingers together as she moved them back and forth, unaware of the nervous action. The Lady Anna consumed her every thought. Even in her night terrors, the half-Earthling appeared. She had taken to watching her during her comings and goings throughout the days, though careful not to cross the village boundaries set by Traun. She had listened that day to the women who lived near her talk about how happy the couple were with each other. Never had they seen such contentment between two Lifemates, they exclaimed as they sighed and ignored her from where she sat beside them. When she abruptly stood to walk away from their conversation, they took no notice of her departure. Avreen was puzzled how her plans for her and Traun had gone awry so fast. If only she'd not given in to that urge to push his Lifemate over the edge that day, to taunt her with her knowledge that he'd stayed away all night from their home. She'd over-played her hand. With Nevin no longer around to watch and scold her on her expressed hatred for the woman, which she realized now, in hindsight, had held her behavior in check, she'd grown too confident.

That servant must've brought Traun to the hut. She even had the nerve to smirk when I was led away. Fresh anger at the woman rose again.

As Traun had ordered, Lady Anna's brother had gathered several men in the village that day to help relocate her. The couple whose hut he selected to move her into had expressed their delight to be reestablished closer to their High Commander and the half-Earthling. Everyone in the settlement realized she'd drawn the disfavor of their High Commander, and they turned away from her.

Avreen stared across the inside space of her home. *If only I'd waited one day longer or a few minutes more. That stupid servant might not have caught me and summoned Traun. And that half-Earthling might be out of his life as planned and him coming to me for comfort. I would now be the one everyone would have to bow to or meet with his disfavor.* Avreen looked down at her fingers, which she'd twisted together. Frowning, she parted her hands. She drew her lips back tight over her teeth, her gaze narrow.

***

Anna studied the handwritten communication held. A servant had appeared at her door to inform her that he'd been instructed to give her the sealed missive. Traun's note was short and to the point. She was to meet him in the food storage building. Anna laid the small slip of paper aside. He probably had something he wanted to ask her about with the storage of their food supply. He worried over it. She had been in the storage hut the day before, and everything was fine. The cold weather and blanket of snow covering the ground would not affect how the food needed to be stored. All of it was protected from the drop in temperature.

Dragging on her snow boots and heavy coat, Anna headed toward the storage hut. Snowflakes fell, wetting her coat hood; she pulled it up over her head. Arriving at the building, Anna pushed the door of the storage hut open. The door was unlocked, and the lock was gone, but no light was on.

"Traun," she called out.

There appeared to be a burnt spot on the door. She rubbed her finger over it and frowned; Traun didn't answer. Stepping up into the room, Anna reached out, prepared to turn on the overhead solar-powered light fixture in the darkened space.

"Leave that light off. Stay quiet and turn around." The command came from behind her within the depth of the room. Spinning toward the recognized voice, Anna couldn't stop her eyes from widening.

"Don't make a sound, or I'll cut you in half."

She froze. "What are you doing?" she managed to whisper.

Avreen's lips pulled back into a sneer.

"You and I are going for a walk," she said. She waved the laser weapon she held in her hand. "Now. Turn."

Anna turned. *Where's Traun?* Her panic heightened at the thought of his safety. What had Avreen done? Was he lying somewhere in the darkened space, dead?

Avreen stepped up close behind her to poke the weapon she held into her back to force her to move forward and out the storage building door. She kept at it, pushing her toward a stand of trees that Anna knew a guard was posted by day and night. Avreen must be unaware of it. Relief surged. Soon, the weapon would be handed over to the guard.

"Go, hurry," Avreen said from behind her, speeding her to a trot.

Anna couldn't stop her gasp when they entered the tree grove, and she realized the guard's body sprawled out on the snow-covered ground. Her running steps faltered as she halted.

"You killed him?"

"Oh, don't worry. I didn't kill him," Avreen said from behind her. "I'll wake him on my return. He's going to believe he fell asleep while on duty. Shame…shame."

Anna could tell she smiled by the reflection of it in her voice.

"Did you kill Traun?" Anna needed to know her answer. Avreen laughed. "No! Stupid. Traun is my lover. I only kill those who get in our way."

Anna sucked her breath in and whirled to face her adversary. "You won't get away with this."

"Go," Avreen commanded. A harsh look settled over her features. She brandished the weapon she held.

"Turn around and walk, stupid." She gave Anna a hard shove when she didn't move.

Sweet Jesus in heaven, please save me from this evil woman, Anna prayed. After what seemed an eternity, she was ordered to halt.

"Turn around, stupid."

Anna rotated to face the woman whose hatred reached out in a suffocating wave of energy. Avreen gave a queer laugh when their gazes met, and she jeered, "Yeah, you should be afraid. I'm going to kill you right here."

She waved the weapon she held to indicate a spot behind Anna. "I prepared a burial hole just for you. Which, I'm more than confident, will keep your body hidden and no one the wiser as to what happened to you, their precious Lady Anna."

Avreen gave that strange gurgle of laughter again. "I'll be back, snug in my new hut before anyone realizes you're missing. When you're invisible like I am, no one pays attention to your movements," she taunted.

As Anna studied the woman before her, she feared her knees would buckle beneath her.

"You are not the first person I've had to kill to be with Traun," Avreen continued.

Anna stared in horror at the woman. Avreen was obsessed with Traun to the point of insanity.

"Left you speechless, have I?" Avreen found the thought funny, and her strange laughter spilled forth again. It abruptly stopped.

"Each time gets easier," she said with a faraway look rising within her gaze. "The first time was the hardest. I will admit to it. I took to my bed for a week afterward."

With a shake of her head, she focused back on Anna.

"The stupid girl refused to tell the High Council members she had decided not to come to this planet as I instructed her to do."

Avreen shrugged. "I tricked her into swallowing poison, and thus, she took her own life. I had her write a suicide note to her parents before she died. I thought it was a touching gesture on my part. Don't you agree?" She looked at Anna.

In confusion, Anna wondered if the woman expected her to answer.

Avreen shook her head again. It was as if she was clearing it of cobwebs. "Then Nevin got in my way."

Anna's gasp came out, even though she tried to restrain it.

Avreen's eyes narrowed as she focused on her again. "Oh yes, you and my Lifemate. He always looked out for you."

Her words sounded almost tender, as if she and Anna were close friends. She frowned. "He knew I hated you. Yet he always defended you.

"I thought if he weren't around, my beloved would look my way again." She scowled at Anna. "But you stole Traun from me. I have to get rid of you. I worked for a year on Garr to capture my beloved's attention, and I kept it for two years before he came here and before *you* became his Lifemate."

The web that clouded Avreen's mind was unmistakable. She stared at Anna as if suddenly bewildered that she was standing before her.

"Lady Anna?"

The dark evil of insanity that cocooned Avreen began to recede. Anna saw Avreen recognize it, and the weapon she pointed toward her lowered.

"He never loved me. With everything I put into our relationship, he never came to love me." Her voice held a whisper of sorrow and tears.

"Avreen," Anna said, her voice soft. "Hand me the weapon. We will forget this ever happened. Let's get you help."

"Shut your mouth!" Avreen raised the weapon again, and the evil within her, Anna thought, actually hissed. It twisted Avreen's facial expression, pulling her back into its darkness. Anna grasped her mistake and, snapping her eyes shut, a sick feeling rose. She was unable to watch the button on the weapon being squeezed, ending her life; a whoosh sound sliced through the air beside her head. Avreen grunted.

In astonishment, realizing she'd missed her, Anna opened her eyes, prepared to pounce to wrestle the weapon from her. To fight. She froze in her step instead. Sprawled on the snow-blanketed ground, Avreen lay unmoving, her right arm at an odd angle out from her body. Three of the wild men Traun had described stood over her prone form.

A large hand clamped across Anna's mouth.

It stopped her rising scream.

She clawed at the hand of the creature behind her. She twisted and turned to try to escape it and its hair-enveloped arm that encircled her neck. Thrown to the ground, she was pinned there with a knee pressed into her chest. In a smooth and swift motion, a wide piece of leather was wrapped around her head and over her mouth and secured in place. The savage standing over her tied her hands together. Jerked upward to an upright position, he grunted at her, his coarse face close to hers. Grasped by the waist, Anna was lifted onto his broad shoulder. The savage's body odor engulfed her. The creature closest to Avreen heaved her unconscious form up to sling her behind his head and position her across his back.

The savages took off at a hard and fast trot away from the settlement.

Their running lopes soon put distance between them and the village. Anna flopped about loosely on the shoulder of the being who held her;

the blood that rushed to her upside-down head, combined with her fear, caused her to lose consciousness and, for a time, she became unaware of what was happening to her.

***

"High Commander, you need to come check this out."

Traun turned toward the guard who called out to him, the one he had scheduled to replace the sentry at the south entrance of their village. Frowning, Traun followed the man through the trees to where he should have been stationed. The man who was to be relieved sat on the ground—his head between his hands.

Traun walked over to him.

"What's happened to you? Are you sick?"

The man staggered to his feet to stand before him. "High Commander, I think I have been drugged."

Traun's frown deepened. "What makes you believe you've been drugged?"

"That widow of Nevin's came by at noon with my lunch. She said the servant, who usually brings the guards their meals, was sick today. I didn't think anything of it. However, it was hard for me to stand right after I ate. Next thing I know, I'm being awakened by my replacement."

"Go to a Learned One and get checked out," Traun instructed the man. He turned from him. He couldn't think of any reason why Avreen would want to drug the man, but he needed to locate her and demand some answers.

"High Commander," the sick guard exclaimed.

He turned back toward him.

"It seems that my weapon has been taken."

His words startled Traun, and he quickly scanned the area. Two faint impressions of tracks were present, and they led away from where they all stood; the falling snow had almost covered them.

Traun walked out from the wooded area to motion toward Andrew.

"Come with me," he said when he approached. Drawing his weapon from the pocket holder at his waist, Traun turned its safety setting to the off position. Andrew did the same with his weapon. Traun pointed out the tracks to him. "Let's follow those.

"You stay at your station," he instructed the replacement guard. He and Andrew shadowed the tracks where there seemed to be some struggle. They separated to inspect the area further.

"Here's the guard's weapon over here in the snow. It's set to fire," Andrew hollered out. He picked the weapon up to flip its safety switch on. He walked back to Traun.

"There is a shallow hole dug over there, too. What do you think is going on here?"

Traun gazed around the area for a moment more. He turned to look at Andrew. "I don't know for sure, but I think our wild men have come for a visit, and Avreen and whoever was with her got themselves taken captive.

"Come on, let's head back. A search party must be assembled to rescue them both. Though I'm tempted to leave them to their fate since it seems they were leaving the settlement." Traun was angry. Furiously so. From the looks of the tracks, there seemed to be six savages who'd come to check them out. He would need to gather at least ten men besides him and Andrew to begin the hunt. Andrew voiced his agreement.

At the sound of the clubs held and being pounded onto the back of the tubs, the people in the village gathered in quick response. Seeing Charlee approach from the direction of their hut, Traun looked for Anna. *She should be here any moment,* he thought. He held up a hand for the crowd to quieten.

"It seems we have two in our group who wanted to leave us. They drugged a guard and took his weapon before they left. However, they didn't get far before the wild men we told you of captured them. I need ten men to go with me and Andrew to help get them back."

Someone yelled from the back of the crowd, "If they wanted to leave so bad, I say let them stay with the savages."

Traun shook his head at the comment. No one raised their hand to volunteer in the search. Anna still hadn't arrived. She should have been there by now. Traun motioned for Charlee to come forward.

"Where's Anna?" he asked when she got to him. For some reason, he felt uneasy.

"She hasn't been around all afternoon," Charlee said. "I thought she was with you. When she stopped by my hut, she told me you'd sent her a note to meet you at the food storage hut. She thought you were probably worried about the recent freeze ruining the food."

"I didn't send her a note to meet me."

Charlee's eyes grew round.

Traun took off at a run for the food storage building. The crowd followed. The storage hut was unlocked, with no one inside or around it. Its latch had been tampered with. Traun could make out the faint outline of two sets of tracks that led away from the storage hut toward the area of the found unconscious guard.

He staggered and almost fell as he realized Anna was the second captive. She would not have left the village voluntarily.

He roared the names of ten of his most dependable men. This time, there was no shortage of volunteers eager to help their High Commander.

***

"I'll kill that bitch myself if the savages don't do so," Andrew said to Charlee in his anger and fear as he packed the essentials needed for the mission. He'd had a bad feeling about Avreen for a long time. He hoped his sister stayed alive for her rescue.

***

Traun secured the wanted supplies and, when done and in his home, he slid a long steel-bladed knife into its sheath strapped tight to his thigh…all copied as he'd seen the savages' wear. He had removed his laser gun while preparing to leave and now shoved it back into its small square-holding holster at his waist. He lifted his packed backpack to sling it behind his shoulders. He gazed down at his hands afterward, which continued to shake. He needed to get that under control, or he'd not be any help with Anna's rescue. With a swift move, Traun exited the hut. His handpicked men gathered around him, their faces hard masks. They followed when he took off at a fast trot.

***

Anna sat huddled within her coat, and with a grimace at the weather, she reached to pull its hood further down over her face. The bite of the cold wind stung her exposed face. She was starving, and the smell of the food the savages cooked made her stomach growl. The savages didn't always remember to feed her and Avreen. It had been over two days since they'd last eaten. Sixteen days had come and gone since they'd been taken captive. Anna knew it had been precisely that because she counted off each day every morning and prayed for rescue. Traun and Andrew would be searching for them. She hoped they'd be able to find the trail left behind—a trail that, some days, was quickly concealed by the heavy falling snow. Anna glanced over toward Avreen.

She looked bad that evening, even worse than before, her face covered with a bright flush. Anna knew a fever raged in her. Avreen cradled her broken arm and mumbled about being hot. She had barely eaten the small amount of food offered them over the days and now frowned with a permanent glassy-eyed gaze.

Anna watched as the savage who had captured and carried her that first day stood to withdraw his knife from its sheath strapped to his thigh.

He sliced two chunks of meat from the skinned animal cooking over the open fire. The enormous white dog who'd waited in the woods while his master had captured her stood to walk with him. In apprehension, Anna watched the two approach her and Avreen.

Squatting before her, the wild man held his hand out to offer her one of the chunks of meat he held. When she hesitated, he grunted, shaking his hand that the meat held. Anna snatched the piece even as her mind rebelled at the thought of the half-cooked substance. She had to eat for the baby and to keep her strength up; survival was important. The being rotated on his heels to stretch a hand out with the rest of the meat he held toward Avreen. Avreen looked at the offering, then lifted her gaze back to his to spit with force in his face.

Anna drew back in alarm when the wild being lunged upward. Rage reflected on his rugged features. The power of his backhanded slap to Avreen's face divided her bottom lip, and blood flew as her scream rang out; she sprawled on her side at his feet. She didn't move afterward, her eyes glued to his. The savage bent at his waist toward her to grunt down at her. Anna thought he was about to kick Avreen in her side with his booted foot when he straightened instead to throw the meat he held over her head to the ground behind her.

The dog at his side scrambled to obtain the discarded piece.

The savage stomped back to the fire to where the others of his kind ate and watched the commotion. He squatted down in front of the fire.

Avreen's sobs quietened as she lay huddled under her coat. Anna saw that she shivered uncontrollably and felt sympathy for her rise, even knowing what she'd done to Nevin and the unknown woman from Garr and what she planned to do to her. She had to be going through enormous pain with that broken arm, and now maybe more broken bones. The savage had hit her hard enough that her cheekbone could be shattered.

Curling up on the cold ground as tight as she could and with her legs drawn up to her chest, Anna was thankful to have donned her heavy coat that awful afternoon and her snow boots; both items comforted her from the frigid weather. Awakened the next morning by another savage with a kick to the center of her back, Anna managed to stand. Woken the same way as she'd been, Avreen staggered upward, her broken arm cradled under her hand. Herded forward, Anna, with Avreen right before her, fell in line behind the savage offering the food the previous evening.

***

Avreen, in her pain-filled and fever-hazed world, knew her hatred for Lady Anna. It tormented and whispered at her. She rotated her jaw. It wasn't broken as she'd believed. She realized Lady Anna remained unhurt even after being with the savages for over two weeks now, while she felt pain in every conceivable place on her body. Why wouldn't the beings persecute Lady Anna like they did her? *I don't deserve what I'm going through,* Avreen thought in bewilderment. *Why hasn't my beloved rescued me?* Her mother's voice rang out. She scolded her for demanding a trinket she'd wanted as a child.

Avreen looked around in puzzlement.

"Mommy? Mommy, where are you?"

She gazed in confusion at the strange faces which surrounded her.

***

The savages halted walking. They watched Avreen as she twisted and turned about. Anna also studied her as she repeatedly cried out for her mother in the language of the people of Garr. Avreen was unrecognizable as the beautiful woman she'd been. Had she sunk further into her insanity, or was it the fever that raged through her body that made her shriek for her mother, Anna wondered as she watched her. The savages grunted at each other before forcing her and then Avreen to begin walking again.

***

Avreen found she could bear the pain that racked her body with a total concentration on her abhorrence of that of Lady Anna, who now walked before her. It blocked out her mother's scolding voice, too. She began to taunt Traun's Lifemate as they were forced forward. She described in minute detail how the savages would kill Lady Anna and the baby she carried. She stressed how Traun wouldn't find them and probably wouldn't want to find her after the savages were done with her. She spoke about his and her two-year relationship while on Garr, and with intimate details given. She narrated everything repeatedly and with glee.

***

Anna collapsed to the ground, where she was pushed when the savages finally halted for the night. She was numb in both spirit and body. Avreen hadn't shut up all day, and she wanted to sob at the fear that coursed through her from the repeated and detailed narrative of how the baby growing within her was to be ripped from her body; all the while, Avreen said, she'd wish for death as the savages took their turns with her. Everything she told was described with specific clarity. Avreen was shoved to the ground, not four feet from her. She began her torture again.

"Shut up," Anna screamed, unable to take any more verbal abuse. "Shut your filthy mouth!"

The savage, who seemed to consider her his, looked up, and with a blur of movement, he stood before Avreen to kick her in the face with a large fur-booted foot; with the popping sound of her jaw, as it shattered, Avreen tumbled backward. Anna couldn't stop her scream of terror from her lungs and into the surrounding air as she jumped to her feet to take off into the immediate forest. She couldn't wait any longer for rescue; she needed to take action to save herself. She didn't make it far before the savage caught up to her, and with a shove to her back, he sent her tumbling. Rolling across the snow-covered ground, Anna kicked out to catch the being in the chest with the heels of her boots when he followed to grab her coat. He stumbled back; his hold of her released. Unable to rise, Anna scrambled backward with the use of her elbows, and her screams continued. She couldn't cease the screeching once it had begun.

The savage lunged again, and reaching her, he stood over her. He slapped her across the mouth.

It silenced the noise she made.

Grasped by a wrist, Anna was dragged across the rough ground back to where the thing planned to bed for the night. With a fistful of her hair caught up in his hand, he raised her face toward his to shake her head. His hold of her released. He let her fall to the ground to stomp away from her to the campfire now built by the others of his kind.

Lying on the ground, shivering with her fright, Anna whispered a prayer for rescue to happen soon. The sting of her busted lips was felt, as well as the salty tang of blood on them and in her mouth. Spitting the red liquid onto the ground, Anna glanced over to where Avreen lay so still. Turning her back to her, she curled up into a tight protective ball to close her eyes in exhaustion.

The next morning, the savages left Avreen, where she'd crawled to in the middle of the night. The being beside Anna yanked her upward, so she stood beside him. With a shove of her back, he indicated that she was to follow behind the others as they were leaving camp. He prodded her on throughout the day if she happened to slow down as they walked at a fast pace. They moved that day without ceasing to rest or eat.

Looking down at the snow-covered ground, Anna didn't think she could take another step, but she did. Her legs were heavy, made of lead, it seemed. With each step moved forward, it took her total concentration. The image stuck in her mind as she walked that day was of Avreen left behind as she and the savages departed camp that morning. *Was she alive? Or dead?* Anna shivered at her thoughts, not from the cold but from her fear. The savage behind her said something to the others, and he grasped her arm to halt her agonizing step forward.

The other beings stopped.

They began to prepare the camp.

Anna collapsed to the ground, where she'd been pulled to a stop. The savage beside her reached down to rip her coat from her shoulders. She didn't care. So, she froze to death. It would be preferable to what she was sure would happen when they arrived wherever they headed. The being beside her lumbered from her side to where the others were creating a fire.

He spread the coat out on the ground beside it. He turned to motion for her to come to him. Anna stumbled upward.

He aimed a short finger at the coat at her approach, and she sat. The savage gathered the animal fur he slept with to drop it beside her. Anna stared at it briefly before pulling it around her shoulders. She shook from the cold wind and the swirling snow. Looking up at the group who busied themselves around her, Anna realized that one of the six was missing. Swiveling her head, she failed to locate him anywhere within the camp. She had been unaware he'd dropped off behind them.

Oh well. Good riddance. One less savage Traun and the others will have to deal with, she thought. Curling up beside the now-blazing fire, she slipped into a light sleep. The savages talking with excitement amongst themselves woke her. Rising to a sitting position, Anna watched them. The one she'd not seen was now back in camp, and he waved a hair-covered hand as he pointed a stubby finger back toward the trail where they'd all advanced from earlier. Anna tensed as the one who acted as her keeper turned to approach her, his short-spread legs massive-looking. Her heart began to pound when he pulled two pieces of woven rope from under the loose animal skin he wore as a covering. His eyes made contact with hers as he grabbed her hands to tie them together with one of the ropes he held; he snatched her snow boots from her feet to bind her ankles together with the other. Afterward, he grunted something to his dog before he walked away. Anna had sat frozen. Her fear had paralyzed her. The animal had moved to plop down across the fire from her.

Numbly, she watched the savages leave. When they were out of sight, she became alive and began to gnaw on the rope that bound her hands. The dog lunged to his feet, growled low in his throat, and exposed his teeth. Anna promptly lowered her hands. Her heart raced as she crooned, "Good doggie…good doggie…pretty doggie."

The animal lay back down, yet his eyebrows twitched: one up, the other down as he watched her. Ever so slowly, Anna inched her hands toward her feet. She could run with her hands tied. The dog growled deep in his throat again. She pulled her hands back to her lap. It was there to prevent her escape.

***

Traun and the other men quietly walked into the empty campsite they'd come upon. The savages traveled quickly before them, but he and his men had gained ground. As all inspected the area, each looked for the direction the others had taken that morning and not so long ago, as evidenced by the still smoldering ambers of their built fire.

"Holy shit," Andrew exclaimed from where he was.

"There's someone over here," he yelled out.

Traun and the others hastened to where he'd squatted down. Andrew shook so hard he had to brace himself with a hand on the snow-covered ground where he knelt.

Reaching up under the branches of the large bush before him, where the individual had dragged themself, he pulled the body out from under it.

"It must be Avreen. I've seen her wear that coat," Traun said, and he wanted to fall to his knees and weep in his relief at knowing Anna wasn't the one who lay before him. Andrew turned the body face up. The hood on the coat fell back to reveal dark hair and Avreen's face. Traun and the men around him cringed at the battered woman before them. Her right arm had flopped loosely. Andrew felt at her neck for a pulse. He looked up at Traun to shake his head. She was dead.

The sight of Avreen and what she'd gone through sickened Traun, yet his anger at her also coursed through him. What had happened to her was her fault. And it would be her doing if Anna came to a bad end.

"Let's move her over between those two boulders, Andrew. The body will be protected there. When we come back through, we'll bury her then. I won't lose precious time on a dead body when Anna is still with those savages," he said.

Within moments, everyone was ready to follow the trail, which was found again outside the camp area. Traun knew he and his men were close behind the savages, as no fresh snow covered their tracks, and no animal imprints were seen across the trail. He took off, determined to close the gap between their two groups.

After several miles being covered, Traun halted his swift walking pace to stand in place. He studied the area ahead. The others halted beside him. There were plenty of places up there for a person to hide with its overhangs of rocks and trees and brush on each side of those towering cliffs.

It was an ambush ready to happen.

Traun turned toward the men who waited for instruction.

"I have an uneasy feeling about us going through that pass, but I can't see any other way, and the savage's tracks lead right up to it. Get your weapons out and ready to fire, and keep your eyes peeled for any movement. Don't hesitate to shoot to kill if we're jumped."

The men nodded as they withdrew their weapons from the holsters at their waists. With his firearm palmed, Traun turned again toward the passageway.

He and the others moved slowly and cautiously forward. No attack was forthcoming. As the end of the narrow trail drew nearer, Traun's tension began to leave him, and his breathing grew easier. Screams rent the air—one above and still more behind him. The being who'd lain in wait at the trail's end landed heavily upon his back. Traun's laser weapon was knocked from his hand with its fur-covered booted foot, making hard contact with his arm. Traun watched as the weapon flew through the air to skid across the ground with a desperate sickness at the sight. Swiftly, he reached upward to wrap his arms around the squat body latched onto his shoulders. He and the screaming savage rolled forward to tumble end-over-end. Rocks covered with snow were felt by Traun, as was the sting of a sharp-bladed knife sinking deep into his right shoulder before the blade scraped across his shoulder bone to slice downward through his coat sleeve and the fleshy meat at the back of his arm. Shaking the savage loose, he stumbled upward. The long-bladed knife in its sheath tied at his thigh, he withdrew swiftly.

The savage lunged, and hastily, Traun brought the knife up. With a sidestep, he avoided the rapid downward slash of the weapon the savage yielded even as he gave a stab at the thing. The being jumped backward, but then, in a swift move, it jumped high in the air toward him with a shrill scream. Rolling on the ground with the thing attached to him again, Traun jabbed the knife he held upward, deep into the flat stomach above him, and pushed it with determination to its homemade hilt to give its handle a hard twist.

The wild man slumped—dead weight. Traun heaved the thing up and away even as another one of the beings raced past him.

Jumping to his feet, he glanced back at his men. They were engaged with the other beings. He decided to give chase to the one who'd run by. His men were doing fine. He was sure the one who fled would lead him to Anna.

Snatching his laser weapon from the ground where it had spun, he sprinted after the wild being.

***

Anna could hear something happening down the trail from where she sat tied. She began to scream when the savage who claimed her rushed through the trees toward her and was covered in blood. The dog lunged to his feet to snarl at her. The wild being grabbed her by her tied wrists and continued to run. Anna bounced along on the rough ground alongside him and cried out with her pain as she was dragged across the sharp rocks he sprinted over. Her arms that were stretched above her head, she thought, would come out from their sockets. She expected to feel the dog's powerful teeth sink deep into her flesh at any moment as it ran beside her flailing body and snapped with excitement at her with its white, pointed teeth.

***

Traun raced through the trees and brush as he swung this way and that to dodge their branches. Anna's terrified screams could be heard ahead of him. Fear clutched at his chest. He caught sight of the savage through a clearing. Anna bumped along beside him as the being ran with her in tow. He had a clear shot, not a shot to kill, but a shot that would make the being lose his hold of her. Dropping to his knees, Traun raised his weapon to squeeze its trigger button.

The wild man roared with rage. Traun knew intense burning pain ripped through his arm. As he'd planned, the savage lost his tight hold of Anna. In a swift and unexpected movement, though, the Neanderthal turned to grab a fistful of her hair in his uninjured hand, and he pulled her up to him to wrap a hairy arm around her neck from behind her.

He faced him; his teeth bared like the dog's. Anna's screams died to a whimper. She kept her eyes glued on him. Traun was afraid the savage would squeeze the breath of life from her in his agitation if she tried to escape. He prayed she remained still and silent. If he shot the thing holding her full blast with the laser, the heat of it would engulf her also. Rising to his feet, Traun watched the being. The wild man breathed heavily, his eyes wide, his attention focused on him. The dog quieted beside his master, although he still growled low in his throat. Traun could tell the savage didn't want to lose his much-wanted prize as the being continued to watch him. It seemed the savage looked at him as if he wondered how he'd injured him. The being looked at his knife in its sheath at his side and then down to his injured arm; his expression held a bewildered appearance to it. The Neanderthal motioned with his head, indicating for him to leave him and his captive; he yelled guttural sounds out as if he ordered him away. Andrew and the other ten left behind skidded to a halt beside Traun when they burst onto the scene.

The savage watched their arrival with seemed desperation.

As one unit, Traun and his men began to walk toward it. The savage screamed to stomp his feet on the ground. He bared his teeth. When they continued to advance, he looked down at Anna with seemed regret.

With a roar, he slung her to the ground to bound into the forest, his dog at his heels. Traun sprinted to Anna's prostrate form. Kneeling onto the frozen ground beside her, he pulled her onto his lap. He tried to calm her hysteria as she sobbed her face pressed against him. Andrew and the other men sprinted after the lone savage. They returned moments later.

Andrew relayed that they'd given up their chase when they feared the remaining savages might double back upon him and Anna.

"Although, the injuries we inflicted upon the others before we left them should keep them busy," he added.

"Shh…darling, shh…," Traun crooned to Anna while Andrew talked. His heart still slammed against his ribs. He untied her hands and feet and smoothed back her hair from around her face.

"You're safe now, shh…yes, I know. We found her body," Traun said when, in her hysterics, she panted out that the savages had left Avreen behind that morning. He pulled her tighter to him as she sobbed out how Avreen had planned to kill her and had told her she'd killed Nevin and a girl who'd been scheduled to come to the new world. Traun's nausea rose as he listened to what Avreen had done to try to be with him. He wondered what could have gone so wrong with her to cause her deadly actions.

Anna, it seemed, gained control of the panic that gripped her as her sobs grew quieter. Keeping his arms wrapped around her, Traun continued reiterating she was now safe in a hushed voice. She fainted upon seeing his blood-soaked hands and the blood that covered the front of his coat. That same blood now smeared all over her. Traun rose to his feet, her limp form within his arms. His injured shoulder and arm burned with remembered sharp pain at her weight. He could feel the blood from the wounds flowing down his back and his arm.

"Let's get away from this place," he said to the others. "We can make it back to the small cave we came across and hole up there.

"Injury report," he said upon noting the stain of blood on several of the men's clothing. Traun couldn't tell if they were covered in the blood of the savages they'd fought or their own. Or both, as he was.

The men assured him they'd received minor cuts.

Andrew, with the others, laughed with merriment as he and the others relayed of them banging two of the savages' heads together after he had left them to chase the one. The men reported with glee that they'd knocked both beings out cold with their actions. They'd decided not to give chase to the others who escaped and to let the savages' companions drag the two away, running to help him rescue Lady Anna instead upon hearing her screams of terror. Traun knew the adrenaline rush from the recent intense fighting flowed strongly within each man as they slapped at each other's backs and grinned broadly at each other.

***

Andrew sobered from his laughter, as did the other men around him, and he realized his brother-in-law must be in intense pain from his injuries while he held his sister in his arms. Blood flowed freely from the High Commander's coat sleeve and down over his hand. Andrew had noted his slashed coat earlier. The front of his coat was saturated with blood. Andrew didn't know if all the blood was from wounds or the savage he'd killed. Traun hadn't commented since he'd asked for their injury reports. The special winter material of their uniforms and jackets might have been designed to keep a person warm in extreme cold exposure, but their thinness didn't protect them from knife attacks.

"Give me my sister, High Commander," Andrew said. He reached out, and when Traun hesitated, he pointed to his blood-soaked uniform.

"If all that is from injuries, you need to try to stop the bleeding before you lose too much of it."

***

Traun handed Anna over to her brother. Although he wanted to keep her close, his wounds made it impossible for him to carry her. He had one of the men help him remove his coat. Gingerly, he removed his shirt and grimaced with pain when the torn garment snagged the open wound on his shoulder. At his instruction, the men ripped the shirt into large strips after he handed it to them. One man pulled his shoulder wound together and the wound behind his upper right arm, while others tightly wrapped and secured the torn strips of the shirt over and around the injuries. It staunched his bleeding out as much as possible. A sling was made with his shirt's sleeves to support his arm. His coat was laid loosely back over his bare shoulders. The small group of unlikely medics stepped back to watch his face.

"Let's go," Traun said, his words sharp. He wanted to reach the cave before nightfall. It would be a safe place to hole up until they could begin their journey back to their settlement.

Chapter 27

Andrew walked over to where his sister lay. She was asleep, but it seemed restless. The imprint on her wrists showed the result of the rope used.

They had made it to the cavern with no other incidents, and the High Commander had cleaned her up, hidden within it with a fire built to warm her by him. He'd stripped her bare to throw her clothes out to them all to be scrubbed. Andrew and the others had melted snow and left the small heated containers at the cave entrance for him to clean her. The High Commander had rubbed healing ointment over her badly bruised back and wrists. With her coat placed back over her as she slept, dead to the world around her, only then had Andrew been allowed in to see her, the other men not permitted within the cave to witness their Lady Anna in her current condition.

Returning to the mouth of the cave and a second fire now built at its entrance, Andrew watched as his brother-in-law worked to clean his wounds meticulously. The medical kit sat open beside him, and its paraphernalia was spread out on the ground around him. Andrew took the rag Traun held out toward him. He bent to re-wet it as instructed and then squeezed out the water soaked up over the wounds on his shoulder and arm. They were deep, the bone of his shoulder blade exposed. Andrew looked at him in question with the lacerations flushed out as well as they could be.

***

Anna became aware of the sound of men's voices quietly talking. She picked up the timbre of Traun's voice, and it comforted her. She knew he had doctored her and that they had reached a cave. She drifted back to sleep.

***

Traun gritted his teeth as he nodded at Andrew after his instructions to him. Andrew shot the liquid from the container he held into the gaping wound at his shoulder. The liquid's sting was intense. It had to be done. The medicine would stop any infection from setting in. Unmoving, Traun nodded toward him again. Andrew repeated his prior action to the wound at the back of his arm. He then bent to pull his shoulder wound together and to begin sewing the flesh's edges into place with the needle he held. The sight and smell of his own blood and the scent of the applied medicine sickened Traun. He feared he'd faint before he heard Andrew murmur, "Finished."

"Pay up," he said as he stood. Fighting his nausea, he walked to where Anna lay asleep on the pallet he'd made for her. Stretching out beside her, he closed his eyes and promptly passed out.

***

Andrew watched his brother-in-law in amazement. The man was made of steel: calm and collected as he rested. The men had bet him that the High Commander would not show that he felt any pain or emotion while he doctored his wounds. He had bet them he would. He had lost the bet.

The only noticeable sign that their High Commander was affected by his wounds and his administration to them was the bead of sweat that had popped out on his forehead when he'd begun to sew the gaping flesh of his shoulder wound together. Andrew hadn't realized that Traun knew of the bet between him and the other men until he'd heard his words when finished. Shaking his head, he turned to meet the gazes of the other men. They grinned at him. He guessed he'd better start the evening meal for them all. It looked like he would be the cook until they reached home.

***

Anna woke to sharp pain in her lower back late the following day. She gasped at the sudden tightening of her stomach muscles. Lying still, she wondered at the new pain as it receded and her stomach muscles relaxed. Minutes later, the pain began to radiate from her back again and spread around to her stomach. Her stomach muscles tightened. She cried out at realizing what was happening. She was going into labor at five months along.

***

Traun stood outside the mouth of the cave talking to the men when he heard Anna's hoarse call for him. With a quick stride, he entered the cave to hurry toward her.

She stared up at him. "I'm losing the baby!"

With alarm, Traun pulled her coat back from where it lay on top of her. Blood was spreading out on the blanket beneath her. With a hiss of anguish, he knelt to check between her bent legs. He wept at what he found.

"Stay out," he ordered Andrew and the other men when they started to enter the cave. Gathering a thick cleaning cloth, he lifted the exquisite, tiny, dead infant girl with a gentleness. Traun wrapped her up tight within it, and, walking to the mouth of the cave, he tried to call out to Anna's brother.

The words caught in his throat.

***

Andrew realized what had happened when he approached Traun. His brother-in-law's face was drawn tight with his pain, and it let him know, without words, what had occurred within the cave. Traun, a shimmer of tears in his gaze, said, "Bury this precious child and mark the grave so I can show it to Anna when she recovers."

Andrew nodded, taking the tiny bundle from his outstretched hands, his throat tight with emotion. The other men lowered their gazes from their High Commander's obvious sorrow. They knew he would not appreciate them seeing him in what he would consider a personal and private moment. They went with Andrew to help dig a small grave for the bundle he carried.

***

Traun cleaned up Anna as she continued to weep. Afterward, he sat beside her with another pallet made and her coat placed back over her. Reaching out, he stroked her hair until she quieted. He stared across the interior space of the cave at its gray and moss-covered walls. His shoulders shook as, in silence, he mourned the loss of the child.

Rising, he exited the cave when she fell asleep.

Andrew showed him the grave of his firstborn. Traun began to hunt until he found the right size of stone; his men watched him, and he knew they wondered at his actions. Sitting down, he began to carve.

***

A week had passed since her miscarriage. Anna wanted to see the burial site of the baby. She hadn't recovered her strength yet, but she needed the emotional closure of it. At her request to do so, Traun helped her to her feet and then out from the mouth of the cave. Anna grasped his hand tightly within hers when they approached the grave, and she noted the large stone that had been placed over it, with the words, *Our Precious Baby Conceived in Love,* carved into it. She looked up to meet Traun's gaze. He turned his away from her as he relayed that her brother and the other men had buried the infant beneath the branches of the huge tree before them; they had then constructed the two-foot-high stone wall fence, which encircled and secured the tiny grave within it.

Anna swallowed back her rush of tears and wondered if she'd ever get over the feeling of loss that consumed her. She needed Molly's comfort.

"Let's go home, Traun," she said. She took in his somber expression again as he stood silently beside her.

At her words, he shook off whatever feeling he was experiencing and looked down at her. "I'm ready to go home, too," he said.

The men fashioned a carrier, and when Anna was settled onto the top of it, a man at each corner lifted it. With a handle resting over each of their shoulders, they gripped it between capable hands.

Their solemn group began the journey back to their waiting village.

With an arm placed over her eyes, Anna tried to hide the tears that began to slide down the sides of her face. Left behind was her loved and much-wanted baby.

* * *

Traun noticed her tears but quickly walked ahead of the carrier to lead his small group home. If he stopped to comfort her, he'd break down in front of everyone. His grief and anger over what occurred still gripped him and twisted his insides into tethered knots. He needed to focus on a safe return to the settlement.

Readjusting his injured arm within its sling, Traun welcomed the pain he felt at the movement. It forced his attention away from his Lifemate. He flexed the arm muscle with deliberate intent as he walked. He blamed himself for what had happened to the child and Anna.

Chapter 28

The weary group trudged with slow steps into the settlement amidst a loud banging of metal tubs that announced their arrival. Walking beside Traun, Anna watched Molly run toward them, and her eyes began to fill with tears. She always seemed to cry now, and she knew Traun hated it. Her sadness engulfed her. When Molly reached her, she gazed silently at her as she fought back the tears.

"I lost the baby," she choked out.

Molly looked at Traun. Anna saw her swallow before she enfolded her into her arms. Anna couldn't hold back her emotional response as she wept on her shoulder.

"Aunt, take Lady Anna to her Learned One so she can give her a physical," Traun ordered. Anna jerked away from Molly's comfort, hurt because she knew he wanted to leave her side. She swiped at her wet face.

"What about your arm and shoulder? You need to have the Learned One look at you also." Her voice held her tears. She avoided looking directly at her Lifemate.

"I will have everything examined later. Right now, I want to see what has happened here since we've been gone." He looked everywhere but at her. He turned abruptly to walk away, leaving her to stare at his retreating backside.

Molly gently took her by the arm. "Let it go, honey. He is grieving in the only way he knows how."

Anna wondered helplessly if he blamed her for the loss of their child. He had spoken to her with as few words as possible the past two weeks. Several times, as now, he'd left her side with abruptness when she began to cry with the sadness that enveloped her. In silence, Anna stood beside Molly as Molly turned toward Andrew to hug him. Anna froze when she softly informed him that Charlee had delivered a darling little boy three weeks past. With a heavy heart, Anna watched as her brother bounded away toward his home, and she decided then and there to make sure she kept clear of Charlee. She couldn't handle any more pain. She was glad for Charlee and Andrew, yet knew she couldn't see the baby without falling apart.

Anna took off toward the Learned One's visiting room. She didn't look at Molly when she followed beside her. She had believed she needed comfort, but now, she wanted to be alone.

***

Andrew's heart pounded with the news Molly had relayed. Charlee had refused to be told the sex of the child, telling him she didn't care whether the child was a boy or girl; she'd be as happy with either. When she'd inquired what he wanted, he hadn't said much, and had only mumbled that either would be fine with him too. At the time, he'd worried if he would be able to love or accept the child as his own, whatever its sex was. He was anxious to see Charlee and tell her how much she meant to him. When Molly had informed about the child's birth, he'd noticed Anna's stricken look, and he knew how lucky he and Charlee were to have a healthy baby. He was still worried at the jealousy he experienced over this unknown man whose child he would now be required to raise as his own offspring. Would he be able to view this boy as his, or would he always be unable to forget he was another man's and not his own?

No matter how hard it may be. If I can't love this child, I'll do everything I can to keep my feelings locked down deep inside me, Andrew silently vowed as he stepped up to open his home's door.

Charlee would be unable to contain her hurt toward him if he couldn't overcome this weakness of character he had.

"Charlee," he called out, his voice low and soft. Andrew shut the door to their hut behind him with a gentle click. Charlee lay on her side, her back to him. He glanced around the interior of the small hut. He wasn't able to locate the baby. He approached the bed.

"Charlee."

With a gentle touch, Andrew shook her shoulder. She was sound asleep. He hated to wake her, but he wanted her to know he was home and with her now. Charlee turned her head to gaze up at him sleepily. Her eyes snapped open, and her face broke into a beautiful smile.

"Andrew, you're home," she breathed out. "Anna? Is she here?"

Andrew bent down to kiss her with a soft touch to her cheek.

"She is back home.

"Where's the baby?" He needed to see the child. With shame, he admitted to himself that he was scared to look at the newborn, afraid of what he might feel.

"Come over to the other side of the bed," Charlee said.

Andrew walked around the bed, and she pulled back the covers.

She watched his expression with a sudden stillness as he gazed down at the plump-cheeked baby beside her in the middle of the bed. The child had a shock of thick reddish-brown hair covering his head. He opened his sleepy eyes to lock a dark brown gaze with his. Reaching out, Andrew stroked the fat cheek before him with a forefinger. Small fingers waved into the air to grip tight around it.

Andrew felt the air leave his lungs at the infant's firm grasp. It was as if the child declared boldly, "Here I am. Take me or leave me. Either one makes no difference to me."

Incredible tenderness filled Andrew for the tiny thing. This child was his and Charlee's. Andrew raised his eyes to Charlee and realized at that moment that she'd known all along the demons he had fought. He smiled with love for her as he climbed onto the bed alongside the baby, who refused to release his finger.

"Our son is going to be a fighter." He was proud of the thought.

Leaning over, he kissed Charlee full on the mouth. He knew he would love this tiny infant as his own.

Charlee wiped at her eyes.

"I was so afraid you wouldn't feel anything," she whispered.

Reaching over the baby with his free hand, Andrew cupped her cheek. "I love this baby, and I love you, honey."

Charlee turned her face into his open palm.

"Oh, how I love you, my wonderful husband," she said, smiling with a teary-eyed gaze back at him.

***

After he'd walked away from Anna, Traun felt like a heel. Every time she started to weep, it seemed he cracked into a million shattered pieces. Unable to bear her pain, he always ducked away from her. His guilt ate away at him. Traun watched and waited until she left the Learned One's office with Molly at her side, and then he went to get his arm and shoulder checked out. He grilled the Learned One on Anna's condition while there.

***

Anna pretended to be asleep when her Lifemate came home that night. It was midnight before Traun opened their door to step into the hut to ease it closed with a soft click behind him. She lay unmoving as he crept over to her. She wondered what he was about when he stood beside the bed to stare down. Anna felt him brush her cheek lightly with his fingers before he stepped away to recline in the chair beside the fireplace. Opening her eyes, she watched him as he stared into the flames of the fire. The next morning, she woke to find him gone.

He had come to their bed sometime during the night because his side of it was messed up. Anna sighed. The Learned One had informed her that she was healing normally at her visit. She had instructed to wait at least six weeks before becoming intimate with her Lifemate again. This would give her body time to heal, she'd said. Rolling over onto her back, Anna gazed at the hut's ceiling. She had woken up angry: angry at the senseless loss of her child and angry with Traun for always walking away when she broke down and began to cry. With a start of surprise, Anna realized that, deep down, she blamed him for what had happened to her and the baby. If he had not had a relationship with Avreen, the sick woman wouldn't have followed him to the planet and caused the death of so many.

Reaching across the span of the bed, Anna picked up the bed pillow, which still held the indentation of his head where he'd lain upon it, and she slung it toward the wall beside her with a savage hiss. She ignored Klinn when the woman knocked and then, as usual, brought in her bathwater without being told she was welcome to come in.

Klinn glanced at her several times, but the silence in the room remained unbroken as she went about her duties. Upon leaving, she closed the door softly behind her.

***

Traun made sure he fell into bed exhausted each evening after arriving home, only to rise early the next morning to begin it all again with a vengeance. Eight weeks had passed since he and his small group had arrived back into the settlement, and he and Anna hadn't regained the happiness of life between them as before. He had taken to visiting with Andrew and Charlee at their hut in the evenings to avoid going home as long as possible to her silent pain. Traun enjoyed holding Charlee's tiny infant boy, whom they'd named Rowan. Andrew bragged about the newborn doing this or that, as if none of the others did the same thing. Traun knew Anna hadn't looked upon the baby, even as the weeks passed.

He gazed down at the chubby little thing he held in his arms, and his heart clenched at the innocent sleeping face before him. Deep in the night, he would reach out to Anna to try to comfort her, but after a moment of being in his arms, she always pulled away to turn and lie with stiffness on her side of the bed. Traun felt his loneliness. He was at a loss on how to help his Lifemate deal with the death of their child.

***

Charlee studied the forlorn expression on Traun's face as he gazed down at the baby, which he cradled against him. She glanced over at Andrew. He shook his head at her. She didn't know what to do to help Anna work through her grief. She had tried talking to her about her loss, but her friend hadn't wanted to discuss it. At least Traun was attempting to get on with life. Anna had shut everyone out, even her Lifemate. Charlee sighed. She hurt emotionally for her sister-in-law.

Looking up, Traun rose. He handed Rowan over to her. "I should be going. It's getting late," he said. He must have heard her sigh and thought he'd overstayed his welcome.

Andrew stood with their goodbyes and locked the door after he stepped out into the night. Charlee rose to place Rowan in the homemade wooden cradle beside their bed. Rising from the sleeping infant, her gaze met Andrew's blue-eyed stare. He walked over to her.

"I love you," he said, slipping his arms around her waist to pull her close. "And I need you, Charlee."

Wrapping her arms around his waist, Charlee raised her mouth to his. He was her anchor in life, and she needed him, too.

***

Walking from his in-laws' home to his own, Traun wondered how long Anna had stayed at the House of Reflection that day. She seemed to find comfort in being on top of the mountain ledge.

Daily, he wanted to wrap his arms around her and tell her to cry until her sorrow eased and not to stop because it made him uncomfortable; he would not walk away from her again.

She had stopped crying the day after their return to the settlement, and it was when she began to draw away from him. There were days when she would look at him for several moments without saying anything and then abruptly turn away from him.

He had blamed himself for her capture and the loss of their child; if only he'd kept a better eye on Avreen, if only he'd ordered the killing of the savages when they'd first hunted and found them.

One evening, he'd expressed his belief to Andrew and Charlee that all fault lay with him as to what had happened. Surprisingly, Charlee had been angered over his self-blame. She had torn into him, with harsh words, that he was to stop blaming himself for the actions of others. Traun smiled to himself. She made a believer out of him that night. It had surprised him, her defense of him.

With a slowness, Anna stood from where she reclined in their chair as he closed the door to their hut behind him. She was awake. Traun's eyes widened at what she was wearing. The silky nightshirt she'd donned hit her high on the thigh. Its sheer material left little to the imagination. Her nipples could be seen.

"Are you sure, sweetheart?" A nervous tension tightened within Traun. They had been down this road twice this past week, and she'd pulled away from him each time at the last minute, leaving him aching with unrequited need.

"I am positive this time, Traun. I want to get pregnant again."

Traun felt his insides constrict. There was no *I want you,* or *I need you* from her, only; *I want to get pregnant again.* He studied her closely. She smiled with seeming tentativeness back at him. *Maybe this is what she needs,* he thought as he watched her. Getting pregnant as soon as possible with another child might help to heal her sharp grief.

***

Anna lay beside her Lifemate in the middle of their bed. He hadn't taken her into his arms yet. She had noticed the smile on his face when he first entered their home, and she wondered about it. That day, she'd come to the firm conclusion that she was determined to get pregnant again. There would be no turning back this night for her. More than eight full weeks had passed since she'd lost the baby. Another child would help to ease her grief.

When Traun still didn't move toward her, Anna rose to face him and leaned against him. He watched her. Stretching upward to kiss him open-mouthed, she ran her tongue lightly across his lips. He issued a groan.

He raised a hand to smooth his palm down over her bare backside. He still didn't take her in his arms. Anna curled against him, running her hand across his stomach muscles. Traun swiftly flipped her with him above her and devoured her mouth with his. He drew back.

"I don't want to rush you, sweetheart. I want us to take it slow. But I don't know if I can," he rasped.

Raising her legs, Anna wrapped them around his waist. She urged him on. Anna knew he tried to pull back to slow his taking of her. In the end, he surrendered, but when his need pressed against her, she stiffened.

I can't do this, she thought, in panic. *I am not ready. I am disloyal to the baby we lost, with my wish to replace her with another.*

She pushed with her hands at his waist.

"Get off! I can't," she sobbed.

***

Traun froze, gripping the sheet on each side of Anna's head, and his anger boiled up. With a vile curse, he lunged from the bed to grab his pants to jerk them on.

"I can't keep going through this, Anna! I lost a child that day, too. You're not the only one suffering."

Angrily, Traun gazed down at his Lifemate as she gulped and tried to stop sobbing. She turned her back to him and rolled to her side of their bed. He raked his trembling fingers through his short-cropped hair as his anger drained. Walking to the other side of the bed to sit on its edge, he stroked her arm.

"Cry if you need to, sweetheart." He didn't know what else to do. His shoulders felt heavy from the weight of her pain.

She shrugged his hand away.

"We wouldn't have lost our child if it wasn't for you and your lover," she said, her tone bitter. She looked up at him accusingly.

In a swift move, Traun rose. He jerked the rest of his clothes on and slammed the door shut on his way out of their home.

Chapter 29

"Andrew, what are we going to do about Anna?" Charlee looked down at the baby as he nursed and then switched him to the other breast. He noisily latched on to her, his tiny hand waving in the air with his contentment. She stroked the child's fat cheek with her finger for a moment before she looked back up. Andrew eased his muddy boots off at the door. *Damn, I'm tired*, he thought.

Traun worked all the men hard, from daylight to sundown, almost like he was possessed. Andrew knew their High Commander started and ended his day long before and after everyone else was expected to report for duty or retire home.

From the abundance of trees that grew within the area, they built better and sturdier new pens for all the animals and birthing sheds for any newly born ones. Once the animals began birthing in the spring, the High Commander wanted to separate the expectant mothers from each other in case any problems arose.

Not only had all the men been busy constructing the pens for the animals for the past two months, but they were also expected to practice hand-to-hand combat for three hours each night. The High Commander drilled them on what to do if the savages returned, and procedures were put into place to be followed without exception.

Andrew knew Traun felt some relief when they figured out the problem with the power bases. The alarm system around the village and the communication system between the night watchmen were now back in place.

He frowned at Charlee's question concerning his sister. Hell, he didn't know what to do for Anna. His sister was hurting, and only she could deal with the pain she felt in the only way she knew how. Same as he knew Traun was doing by working until he dropped.

Walking over to where she sat and nursed Rowan, he bent to kiss the top of the breast that the baby noisily sucked on with an eager appetite. Rising, he then kissed her on the mouth.

She studied him, and her worry caused her brow to crease. Sighing, Andrew turned to sit down in the other chair before the warm fire. "I don't know what to do, Charlee. Anna and Traun are both going through a hard time right now. They are each handling their grief in the only way they know how."

Charlee's eyes shimmered with unshed tears as she looked back at him.

"But that's just it, Andrew. Anna is not handling her grief. Traun is keeping busy, working and interacting with you men. She's drawn into herself. She won't even look at Rowan." She glanced down at their nursing son for a moment before she looked back up at him.

"All she wants to do is sit up at the House of Reflection. Molly came over today all upset. She said she'd tried to get Anna to go with her to check on one of the women in the village who had been under the weather the past few days. She said Anna turned and walked away without an expression or a response."

Andrew already knew what Charlee was telling him. Molly had also come to him. He didn't have a clue as to what he could do to help his sister. He watched Charlee pull the sleeping baby from her breast and button her shirt.

He motioned to her. "Give me my son."

Charlee looked at him in surprise. "He's sleeping, Andrew. I was going to lay him down on the bed."

He gestured to her with his hand again. "I want to hold him. I won't wake him, I promise."

With a smile, she stood. She handed the sleeping baby to him.

***

Anna gazed out at the magnificent view from the backside window of the House of Reflection, from where she sat within the building. From her vantage point, the mountain on which the House of Reflection was built had a steep drop downward, allowing her a clear view of the towering mountain behind it.

The heavy pile of powdery snow on the massive tree branches near the open window where she rested was a pure, glistening white. The sunlight that flowed down from the clear sky and through the tree's branches gave the snow before her a sparkling, magical appeal.

It is so peaceful up here, she thought, leaning forward to prop her elbows on the open window. She always felt comforted and at peace in the quiet, holy house. Anna realized the intensity of her grief had faded as she continued to gaze out at the scenery. She knew her family worried about her, but she didn't want to talk about her loss with them or anyone else.

She knew she'd hurt Molly's feelings when she'd abruptly walked away from her the day before. The sick woman Molly had requested for her to visit with her was huge with her pregnancy. She had not wanted to hear the woman talk about her excitement of the coming birth. Anna smiled with a wry acceptance that everywhere she turned now, there were pregnant women. She prayed for all to have healthy babies. She wouldn't want any of them to experience the pain she was going through. She knew Charlee's feelings were hurt over her not having anything to do with baby Rowan, although she hadn't said anything to her. Right now, it hurt too much to even think of holding a baby that wasn't hers. Anna continued to gaze out at the snow-covered trees.

Surprised, she registered the grayish-white birds that now flew overhead and among the treetops. They swooped and circled and then dove to settle with a rush, landing in the tree branches not far from where she sat. It was the first time she had seen any bird in the area. There had been none during the summer months that she or the others had ever noticed or heard. Anna wondered what these ate in this part of the woods during the winter that would cause them to fly down to where she sat.

The birds cooed for a moment before their voices lifted, and they sang together with a multi-layered series of sounds and mini trills. It was an orchestra of music as if they were singing it for her. As abruptly as they landed, the flock took off again. Anna smiled at their graceful flight up into the air. Their serenade had cheered her. The Keeper strolled into the House of Reflection, and his appearance pulled her away from her silent musings.

Anna realized the holy man had never imposed himself on her in her solitude while she was there. He might wander in from time to time to where she sat and played his musical instrument or read in quiet solitude from the Book of Wisdom, but not once had he disturbed her. Anna liked the old man tremendously and his young trainee, who was as quiet as he was when he drifted in and out of the House of Reflection. She hoped the Keeper planned to play his musical apparatus.

When he withdrew the instrument from its velvet-lined holding case, she returned to her view of the mountainous range and the snow-covered tree branches that graced the hillside outside the window.

Music began to flow around her.

It had the haunting sound of a Celtic composition, beautiful in its simplicity. With her eyes closed, Anna let the arrangement the Keeper played soak into her pores and soul. He continued playing until the piece was finished, with a slow, drawn-out ending. She didn't move even though she heard him replace the instrument into its case.

After a moment, Anna knew she was alone again. Opening her eyes, she glanced over to where the holy man had sat.

He had left as he'd entered the building without a sound made. It was time for her to go home. Turning to stand, a book on the bench beside her fell onto the floor at her feet.

Puzzled, Anna gazed down at the Book of Wisdom.

She didn't remember it being on the bench when she'd sat down. Reaching down to the floor, she retrieved the thick volume. When she straightened, Anna read the first passage on its open pages. She then reread it. *When sorrow is at its deepest, look to your loved ones for comfort. See who has been beside you, ready to embrace you should you turn to them; open your heart. This trial, too, shall pass. Your pain shall ease with each passing moment in time.*

Anna sank back down onto the bench to place the book beside her.

She had clutched her pain to her. Selfish in her sorrow and unwilling to allow her family to comfort her, she realized. She'd turned her back on Traun and the grief he was going through and had even blamed him for the loss of their child. She'd condemned him for something he had had no control over. Anna felt ashamed of her behavior.

She could lay the fault for the loss of their child at Avreen's feet or the wild men, but not Traun, never Traun.

Yes, this trial, too, shall pass, she thought as she stood with a firm decision made. It was time for her to go to her Lifemate to ask for his forgiveness and to draw comfort from his presence. And Anna knew she would, in sudden unexpected moments, feel sadness again by the loss of their child, but her pain had and would ease even further with time, and the memory of her and Traun's firstborn would never fade.

Anna walked out from the House of Reflection to find her Lifemate straightaway. Her apology to him was something that couldn't wait until after their dinner with the entire family that night. Molly had requested they all meet around a campfire that evening for a family get-together. She always wanted to gather the family close to her when the evenings were not too cold to eat outside with the help of a blazing fire. With careful concentration, Anna descended the rocky sloped footpath made by the visitors of the mountainside. Upon reaching its end at the edge of the village and from which it had led up to the House of Reflection, she glanced around the settlement and spotted Traun, speaking to several men alongside him, working as he did.

With her gaze pinned on her Lifemate, Anna was single-minded in her course of direction. *He is so handsome, a beautiful and welcome sight,* she thought as she walked toward him. She noticed the men around her Lifemate stop their work at her approach, and they watched her.

*****

Traun turned to see what Andrew and the other men beside him were gawking at, and he stared as Anna began to run toward him. Alarmed, he wondered what was going on. She never came and interfered when he was working. She ran straight to him, flinging her arms around his waist, and squeezed him tightly. Raising her gaze to his, she said, "I love you, Traun. I'm sorry for what I accused you of."

Standing on her tiptoes, she wrapped her arms around his neck and kissed him deeply on the lips. As swiftly as she'd approached, she turned and, with quick steps, walked away.

Stunned, Traun gazed after his Lifemate. The men around him began to snicker and elbow each other. In a daze, he turned to encounter their smirking faces.

"Get back to work, the lot of you," he ordered. He was unable to stop the wide grin that spread across his face. The men roared with their laughter, and it caused several heads across the village to turn in their direction.

***

Anna lifted her hand, rapping her knuckles against the door of Klinn's home. The woman opened it. She looked directly at her servant for the first time in months.

"If it wouldn't be too much trouble, I wish for bath water to be drawn and heated early this evening. Oh, and please prepare an early bath for the High Commander, too," she added with a smile toward the woman. Klinn appeared to do a little happy jig before she quickly told her that she would see to it.

Anna soaked in her hot bath water.

The servants were gone, and Klinn chattered away again about anything and everything. In another couple of hours, it would be time to meet with the family around the campfire for the evening meal. Anna soaped her arm and then rinsed it off in slow motion.

Tonight will be Traun's night, she promised herself as she washed. With her hair clean and the water now cold, she stepped out of the tub.

Drying off, Anna began to towel dry her hair. She brushed the strands until they shined. She pulled the red ribbed sweater Klinn had laid out on the bed at her request over her head. Its form hugged her full, high breasts.

Next, she donned a long gray wool skirt that swirled around her booted ankles when she moved. She wouldn't need a coat, she realized. The clothes she'd chosen to wear would keep her warm enough by the campfire. Anna glanced in the mirror beside her and moved her hand back and forth as she studied the ring Traun had given her for her birthday.

The stone's glow seemed more intense that evening. She looked good, she realized, and she smiled with happiness. After a dab of perfume on her wrists, she turned toward the door, ready to embrace life again.

Traun had stepped up to their door just as she pulled it open. He was still in a position of reaching for the door handle.

"Your bath water waits for you," she said and passed him by with a smile directed his way. Anna knew he watched her walk away from him toward the campfire the family and the servants had begun to gather around. Sitting beside George when she arrived at the area, she reached for the strong hand attached to the person who had always been loving and generous toward her. She raised his hand to her mouth to kiss the back of it.

"Girlie?" George said. He smiled in question at her and her action.

"Nothing, George. I'm glad I have you, is all."

He raised his arm to wrap it around her shoulders and squeezed them. "You are back with us," he said.

He looked up at Molly, and Anna saw Molly's eyes tear up before she quickly turned away to direct the meal cooking over the open fire.

"Go sit with your Lifemate," George instructed when Traun strolled into the area to sit down alone across the fire from them. Smiling at the man by her side, Anna stood.

***

Traun watched Anna approach with a graceful swing of her hips. *She is beautiful tonight*, he thought, and he realized there was an air of maturity about her she hadn't had before. She seemed almost serene. She met his gaze with a new boldness when she settled beside him.

"I have missed you these past few months," she said as she clasped his hand tightly. Traun felt his breath catch in his throat, and he couldn't stop the curl of his fingers from tightening around hers.

"I have missed you too, Anna," he replied. He watched her for any sign that she forced herself to behave unnaturally.

She looked back at him.

"I still hurt within, Traun. But my pain has faded. I needed time to grieve. Today, I noticed my sorrow wasn't as intense. It made me realize that the rotation of life does go on. I also know that I want to be with you during our cycle of life."

Traun couldn't stop his wide smile toward her. Her lips stretched into a smile back at him. Turning from him, she watched her brother and Charlee arrive at the cookout. Charlee carried the wrapped-up baby Rowan. Traun watched Anna's beautiful smile fade as she took in the bundle her friend carried. He realized she still had a hurdle to overcome. He squeezed her fingers held within his.

She turned back to him. "I guess I'm not ready to see the baby yet."

"All in good time, Anna," he said, his words as soft as hers. "All in good time."

***

Charlee gazed across the campfire flames over to where Anna and Traun sat beside each other. Andrew had told her about Anna's actions earlier that day. He was convinced she'd overcome her deep depression. Charlee hoped so. She had noticed Anna take in Rowan bundled up in her arms before quickly turning back to speak to the High Commander.

She frowned.

"Don't scowl so, Charlee," Andrew said beside her. "Everyone will think you're mad at me."

Turning toward him, Charlee wiped the frown from her face. She smiled wide at him as she held their child out toward him.

"Sit down, Andrew, and hold the baby for me. Molly motioned that our food was ready. I'll go get us both a plate," she said.

Andrew took the baby while watching Traun and Anna stand together to collect their plates. *At least they look at each other again*, Charlee thought. Andrew smiled down at the baby in his arms as he sat down.

***

"The food tasted exceptional tonight, didn't it?" Anna said when she returned after taking their empty plates to the servants.

"Yes, it was good," Traun replied as she sat beside him. Watching her, he thought everything about the evening was exceptional. She glanced across the fire at the baby again before she turned toward him.

***

"I will push her to face her fear!"

Charlee stood up with Rowan held in her arms. She had noticed Anna's quick, frequent peeks toward the baby all evening.

"What are you up to, Charlee?" Andrew asked. His alarm felt was obvious.

"I plan to do something that needs to be done." Charlee walked away from him and knew Anna watched her with unease as she approached her. Her friend glanced at Traun. He wrapped an arm behind her back to pull her close to him. Charlee hoped what she planned didn't backfire and cause her to slip back into her depression. When she reached her, she, in one swift move, laid the baby into her arms.

"Hold him for me, please. I forgot something at home." She hurriedly walked away and ignored the stuttering *no, no,* said behind her.

***

Anna held tight onto the bundle dumped into her lap and looked desperately at Traun, afraid to look down. Rowan began to coo. With hesitation, she lowered her gaze to the squirming bundle she held.

"Oh, Traun, isn't he beautiful," she whispered. Her heart melted as little eyes stared intensely up at her. She stroked the baby's fat little cheek with a finger.

Traun looked over to where Charlee now stood. He smiled at her. She smiled back. She walked over to sit down beside Anna. Anna shook her head at her. She then laughed. "You knew what I needed."

After a time, everyone around the campfire began to make motions to return to their huts. The day for all had been a long one. With reluctance, Anna handed the baby she held over to his mother.

"I will be over tomorrow to see him again," she said, smiling at her friend.

"Welcome back, Anna," Charlee said. She stood to hand the now sleeping infant to Andrew. He reached out to rub a knuckle against Anna's cheek before he walked away, the baby in the crook of his arm. Traun sat quietly as all said their goodbyes, only inclining his head toward them.

"Should we put out the fire and go home ourselves?" Anna asked after a moment had passed and everyone around the campfire had walked away. She and Traun were alone now before the fire. He encircled an arm around her shoulders.

"Let's sit here for a time longer and enjoy the fire and the quietness of the night."

Anna leaned against him, wrapping her arms around his waist. In silence, she gazed into the crackling fire, as did he.

"This planet we have occupied is beautiful, isn't it," he said after a moment.

"I thought it was from the beginning when we transported down," she responded, looking up at him.

"Do you miss Earth, Anna, and the life there left behind?" He turned his head to gaze down at her.

"Sometimes, yes. I miss the modern conveniences known. However, I wouldn't give you up to return to it."

Traun lowered his head to kiss her. "Let's go home," he said when they parted. With the fire out, he reached for her hand to hold it within his and pulled her to his side. He raised it to kiss its black marriage tattoo mark. Turning, they walked home, hand in hand.

***

Anna rolled to her side on their bed to face her Lifemate.

He lay on his back, his arms behind his head. He hadn't made any sexual overtures toward her once they'd arrived home or had gone to bed. She supposed he waited for her to make the first move, not wanting to assume she was interested in making love because she'd come out from her depression.

"I love you," she said as she watched him.

"I love you, too," he replied, smiling at her.

Anna rose to lean toward him and to kiss the ugly scar on his shoulder.

"I could have lost you that day," she said. How lucky she was to still have him with her. When she leaned to kiss the back of his arm that the savage had ripped open and its resulting scar, his arm muscle contracted, and his breathing grew labored. Anna smoothed her hand across his chest. Her Lifemate didn't move. Rising, she kissed the side of his mouth, then nibbled on his ear and breathed heavily on it so he'd feel the air of her breath.

With an abrupt move, Traun rolled to his side, wrapping his arms around her. "You're killing me, Anna," he said before he devoured her mouth with an onslaught of his. He slung a leg over hers to hold her in place and lifted his head so his eyes met hers.

"If you try to pull away this time, Anna, I won't be able to let you." His tone was rough. His words rasped out.

Anna urged him on as she curled up against him. "I love you. Don't stop."

"I am too far gone to do that now," he groaned.

With a smile, she reached up to pull him toward her.

"Love me till I beg for mercy then," she whispered.

Epilogue

Traun gazed down across the vast valley he ruled over from where he stood on the hilltop he'd climbed. His reign stretched as far as the eye could see and even further. This day began a three-day feast to celebrate life and survival: a yearly celebration that all the people of Garrearth gathered to enjoy. The tradition started after the first three hundred and sixty-five days he and his people landed on this planet and survived. *Now, a swift one hundred years later, look at what has been accomplished,* Traun thought with pride.

After ten years in the valley where they first settled, they relocated to the current area. The original six hundred and ninety-five pioneers' descendants numbered in the hundreds of thousands of Garrearth people. Over time, some married into another race of people Andrew's oldest son had come upon during his travels and introduced them to.

The Neanderthal men they'd encountered that first year and had continued to fight from time to time had become extinct. Traun watched the many people below him who had set up camp in the valley. Some even spilled over into the palace courtyard. All were there for the celebration, plus the handing over of leadership to his eldest son. Traun was ready for the transfer of power. After one hundred years of leadership, it was time to hand the reins to someone younger with his ideas of leading the people into the future.

The prior evening, he'd been reminiscing about his home planet, Garr, and realized that his parents had long passed. It had saddened Traun. His brother ruled over planet Garr now unless he, too, had passed on. Bran would be one hundred and sixty-five.

Traun noticed Anna walking toward a group of servants with a determined stride, pulling him from his musings. He laughed aloud when he noted what she handed to one of them. The servant took the dangling bird from her hand and nodded his head at Lady Anna's instruction given to him.

Looks like I will be having poultry for my evening meal, Traun thought with amusement. He continued to watch his Lifemate when she turned and began to climb the hill to where he stood. After all this time, his Lifemate could still make him pause in whatever he was doing when she happened to come into his line of view, just as she'd done with that first time meeting her on board his spaceship.

She was still the love of his life. His desire for her had never faded in intensity as the years passed. She had birthed eight healthy children for him after they had lost their firstborn, an eight-pound boy first, and then a healthy bouncing girl seventeen months later, four boys and four girls in total over the years. The third daughter born to them married Andrew's oldest son, Rowan.

He had almost lost two good friends over the union of his daughter Catalena with Rowan.

His stubborn resolve that no child of his was to be united with someone of complete Earthly origin had caused a wide rift between Andrew, Charlee, and him at the time. Anna fought with him privately over his stubbornness, but never during that difficult time had she come out publicly with her discontent over his hardheadedness. Years later, she'd been able to crow with delight when her friend Charlee aged no faster than either Anna or he did or had any unknown illnesses crop up with the children she and Andrew had born. *Maybe Charlee's unaged look has something to do with the atmosphere on the planet*, Traun thought. He didn't know. He should give up trying to understand its mystery.

Anna walked up to him. "What are you doing up here by yourself, Traun?" She took the hand he held out to her.

"Thinking back over our years here, Anna."

She rubbed her fingertips over the top of his hand that held hers. "They have been good years, haven't they? Do you regret the decision to hand over the reins of leadership to Allon?"

"No, Anna, he will be a good leader. Our eldest son and Rowan will build their two kingdoms into powerful forces. A powerhouse to be reckoned with. The unknown people who've begun to attack our settlements won't know what hit them."

He and Anna watched as Allon and Rowan walked across the palace courtyard, deep in conversation. Traun knew Anna wished Molly and George were there to watch the power exchange ceremony. They would have enjoyed seeing the passing of leadership to the next generation of children born on Garrearth: descendants of a people who'd escaped extinction. George passed at one hundred and ninety-four, and Molly followed him two years later. They both had lived long and happy lives. Traun turned toward his Lifemate.

"How do you feel about us going with Catalena and Rowan when they return home? Rowan asked me if we would like to live with them for a while. I think it would make the new leadership role easier for Allon if I weren't still here for the people to continue to look to for guidance. It would also give us a chance to get to know our grandkids better, and great grandkids, and great, great grandkids from the union of Catalena and Rowan. What do you think?"

Anna laughed and turned, standing within the circle of his arms. She hugged what she declared was his still-trim waistline.

"I think that is a wonderful idea, Lifemate of mine."

They turned to walk arm in arm back down the hillside to join their large, extended family.

THE END

Other books by L. J. Vant
An Unfair Division
Across All Boundaries